The Witch of Wanchai

David Harris Lang

Library of Congress Control Number: 2015939872

ISBN: print: 978-1-945756-30-6

Published by Merrimack Media, Newburyport, Massachusetts

Contents

Dedication

Dedication

    This novel is dedicated to my incredible wife, Christine,
and my three amazing daughters: Samantha, Alexis, and Michele.
Your support and love is so valuable to everything I do.

Bio

Bio

David Harris Lang, a current resident of Hong Kong, has lived and worked in Asia much of his life. His deep understanding of Asian cultures and locales informs the writing of *The Witch of Wanchai*, where unforgettable characters uncover layers of mystery in the underworlds of Hong Kong, China, Thailand, and Myanmar. Mr. Lang's father and grandfather were fur traders living in Tianjin when the Japanese military invaded China in 1937. Their history, which was relayed to David over a lifetime of stories told over plates of herring and glasses of vodka, was the inspiration for his first book, *The Journal of Rabbi Levy Wang*, and was the foundation of his natural storytelling skills.

www.davidharrislang-books.com

Chapter 1

Geoffrey MacMillan remembered the exact moment that he realized his dad was insane. He was thirteen, sitting on a rock in the shade of a teak tree to escape the intense Burmese sun. He could recall the fragrance of the teak's petite, white flowers. The year was 1973. Geoffrey watched as his best friend, his *only* friend, Khin Khin, tried to catch a lizard dashing away in the dirt. Both boys wore baggy cotton shorts and flip-flops. A blue tiger butterfly fluttered aimlessly above Geoffrey's head and then landed weightlessly on a teak branch. Folding back it's delicate wings, it seemed confused as to where to go next. *Just like me*, Geoffrey thought. *I wish that I were back in 'The World'.*

Geoffrey considered England 'The World'. *'The World' has the good clothes, the good music, the good food. They're eating fish and chips in 'The World' and I'm here eating* khauk swe thoke. *I will be considered a freak when I finally go back to 'The World'.* He and his dad, Arthur MacMillan, as far as Geoffrey knew, were the only two Westerners living in Burma at that time. It had been like that his whole life, although he wasn't exactly sure when his mother had left. That would have made it three Westerners.

Arthur MacMillan had come to Burma at the invitation of the country's first Prime Minister, Thakin Nu, just before Geoffrey was born. Arthur had met the Prime Minister, known as U Nu, 'U' being a common Burmese honorific for men in a senior position, at a tourism convention in Whitehall.

Arthur, sole proprietor of MacMillan Travel, had spent much of the afternoon at the convention's free open bar before deciding to wander the convention floor looking for someone to converse with, a Jameson whiskey clutched firmly in his hand. "Heigh-ho, time for a bit of the old promotion," he said out loud as he pushed away from the stand-up bar. Like a circling hawk studying the forest floor for a rodent he weaved his way onto the convention floor, scanning the booths for a likely recipient of his gregariousness.

The modest stall promoting Burmese tourism was in an obscure corner of the hall out of the main traffic flow of conventioneers. The prime spots had been given to countries like France and Japan who had expensive exhibits, sexy booth-bunnies, and glossy pictures of popular destinations such as the Eiffel Tower or cherry blossoms in Kyoto.

Ah, a likely initiate for the bespoke services of Macmillan Travel, Arthur thought as he zeroed in on the Burmese booth. He switched the Jameson to his left hand as he soared in the direction of the unpretentious booth, his right hand extended towards an Asian man standing in the stall. "Arthur MacMillan here, MacMillan Travel."

The man shook Arthur's hand, a smile on his broad, affable face. His grip was weak compared to Arthur's hearty Western squeeze, U Nu from a culture unused to shaking hands. He beamed at the larger Westerner standing before him and said, "I am U Nu."

"You knew what?" Arthur laughed at his own joke, slapping his leg and taking another sip of whiskey. The Burmese man did not get the joke, but continued to smile.

"So you are from…" Arthur continued, looking up at the letters above the booth, "Burma! That's great, I love Burma!" Arthur had never been there.

"Yes, I am from Burma," U Nu said.

"What is your slogan? To promote your country for travel I mean," Arthur asked his new friend.

"A slogan….?"

"A slogan. You know. Every successful tourism campaign needs one. You really don't have one? Like, 'Visit Burma – The Unspoiled Asia', or 'Burma – The Exotic Asia'. How about, 'Burma – The Real Asia'?" Arthur expounded.

"That's fantastic! We *do* need a slogan! You really know about tourism, Mr. MacMillan," U Nu said. The two hit it off well, and the afternoon turned into a night of revelry, Jameson whiskey, Cohiba cigars, and deep discussions about promoting Burma as a tourist destination. Within a month Arthur and his pregnant wife were living in Burma. Arthur's title was Minister of Tourism. He became the foreign face of the Burmese tourist industry, such a visible and indispensable figure that even when U Nu was deposed by Ne Win's Socialist Movement in 1962 Arthur retained his position.

Khin Khin had given up trying to catch the lizard and, still on his knees in the dirt, was now picking the bark off of a fallen log, watching armies of surprised insects scurry away as they were suddenly exposed to the sunlight. "Run, you bastards!" Khin Khin ordered the fleeing black bugs in English. With no one to speak English to except his dad, Geoffrey had taught Khin Khin English. It had become their special language, especially at school.

School was a nightmare for both boys. Both were ostracized for being different. Geoffrey, white-skinned and giant compared to his classmates, was called 'Bilu', an ogre. Khin Khin's diminutive size also made him the brunt of his classmates' scorn. He was a perfectly proportioned person, just tiny. They called him 'Shrunken Boy'. Bilu and Shrunken Boy became fast friends, each coming to the other's defense when needed, which was often.

Geoffrey, watching his friend harass the insects from his seat in the shade, announced, "My dad is insane."

"No he's not," Khin Khin said. "He is smart. He makes lots of money. *My* dad is insane. He works in a bicycle factory. He makes no money."

"No, it's different, Khin Khin. My dad could be working in England. He doesn't have to be here. What does he do? How many tourists have you ever seen in Burma? My mom was smart, she left. I'm stuck here because my dad is insane. I should be living in 'The World'. "

Khin Khin shrugged. He had tired of annoying insects and was now throwing pebbles at a black-and-yellow Broadbill on an upper branch of the teak tree. The bird nonchalantly ignored the assault. "Hey, let's see what there is to eat at your house."

There was always food at Geoffrey's house, cooked up by Arthur's latest Burmese girlfriend, a long line of woman in their twenties who paraded through the MacMillan residence and Arthur's life. "OK." Geoffrey wasn't particularly hungry but he realized that food was a scarce commodity in Khin Khin's home and was glad to share his relative abundance.

They knew that something was wrong as soon as they walked in the front door of Geoffrey's two-story, wood-sided house. The girlfriend du jour was frantically packing her belongings, drawers left open, clothes strewn everywhere, pots and pans on the living room floor. The woman's hair was wildly unkempt, her eyes frantic, tears glistened on her cheeks. When she saw Geoffrey she screamed at him in Burmese, "Run! Your father has been arrested! Ne Win's puppets have decided that he is anti-socialist! They'll be coming for you soon!" She pushed past the boys, two suitcases in hand, the screen door slamming shut behind her.

The two boys stared at each other. "Geoffrey, we've got to run away!" Khin Khin exclaimed. "Right now!"

" 'We'? You're OK, you're in no danger," Geoffrey said.

"Shrunken Boy goes wherever The Bilu goes. I am going with you!"

"OK, but where? No place is safe."

"Not in Burma, that's for sure. We need to get across the border to Thailand," Khin Khin said."Hurry!"

"Wait, I've got to get something." Geoffrey dashed upstairs to his dad's bedroom. The picture of London's Big Ben was already lying on the floor where Arthur's girlfriend had tossed it, exposing the safe built into the wall, still closed. *Hah, the bitch came here first, but couldn't open it!* Geoffrey thought. The one romantic act ever committed by Arthur MacMillan was using his wife's birth date as the combination of his wall safe; 5-23-38. Geoffrey had it open in a flash and pulled out an envelope of money plus his and his dad's passports.

Before leaving his father's bedroom Geoffrey picked up the picture of Big Ben from the floor and placed it gently on the bed. The picture had been meaningless to him before, but now, ripped from the wall and unceremoniously tossed to the floor, it seemed like it was a fellow victim, a compatriot of British sensibilities suddenly the victim of a brutal foreign assault. He then ran to his room and shoved the envelope and passports in his daypack along with some random clothes. *What else, what else...?* He pulled open the drawer of his desk and snatched a map of Southeast Asia.

He passed through the kitchen on his way back to the living room and grabbed a twelve-inch carving knife. With the knife stashed in his pack he yelled, "Let's go Shrunken Boy! What are you waiting for?" The two youths bolted out the door and headed for the jungle, northeast towards the Thai border.

Chapter 2

It took three days for the boys to reach the Moei River and cross over into Thailand. The Burmese jungle was a familiar place to the boys. It had been their backyard, their playground. They knew how to find food and water, how to make a fire. They skirted the Gulf of Martaban and then headed due east. Whenever they passed through a small village Geoffrey would take some money out of his daypack and they would buy food and supplies. Both boys felt exhilarated, free and finally on their own, not constricted by a world where they did not fit in. Their spirits were high as they trudged out of the muddy waters of the Moei River onto Thai soil.

"Which way?" Khin Khin asked.

Geoffrey pulled out the map of Southeast Asia, turning it around a few times until he was orientated. "That way," he said pointing. "Southeast, towards Bangkok."

Within a few hours they came to the town of Mae Sot, which had a train station. Neither boy spoke Thai but with a combination of charades, Burmese, and English they successfully purchased two tickets to Bangkok. Clutching their five baht ticket stubs Bilu and Shrunken Boy stepped up into the cream and green coach. The whistle of the steam-powered locomotive blew and with short, powerful chuffs they were propelled towards a new world.

They exited the train at the Krungthep Station in central Bangkok. Nosier and more crowded than Yangon, Bangkok was a bombardment to their senses. The smell of the city embraced them: smoky, sweet, spicy, and sour all at the same time. They stood on the train platform and inhaled the perfume of unimaginable adventure combined with the underlying stench of extreme danger. Bangkok led them into her grasp by their noses.

Their attention was captured by a line of street stalls from which emanated the delectable aroma of grilling chicken. Seating themselves on wooden stools in front of one of the stalls they ordered plates of golden-hued legs and thighs along with colorful bowls of spicy papaya salad with dried chili peppers and limes. They voraciously dined, a celebratory meal to launch their new lives.

They then wandered the *soi's*, the back streets, until they found a youth hostel catering to foreign backpackers, The Vipassana. It was a moldy two-story structure with a weedy, cracked front patio. Thailand in the 1970's was a popular destination for hippie tourists from the West: colorful backpacks, torn jeans, Rasta hair, globetrotting youths looking for a dose of spiritual enlightenment while getting high in exotic locations with powerful Asian drugs. Geoffrey and Khin Khin after a few days at the Vipassana Youth Hostel had become friendly with a number of them.

From their tiny, cockroach-infested room, BS Enterprises was launched. "Bilu-Shrunken Boy Enterprises is an awkward name," Geoffrey announced. "Therefore, we will use the initials 'BS'. Our company will be BS Enterprises." When no reaction came from Khin Khin, Geoffrey said, "In English 'BS' means 'bullshit'. So it's a really cool name."

Their first business venture involved buying two cartons of cigarettes, shredding the tobacco from the cigarettes into a plastic bowl, and then pouring elephant tranquilizer over it. They then let it dry in the sun and packaged it in small, red plastic bags that Khin Khin had stolen from a betel nut vendor.

Geoffrey's first sale was to a ratty group of three Canadians, two men and a woman who were sitting on a rusted metal bench in the front yard of the Vipassana hostel. Geoffrey sat down on the ground next to them and said, "Hey, I've got the most powerful weed in Thailand. Interested?"

"Huh? Right, Kid. You do not look like a weed dealer. Go away."

"Of course I don't look like a drug dealer. This is actually my brilliant disguise. Look, the stuff comes from Lampang up in the north. Special nutrients in the soil amps it up. The locals up there use it for religious ceremonies. It's called Golden Glory. You never heard of it?"

"Golden Glory? That sounds cool. How much?" The second Canadian man said.

Geoffrey and Khin Khin made a five hundred percent profit on the sale. Word of Golden Glory soon spread rapidly through the Vipassana and to the other hostels in Bangkok. *Two hits and you cannot even stand up, Man!*

They quickly had so much business that they had to hire four Thai street people to help them produce and bag the toxic mixture. They moved out of the hostel and rented two apartments off of *Soi* Thirty Nine. One apartment was for them to live in, one to produce Golden Glory. After a month of exceptional profits, however, news started to surface that Western hippies were being found dead around Bangkok.

"Khin Khin, I think that we need to move on," Geoffrey said reading an article about the deaths in the *Bangkok Sun*. "Elephant tranquilizer is evidently not that good for people."

"OK with me. Selling drugs to stupid hippies is getting boring anyway. What should we do to make money now then?"

"We will sell fake gems to greedy, idiotic tourists," Geoffrey said. "I have been thinking about this." The boys moved apartments again, this time to a flat on Silom Road between the Chao Phraya River and Lumpini Park. The money flowed easily as they passed off green glass as jade. Geoffrey and Khim Khim started exploring Bangkok in earnest, walking the narrow back alleys and the *soi's*, investigating new wonders and dark holes.

One morning as he walked down a narrow *soi* close to their apartment Khin Khin heard the sounds of a Muay Thai gym: jumping ropes swishing the ground, the thwack of fists and shins striking bags and pads, the hissing yells of the fighters. He followed the sounds and found himself standing in a courtyard with a covered ring. It was a world of punching bags, pads, weights, and lean, dangerous men. Khin Khin was hooked.

Every morning at dawn Khin Khin would run three miles, taking a loop around Lumpini Park and ending up at the Muay Thai gym. He would then work out for two hours before returning to the apartment, repeating the process at 4:00pm. Every day, rain or shine, he followed the rigorous regime, his undersized body soon laced with ropy, taught, powerful muscles.

As the 1970's slipped into the 1980's BS Enterprises' jewelry business evolved. Instead of selling costume glass to gullible Western tourists as real jade, they were now selling poor quality jade as high quality jade to gullible, wealthy Hong Kong buyers. Much bigger amounts of money were involved.

This was easier than they thought it would be. The fact that the boys had escaped the Burmese government's clutches made them quite popular with the anti-government Kachins who controlled the jade mines in northern Burma. From their new Kachin friends they would purchase worthless jade very cheaply, jade of such low quality that it would have been discarded. They would then have it 'quench crackled' and dyed in China, an art of the Middle Kingdom since the 13th century.

Geoffrey traveled to Hong Kong monthly, an economic boom city in the 1980's. Within the city's new finance and entertainment sectors Hong Kong millionaires were created every day. There were those as well who were becoming wealthy in the thriving government corruption business. It was a ripe market for nefarious jade deals. BS Enterprises flourished. The boys were in their early twenties, and they felt like monarchs.

Chapter 3

With the abundance from BS flowing into their pockets Geoffrey and Khin Khin became regulars on 'The Sukumvit Crawl'. Sukumvit Road, one of Bangkok's major thoroughfares, and the narrow side streets, the *soi's,* that branch off of it, come to life at night with a sparkling and sinful magnetic decadence unmatched anywhere else in the world.

Bilu and Shrunken Boy would usually start 'The Crawl' at Soi 39, at 'the artists' bars': Monet Bar, Renoir Bar, Van Gogh Bar. They would then continue down Sukumvit to the Dubliner for some Irish pub atmosphere, live music, and Guinness. After the Dubliner they would wander in and out of various watering holes, all remarkably the same: pool tables, red and blue colored lights, bikini-clad dancing girls, ladyboys, blaring rock and roll, and of course the fuel that drives it all, the paying customer, the Westerners, the *farangs.*

Stops would be made between bars for snacks at festive street stalls, sitting on wooden stools eating bowls of noodles or grilled chicken while watching the Sukumvit parade of huge, middle-aged *farangs* holding hands with comparatively tiny Thai women. Giant water buffaloes with small exotic birds. Then back to barhopping between the myriad of establishments on Soi Cowboy, such as Loretta's, Our Place, Moonshine, Honeymoon, Old China Hand, and Pam's. Then on to Nana Plaza and stops at Three Roses, Hog's Breath, and Rosemary's. 'The Crawl' would continue down Sukumvit into the early hours, ending in the basement level of the Erawan Hotel a few hours before dawn at Spasso, a capacious bar with a live foreign band.

Before staggering into the Erawan Hotel, Geoffrey would always stop at the small Erawan Shrine at the corner of the hotel property, crowded even in the early morning hours. The shrine had been built in 1956 during the construction of the hotel when the project had been plagued with a series of cost overruns, missing materials, and construction deaths. Believed to be the work of evil spirits, the shrine was built to placate the spooks and bring good karma to the project site. No further misfortunes occurred after its erection, and the Erawan Shrine became one of the most sacred shrines in Thailand.

A statue of Phra Phrom, the four-faced deity of good luck, sits serenely at the center of the shrine in an elaborately-tiled altar, surrounded with offerings of incense, candles, carved wooden elephants, and garlands of flowers. Geoffrey had no feelings about religion or an afterlife, but he did believe in luck. Therefore, at the last stop on 'The Crawl' he would always purchase a small wooden carving of an elephant from one of the vendors on the edge of the shrine, walk up to the altar, place the elephant on the dais before Pha Phrom, bow, and say, "Please grant me luck, my four-faced friend."

It was on one of these 'Sukumvit Crawls' that Geoffrey had noticed that Khin Khin was spending more time with ladyboys than 'real' girls. Years of daily Muay Thai workouts had made Khin Khin wiry and flexible. He was still small and thin, still Shrunken Boy, but a very fit Shrunken Boy. By now the two boys had separate apartments on Silom Road, so Geoffrey did not know whom Khin Khin was bringing home. He kept his observations to himself, however. He really did not care.

One of their favorite stops on 'The Crawl' was The Richard Nixon Bar, an open-air bar located on a small plaza next to The Miami Hotel and two doors away from the popular Thermae Bar. The owner of The Richard Nixon, Reggie, a mustached ex-mailman from Petaluma, California, would sit with Geoffrey and Khin Khin, all three smoking Cuban cigars and sucking on frosty bottles of Singha Beer.

*****

A steamy Bangkok evening just after a brief shower, the smell of coriander, jasmine and chili hanging in the air, Reggie was complaining, "I can't effin' compete. Soi Cowboy has glitzier bars, colder beer, prettier women, I don't know…. They're crankin' busy all the time, whereas I'll be lucky just to sell just fifty beers tonight."

"You don't have a hook, Reggie, that's your problem. You need a hook to pull customers in," Khin Khin said.

"What kinda' hook you talkin' 'bout?" Reggie asked, taking a puff on his Cuban.

"Reggie, see that empty plaza in front of us?" Khin Khin pointed with his beer bottle to the deserted courtyard in front of The Richard Nixon. "Could you grease whomever needs to be greased so that BS Enterprises can use it? If you can, we can provide a killer hook for you. You will be overwhelmed by customers, trust me."

"No shit?" Reggie asked. "What hook you talkin' 'bout?"

"I haven't discussed the plan with my partner yet. Actually, I just thought of it." Khin Khin looked over at Geoffrey. "So until we work out the details, I cannot reveal the nature of this venture. Believe me though, it's brilliant. You just get the approvals to use the plaza, we'll take care of the rest, Reggie."

"OK, I'll work on it." Geoffrey and Khin Khin finished their beers and continued on 'The Crawl'.

After they left Khin Khin described his plan to Geoffrey. "Wow, great plan! I love it," Geoffrey exclaimed. "But are you sure? You will be alone out there, the one taking all the risks."

"Bilu, the odds are in our favor. Our 'customers' will be drunk, I will be sober. Buy another of those carved wooden elephants when we get to The Erawan and we'll be fine."

*****

A week later they stopped back in at The Richard Nixon. "I got it," Reggie said when they entered the bar. "Permission to use the plaza. They wanted to know what I was gonna do there, so I told them 'entertainment' and left it up to their imagination. I had to grease the landlord *and* the local cops, so this better be effin' worth it."

"It will be, Reggie," Khim Khim said. "OK, exciting! We will launch in one week then, next Saturday night!"

"So what exactly will you be launching?" Reggie asked.

His question was ignored. Geoffrey said, "I am going to put an ad in *Bangkok After Dark* as well as signs in Nana Plaza and Soi

Cowboy. Reggie, you're going to need more outdoor seating, and up your staff of waitresses too."

"Hey! I asked, 'What the eff will you two mother-humpin' lunatics be launching?'" Reggie yelled.

"Oh," Geoffrey said, as if he just noticed Reggie had asked a question, "We are going to set up a ring. Khin Khin will fight drunken *farangs*. Last more than three rounds, win 1,000 baht."

Chapter 4

Khin Khin found a Muay Thai camp that was upgrading in the outskirts of Bangkok and he was able to cheaply purchase their old boxing ring from them. On Saturday morning he and three of his gym friends rented a truck and brought the boxing ring to the plaza, which Geoffrey had renamed Richard Nixon Plaza. He had Reggie erect a blue and red neon sign at the entry to the plaza from Sukumvit which read '*Reggie's Richard Nixon Plaza*'.

It took most of the day for Khin Khin and his friends to set up the sixteen foot square Muay Thai ring and rig a canopy over it. Geoffrey meanwhile had a team of laborers stringing lighting above the ring and installing red and blue twinkle lights around the perimeter. Reggie had quadrupled the chairs and tables that he had out in front of The Richard Nixon.

"What time does the fighting start?" Reggie asked.

"10:00pm. The crowd needs to be hyped and lubed by then," Geoffrey said.

"So what makes you think that anyone will want to fight Khin Khin? He's a little guy."

"Precisely. *Stay through three rounds with the little guy and you win 1,000 baht.* A piece of cake. What drunken, testosterone-fueled *farang* asshole wouldn't want a piece of that action?"

"I know how I will make money from this adventure, beer sales, but how do you two profit from this?" Reggie asked.

"Gambling, my friend. You'll see. But I want the crowd really lubed. Do you think that you could have some of your girls circulating through the crowd offering half-price shots?"

At 8:00pm Geoffrey's new employees-for-the-evening showed up, ten of the most striking hustlers that he could find working Soi Cowboy. He had told them to bring their bikinis, and by 8:30pm ten gorgeous Isaan girls were strutting up and down Sukumvit in high heels and bikinis holding signs above their heads which read, '*Win 1,000 baht. Follow me.*'

By 10:00pm the tables around Richard Nixon Plaza were packed with sloppy, loud drunks celebrating a privileged life in a foreign land. Where the cash cows go, so do the working girls, and the courtyard was also soon filled with brown-skinned woman in suggestive outfits.

Khin Khin paced the ring with the gaze of a warrior, barefoot, wearing only shorts, with six ounce gloves on his hands. Next to the ring Geoffrey had placed a large sign, '*Survive 3 rounds and win 1,000 baht*'. Musicians had been hired to play traditional Muay Thai music during the bout and they were set up behind one of the ring posts, a man with a Javanese clarinet, the *pi Java*, a drummer with a set of traditional double drums, the *klong kaak*, and a man with the *ching*, the brass cymbals.

Geoffrey climbed into the ring with a megaphone. "OK, Ladies and Gentlemen, who will be first? Who wants to take the challenge? Which one of you thinks that he can last three rounds with my man here?" The musicians started to play their haunting music.

Catcalls and whistles came from around the plaza, "That guy is tiny! Anyone could beat him!" Within seconds an intoxicated group pushed one of their buddies towards the ring. The man climbed through the ropes into the ring. Geoffrey froze in terror. The man had to be over 300 pounds, a wide, tall farm boy that looked like he grew up bench-pressing cows and tossing hay bales. *I hope that Khin Khin can handle this!*

"OK, Sir, very good, my assistant here will get you more comfortably attired and fitted with some gloves." One of the bikini clad Isaan girls unbuttoned the giant's shirt, slowly and suggestively. The crowd loved it, yelling their approval while downing half-priced shots one after the other. She then kneeled before him and removed his shoes and socks. Obscene yells from the crowd. Finally she put a pair of six ounce boxing gloves on his massive, country boy hands.

Geoffrey then said into the megaphone, "Before we begin, let me remind everyone that this is Thailand, where betting on sporting events is totally legal." Geoffrey wasn't completely sure if this was true. "Therefore during the match, my lovely assistants will be circulating amongst you to take your wagers. The system is very simple. If you bet five hundred baht and your fighter lasts past round 3, you get 1,000 baht back. The lovely lady will give you a ticket. Every ticket has a value of 500 baht, so if you bet five hundred baht she will give you one ticket. After the fight, if your fighter is successful, you can cash your tickets in at The Richard Nixon. Also, Guys, if you place a bet of 5,000 baht or more the lovely lady will not only give you ten tickets, she will give you a kiss as well!"

Yells, whistles, and hoots came from the crowd.

"The fighting rules are simple. Kicking, punching, knees, elbows; all cool. The rounds are three minutes long, with a one-minute rest between rounds.

"OK? You guys ready? Good." Geoffrey climbed out of the ring and a referee climbed in, one of Khin Khin's buddies from the gym. Another man who was working the timer and bell, as well as twenty security guards, were also from Khin Khin's gym.

The bell rang. Khin Khin's shirtless opponent flexed his muscles at his hooting buddies and then charged out of his corner, his substantial stomach jiggling as he tried to jab at Khin Khin. It was like a rhinoceros trying to catch a Jack Russell Terrier. Khin Khin effortlessly danced out of the giant's reach.

Khin Khin and Geoffrey had gone over the strategy in detail. Khim Khim was to look like he was losing for the first two rounds. Bob, weave, and slip to avoid the power punches, cover up and take the weak shots. Throw a few shots that will not damage the opponent. While Khin Khin's demise during the first two rounds looked imminent, their gorgeous bet girls would be circulating through the crowd taking the *farangs'* wagers. Round three would be a different story.

The giant had no defense, swinging his enormous arms in wide haymakers. Khin Khin, controlled and balanced, slipped the blows easily. If it looked like one of the punches did not have his weight behind it, Khin Khin would take it on his shoulder or glove. Every once in a while Khin Khin sent a half-power round kick to the man's midsection or a few light jabs to his ribs.

The man quickly became winded, swinging his arms wildly, off balance, chasing the elusive Khin Khin into a corner where Khin

Khin would slide around behind, and the dance would continue to the other corner. Geoffrey worried as Khin Khin, his hands over his ears and his forearms protecting his torso, took what looked like powerful blows.

The choreography went on for two rounds, the discordant sounds of the Thai instruments and the cheers and hoots of the crowd in the background, the man's friends yelling encouragement, "Clar-rence, Clar-ence, Clar-ence!" Clarence was hoping that his friends were taking good pictures so that he could show them around when he returned to Kansas. *Here I am whuppin' up on one of those Muay Thai fighters, giving them a little taste of how we do it back in Kansas, yeah!*

The bell for round three sounded. Both fighters left their corners. Clarence charged out into the center of the ring, "This is where I finish you, Pipsqueak." To his surprise, he ran into a powerful straight front kick to his solar plexus, followed by the resounding 'thwack' of a round kick to his thigh. Then a second devastating round kick smashed into his ribs. Khin Khin generated power from the ground, pushing off with his back leg and transferring his weight to his front leg, powerfully pivoting his body into the kick, snapping his shin into Clarence's body.

Clarence's leg collapsed as a third round kick landed on his thigh, going down on one knee, confused, winded, arms at his waist. Khin Khin delivered a short, chopping left hook to his jaw. Clarence's eyes rolled up and he hit the canvas like a felled tree. It was over.

Geoffrey acted quickly, jumping in the ring with his megaphone, as four of his security guards carried the unconscious man out of the ring and handed him to his friends, who were now quite concerned for Clarence's well-being.

"OK, that was close! Great fight!" Geoffrey said into the megaphone. He paused to make sure that he had the crowds' attention, and their minds were off what just happened to the unconscious Clarence. "Now, Ladies and Gentlemen, we have a special treat for you before our next Muay Thai bout, when another one of you will have a chance to win 1,000 baht and show off your fighting skills. Who would like to see a couple of these Isaan girls fight?"

The crowd of drunken *farang's* hooted, whooped, stamped their feet, and screamed their approval. The Muay Thai musicians started up again, as two slender, brown-skinned women climbed between the ropes and entered the ring. Barefoot and wearing bikinis, the woman put on six ounce gloves. They waved to the cheering crowd. No one remembered Clarence anymore, who had been carried off by his friends, escorted out of Reggie's Richard Nixon Plaza by security and given directions to the nearest hospital.

Geoffrey announced over the megaphone, "The betting is on for the girls' bout too, Gentlemen! Pick a girl and win some money!"

The bell rang, and the women shuffled around each other, jabbing and kicking. One of the women, who had a large tattoo of roses surrounding a skull covering one shoulder, was more aggressive, and delivered a solid straight right to the other's face. As the crowd howled and whistled, Geoffrey went into the Richard Nixon Bar to talk with Khin Khin who was resting in the back office.

"That was an amazing performance, Shrunken Boy! We made a ton on the betting. Are you OK?"

"Yeah, no problem, barely broke a sweat."

"Are you sure that you want to fight another match? That guy seemed dangerous. You don't have to, you know."

"I am good. I love this. Every insult from every motherfucker that ever accosted me is getting paid back. For every one of these big water buffaloes that I chop down it is like I am erasing one insult," Khin Khin said.

"Yeah, but I worry that one of these water buffaloes will accidently connect with a good shot."

"Slim chance. Anyway, remember life at school? I have a lot of insults to erase."

Chapter 5

The methamphetamine trade between Myanmar and Thailand had blossomed into a big business in the mid-80s. The little orange pills, called *Yaa Baa* in Thai, were manufactured on the southern Burmese border, and the bulk of the trade was controlled by the Burmese Generals. It was easy for Geoffrey and Khin Khin to expand their network from jade to drugs, and BS Enterprises became the largest distributer of *Yaa Baa* in Bangkok.

Bilu and Shrunken Boy's network of distribution was simple. They had twenty motorcycle delivery boys whom they dressed in yellow and black striped outfits and who would weave like mad bees through Bangkok traffic on dented, smoke-belching 50cc's, delivering plastic bags of the orange pills. Orders were taken through a call center. The drugs were stored in a warehouse on the outskirts of Bangkok.

The *Yaa Baa* business, however, became problematic. The Thai police would not look the other way when it came to the drug. '*Yaa baa*' in Thai translates literally to 'crazy drug', and that is exactly the effect that it had on the population, causing kidnappings, killings, and suicides by paranoid, delusional addicts. The police pursed *Yaa Baa* dealers with uncharacteristic zeal.

The warning came by way of a telephone call. Geoffrey never found out who the caller was, but it no doubt kept him from a life behind bars in Klong Prem Prison. His best guess was that it was a police official who was greased by one of BS Enterprise's other ventures.

"They all dead!" The Thai-accented voice said in English.

"Who's dead?" Geoffrey asked into the receiver.

"Delivery boys."

"What? Who is this?"

"Yaa Baa no good. You next!" The caller then hung up.

The telephone rang again. Geoffrey snatched it up. This time the caller was a Brit, a bar owner who was a friend. "Hey, Man, you and Khin Khin have got to get out of Bangkok fast! The word on the street is that the police are coming for you!"

Geoffrey raced over to Khin Khin's apartment. Khin Khin had also been warned. All twenty delivery boys had been shot, executed, by the police.

"Sit down, stay calm," Khin Khin said. Geoffrey took a seat next to him on the couch. Khin Khin's serenity was contagious, and Geoffrey felt his breathing return to normal and his body relaxing. "We need to exit Bangkok."

Geoffrey said, "No shit. Anyway, the Hong Kong jade and drug business is going well. I've got some good Triad relationships there. I think that moving to Hong Kong would make sense for us."

"For you, makes sense, good move, but not for me. I love Thailand, I want to stay here."

"Stay in Thailand and be arrested?" Geoffrey asked.

"I would be arrested in Bangkok, yes, but I am moving to Pattaya."

"Pattaya? Are you serious? You have no connections there," Geoffrey said.

"Wrong, my friend. Shrunken Boy has connections in Pattaya. In fact, I am untouchable in Pattaya."

"You would choose a sleepy Thai jungle town over the sophistication of metropolitan Hong Kong?"

Khin Khin laughed. "Not a sleepy town at all! The Americans stationed their forces near Pattaya during the Vietnam War, which resulted in a huge demand for sex and drugs. When the war ended and the G.I.'s left in 1975, the sex and drugs stayed. Pattaya is wild: criminal gangs, a huge drug and sex trade, and a popular retirement and tourist destination for *farangs* begging to be fleeced."

"OK, but I love Hong Kong, so it looks like BS Enterprises gets disbanded. Tell you what, why don't I accompany you to Pattaya and spend a week there on my way to Hong Kong?" Geoffrey said. "Meanwhile, we need to be out of Bangkok fast!"

"Very welcome to join me in Pattaya, Bilu. The Thai police, if they are checking, will be looking for us on international flights rather than domestic anyway, so it's a safer route."

*****

When Geoffrey and Khin Khin walked out of the airport gate at U-Tapao Airport in Pattaya, a tall, stunning Thai woman was holding up a sign reading 'Khin Khin' written in black letters. She was dressed in a low-cut pink blouse and a tight black skirt. Khin Khin walked up to the woman, who was at least a foot taller than him, and said, "I am Khin Khin."

The woman smiled and took Khin Khin's bag. "Please follow me, sir," She said in excellent English. Her high heels clicked smartly on the airport's granite floor as she led the way to the parking lot. Geoffrey looked at Khin Khin as if to say, '*What?*' Khin Khin shrugged and laughed.

The woman led them to a 1968, alabaster-white, Plymouth Barracuda convertible. She opened the rear trunk and put the boys' suitcases in. "Wow, what a cool car!" Geoffrey exclaimed.

"My people here have style, Bilu."

Khin Khin pulled the front seat of the two-door Plymouth forward, and he and Geoffrey climbed into the back. When they were seated the woman pushed the front seat back into position and got into the driver's seat. Driving down Beach Road in the convertible was exhilarating. It was a brilliant Pattaya day, a tropical wind scented with curry and ginger, the rich aroma of the ocean and the sand. A double row of palm trees lined Beach Road. The vivid blue water of the bay was on their right side, single-story shop fronts on their left. When they were almost to Mueng Pattaya Park the convertible turned into a narrow driveway, a large carved wooden sign at the entry reading, 'Billion Dollar Real Estate Company, Inc.'.

The offices of Billion Dollar Real Estate was on a half an acre of land surrounded by multi-hued greens of dense tropical landscaping. There was a magnificent view of the ocean from the entry terrace. The building itself was traditional Thai, the graceful structure made entirely of oiled teak. The walls leaned slightly inward as it rose to steeply pitched, upward-arching roofs, the rafter ends curling upwards towards the sky. From the terrace they walked through intricately carved wooden doors into a great hall. Carved teakwood panels in a snake motif lined the walls, and in an alcove was a Khmer statue of Buddha.

At the back of the hall an elegant woman, professionally dressed in a tight tan skirt and white open-neck blouse, stood waiting to greet them. Behind her on an Italian leather couch were seated five other women, all thin and tall. Their driver joined her colleagues on the couch, as the standing woman walked over to Khin Khin, shorter than her by a head, and gave him a hug and a kiss on the cheek. Geoffrey had never seen a woman project so much strength. Her muscles rolled beneath her tanned skin, her movements graceful as a jungle cat. She turned to Geoffrey and held out her hand. "I am Eggplant."

"Your name is Eggplant?" Geoffrey asked.

"Yes. Thai curry very spicy for foreign man. Put eggplant makes sweeter, take some spice out, easier to eat for foreign man," Eggplant said smiling.

"A pleasure to meet you, Eggplant, I am Geoffrey."

"I know, Khin Khin tell me about you." With a sweep of her arm towards the couch and the six seated ladies, Eggplant said, "These my real estate agents." She then pointed to two chairs opposite the long couch. "Please, you sit down."

Eggplant sat down on the couch between her agents, three on each side. A waitress immediately appeared with a tray of martinis, offering the drinks first to the two guests, then Eggplant, and then the agents.

"I am afraid that I am at a slight disadvantage here, Eggplant," Geoffrey said, taking a sip of his martini. "Khin Khin has rudely not told me anything about you or your business. Could you please enlighten me?"

"Hah, Khin Khin very rude. No problem, I 'lighten you." Everyone laughed. "My business sell real estate in Pattaya to *farangs*. It nice place for *farang* retire."

"How do you know Khin Khin?" Geoffrey asked.

"I am Muay Thai fighter, train with Khin Khin before in Bangkok," Eggplant said.

"A lady Muay Thai fighter? I have never heard of that."

"There are some lady Muay Thai fighters, but no me. I am ladyboy. I ladyboy Muai Thai fighter. I fight men."

"That is very cool, Eggplant," Geoffrey said.

She swept her arms again to either side, indicating her agents. "We all ladyboy."

"Could you tell me more about your real estate operation?" Geoffrey asked.

"It most professional and successful in Pattaya. For foreigner to buy real estate in Thailand it against Thai law, illegal, never happen. So how they do? Very complicated. If no Thai wife or girlfriend, they need to buy leasehold from Thai company. They put up money and I buy, then lease back to them thirty years," Eggplant said.

"I see, no way to do it unless they cheat the system, and once they cheat the system they leave themselves open to be cheated by you. No offense meant, by the way," Geoffrey said.

"No offense, I proud. I are only one on deed, and only one with any rights. I raise rent whenever want, and if they don't like, I kick them out. I can even sell to someone else any time, and they out of luck."

"That is brilliant!" Geoffrey exclaimed.

"Geoffrey, you very quick learner. Many other ways to make money Pattaya too. It good business here."

"And you are going to go into this real estate business with Eggplant?" Geoffrey asked turning to Khin Khin.

"No, no, not at all, going into another business venture. We are going to start a new bar street here. There are some good bars already in Pattaya, but nothing like Soi Cowboy or Nana. We are going to bring the neon and sparkle of Bangkok to Pattaya. It is ripe for it," Khin Khin said.

"No more business questions? Good! Now we party!" Eggplant exclaimed.

The party lasted five days, at the end of which time Geoffrey's hung-over, abused body was transported, via Plymouth Barracuda, back to U-Tapao Airport. He gave Khin Khin a hug and boarded his flight to Hong Kong. Thirty years would go by before he would see Khin Khin again.

*

Chapter 6

Sunday night in Hong Kong, a light rain making the streets of Wanchai glisten. Inside The Surabaya Club Lilly spun her body around in circles to the music, her arms flung high above her head. She could feel the '*whump, whump*' of The Surabaya Club's techno beat in the packed lesbian bar vibrating deep inside her body like a tuning fork. Around her other Indonesian Tommy-boys and Girly-girls gyrated to the music.

Sunday in Hong Kong, *the* day for Hong Kong's Indonesian and Filipino domestic helpers, the day that they have off. Migrating as a herd to Central and Causeway Bay, and particularly to Wanchai's wild bars and clubs, intent on partying hard enough to last them for the rest of the week. The Surabaya Club was one of these clubs, the only difference being that Surabaya catered to women who preferred women.

Lilly danced and spun, her senses bombarded by flashing strobes illuminating images of asymmetrically cropped hair appearing and disappearing around her, bouncing heads on compact bodies. Lilly's soul felt temporarily liberated from a week of demoralizing servitude as she surrendered to the driving beat. She danced with abandon.

Next to Lilly, wearing a baseball cap with an extra-large brim, embroidered with '*AC* lightning bolt *DC*' and worn backwards on her head, Bella hopped to the music. As one song evolved into the next Bella stopped dancing and beckoned Lilly to follow her to a dark booth along the perimeter of the bar. Lilly slid in next to Bella, close, inhaling. She liked that Bella smelled like a man.

Her hand resting on Lilly's thigh, Bella signaled the waiter, "Two tequila shots." When they came the two girls smacked glasses and slammed back shots of Jose Cuervo Gold. "*Santi!*, Cheers!" Lilly grimaced from the after-burn.

The chaos of The Surabaya Club's body-piercing music, flashing lights, twirling shapes, and a woman instead of a man sitting next to her, blurred into the background as Lilly's thoughts drifted back to her life before Hong Kong. She thought about *The Dream* and the promises that had sounded so real back in Indonesia, so achievable.

She had been, like most girls in her village, pulled out of school early; no marketable skills, no hope of finding work. A Sponsor had visited her parents' home, as he did all the homes with young girls. The Sponsor, bad teeth and bad breath, a crocodile with his mouth open waiting for a small animal to stroll in, sat on her mother's flower-patterned couch sipping tea. He had described a vision of wealth. *Work overseas as a maid for a few years and soon you will be buying property, have a house, a future.* They had bought *The Dream*.

Lilly immediately had found herself sitting in a training center in Jakarta learning the four 'C' skills: 'Cantonese, cleaning, cooking, and courtesy'. Cantonese was the only challenge, but after three months of study, she had reached an acceptable level of competence, and, as if a tsunami wave had suddenly rolled in from in the ocean and ripped her from Indonesia, Lilly was whisked off to Hong Kong to meet her agent and to be introduced to an employer.

It was her first trip on an airplane. Lilly gripped the armrest as if it was her tether to solid land. The sleek metal tube powered into the sky, Lilly staring out of the circular window at the clouds below them. *What sort of magic keeps us from plummeting into the ocean below?*

The agent, a short woman in a gray suit, each fingernail painted a different color, met Lilly and three other village girls at the gate. The Agent seemed to Lilly to be an incarnation of *Rangda*, the mythical, child-eating demon queen: large fangs, claws, pendulous breasts, and protruding eyeballs. "You four, follow me, quickly." *Rangda* spun and took off through the crowd.

The four girls followed the Demon Queen through Hong Kong's Chek Lap Kok Airport to a waiting shuttle bus which, with slipping gears and the sharp odor of a burning transmission, transported them to a moldy boarding house in Sheung Wan. *Is the world spinning faster? Everything is moving so fast,* Lilly thought as she looked out of the dirt-streaked van windows at Hong Kong's complex urbanity. She calmed herself by thinking about *The Dream*. *I will soon be sending great sums of money home to my family.*

In the morning, after an indoctrination speech to the group, which sounded to Lilly like a scolding, the agent, same gray suit and clicking heels, strode over to Lilly and, pointing her finger in Lilly's face, said, "You, Lilly, come with me." Lilly followed, the agent setting a pace as they wove their way through the crowded streets of Sheung Wan that Lilly found difficult to match, finally arriving at the Metro.

Mr. and Mrs. Chan, their two children, and an elderly Pomeranian, lived in East Kowloon in a six hundred square foot, fifth floor walk-up. The Chan family was not wealthy, but having a helper allowed them to be a two-income family. The two children and the Pomeranian watched from a corner with lemur-like eyes as the new 'Auntie' was sized up by Mrs. Chan. As the agent bent and bobbed deferentially while introducing Lilly to her new mistress, Mrs. Chan eyed Lilly like an accident the Pomeranian had left on the living room floor.

When the Agent left, Lilly was shown to the laundry room, which would also double as her room. A mat on the floor amidst the detergent boxes and brooms was to be her new bed. "This your schedule." Mrs. Chan said in Cantonese, thrusting a typed list at Lilly which detailed her daily activities from 6:00am to 11:00pm every day.

Looking at the list, Lilly said in broken Cantonese, "But, Madame, I was told that I would only work six days per week, with one day off. This list says that I work seven days."

The hard slap across her cheek shocked her. Lilly had never been hit before. The pain of the violation stung the most. Mrs. Chan gave a brief half-smile, and said, "Oh, yes, six days, my mistake." She then spun and walked away, leaving Lilly with tears welling in her eyes, *The Dream* collapsed on the floor around her feet.

Sundays became Lilly's one day of relief, the one day that belonged to her. On Sundays she joined the thousands of other domestic workers in Hong Kong who gathered to make and meet friends, the Filipinas in Central, and the Indonesians in Causeway Bay. Cardboard and blankets were set out on concrete, turf staked out, gossiping, playing cards, and eating home-country food from Styrofoam boxes, Sunday was for washing away the humiliation. Sunday was a day to be relished.

Months of isolation, loneliness, abuse from her employers, and a scarcity of Indonesian men in Hong Kong had left Lilly ready to seek comfort wherever it was available. She had met Bella in Victoria Park. Bella was total Tomboy, masculine gestures and body language. There was no way that she could be mistaken for someone who liked men. Lilly had felt awkward at first, but now, after three months, she was comfortable. She and Bella knew that one day Lilly would return to Indonesia, find a husband, and have children. Bella, however, would forever be a Tomboy.

Lilly's consciousness came back to the present as a man slid into their booth opposite the girls. Bella growled, "Who do you think you are?" in Indonesian.

The man smiled, showing tobacco stained teeth, and replied in Cantonese, "Hi, Girls."

"You are not Chinese, not Indonesian, not Thai, and not Filipino. What the hell are you?" Bella said in Cantonese.

"I am from Myanmar," the man said.

"Go sit someplace else," Bella snarled. Lilly noticed that Bella fingered the six inch knife that she kept strapped inside the waistband of her jeans.

"I just want to let you girls know of a money-making opportunity, that's all," the man said, flashing his ochre-streaked smile again. He removed a flyer from a cloth bag and placed it in front of the girls. One more smile and he moved on to the next booth and another couple.

Bella and Lilly looked at the flyer. In Indonesian it said, '*Teach Indonesian to Chinese businessmen on Sundays. Two hour class. Good money.*' At the bottom of the flyer was a telephone number.

"Sounds like easy money," Lilly said. "I don't want to take away our precious Sunday time though."

Bella shrugged. "You could try. Only two hours."

"Maybe." Lilly folded the flyer and put it in her pocket. "Let's dance."

At 1:00am Lilly and Bella walked past the bouncers in black T-shirts at the front door. They held hands as they exited The Surabaya Club onto the still-busy Wanchai sidewalk. Lilly gave Bella a kiss on the cheek and said "See you in a week." She walked towards the Wanchai metro station. It was the last time Bella ever saw her.

*****

In the Sham Shui Po neighborhood of Kowloon, a twenty minute subway ride from The Surabaya Club, a lean Burmese man was working late. On the long butcher block table before him lay the body of an Indonesian woman. A streak of bright blue highlight in her short hair and a tattoo of a Jasmine flower on her calf, vestiges of how she decorated herself in life, were now irrelevant. The man did not view her as a being once alive. Ever since becoming a minion of The Witch he had trained himself this way. It made the butchering easier.

With a German boning knife he carefully sliced out the rib cage. This would be the only part of the woman retained, refrigerated for Feast Day. The remainder would be disposed of in black plastic garbage bags, weighted to sink into the murky obscurity of Victoria Harbor.

Chapter 7

Lantau Island is the largest of Hong Kong's two hundred and sixty three islands, a twenty-five minute ferry ride from the skyscrapers of Central. On one side of Lantau Island is the modern Chek Lap Kok Airport and on the opposite side is Discovery Bay, a resort-like community of ex-pats and wealthy Chinese. Other than these contemporary developments and some fishing villages like Mui Wo, the majority of Lantau Island is natural, steep craggy pinnacles and thick jungle; home to six foot long cobras and Golden Orb Spiders as big as a pancake.

Mui Wo, tucked into a natural bay, is connected to Hong Kong Island by ferry. Clustered around the ferry pier and the town's central plaza are a few Western restaurants, such as the China Bear, which serves the best milk shakes in Hong Kong. Outside of this small accommodation to Western tastes is the real Mui Wo, a town of fishermen and shopkeepers. Packs of lean, curly-tailed village dogs have free run of the streets, in-bred so much that the only distinction between them is their size: small, medium, or large.

Like muscular green arms embracing the narrow streets of the village is a luxuriant jungle of vines, ferns, thorny bushes, and tropical trees, all tightly packed and jostling each other for a bit of sun and space, the tangle impassable except by a few well-used hiking trails. Besides the popular trails of weekend hikers, such as the hike from Mui Wo to Poi-O Beach along the coast, with its views of idyllic coves, Peng Chau Island, and in the far distance the high rise towers of Kowloon, there are also a network of invisible, overgrown pathways crisscrossing the island.

Through such a concealed byway, four Burmese men had traveled deep into the Lantau backcountry, and in a protected valley they had found a clearing within which they had built two simple huts in traditional Burmese style. Made out of branches, bamboo, and thatch, they had also added a door and jamb for each hut so that they could be secured when the men were absent. The four men lived in one hut communally. The other hut was for The Witch.

Most Burmese, even those living in modern cities, have an ingrained belief in witches, ghosts, and spirits. From childhood they are introduced to tales of ogres that eat bad children, of half human-half animal creatures of the underworld, and of shape-shifting creatures that hunt humans lost in the jungle. To the four Kachin tribesmen who lived in the Mui Wo jungle on Lantau Island and who served The Witch, the Spirit World was very real.

The Witch would visit the camp each weekend, arriving at Mui Wo by ferry from Central. He always carried with him a blue and white duffle bag which contained his ceremonial outfit and vials of esoteric substances, the trappings of superstition and malevolence. When he arrived at the camp The Witch would enter his hut and change into his ceremonial garb, which consisted of a maroon and blue cloth skirt, a headdress decorated with red feathers and boar tusks, and red cloth bracelets wrapped around his biceps. Bare-chested, he also put on his favorite necklace, a mummified human hand.

The men were forbidden to enter The Witch's hut. He had put no lock on the door. His word alone was sufficient to keep his men out. Each time that he left to return to Central, however, just to be sure that his power still held, The Witch would pluck a hair from his head and secretly tie it between the jamb and the door of his hut.

*****

What began as a gentle Saturday dawn had turned into a merciless scorcher by 10:00am. The Witch felt like a Burmese steamed bun, a *pauk see*, as he hiked the trail to the camp. The four Burmese men who served him, sitting in the center of the camp's clearing, smoked and chatted. A small fire smoldered in a pit in the center of the clearing, a kettle balanced on a metal grill for their tea.

When the Witch exited the jungle into the clearing, his T-shirt stained wet from the hike, the men bowed low in respect. The Witch nodded and strode to his hut, duffle bag slung over his shoulder. He stopped short at the door. The hair had been broken.

The four noted his hesitation, and their stomachs dropped. Curiosity and a six-pack of beer had gotten the better of them. *How would he know? Just a peek inside could not hurt.*

The Witch walked into his hut and shut the door. He had been violated! A violation not as much of the hut but of his power. He glanced around. Nothing was missing or disturbed, but of course he had left nothing of value there anyway. In silent anger The Witch changed into his outfit. He then took a small glass jar filled with a clear liquid from the duffle bag and tucked it into the waistband of his skirt. *They dare challenge me?* The Witch invoked Nat, his protector in the Spirit World. He pictured Nat as a sleek, golden cobra, lustrous eyes emitting a soul-penetrating, venomous white light. *Nat, I am host to your spirit.*

The Witch exited his hut howling in displeasure. He thrust his arms skyward, the feathers on his headdress vibrating as his body trembled with rage. The four men instantly prostrated themselves on the ground. They had been so careful, just curiosity, *How could he have known?*

The Witch did three circuits around the clearing, growling and bellowing as if possessed, a rabid animal released from the hell-fire of the underworld. He then strode to the men's hut, flung the door open, and disappeared inside. The men remained face-down in the dirt.

Looking around the room he surveyed the men's meager possessions in separate piles by each one's sleeping mat: clothes, combs, toothbrushes, and the metal water bottles that he had provided them. He did not know which bottle was whose, but no matter. He removed the glass jar from his waistband, took the lid off one of the water bottles, and poured in the liquid from the jar, swirling it around for a minute until he was sure that the inside of the bottle was well coated.

The Witch then exited the men's hut and walked past the prostrate men to the stone fire pit in the center of the clearing. He kicked off the tea kettle. "The rules have been broken! I have put a curse on you! One of you will die! I will leave it up to Nat as to which one!" A final howl and The Witch went back to his hut, where he changed into his jeans and t-shirt. With duffle bag slung over his shoulder, he then left the camp and hiked back through the jungle to the Mui Wo ferry pier.

On the thirty minute ride back to Central, The Witch watched the passing cargo ships from the ferry window. As the boat bucked in the choppy waves, he remembered back to when he first learned at the age of twelve that he could invoke the spirits of the underworld.

Raised by a mother who, whenever he misbehaved, had called on the goblins who ruled the world of mortals to punish her naughty boy, bedtime would involve stories of child-eating ogres. In the morning, waking up to discover that he had not been eaten, he would say to his mother, "Mom, the goblins did not eat me."

"A Nat spirit must have protected you, although I have no idea why a Nat would protect such a naughty boy as you," his mother would answer.

He came to think that Nat was his personal protector, and would speak with him every day. Nat came to be a very real ally, someone who would shelter him from the myriad spirits and humans that were out to do him harm.

His life had changed one day in July not long after his twelfth birthday. He knew that it had been July because he distinctly remembered the deafening call of the Cicadas. It was July when their song was the loudest, after the monsoon rains. He was walking home from visiting his Auntie. The red-dirt village lane, damp from rain, was crowded with the life of the village. In the huts that lined the path gaunt, brown women were milling grain, weaving cloth, making baskets from thatch, everyone barefoot. Mud-crusted black piglets and bone-thin dogs were being chased by laughing children. In the misty distance lanky men lead somnambulant water buffaloes through the verdant rice fields.

An older boy had suddenly appeared on the path in front of him blocking his way. Perhaps two years older, and motivated by nothing more complicated than a desire to exert the power he felt as his hormones turned him from a boy into a man, the boy, hands on his hips, sneered, "Why are you looking at me, Water Buffalo Shit?"

"I am not looking at you."

"You say that I am a liar? I will teach you!"

Hearing no retort to his challenge, the older boy had slapped him hard across the face and then pushed him to the ground, where he had unceremoniously landed in a puddle, splashed brown with mud like the piglets. Everyone on the street turned as he picked himself up. He remembered their laughs. The women, the children, he even imagined the underfed dogs and lethargic water buffaloes giggling at his embarrassment, his weakness. He pointed his finger at the bully and screamed, "I curse you! I curse you! In the name of Nat, I curse you!"

Where did those words come from? From Nat for sure. Suddenly the background call of the cicadas had increased in volume, the sky turned black, and a late-season monsoon drenched the village. The next day the bully had stepped on a land mine, and the boy suddenly had a reputation. He could see the fear in superstitious eyes as he walked through the village, everyone careful not to cross him. He reveled in his new power; he had become 'The Witch'.

Joining the army at an early age, and with the power from Nat and a ruthless nature, it was easy for him to dominate men. He rose in the ranks, he grew in stature, and using his troops to run drugs from Myanmar through Thailand and China to Hong Kong, The Witch had amassed a personal fortune.

The drug business had brought him to Hong Kong and he had fallen in love with the city. The world-class architectural towers of vibrant commerce, the unapologetic display of personal wealth, The Witch had felt his power grow in Hong Kong. He heard the messages from the spirit world clearer amidst the crowded skyscrapers hugging Victoria Harbor.

It was then, after he moved to Hong Kong, that Nat had instructed him to create 'Feast Day'. Nat was very explicit in his directions, '*The weak of the earth are here for you to harvest. You honor me as well as strengthen yourself by consuming them.*'

As the ferry docked in Central, The Witch thought how right Nat was. Or was he, was Nat a fabrication of his mind? He glanced at the closest seats to him. A Chinese woman was engrossed in her iPad. Next to her a Filipino helper with two blonde Western charges was napping. Another domestic helper in the next row of seats was having an argument in *Tagalog* on her mobile. The Witch partially unzipped the duffel bag on his lap and surreptitiously reached in, feeling around until he felt the mummified hand. He stroked it with his thumb and forefinger as a child would satin a blanket. *Yes, I feel the power! Nat is real, Nat is real!*

Chapter 8

Ian Hamilton's police cruiser rolled slowly through the congestion on Gloucester Road. Ian knew that he could part the traffic like Moses parting the Red Sea by putting on the flashers. However, the call had come in '*D.B. at the Queen Victoria*'. A few extra minutes would not make the body any less dead.

Ian had seen plenty of fights at the 'Queen Vic' over the years, staggering drunks swinging at air over some perceived insult. However he had no memory of there ever having been a murder there before. *Maybe the dead body is a heart attack, some ancient fossil that smoked one cigarette too many and keeled over. No, there had to be suspicious circumstances, a suspected homicide, for our department to get the call.*

The Queen Victoria, an iconic Wanchai British pub located at the epicenter of the Wanchai party scene on Lockhart Road, was a bar for those with a propensity for downing serious amounts of alcohol. The front of the bar opened to the street, and depending on the night and the crowd, it pulsed with an energy not found in newer pubs. It was sleazy and classy all at the same time. It was one of Ian's favorite bars.

Ian was a native Hong Konger born of British parents, inheriting their fair complexion and a face sprinkled with freckles. In his twenty eight years he had lived outside of Hong Kong only once while attending the London College of Communications, where he had decided that a career in the arts was not for him. As soon as he got back from London he had immediately joined the Hong Kong police force. Hong Kong was Hong Kong, and it was his home. He loved it.

Next to Ian in the passenger seat of the cruiser sat Detective Nigel Ho, Hong Kong-Chinese, two years Ian's junior. Nigel was tall, a good head over Ian, and a jogger.

Ian turned to Nigel, "I was just in the Queen Vic last weekend. You ever go there?"

"It's a *gweilo* bar, not for me," Nigel said.

Ian shrugged, "I've seen Chinese in there."

"Chinese who like to drink themselves stupid," Nigel said.

"Have I ever mentioned to you that if you loosened up once in awhile you might get yourself some pussy?" Ian smiled. Ian's signature smile was a boyish smirk, his eyes glowing with sarcasm and mischief, a promise of trouble ahead.

Nigel continued looking out the window of the cruiser. Finally he responded, "How much pussy I get is my business, but the kind of *gweilo*-loving slappers who hang out at bars like the Queen Victoria are not my type."

"Point taken. Just saying…" Ian said with another smirk.

They parked on Lockhart Road in front of the Queen Victoria. A group of afternoon drunks were standing outside befuddled, starring at the yellow police tape across the open front of the pub wondering why they had been evicted from their favorite bar just because a dead body was sprawled on the floor. Ian flashed his badge and he and Nigel ducked under the tape line.

The man lying on the tile floor was Southeast Asian. A wooden stool lay on its side next to him. Four full beer glasses were untouched on the table next to the body. No one had turned off the jukebox. *ZZ Top* was singing 'Sharp Dressed Man'.

The Coroner, Cindy Chow, squatting flat footed next to the body, was examining the dead man. Ian thought, *How do they squat like that? My knees would collapse.* "Hi, Cindy. Cause of death?" he asked.

Cindy stood up. "Good afternoon, Gentlemen. Nothing obvious. I'll update you as soon as we've studied him in the lab. We're finished with our field work here, so let me know when you're done and we'll ship him out."

"OK," Ian said, putting on latex gloves. He kneeled next to the body and ran his hand over the man's arm looking for track marks. Pushing up the victim's sleeve, Ian noted a striking tattoo on his shoulder. It was of a pair of crossed white machetes with a background of two bands, one red and one teal. Ian also noted that the man was thin but his arms were toned with muscle, and pulling the man's T-shirt up to look for wounds, saw a six-pack stomach.

"This guy was in shape," Ian said to Nigel. He went through the pockets. No wallet, just a few crumbled bills and some change. No mobile telephone. Ian stood up as the jukebox blared, *'They come runnin' just as fast as they can, cause every girl's crazy 'bout a sharp dressed man.'* "Nothing was sharp dressed about this guy, just an old T-shirt and jeans."

In a far corner of the bar an animated, plump Filipino waitress, hair dyed reddish blonde, was talking with two street officers. Ian walked over, the waitress was gesturing vigorously with her thick arms as one of the officers took notes.

"Hi, Mandy," Ian said to the waitress.

"Ian?" Mandy said, surprised at seeing a familiar face. Mandy spoke fast, her conversation like a machine gun firing a barrage of words instead of bullets, "What are you doing here? Oh yeah, you're a cop. Can you believe this shit? What is this going to do to the afternoon business?" She stopped gesturing and parked her hands on her ample hips.

"Can you tell me what happened here, Mandy?"

"Four men man came in like anyone else, nothing special, sat down at that table." Mandy pointed to the table next to the body. "I figured that they were drunk already, stupid look on their faces and all, but typical, right? Who isn't drunk in here?"

"Then what?"

"I went over to take their orders. One of them mumbled something that I did not understand. It sounded like 'Kilkenny', so I brought them each a Kilkenny draft." Ian noted the four untouched mugs of beer on the bar table. "They didn't send them back, so I assumed that I had understood correctly," Mandy continued. "The dead guy had an expression on his face like he was going to crap his pants. I was hoping he wouldn't, but it would not be the first time in this bar."

"And then?"

"I turned my back to take some other orders, and when I turned around a few minutes later, he's lying face-up on the floor. Thought he just passed out, too much booze, but when I tried to get him up…..shit, Ian, the man was dead!" Mandy said.

"What about the other three guys with him?" Ian asked.

"Gone. Disappeared."

Ian turned to the two police officers, "Any other witnesses?"

"No one that wasn't slurring their words, but we got their names for follow-up," one of the officers said.

"OK, thanks," Ian said. He turned and looked around the room for anything that seemed out of place. He had been in the Queen Victoria a thousand times. The British flag on the wall, the 'Pizza of the Month' sign, the bottles of Del Monte ketchup and HP Sauce on the tables, the framed map of 'The Queen's Dominion at the End of the Nineteenth Century'. It was all there as always.

Ian walked back over to Nigel. "Nigel, go through the back rooms, especially the restrooms. Look for a hypo just in case he had gone back there to shoot up. No signs of needle use on his arms, but you never know. I'll collect the evidence from the table."

As he was working Mandy called across the room, "Hey Ian, there is one more thing that I remember." She beckoned him over.

"Oh, yeah?" Ian walked back over to her. Mandy, just like the bar, smelled of stale beer and cigarette smoke.

"Yeah. Each one of the men had a cloth bag strapped over his shoulder when they came in," Mandy said. "Like they worked together. I mean, why would four guys each be carrying identical bags if they didn't work together?"

"But the body on the floor does not have one, so the other three must have taken the victim's bag when he fell. That's important, Mandy. Thanks."

*****

Two hours later Ian and Nigel had finished collecting what evidence they could and left. As Ian walked out of the bar his phone vibrated. The text message was from his sister, Sarah. Sarah Hamilton, two years younger than Ian, had graduated with a degree in art history, which she had parlayed into a job with Julie's Auction House.

The text read, '*Tott's. 7:30.*'

Tott's Bar and Restaurant on the thirty-fourth floor of the Excelsior

Hotel was one of those places that used to be un-cool, patronized only by tourists in their fifties. However, just because it was so 'un-cool', it had suddenly become 'super-cool', a great place to start the evening with some dinner and drinks before heading out to Lan Kwai Fong.

Ian texted back, '*OK. George coming?*'

George Washington Smith, Sarah's boyfriend, was an American architect. He was the same age as Ian but an opposite in looks and style. Ian looked like he could bench press a hippopotamus. George appeared more pedantic than athletic. Ian's dress and grooming were on the conservative side, where George's attire could best be described as 'experimental'. However, the two got along well.

'*Yes, George and also another friend.*' Sarah texted back. Ian knew that '*another friend*' meant that Sarah was bringing a girl with her whom she hoped he would fall deeply in love with, and that they would live happily ever after. *Right, that never works out*, Ian thought.

Ian returned to headquarters with Nigel, filing the evidence and completing the paperwork. He then walked to his apartment in the Mid-Levels. He could not get the image of the dead man's tattoo out of his mind. He sensed that it was a clue. He also was annoyed to find he could not stop his mind from running a constant replay of 'Sharp Dressed Man'.

A shower and a change of clothing, and a short ride on the Metro to Causeway Bay, 'Sharp Dressed Man' was still playing in his head as the elevator rose to the thirty-fourth floor of the Excelsior Hotel. He exited the elevator and walked into the luxurious, wood paneled dining room of Tott's. A live jazz band was setting up in a corner of the room. Ian spotted Sarah and George sitting at a table by the window with an attractive Asian woman in a red silk blouse and blue jeans. A string of pearls around her neck contrasted brilliantly with her cappuccino-colored skin.

Ian walked up to the table and Sarah, fair and with freckles like her brother, bounced up and gave her brother a hug. She said, "Ian, this is my friend Tika."

Tika, tall and graceful, stood and extended her hand, "Hi, Ian. Sarah told me that you are a detective with the Hong Kong Police Department, right?"

"Yes, nice to meet you. Tika, I like the name," Ian said. *This girl is gorgeous! Nice work, Sarah!*

"It's short for Atika. It's an Indonesian name."

"You are Indonesian?" Ian asked.

"Canadian, but my parents are Indonesian."

Sarah added, "Tika is an attorney with the Indonesian Legal Aid Foundation."

They sat down. "Hey, George, how is it?" Ian said.

George, scruffy beard, wearing a suit from the 60's, a thin tie, and Converse All Stars, was sipping a martini. "Hey, Ian."

From Tott's over-size windows Ian watched the sparkling lights of the numerous ships traversing Victoria Harbor. Three festive cruise liners were docked across the harbor at Tsim Sha Tsui. He ordered a beer and admired the distinctive skyline of Kowloon: the Hong Kong Museum of Art and the Promenade, the Kowloon Station Clock Tower, and the ICC Tower. His beer arrived, and Ian said, "Glad that it's Friday! Cheers!"

"Amen!" George exclaimed. "*Gambei* that shit. It's the weekend!" He raised his glass above his head and then downed his martini in one gulp.

Ian followed, draining the mug, and then called for the waiter. "Tika and Sarah, what are you ladies drinking?"

"Wine." Sarah said.

"Unless you boys want to do some shots instead?" Tika added.

"I am all over *that*, Tikarina," George said. "Waiter, four shots of Tequila, *Herradura* please."

The waiter brought the shots, and also placed a sheet of paper with a list of tequila brands and a pen on the table. "This is our list of available tequilas today, Sir. You can just mark off which ones you would like to try."

"Wow, just like a sushi bar, only with tequila!" George said as he perused the list. "I like this."

After they downed the shots, Tika said, "Ian, I have a confession to make."

"Really? A confession?" Ian smiled.

"I asked Sarah to introduce us because there is an issue that I want to speak with you about in your professional capacity." She then added, "Not tonight when we're drinking, of course, another time."

"Sure. No problem, Tika."

"Can I call you tomorrow morning then?" Tika asked.

The next round of shots arrived at the table, and Ian said, "Be glad to talk with you tomorrow, Tika, but we had better make it tomorrow afternoon if these shots keep coming."

"Deal." Tika said, raising her glass and knocking back the drink. "Thank you."

Ian realized as he downed his shot that for once Sarah had introduced him to an interesting woman. *This girl can drink!* Ian thought, *and she looks amazing.*

The shots kept coming, and George started to talk about his latest assignment at work. "Guys, check out this coincidence. Sarah and I have the same client."

"Yeah, but not just any client," Sarah said. "A real bad guy."

"Congratulations," Ian said. "But, why would either of you take on a client that you know is a bad guy?"

"Money, of course. Money and opportunity, my friend," George said, holding up his shot.

"Tell us about this horrible client of yours," Tika said.

"He is an illegal jade dealer as well as a drug dealer," Sarah said, leaning forward. "He is some high-up guy connected to the Burmese military, and he runs jade mines in Myanmar. He makes slaves of whole villages of laborers, pays them in heroin and makes HIV infected addicts out of them. After the jade travels from Myanmar our 'bad boy' puts it on auction at Julie's. The twice yearly Julie's Jade Auction has become quite the international event."

"Very nice, but doesn't that make Julie's complicit in the whole illegal jade trade business?" Ian asked, slamming back his latest shot of tequila. "And why is this exemplary citizen also your client, George?"

"Well, the boogieman's name is Zaw Than.' George said. "He has come up with the idea to build a hotel in Hpakant, and he has hired my firm to design it."

"Hpakant? Never heard of it," Ian said.

George explained, "Ninety nine percent of the jade in the world comes from a relatively small area in Myanmar called Jade Land. Hpakant is at the center of it. No foreigners are allowed into Jade Land except the Chinese buyers. These buyers have no decent place to stay in Hpakant. A world-class hotel in Hpakant would have zero vacancy, no competition, and could charge whatever exorbitant room rates they wanted."

As George spoke, Ian absentmindedly was doodling on the tequila list that the waiter had left. George suddenly looked down at Ian's sketch and pointed, exclaiming, "Hold up, you know more than you have let on, Ian, that's KIA!"

"KIA?" Ian looked down at his sketch. He had drawn the tattoo of the crossed machetes that was on the dead man's shoulder at the Queen Vic.

"Yeah, KIA, Kachin Independence Army. That's their emblem," George said. "They run the jade mines in Myanmar and control the Jade Road through China. Hpakant is in Kachin territory. Not only that, there is a constant shooting match going on between the Burmese government and the KIA for control of the jade mines. The Chinese are in the mix too, trying to buy mine rights from both groups."

"Serious?"

"Yeah."

Ian thought, *A connection with the Myanmar jade trade and my Queen Victoria dead body? If my victim is a Kachin rebel from some area called 'Jade Land', and this client of George's and Sarah's, Zaw Than, controls the jade trade to Hong Kong, then I wonder if Zaw Than might not soon become a client of mine too!*

Chapter 9

Ian woke up mid-morning feeling like he had been cracked in the head with a bat, awakened by the vibrating iPhone next to his bed. The screen showed that he had a text message. It was from Tika. '*What time meet today?*' Ian noted that the text had been sent at 8:00am. *She was out as late as I was and matched me drink for drink, and yet she's sending texts at 8:00am? That girl can drink!*

'*Lunch?*' He texted back.

Ten minutes later the answer, '*Good.* Sedap Gurih *on Sugar Street, Causeway Bay. Noon.*' Ian's stomach took a bounce at the thought of Indonesian food after the night's tequila.

******

A crowded Saturday in Causeway Bay, locals moving like zombies while staring at their mobile phones or reading the newspaper as they walked, oblivious to their surroundings. *Gweilo* tourists stopped to window shop or glance upwards at the tall buildings, blocking the flow of sidewalk traffic like boulders in a stream with their huge Western bodies. Groups of Muslim women wearing colorful head scarves, their un-made-up faces the only part of their bodies exposed, darted through the slow strolling crowd in small, quick groups, like schools of colorful fish. Indonesian Tomboys and Girly-girls walked hand in hand, or sat on the stairs at the Yee Wo pedestrian overpass eating pungent dishes from Styrofoam containers. Ian navigated his way through the obstacle course, his head still battered from his hangover, making his way from the Metro towards Sugar Street.

At the corner of Yee Wo and Sugar Ian spotted the bright red sign of Sedap Gurih. He walked into the open doorway. The pungent smell of shrimp paste hit his nostrils, and his stomach took a jump. Tika was sitting at one of the booths along the wall. Next to Tika sat an

Indonesian woman, about twenty years old, half her head shaved bald. The hair on the other half was chopped short and dyed with streaks of gold. She wore no makeup and had a small silver ring in one eyebrow. Ian slid into the booth. "Good morning, Ladies."

Tika said, "Thanks for coming, Ian. This is Ruby."

Ian looked at Ruby, smiled, and nodded. She fleetingly smiled back, but Ian noted that the smile was only a flash, a pretense. Her eyes were not smiling.

"I hope that you don't mind my bringing Ruby along. Ruby doesn't speak English, so I will explain the situation to you first and then will translate as Ruby gives you the details."

"OK," Ian said, staring at Ruby's hairstyle, thinking, *How can she think that looks good?*

The waitress came over with menus. "Shall we order first?" Tika asked.

"Great, it has pictures," Ian said as he opened the menu. "I'll have the Nasi Goreng and a coffee." The girls ordered in Indonesian. As Tika spoke to the waitress in Indonesian, Ian watched her. *She still looks hot today.*

After the waitress left Tika leaned towards Ian and said, "Someone is preying on the Indonesian Tomboys and Girly-girls."

"Preying on…?" Ian asked.

"Abducting, or maybe worse. Every month one or two disappear."

"Tomboys and Girly-girls…?"

"You know, the lesbians."

"Oh," Ian said. "How do you know they're abductions? Maybe they just decided to go back to Indonesia?"

"And leave their few possessions? And not tell their friends? Just walk off and disappear? Not likely!" Tika said with a dismissive wave of her hand.

"How long has this been going on?"

"About four months. It's hard to judge. A lot of it probably goes unreported. Ruby is one of the vocal ones. Many just move on to the next girlfriend and say nothing."

"So how did you get involved, Tika?" Ian asked.

"The foundation that I work for defends the rights of the Indonesians who come to Hong Kong as domestic helpers. The girls distrust the police, they would never talk to someone like yourself alone." Tika said. She reached into her bag and pulled out a file folder, handing it to Ian. "I have interviewed those that came forward. The details of twelve of the disappearances are in here."

Ian quickly thumbed through the papers in the folder, closed it, and placed the file on the table.

Ruby suddenly erupted into a flurry of angry Indonesian, pointing her finger at Ian and then slamming her hand on the table. Ian looked helplessly at Tika. "What?"

Tika smiled, "Indonesians are calm and submissive, until they are not. When you piss one off, watch out. She interpreted the way that you so casually looked through the file that I gave you as meaning that you are disinterested."

"No… I didn't mean anything by it. I'll read it in detail later," Ian said, looking directly at Ruby as he spoke.

Ruby unleashed another barrage of fiery Indonesian.

"She says that you disrespect us. Her people come here and are abused and treated like slaves every day and the police only turn their eyes the other way. Now someone is systematically killing them. What justice will they get?"

"I will seriously investigate this, Ruby, I promise," Ian protested.

Ruby shrugged and frowned. She looked away, saying something more in Indonesian.

"I would rather not translate *that*," Tika said.

Ruby's expression suddenly went from anger to terror as she looked over Ian's shoulder. Framed by the open doorway she saw three Southeast Asian men coming down the stairs of the pedestrian overpass that crossed Yee Wo Street. The men split up at the bottom of the stairs and one walked into Sedap Gurih. Without a word Ruby jumped up, dashed through the restaurant's open kitchen, and bolted out a side door.

Ian watched her small frame disappear and then looked at Tika, "What happened?"

"Don't know." Tika said, frowning and shrugging. "Sometimes these girls are more feral than logical. They can only depend on themselves for survival."

The Southeast Asian man, unnoticed by Ian and Tika, looked the patrons of the restaurant over and then slid into a booth where a Tomboy and her girlfriend were eating from a plate of rice and vegetables with their fingers. He spoke to them in Cantonese, smiled, reached into a cloth bag, and handed them a flyer.

Chapter 10

George had his feet up on the desk of his cubicle on the twenty-fourth floor of the steel and glass edifice of Pacific Place 3. From the window of the Hong Kong headquarters of Robison Whitehorse and Grant he had a view of some of the world's most magnificent skyscrapers. Telephone to his ear, he said to Sarah on the other end of the line, "Going to be gone for a while, Saralita. Doing a site visit for Zaw Than's hotel project. Back in a week."

"You are going to Myanmar?" Sarah's asked.

"Yep. Not just Myanmar though, Babe. Going to Jade Land, way outside of the tourist triangle."

"Alone?"

"Not alone. Tan Lam, my project manager, will come too. And we are being taken by Aung. You know him, he is Zaw Than's assistant, the only one who speaks English."

"I am jealous! No one from Julie's has ever been to Jade Land, other than my boss," Sarah said.

"I am special," George joked. "You are lucky to know me."

"No, seriously, George, it's a big deal. Except for the Chinese buyers, no foreigners are ever allowed into the jade mining district," Sarah said. "How are you getting there?"

"We fly into Yangon from Hong Kong and then take a local airline to …," George picked up the piece of paper on his desk with his itinerary, the Burmese names still strange to him, "Myitkyina. I am probably killing the pronunciation. Then we drive to Hpakant."

"How cool! I can't wait to see your photos! Send them to me daily. We can also Skype."

"No can do, Sarah. Government blanks out all internet service for the public in Myanmar outside of Yangon, keeping the masses under control and all that. We will be off the grid, Baby."

Tan Lam, George's project manager, walked into George's cubicle and interrupted the call. He said, "Sorry, George. They are here."

"Got to go, Sarah. I have a design meeting with Zaw Than and his boys. See you in a week." He hung up the telephone.

"They are in the lobby," Tan said. Tan was three years out of Hong Kong University. Robison Whitehorse and Grant was his first job.

"Did you get all the drawings up on the walls in the conference room, Tan?" George asked.

"Sure."

"Ready for *Shock and Awe*?" George had borrowed the military term *Shock and Awe* from George Bush the Second's presidency. George Bush had used the term to mean overwhelming the enemy with so much fire power that they would recognize America as the most powerful force on the planet. In architectural terms, George Washington Smith had adopted the term to mean overwhelming the client with so many fully-worked out design concepts in the initial presentation that George Washington Smith would be recognized as the most powerful architect on the planet, or at least in Hong Kong.

George and Tan walked into Robison Whitehorse and Grant's plush lobby where five Burmese men in ill-fitting gray suits sat awkwardly on a plush French couch, a glass coffee table in front of them supporting five untouched cups of coffee in delicate white cups. The men stood up as the two architects approached.

Aung, the leader of the group, beamed as they shook hands. In broken English he said, "George and Tan, good see you." Pointing to his colleagues, "These four, me, are Design Committee. I only one speak English."

The architects handed out business cards. The men of the Design Committee did not respond with business cards of their own. "I am George Washington Smith, and this is my project manager, Tan Lam," George said. "You are..?"

"Don't worry their names. Burmese people change their names all the time," Aung said laughing.

George was expecting jade dealer/drug lord Zaw Than to attend the meeting. Not seeing him, he had difficulty hiding his disappointment. "Is Zaw Than not going to be here then? Should we wait for him to begin?" George asked.

"He set own schedule," Aung shrugged. "Start please without him."

George led the five Burmese men into Robison Whitehorse and Grant's main conference room: huge marble table, the latest Herman Miller chairs, warm gray carpeting. All along the walls Tan had taped up their conceptual drawings.

Aung had previously sent George a brief program for the project: the boundary and size of the site, the need for a hotel of about two hundred rooms, not too many amenities, a businessman's hotel. With only this rudimentary program George had launched into his *Shock and Awe* program.

He had assembled his design team, which included Tan and two interns. "OK, Team, prime programmatic element of this project is capturing a sense of place. Myanmar. Not just anyplace Myanmar, however, but deep-in–the-jungle Myanmar. 'Comfort in the Jungle', that's our theme. I have pulled classical Myanmar architectural elements and details off the internet. I will e-mail the files to all of you. We are now officially in *Shock and Awe* mode, Gentlemen. Do you know what that means?" George had paused and looked at the younger architects. They had stared backed blankly. "It means that you are working with George Washington Smith, Gentlemen, and we will exceed all expectations. We will blow their Burmese socks right off their feet!"

As the Burmese clients lowered themselves tentatively into the conference room's ergonomically advanced Herman Miller chairs George looked around the conference room in satisfaction. The walls were covered with over thirty drawings of a hotel styled in all the faux Burmese architectural details that Google Images could provide. A computer connected to an overhead projector flashed images of a resort-like hotel with happy businessmen, briefcases in hand, strolling through luxurious landscaping past swimming pools and fountains and into a spacious lobby. The Design Committee, in their over-sized suits and seated at the gigantic marble conference table, stared vacuously at the images.

George, armed with a laser pointer, proceeded with his presentation. "So, Aung, if you could please translate for me I would appreciate it."

"No problem," Aung said.

George talked for about ten minutes, starting with options for the location of the building on the site. He spoke about the structure fitting naturally into the topography, about taking advantage of the best views, about vehicular, pedestrian, and back-of-house service circulation. He described the need to provide the hotel guests with a memorable experience. George then paused and nodded to Aung to translate.

Aung said only two short sentences in Burmese, and then nodded back to George.

"You translated all that?"

"Yes."

The Burmese men fidgeted in their Herman Miller chairs. George continued, "The floor plan, designed to enhance clear way-finding..."

Suddenly the double doors of the conference room opened and a tall Burmese man with a crew cut wearing an Armani suit strode in. To his left, right, and rear were bodyguards whose eyes scanned everyone in the room. Aung and the Design Committee instantly sprung to their feet. George was surprised when the Design Committee saluted. Zaw Than saluted back crisply.

Ahh, George thought, *The Big Dog arrives. Now this will be more like it.* George walked over to Zaw Than, extended his hand, and said, "I am George Washington Smith, the Director in charge of your project. It is a pleasure to meet you."

Zaw Than nodded, shaking George's hand. George noticed the deep green of a jade ring set in white gold on his pinky finger. Zaw Than then looked at the walls and walked slowly past all the drawings until he had completed the full circuit of the room. George opened his mouth to explain the design, but before he could get a word out Aung said, "Shut up."

When he had completed his circuit Zaw Than stopped in front of the Design Committee and had a short discussion with them in Burmese. He then strode out of the room followed by the three bodyguards. The room suddenly seemed emptied of energy. "What did he say?" George, surprised, asked.

"He asked if I had given you the picture yet," Aung answered. "I told him not yet."

"The picture? What picture?"

Aung reached into the breast pocket of his suit and pulled out a Polaroid photograph. He handed it to George.

"In 1995 we travel to Anaheim in California. We went to *Happiest Place on Earth*."

"You went to Disneyland?" George asked, looking at the picture. The photograph showed the members of the Design Committee standing, smiling, and displaying thumbs up in front of a Motel 6. "OK, so what is this photo supposed to show?"

"Hotel like this. This good American hotel. You design like this," Aung said.

"You want me to design a Motel 6? You're kidding! This is a terrible hotel...Look at the air conditioners sticking out from under the windows! It's a crappy, white stucco box!" George blurted before he could control himself.

One of the Design Committee members walked around the conference table and stuck his finger in George's face. He exclaimed in English, "No way, Jose!" All the committee members exploded in laughter. Aung said, "He learned that on trip to America. Very funny guy."

The Burmese men walked out of the conference room, still laughing. George collapsed into one of the conference room chairs. Instead of *Shock and Awe* George had just blown the entire Conceptual Phase budget for the project, and now he was at point zero. Worse than that, George Washington Smith would be known, at least at Robison Whitehorse and Grant, as the guy who designed the project that looked like a Motel 6 in Myanmar. George glanced over at Tan still sitting across from him, a look of horror on Tan's face.

"George, those guys are very scary. Are we really going to go with them to one of the most dangerous places in Asia?" Tan asked.

"Myanmar, dangerous? No way, it's perfectly safe," George said.

"Are you kidding? Have you ever 'Googled' Myanmar Jade Land, George? Do you not know that those guys are Kachin rebels? They are involved in a shooting war with the Burmese government over the jade trade in an area where a life is considered almost worthless!" Tan exclaimed.

"Well, sure, but people go there all the time and nothing happens to them," George answered.

"*People* go to Yangon, George. *People* go to resorts set up for tourists. No one in their right mind goes to Hpakant with the Kachin Independence Army." Tan walked out of the room.

George sat by himself in the empty conference room, dejected, but then thought, *I can turn this around, just need to educate the client. Reaction based on limited experience, that is what that was. I'll cut back the swimming pool, eliminate the conference center, give them a smaller restaurant. A small jewel of traditional Myanmar architecture nestled in the jungle. 'Comfort in the Jungle' is still on!* He grabbed a roll of sketch paper and a Pilot pen.

Chapter 11

Coroner Cindy Chow stood at the entry to Ian's cubicle and waited until he noticed her. Ian looked up from the file he was reading and said, "Oh, Cindy, didn't know you were there. Please sit down," pointing to the spare chair in his space.

"You wanted to see me?" Cindy asked as she lowered herself into the seat.

"Yes, I have some questions on the report that you sent on the Queen Vic body." Ian picked up the report. "Cause of Death is listed as tetrodotoxin poisoning?"

"Right. That is the toxin in blowfish, specifically in this case the tiger blowfish," Cindy said.

"Isn't that what the Japanese call *fugu*, eat it in sashimi?" Ian asked.

"Correct. In Japan you must be a specially trained chef to get a license to prepare it. Most of the toxin is in the fish's liver. One drop of toxin from the liver can kill a man," Cindy said.

"How would death occur?"

Blowfish poison is a neurotoxin. The victim would first feel a tingling numbness in his lips and fingers, then a general muscle weakness, and in the final stage a paralysis of his diaphragm. The respiratory system would fail. That is what finally killed your victim, asphyxiation."

"So he died from eating a last meal of *fugu* fish?"

"No, his stomach was almost empty. No fish, no *fugu*," Cindy said. "Also, he had a huge amount of the toxin in his system, much more than a few drops. He would have had to have eaten the whole liver to get that much toxin in his system."

"A whole liver? Once it got in his system, how long would it take to kill him?" Ian asked.

"Death could occur in a few hours, but with the amount of toxin that that he had in him, I would say that death occurred within thirty minutes at the most."

"How would he get so much blowfish toxin in his system if he didn't eat it?"

Cindy smiled and shrugged, "You're the detective, but other than by eating it the poison could enter the system by drinking it, injecting it, through an open wound, or by inhaling it."

"Your report also said that there was blood splatter on the victim's clothes?" Ian asked.

"Right. The victim's clothes were covered with specks of human blood from multiple sources," Cindy said.

"It wasn't just one person's blood? It was from many people?"

"Right, we identified at least eight different sources. The splatter pattern also suggests multiple angles. The pattern would be consistent with what you would find on the apron of someone working in a butcher shop, only that would be animal's blood, of course, rather than human."

"Can you tell the ethnicity or ages of the people from the blood?" Ian asked.

"Ha," Cindy chuckled, "I think you have been watching too many detective shows on TV, Detective Hamilton."

"What else can you tell me about our Queen Victoria body?" Ian asked.

"As the report mentions ethnically he is Burmese, and there are multiple scars from old bullet wounds on his body. Violence was not something foreign to this guy, consistent with a military career."

"So our Queen Vic fatality was a soldier-turned-serial killer who butchered his victims, and then he was killed by blowfish toxin."

"That is for you to say, Detective, not me," Cindy shrugged and stood up to leave.

Ian put down the file on the *Queen Vic* body as Cindy left his cubicle and picked up the file that Tika had given him. *Multiple Indonesian girls disappearing. Are they the contributors of the multiple blood splatters?*

*****

The Business Class lounge at Chek Lap Kok Airport was a hushed, dimly lit refuge of serenity and privilege. George Washington Smith and Tan Lam were availing themselves of the lounge's finger-food while waiting for their flight to Myanmar. "I wonder where Aung and the Design Committee are?" George said to Tan, as he filled a plate with sushi, spring rolls, and pork dumplings.

"Oh, I saw them as I was walking to the lounge. They are flying Economy, so they cannot get into the lounge," Tan answered.

George's stomach sunk; his clients were flying Economy and he and his project manager were flying Business Class? That was not a good message to send to the client. "Economy? It's in our contract that we fly Business, right?"

Tan shrugged. "They are more cost conscious than us, I guess."

George had the contract with Zaw Than's 'Kachin Hotel Group' translated into Burmese so he knew that there could be no misunderstanding; Robison Whitehorse and Grant's Business Class air tickets were a reimbursable expense. *But if they are flying Economy, I wonder if they are going to respect the contract? Do they even plan to reimburse us?* he worried.

George called his finance department. "Hi, Claire. This is George. Could you tell me if the Kachin Hotel Group paid their retainer fee for the Myanmar project?" A pause. "No? OK, thanks." George's stomach did another flip.

Tan was sitting in an upholstered chair munching on crackers and cheese. "Tan, I am going to find Aung. I need to discuss something with him. See you on the plane," George said.

He spotted his Burmese clients sitting by the gate. They had all taken off their shoes and all were wearing identical gray and red socks with the word 'Boss' embroidered on them. George was greeted with smiles as he walked up.

"Hi, Aung. Hey, there's something I would like to discuss with you. I hate to bring this up, but I just called my office and you guys have not paid the retainer yet. That was supposed to be paid before we started work, and certainly before we went on any trips like this. It's very clear in the contract," George said.

"Oh, sorry, sorry. Forgot. We give you money in Myanmar. No worry."

"In Myanmar?"

"Yeah, yeah, no worry."

"By the way, I noticed that you and your team are flying Economy. I just want to mention that, per our contract, Tan and I are flying Business Class. I hope that's OK," George said.

"Sure, OK, OK, you guys famous architects, right? Yeah, yeah, no worry."

Their Dragonair flight from Hong Kong to Yangon International was delayed by an hour, which necessitated a quick dash in Myanmar through the Yangon International Terminal to a shuttle bus which took them to the Domestic Terminal. There they caught a Myanma Airways flight to Myitkyina.

Seated in the one-class airplane next to Aung, the plane shaking as it ascended through turbulence, George pulled the Myanma Airways brochure from the pocket in front of him. It was in Burmese. George opened to the map page which showed all the cities that Myanma flew to.

Aung reached over and pointed to a small red dot on the map in northern Myanmar. "Myitkyina, 920 miles from Yangon. Spend night, then morning drive Hpakant."

George looked at the red dot that Aung had pointed too, surrounded by miles of nothingness in any direction. "How long a drive is it to Hpakant from Myitkyina?"

"If not muddy, six hours."

George fell asleep on the flight, waking as the plane was descending. He stuck his nose to the window and looked out at the dark green canopy of impenetrable jungle below, the blue's and orange's of a setting sun on the horizon. Still groggy with the remnants of sleep, George imagined tigers, apes, and elephants concealed beneath the canopy of the intertwined trees below. The wheels of the airplane dropped and George, turning his attention to the interior of the plane, noted that he was the only Caucasian on the flight. Even Tan, sitting next to a Design Committee member, was Asian. There were a few other Chinese and Indians, but everyone else was Burmese. *On the edge of civilization, bringing Western architectural sensibilities to the natives, the International Missionary of Architecture, George Washington Smith, lands in a remote area of northern Myanmar*, George announced to himself.

They got their luggage and George and Tan exchanged their Hong Kong Dollars for Burmese Kyats. Aung and the Design Committee walked George and Tan outside of Myitkyina's World War II-era airport building, little more than a Quonset hut, where a line of three-wheeled motorcycle taxis waited. The heat and humidity were overwhelming even for someone used to Hong Kong's tropical weather. Aung said, "You go hotel. We pick you up morning, hotel lobby. 9:00."

"Which hotel? Where are you going? Where are we going?" George asked, surprised at being abandoned.

"We go someplace. You OK, no worry. Hotel Madira. I tell driver." George, Tan and their luggage were squeezed into the back seat of the small cab connected to a 50cc motorcycle, and Aung unleashed a flurry of Burmese at the scarecrow of a driver.

As the motorcycle taxi lurched away from the curb, Aung yelled at George, "He take you hotel. No let him cheat you."

Already out of Aung's earshot and careening down the airport exit road, George yelled back, "How would I know if he is cheating me or not?" He turned to see Aung and the Design Committee stepping into a gleaming black Range Rover that had pulled up to the curb behind the three-wheelers.

The four story Hotel Madira facade was a disharmonious composition of forms painted Walmart blue. George paid the driver, who had held up four fingers. George knew it would be useless to ask for a receipt so that he could expense the fare. They walked through the aluminum and glass entry doors to the front desk, and with relief found that the staff at the Hotel Madira spoke English.

After checking in, George said to Tan, "Let's meet in the lobby in an hour and get some dinner."

"Are we going to eat in the hotel restaurant?" Tan asked.

"And miss an opportunity to discover the real Myitkyina? No way." George turned to the desk staff, "Is there a restaurant around here that you could recommend?"

"Many Westerners like Kiss Me Restaurant. Not far, ten minute walk, next to the Su Taung Pyi Pagoda."

"That sounds great. Kiss Me it is. See you in an hour, Tan."

Chapter 12

The Kiss Me Restaurant had two sections, each with a different ambiance. The front section was a fluorescent-lit eatery with long wooden tables and benches, sheet vinyl floors, and aluminum framed pictures of Myanmar temples hanging on white-washed walls. To the rear was another room, the bar. Two steps down, carpeted, low lighting, no windows. As they walked in George asked the greeter, "Can we get food in the bar?"

No answer came from the greeter, only a blank stare. George pantomimed eating from a plate and pointed to the bar. The greeter enthusiastically shook his head 'Yes', directed them down the two stairs, and handed them each a menu.

They could see that there were other people at the bar but the lighting was so dim that their forms were only darkened shadows. George used his mobile phone to light up their menus. There were pictures of a variety of unidentifiable items on rice and they each picked one by pointing when a waiter arrived, handing the menus back and hoping that they had chosen wisely. George asked the bartender, "Do you speak English? Do you have any tequila?"

"Speak English little. No tequila. Whiskey, gin, beer," the bartender said pointing to the backlit bottles lined up on glass shelves behind the bar.

George squinted his eyes as he perused the selection of whiskies on the back bar. "Hmm, Johnny Walker on the rocks for me. What about you, Tan?"

"Sure, sounds good," Tan said.

A voice from one of the darkened forms from down the bar said, in unaccented English, "Excuse me, Gentlemen, but are you sure that you want your drinks 'on the rocks'? I have seen many a good man laid flat by ordering a drink in this part of the world 'on the rocks'."

The form rose and came out of the darkness into their light circle.

He was a huge Western man in a white buttoned down shirt and blue jeans. He held out his hand and said, "I am Ruud."

"I am George and this is Tan. We are from Hong Kong. 'On the rocks' is a problem here?" George's hand was dwarfed by Ruud's as they shook.

"The ice cubes in the drinks comes from a water tap, the bacteria is frozen inside," Ruud said.

"Good advice. Bartender, please make those two Johnny Walkers straight up," George said. Turning back to their new friend, "'Ruud' sounds like a Dutch name."

"It is. If you don't mind my asking, what are you guys doing here? Westerners are rare in this town."

"We are architects. We're designing a hotel in Hpakant."

"In Hpakant! You guys must be really connected. No foreigners are ever allowed in there." Ruud exclaimed, seating himself next to George. As Ruud eased his giant frame onto the barstool, George and Tan noticed that he was missing his left hand. In its place was a prosthetic that looked the BBQ tongs George used on his Weber to flip steaks.

Noting their stares, Ruud said, "An occupational accident."

"What is your occupation, Ruud?" Tan asked.

"Global supply chain."

The drinks came with the rice dishes, along with a pint of beer for Ruud. "So you guys are heading out to Hpakant soon?" Ruud said, and he knocked back half the beer. "I admire your adventurous spirit, Gentlemen."

"We're not adventurous, we're just architects," Tan said. "It's safe, right?"

"Righhhht....," Ruud said.

The drinks kept coming. Two hours into it George realized that he was quite pleasantly inebriated. Tan, who did not have much propensity for alcohol at all, was sloppily slurring his words and was weaving back and forth on his stool.

Ruud had launched into a list of dangers to be aware of in Myanmar. "What do you mean, we are being watched?" Tan loudly demanded. Ruud put a finger up to his lips.

Tan, in a hissing whisper, asked the same question again, "What do you mean we are being watched?"

"Do not turn around and look, but those two guys at the table behind you are undercover police. All foreigners are watched in this part of the world."

Tan turned around and looked. "Holy cow!"

"Hey, I have a big favor to ask of you guys," Ruud said. "The last time I was in Hpakant I forgot my mobile phone there. A friend of mine in Hphakant has it. Could I ask him to give it to you guys to return to me? I am in Hong Kong every month. I could get it from you there."

"Sure. How will we find him?" George asked.

"You will be the only Westerners in Hpakant. He will have no trouble finding you. His name is Tony. I will contact him and let him know that you are coming. Thank you so much. This means a lot to me."

George gave Ruud a business card, "Here's my contact information in Hong Kong. Do you have a card?"

Ruud patted his pocket with his one hand, "I didn't bring one with me. No problem, Tony will let me know when he has passed the phone to you and I will contact you the next time that I come to Hong Kong."

"Great. Well, we need to get back, Ruud," George said, signaling the waiter for the bill, using the international pantomime of writing with an imaginary pen on an imaginary piece of paper.

"No, no, I got it," Ruud said.

*****

At 9:00am the next morning, hung over and seated uncomfortably on a couch upholstered in extra-crinkly vinyl, Tan waited with George in the Madira Hotel lobby for the Design Committee. When the Committee arrived, George and Tan saw a transformed group. They were on their home turf, not awkward strangers in a foreign land wearing ill-fitting suits. Here they were dressed in camouflage pants and combat boots, tight green T-shirts showing off their wiry, muscular frames. Each also had a large pistol in a holster strapped to his side. As Aung reached out to shake George's hand in greeting and his T-shirt sleeve rode up his bicep, George noted a tattoo of white crossed machetes on a background of two stripes, one teal and one red.

"Let's go," Aung said.

Outside of the hotel two mud-splattered Toyota trucks were waiting for them. George and Tan were directed into the backseat. Aung slipped into the passenger seat next to the driver. The Design Committee took up the other truck.

Within fifteen minutes of driving they had left the relative civilization of Myitkyina and were enveloped by the vibrant green kaleidoscope of the Burmese jungle. The trucks' tires straddled the narrow, red dirt ribbon of a road, the only passage through a tangle of choking vines and who-knows-what. Step off the path and be swallowed whole.

George inhaled deeply. "What a change from Hong Kong, huh, Tan? The air is so delicious! The colors are so intense, the reds of the dirt, the greens of the jungle, the blues of the sky."

Tan looked at George through his half shut eyes of a hung-over fog. "George, can I be honest with you?"

"Sure, Tan."

"You are a very optimistic person, and that is a good trait. However, I am concerned that you do not notice the small details that might not be positive, like the fact that our Design Committee members are carrying guns."

"I noticed, Tan. Look, let me tell you something about my life, as long as we are being honest. I come from a rural town in California. Have you ever heard of Gilroy, Tan? Of course not. Well, the town calls itself the 'Garlic Capital of the World'. That about says it. Everyone grows up in farming. Nothing, and I mean nothing, ever happens in Gilroy."

"Sounds bleak," Tan said.

"You cannot imagine. Total sensory deprivation."

"So to compensate for a boring youth you get your thrills from extreme situations. I get it, George. However, I had a wonderful youth, and I do not like working on projects where there is the possibility of death, even the most remote possibility. I realize that at this point in our little Burmese adventure there is not much that I can do about it, but I want you to understand that, for me, the sooner we are back in Hong Kong, the better," Tan said.

"Got it, Tan. We'll view the site, have a design meeting with the Committee, and we'll be back on a plane in no time."

*****

They arrived at the first checkpoint an hour outside of Myitkyina. A clearing had been hacked out of the jungle and a few small shacks and lean-to's had been set up. Blocking the road was a gate with a striped arm. About thirty soldiers stood around, machine guns cradled in their arms. As they got closer George could see that they were mostly boys, sixteen year olds holding adult guns.

At every checkpoint the same scenario was played out. Aung, instructing George and Tan to stay in the vehicle, would get out and greet the boy soldiers jovially, handing out cigarettes. After a few minutes an older soldier, a Captain, would appear from the guard shack. Aung would chat with the Captain and then pass him an envelope, which the Captain would slip into his pocket. Aung would then show him their permits to pass. While the Captain was reviewing their permits, the boy soldiers would come up to the Toyota and peer into the windows at George and Tan, pointing and laughing.

At the third checkpoint Tan got out of the car with Aung and said, "Aung, I need to get out of the car to use the bathroom."

"OK," Aung said, "Pee on road, no go into jungle."

"Pee on the road?"

Aung picked up a handful of rocks. He tossed one after the other into the jungle. On the third rock there was an explosion followed by a puff of smoke. "Land mines," Aung said smiling.

"I see."

Back in the car, Tan said to George, "Are you sensing my increasing discomfort?"

"I am sensing it, Tan."

Finally after six hours of driving through endless jungle they arrived at the eighth checkpoint. Aung turned around and said, "We arrive Hphakant soon. Hey, Tan, you speak Cantonese?"

"Yes, I do, of course."

"Good. Many people in Hpakant speak Cantonese so can talk with Chinese traders. You take care George, OK then?" He laughed like this was a funny joke, as George and Tan looked at him in silence.

"It joke, it joke, no worry!" Aung laughed. "I assign Cantonese speaking soldier to take care you. Hpakant is crazy place."

Chapter 13

Just before evening, the remnants of the sun only a sharp, golden outline behind the purple-blue silhouette of rugged mountains, they crested a hill and peered from the windows of the Toyota down into the Hpakant river valley below. The mahogany brown Uyu River undulated through hills chopped bare by open cut mining. The few last rays of sunshine glinted off the dark water. Rubble-piles of mining waste cast long shadows on the hillsides, and gaping mouths of numerous jade mines obscenely scarred what once had been a pristine river valley. Hugging the banks of the Uyu was the town of Hpakant; slapped-together, haphazard architecture with rusty tin roofs. Narrow dirt roads chaotically crisscrossed the assemblage of buildings.

The Toyotas descended into the valley as the dramatic evening sky faded into night. The two architects found themselves driving through unpaved streets congested with motorbikes and bicycles. Open air restaurants with plastic stools and shops illuminated by bare electric bulbs lined the narrow lanes. They passed shuffling, hollow-eyed men, thin brown arms and legs protruding from plaid shirts and shorts. *A town of zombies*, Tan thought.

After numerous turns their vehicles stopped in front of a squat, four-story, cement block building. Aung said, "This your hotel." They got out of the car, and George and Tan looked up at the wood sign hung across the front of the building, carved red letters on a yellow background reading 'Jade City Hotel'.

From the second car one of the Design Committee members walked up to them. Aung said, "This Colonel Tun Tun Ko. He speak Cantonese. He take care you."

In Cantonese Tan said, "Thank you for your protection while we are here, Colonel Ko."

"Please call me Tun Tun," the Colonel replied in Cantonese.

George could see that Tan was visibly more relaxed having Tun Tun as a minder.

Aung said, "We pick you up 9:00 tomorrow morning, tour site."

"That's great, Aung. See you tomorrow," George said, and the three walked into the lobby of the Jade City Hotel.

White porcelain tiles covered the floors and walls of Jade City's lobby. A strong smell of mold, ineffectively masked by burning incense, hit their nostrils. There were two small paintings of Kachin heroes on the walls framed in aluminum but neither George nor Tan knew who they were. Tun Tun checked them in at the front desk.

"We get together for dinner tonight. It is not good for you two to walk around Hpakant alone," Tun Tun said to Tan in Cantonese.

"Yes, sure," Tan replied, and translated for George, adding, "See, I told you that this place is dangerous."

"Meet in fifteen minutes in the lobby. Your rooms are 404 and 405." Tun Tun handed a large metal key to each man. "Sorry, no elevator in this hotel," he said smiling.

George and Tan, suitcases in hand, were out of breath by the time they had ascended the wood staircase to the fourth floor. Tan's room was 404. The stuffiness of the room enveloped him as he entered. He put down his suitcase on the bed, turned on the electric fan that stood in one corner, and opened the double hung window.

Tan looked out at the street below. In the enveloping blackness of night the only illumination in the street was ambient light from adjacent storefronts. Tan saw a small gathering of stick-like men around a wooden crate that had been turned upside down to serve as a table. The man behind the crate took a few crumpled bills from each of the five men who stood at his table and then, as Tan watched, placed a fine powder into a syringe. He stuck the needle into one of the men's arm. As he pulled back on the plunger the syringe filled with the man's blood, mixing with the heroin. Then he pushed down on the plunger to send the mixture back into the man's body.

Tan remembered reading on the internet that this was the preferred method of injection in Jade Land. He forgot why. Each man followed suit, using the same needle, blood mixing with heroin powder. After all were done the seller urinated on the needle, believing that he was disinfecting it for HIV.

Tan turned from the window. "Got to get back to Hong Kong soon!" he said out loud. He then left the room to meet George and Tun Tun for dinner.

*****

George, Tan, and Tun Tun sat on pink plastic stools pulled up to a table with a red laminated tabletop. The outdoor restaurant was a short walk from their hotel. Tun Tun had ordered rice with grilled chicken, beef curry, and a steamed vegetable dish. They drank from bottles of Dagon Beer.

"I really like this beer," George said, looking at his bottle of Dagon, a roaring, golden lion on the green label. "I didn't even know that they made beer in Myanmar." Tan translated.

Tun Tun said, "Myanmar beer is stronger than Western beer, has more alcohol." He raised his bottle, and the three touched bottle tops.

Tan was feeling quite relaxed with Tun Tun, who had been standoffish in Hong Kong as a Design Committee member but had now opened up in a social setting on his home turf. He chatted in Cantonese about his wife and three year old daughter who lived in a Kachin village and his life growing up in a traditional Kachin tribe.

"Tun Tun, I notice that you are carrying a gun," Tan said.

"Well, I am a military man."

"So, you carry a gun just because you are military, right, probably don't really need it?"

Tun Tun broke into a laugh. He took a Cuban cigar from his breast pocket and pulled a knife from a sheath in his boot. He held the cigar up to admire it and then, placing it on the table, sliced the end off, put it to his mouth, and lit it. "The Burmese government and the Kachin are at war: for land, for independence, for the drug trade, and for the jade trade. We also shoot each other occasionally for no reason other than a supposed insult. It has been so all my life. There is only thin cooperation between us."

Tun Tun took a few long puffs on his Cuban. "Also need a gun because there is much money moving around here. All miners are poor, almost all are drug addicts. They would kill you for one Kyat."

Tan translated for George, and then added, "Our project is in a war zone, George. I want out of here as soon as possible."

"Think of the stories that you will be able to tell back in Lan Kwai Fung, Tan," George said.

"I do not hang out in Lan Kwai Fung, George. Please, do not try to put your positive spin on this."

"OK, but you are in it for the next few days. Might as well quit worrying and enjoy it," George said.

Suddenly a skeletal Burmese man with greasy hair and bloodshot eyes, dressed in blue jeans and an orange T-shirt, appeared at their table. He said in Cantonese to Tan, "Hey, you here to buy jade? I can get you a great deal."

Tun Tun answered for them, "No, they are not here to buy jade."

"Perhaps they would like to buy some opium then?" the man asked, pulling from his pants pocket a glass jar containing small brown pellets.

"No. They do not want your mouse droppings," Tun Tun growled. "Go away."

The man disappeared back into the crowded street as if he had been an apparition made of smoke.

"He would cheat you," Tun Tun said to Tan.

"Cheat us, and then probably kill us," the wide-eyed Tan said.

"Hey, Tun Tun, this beer is good, but do they have liquor here stronger than beer?" George asked in English. Tan translated.

Tun Tun laughed. "You want a man's drink, yes? I will take you a place where they have the best man's drink."

"O.K." The three tapped beer bottle tops again. Tun Tun paid the bill while George helped an already-inebriated Tan stand up from the plastic stool.

"That Myanmar beer is powerful," Tan said.

"You are just a lightweight."

They followed Tun Tun through a maze of winding, narrow streets to a small plaza. The plaza was festive, decorated with twinkling, multi-colored Christmas lights strung around the perimeter. Food stalls lined one side of the courtyard. Most were selling pig organ hotpot, smoke rising from steam tables with vats of hot oil into which the customers dipped pig parts on skewers. There were a variety of sauces in plastic jars, plates of green chilies and garlic cloves, and bowls of cold rice noodles. On the other side of the plaza was a giant Wheel of Chance game with blinking yellow, blue, and red lights. A small group of gamblers sat on benches in front of the wheel as a barker took their money and spun the wheel.

"Holy shit, an elephant!" Tan said, pointing at a small elephant with a trainer on his back. The beast lumbered across the plaza, his trunk swishing back and forth.

In the middle of it all was a giant neon sign hung over a bar front, a coiled cobra in bright yellow, its hood expanded and its fangs exposed. Next to the neon cobra the sign had red Burmese lettering. "What's that sign say?" Tan asked.

"It means 'Drink Cobra Bar'." Tun Tun said. "It's where we are going."

The inside of the Drink Cobra Bar was suffused in red light and smoke. George and Tan followed Tun Tun to a table on the far side. A waiter came over and greeted Tun Tun, suspiciously eyeing George. After an exchange in Burmese, the waiter disappeared, returning in a few minutes with a bottle of clear liquid and three glasses.

Tan jumped up in shock. "Whoa, there's a snake in there!" Floating in the bottle, a King Cobra stared blankly out at them through glassy, gray eyes.

"This is a man's drink in Myanmar," Tun Tun said laughing. "First make distilled rice wine, then marinate the cobra for at least three months. This bar is famous for Cobra Wine." Tun Tun filled their glasses. "Cheers!"

"Not bad at all," George exclaimed. The three tapped glasses.

"You two outclass me," Tan said after the first drink. "You guys go ahead, I have had enough."

As George and Tun Tun continued to down shots of Cobra Wine, Tan looked around the bar. He did not realize how large it was when he first walked in. He spotted a group of tables in a corner that had only women sitting at them. The women looked to be in their twenties, short skirts, high heels, vacant stares.

"Hey Tun Tun, those are hookers, right?" Tan asked.

"Of course. Better stay away, they all have AIDS," Tun Tun said. "All?"

"Probably. All miners are addicts, all share needles. Use the same needle hundreds of times. The miners do not use condoms. All girls get AIDS."

"Whoa, terrible situation here." Tan translated for George. Then, noticing a steady stream of people entering a pair of double doors at the rear of the bar, he asked Tun Tun, "What's behind those doors?"

"In the back is Lethwei," Tun Tun said, his eyes lighting up. "You want to see?"

"Lethwei, what is that?"

"It's Burmese martial arts. There is a ring in the back. People gamble on the matches."

Tan translated for George. "Hell,yeah! That sounds cool!" George said.

As the three walked through the double doors George's senses were immediately overwhelmed. The back room was the size of a barn, open windows and lazy ancient fans did little for ventilation, more cigarette smoke than air, the humidity suffocating. In the center of the room was a boxing ring, a raised canvas platform with red ropes, bright lights above. Around the perimeter of the ring were plastic chairs filled with sweating, yelling men waving colorful Kyat notes above their heads. Tun Tun directed George and Tan to sit down.

Yelling to be heard above the din of the room, Tun Tun explained, "Lethwei fighters can use knees, elbows, fists, kicks, and head butts. They can also throw their opponent down. No gloves are worn, only hand wraps. Can only win by knockout or if opponent gives up."

A four man band; two men on oboes, one on a cymbal, and one with a drum, sat ringside playing a whiny, high-pitched music. As the hypnotic music played, from each corner a thin, brown-skinned, man pulled down the top rope and vaulted into the ring, taut muscles glistening with sweat, their fists wrapped in white cloth. They were both in their early twenties, one wearing blue shorts and one red. Each put his hands together in front of his faced and bowed to the audience as they entered the ring. In the center of the ring a referee wearing slacks and a lime green shirt made sure that both fighters were ready, and then gave them the signal to proceed.

The two men approached, throwing a few tentative round kicks to legs and midsections, a few one-two punches, feeling each other out. The clashing sound of the cymbals and the whine of the oboe egged them on. As Blue Shorts threw a left jab, Red Shorts sent a right roundhouse kick over the jab, which landed square on Blue Short's jaw. The crowd cheered loudly.

The two men closed the distance, and both landed punches, elbows and knees. The crowd was on its feet, the noise of their yells, the clash of the cymbals, and the whine of the oboes deafening. Both men soon had blood streaming from cuts above their eyes from head butts.

Blue Shorts feinted and then threw a powerful spinning hook kick. Red Shorts dodged the kick and, moving in close, slammed a devastating elbow into Blue Shorts' jaw. Blue Shorts dropped to the mat, unconscious. The bettors from the Red Shorts' camp howled their delight and collected their winnings as two other gladiators prepared to hop into the ring.

"George, you about ready to head back to the hotel?" Tan asked in George's ear over the noise.

"Yeah. Let Tun Tun know."

Tan signaled Tun Tun, and all three left through the double doors. When they were back outside in front of the bar George said, "Thank you so much for the evening, Tun Tun. It was fantastic." Tan translated.

Back in his room as George started to undress he was startled by a knock on his door. "Who is it?" he asked opening the door. He was surprised to see a Chinese man standing there dressed in a polo shirt and khaki pants as if he had just stepped out of a Marks and Spencer shop.

"Hi, I am Tony," the man said in English.

"Tony?"

"Yes, Tony, Ruud's friend. He asked me to drop his phone off with you."

"Oh, yeah, right. I had forgotten about that," George said.

"Well, here it is," Tony said, handing a Samsung Galaxy to George. "He said that he would get it from you in Hong Kong."

"Great. Thanks, Tony."

"Sure," Tony smiled. George closed the door and threw the

Samsung into his suitcase, having no idea how much trouble that mobile telephone was going to cause him.

Chapter 14

Monday emerged as a brilliant morning in Hong Kong after three days of rain, opalescent clouds traversing pale blue skies. Ian and Nigel were seated in a conference room at police headquarters. The coroner's file was laid out in front of them on a table as well as pictures of the crime scene and the lab results. A white board took up one wall of the room, blue, red, and black markers in the tray below the board.

"OK, review time. Let's start with the biggest unknowns, the key questions that we should focus on first," Ian said, walking over to the white board and picking up a marker.

"Please don't write on the white board, Ian," Nigel said. "You know that I hate it when there is only the two of us and you write on the white board. We can just talk and jot down our own notes."

"I don't know why it bothers you, Nigel. It helps me organize the key points in my mind." Ian picked up one of the markers. "Death was by puffer fish poisoning. However, no visible traces of fish were in the victim's stomach. So, how did it get in our victim's system?" Ian wrote '*1. How Did Poison Get In System?*' on the white board, and then a holdover from his days at the London School of Communications, drew a cartoon-like picture of a puffer fish next to it.

"Please don't draw cartoons next to your points, Ian. You know that really bugs me." Nigel said.

Ian stood back to admire his artwork, "OK, no more cartoons." And then he wrote '*2. Source Of Poison?*' So, if someone made a liquid out of puffer fish organs to dose our victim, where does one get puffer fish organs in Hong Kong? Sushi bars are the first thought, but what about the wet markets?" Ian continued writing, '*3. Who Is The Victim?*' "Also, where did the blood spatter on the victim's clothes come from?" He added '*4. Victim's Connection To Other Crimes?*'

on the white board. "My gut tells me that our victim is connected to the disappearing Indonesian maids' case. OK, let's prioritize getting these answered."

"Good, four key points. Very glad that you wrote them on the white board," Nigel said as he left the conference room.

Ian shut the conference room door, gave another glance at the white board to admire his drawing of the puffer fish, and then dialed the telephone number for the Indonesian Legal Aid Foundation. A secretary answered, and Ian said, "May I speak to…..oh, I am sorry, I just realized, I do not know her last name. Her first name is Tika, I mean, Atika."

"No problem, sir, Indonesians do not generally use last names. I will get Tika for you. Whom shall I say is calling?"

"Ian Hamilton, with the Hong Kong Police Department."

After a short wait Tika's voice came on, "Hi, Ian."

"Hi, Tika." Ian pictured Tika. *Keep it professional, Ian.* "In the file that you gave me on the twelve complainants there are no contact numbers. How can we arrange for me to interview them?"

"I will arrange it. It will have to be on a Sunday," Tika said.

"On Sunday?" Ian asked.

"These girls' employers already exploit them enough. If there was suspicion that they were involved in a police investigation, their involvement could be used as an excuse for further abuse. Sunday is their day off, so their employers will not know. It's the only day that we can do it," Tika said.

"OK. Bring them down to the station."

"No, it should be at a place where they are comfortable, and that certainly would not be your police station. I recommend that we use our Indonesian Legal Aid Foundation office. I will contact them and arrange it. I can also translate. Can I set it up for this Sunday?"

"That would be OK," Ian said, "Except for the translating part. I will use one of our Indonesian-speaking officers for that."

"Sure. As their lawyer, though, I will be present at the interviews."

"We are negotiating now?" Ian asked, smiling.

"No, not negotiating. It is their legal right to have representation," Tika said.

"I know, only kidding, relax. As their attorney you are very welcome to attend the interviews."

"Good. 10:00am?"

"10:00am it is. See you on Sunday." Ian put the telephone down and wondered at the feelings stirring within him. *This is one case that I hope gets solved soon. I am having difficulty not hopping over that professional wall.*

*****

By afternoon the optimistic skies of the morning had turned ominous. When Ian walked into Nigel's cubicle, Nigel, looking up from his computer screen, said, "Did you look out the window? We are going to get smacked with a serious summer thundershower."

"Think so?" Ian replied. "Any info on puffer fish sources in Hong Kong yet?"

"Yes. Getting served *fugu fish* in a restaurant is a difficult task in Hong Kong. There are only two places licensed to serve it here. However, the actual fish is easy to acquire. For one thing, it lives here."

"Puffer fish are native to Hong Kong?" Ian asked.

"Puffer fish live in almost every warm sea on the planet, so yes, it is native here. You could go to Tai-O, Aberdeen, Stanley, Mui Wo, wherever there are fisherman in sampans, and buy a recently caught puffer fish. Easy," Nigel said.

"That is amazing, and daunting. Our killer could get his poison at any fishing village and it would be totally untraceable. A little dissection to remove the liver and the killer has his weapon," Ian said.

"Correct."

"So how did the victim get dosed?" Ian asked.

"Probably it was put into a drink, as he had no food in his stomach. That would no doubt be the easiest way."

"Hmm, the victim drinks the poison and then goes about his normal business, which probably is in Wanchai. However, on his way, he starts to feel the effects of the poison: throat constricting, numbness and tingling around his lips and fingers, salivation, nausea. He ducks into the Queen Vic to sit down, thinking that maybe the symptoms will pass. His friends, or we should say his 'colleagues' because they might have been the ones who gave him the dose, are with him."

"Right," Nigel said, picking up the thread. "They sit down and are brought beers that they did not order. Within minutes, our victim cannot breathe and he drops to the floor. His colleagues disappear, and we are called."

"OK, let's move on. Who is he? Did you follow up with Immigration on the victim's fingerprints and photos?"

"I did. Our victim came in on a tourist visa under the name Khin Khin Htoo, almost certainly an alias. Khin Khin Htoo is a famous Burmese novelist. It would be like saying your name is Stephen King or Dan Brown. He then overstayed his visa."

"Another dead end. If he and his buddies frequented the neighborhood around the Queen Vic, though, maybe someone knew him. Let's walk the neighborhood this afternoon."

Nigel looked out the window. It had started to rain, thunder claps and distant, spasmodic ribbons of lightning suggesting a heavier downpour on the way. "This afternoon? It looks like it is going to rain really hard, Ian."

"We won't dissolve, Nigel. A little rain won't hurt. On our way to Wanchai I also want to stop in at the Myanmar Embassy on Harbour Road. One of their citizens has been murdered. Maybe they'll have some information on him." Ian said. "Oh, and by the way, we'll interview the complainants in the Indonesian Maid case this Sunday. Call down to HR and see if we can get an Indonesian speaking officer who can translate for us."

"Sunday?" Nigel asked.

"Sorry." Ian said.

Chapter 15

The windshield wipers of the police cruiser, even on the 'high' setting, were ineffective under the deluge of the monsoon-intensity rain as Ian and Nigel headed down Harbour Road. Ian peered hard through the blurry glass as he navigated the storm, lightning intermittently electrifying the sky above them, "I can't see much past the bumper."

Nigel said, "A little rain won't hurt, right?" Nigel had to raise the volume of his voice to be heard over the resounding clamor of the heavy downpour.

"Ha!" Ian exclaimed, smiling. "We're almost there." The brown granite exterior of the Myanmar Embassy suddenly materialized like a mirage through the pounding rain. "Good, they have an underground parking garage." Ian directed the cruiser off the flooded road and down a ramp out of the storm.

They took the elevator up from the garage into a no-frills lobby. On the wall opposite the elevator doors was a gold-colored plaque which read, 'The Embassy of the Republic of the Union of Myanmar'. Ian and Nigel identified themselves to the receptionist, an Asian woman with hair dyed bright blond and a ring in her eyebrow.

She pushed a buzzer and a middle-aged Burmese woman in a business suit appeared. "Please follow me," she said, leading them down a grey carpeted hall and into a windowless conference room. On the conference room wall was the emblem of the Union of Myanmar, a white five-pointed star on top of yellow, green, and red stripes. A picture of a fierce golden Chinthe, a mythical creature, half lion, half dragon, was next to the star emblem showing its fangs. With a wave of her hand the woman directed them to sit at a mahogany conference table. "Please wait," she said, and disappeared.

"I wonder why that receptionist dyed her hair blond," Nigel mused as soon as the secretary left. "Doesn't she want to look Asian anymore?"

"You find her dyed hair offensive?" Ian asked.

"I'm just saying…"

The conversation was interrupted as three professionally dressed Burmese entered the room, the men in custom tailored gray suits and the woman in red and black Louis Vuitton heels and a black Versace suit. A jade and gold necklace embraced her neck. An overwhelming aroma of *Armani Acqua Di Gio* cologne suddenly settled over the room. Nigel realized the smell was coming from the stout, middle-aged man with the greased-back hair.

"Sorry to have kept you waiting, Detectives. I am the Myanmar Consul General to Hong Kong, U Kham," the heavily scented man said. He shook hands with the detectives and then introduced his Political Counselor, Nakaji Sein, and Attaché, Mi Mi Tun. Seating themselves opposite the detectives, Consul General Kham said, "How can we help you, Inspector Hamilton?"

"We regret to inform you that one of your citizens in Hong Kong has died under suspicious circumstances. We were wondering if there was any information that you could provide on the man." Ian then looked down shaking his head, and when he looked back up at the General Consul he had on his boyish smirk, "Sorry, that sounds like a line from a bad detective movie. I don't know how else to say it though." Ian laid pictures of the victim, including a close-up shot of his tattoo, on the table.

"No problem, sometimes in our work it does seem like we really are starring in a bad movie, Detective." The three politicians all smiled, but when they glanced down at the photos laid out on the mahogany table the smiles disappeared. Consul General Kham looked up from the photos and said, "We would not know this man. Do you know what this symbol means, Inspector Hamilton?" He pointed to the photograph of the victim's tattoo.

"I believe that it means he was a member of the Kachin Independence Army," Ian said.

"That is correct, Inspector Hamilton, an insurgent."

"An insurgent?"

"Yes. Myanmar is in a civil war. The Union of Myanmar has been in conflict with the Kachins for…, well, my whole life actually," General Consul Kham said.

Political Councilor Sein added, "You have to understand, Detective, that such a man as this would be virtually untraceable, as he was no doubt here illegally. It is, however, indeed unfortunate that this man met a bad ending on your soil, and, insurgent or not, a Burmese is a Burmese. We will help in any way that we can. I will make inquiries to see if we can identify the man."

"That is appreciated, Political Counselor Sein," Ian said. Then going with a hunch, "I would also like to ask you if you know another Burmese man living here in Hong Kong. We do not know if he is involved with this case, but in our minds he is a person of interest. His name is Zaw Than."

Ian noticed another momentary disappearance of the gracious smiles. Political Counselor Sein said, "Zaw Than is indeed a man well known to us. We believe that he is involved with many abhorrent activities, and I would not be surprised if the dead man in your photo was in his employ. I will be glad to reach out to the Burmese community and make some inquiries in regards to Zaw Than's relationship to the dead man."

"Thank you again, Political Counselor Sein."

"The only thing that I ask is that you please keep me informed of the progress of the investigation. Here is my business card," the Political Counselor said.

"Thanks. We appreciate your cooperation. Here is mine," Ian said, handing his card to the Political Counselor.

"Good luck with your investigation, Inspector." The three politicians stood and left the room.

The afternoon storm had stopped by the time Ian and Nigel left the Myanmar Embassy. Hong Kong looked like a black-and-white photo, glossy wet streets and a ceiling of gray clouds. As the cruiser pulled out of the garage Nigel said, "They seemed to not be telling us everything that they knew."

"Of course not. They are politicians," Ian said.

Ian found a parking spot three blocks from the Queen Victoria. As they exited the car he spotted two uniformed officers across the street showing photographs to a local shopkeeper. He nudged Nigel and the two crossed Lockhart, catching up to the officers in front of Bar 109.

"Hey guys, any progress?" Ian asked.

"Yes, Detective Hamilton," one of the officers said. "At The Surabaya Club a bouncer recognized the victim. He said the victim frequently came in there to hand out flyers to the girls."

Jesus, how young are we hiring? These two look like they don't even shave yet, Ian thought. "What kind of flyers?"

"He didn't know. The bouncer's name is…," looking down at his notes, "Tommy Chang."

"Thanks." Ian and Nigel walked the few blocks to Club Surabaya. Three men wearing tight black T-shirts with the word 'STAFF' in white letters on the back, and who obviously spent a lot of time in a gym, were on-guard at the entry to the club.

"One of you guys Tommy Chang?" Ian asked.

"I am Tommy Chang."

"Is there someplace that we can talk?" Ian said showing his badge.

They walked upstairs. It was just 6:00pm, the club empty. The three slipped into a booth, Ian and Nigel on one side, the bouncer on the other.

"One of our officers said that you recognized a photo of a man whose death we are investigating."

"Yeah, used to come in here a lot, usually four of them. They would have cloth bags slung over their shoulders full of flyers. They handed the flyers out to the girls."

"What did the flyers say?" Ian asked.

"Don't know, never read one."

"How did you know there were flyers in the bags if you never read one?" Nigel asked.

"Bags we do take a big interest in. We don't want weapons of any kind getting into the club. Policy is, check all bags. I can tell you all about their bags."

"Go ahead," Nigel said.

"Full of nothing but flyers and a water bottle."

"A water bottle?" Ian exclaimed.

"Yeah, each of the four men had a metal water bottle in their bag." Ian shot a glance at Nigel.

Nigel asked, "Any names? Ever talk with them?"

"No." the bouncer said. "They would stay here a few hours, do their thing, and leave. No trouble."

"What color were the bags?"

"They were green."

"Thanks, you have been very helpful, Tommy," Ian said.

As they walked back up Lockhart towards the Queen Victoria, Ian said, "Let's question Mandy again, maybe she missed something the first time."

"Sure," Nigel said. "A water bottle in the bag with the flyers, the guy's friends took his bag after he hit the floor. I'll bet that the water bottle was the source of the poison."

"But only the victim's bottle was poisoned, the guy's friends were not affected. And what did those flyers say? What were those guys up to?"

The Queen Victoria was already packed at 6:15pm. Ian jostled his way through the drunks until he found Mandy, a tray full of draft beers and tequila shots balanced above her head as she navigated through the crowd. "Hey, Mandy, we would like to ask you some more questions."

"Sure, let me deliver these and I will be right with you," Mandy yelled to be heard over the din of the revelers. Ian and Nigel leaned against the bar while they waited, 'Sweet Home, Alabama' blasting from the juke box. Ian felt like he should be relaxing, having a Boddington at the bar with the other customers rather than be here investigating a case.

When Mandy came back, Ian said, "This place is packed early tonight."

"We have been crowded like this ever since the story broke in the newspaper about the dead guy," Mandy said. She picked up a copy of 'The Hong Standard' from the bar and displayed it to the two policemen. 'Dead Body Found at the Queen Vic'. "Great for business!"

"Can we go in the back and talk?" Ian asked

"Sure, let's go to the office." Ian and Nigel followed Mandy through the bar to the double doors at the rear, past the bank of restrooms, to a cluttered office the size of a closet. There was only one chair, which Mandy sat in. Ian stood and, because the room was so small, Nigel remained in the doorway.

"Mandy, I want to go over it again, see if there were any details that you might have missed the first time," Ian said.

"OK. Well, like I said, the four guys came in, late afternoon. One of them was looking really wasted, and the other three seemed sober, concerned about the wasted guy."

"Right. What were the other three guys like physically? What were they wearing? You said that they were carrying bags? What color bags?" Ian asked.

"Physically? They were all about the same size, like the dead guy. They were dressed similar too, T-shirts, jeans. The bags? I think that they were purple, or maybe gray?"

"Could they have been green, Mandy?"

"Yeah, green! They were green."

"OK, so they sat down at a table, you brought them some beers. What else? Were they arguing?"

"Not arguing. As I said, the other three seemed concerned about the screwed up guy. I do remember thinking that they may have brought in their own booze, though. They kept sipping out of metal bottles, pulling them out of their bags. People do that sometimes, they order one beer and sit here with their own bottle of Johnnie Walker. Cheaper for them, but bad for the bar."

"Anything else?"

"They didn't pay for their beers, but no problem, we've been crazy busy since the newspaper story broke," Mandy said.

"And, just to confirm, you had never seen them in here before, right?"

"Nope."

"Thanks for your help, Mandy." Ian and Nigel shouldered their way back through the raucous crowd of the Queen Victoria and out to the street.

In the police cruiser on the way back to headquarters Ian said, "The victim and his friends were passing out flyers in Club Surabaya. The disappearing lesbians case and the dead Burmese guy in the Queen Vic are definitely related. The girls read the flyers and then disappeared. Why? To what end? What would Burmese criminals want with Indonesian lesbians? To use them as drug mules?"

"Or to murder them, a gang that kills just for the thrill of it. What better group to target than Indonesian lesbian maids. They are so far out of mainstream that they are perfect victims," Nigel said. "But why wouldn't our killers, for whatever their purpose, use women to pass out the flyers? The missing girls were lesbians, and Club Surabaya is a lesbian bar. Wouldn't it seem strange that four guys would be going into a lesbian bar?"

"Not really. Guys go in there all the time," Ian said. "They think that they can 'turn' the girls, or get a three-way going. Some strange things go on in Wanchai, Nigel."

"I guess." Nigel's mobile phone vibrated. He looked at the screen and then answered. "Nigel Ho here." A pause. "Great, thank you."

"We've got our translator for Sunday." Nigel said as he hung up.

Chapter 16

The great Sunday morning migration of thousands of Filipina and Indonesian maids on their day off to Central and Causeway Bay was well underway by 9:00am. As the streets filled with the furloughed women, at Police Headquarters Ian introduced himself to a uniformed policewoman standing in his cubicle, her body compact, her demeanor no-nonsense, her straight, black hair cropped short just below her ears.

"So, Officer... Angela Cheung," Ian read her name badge, "If you don't my mentioning it, you look Chinese, not Indonesian. Are you sure that you will be able to translate for us?" Ian asked.

"I am Chinese-Indonesian, Inspector. I am fluent," Officer Cheung responded crisply.

"OK, let's go then."

As they drove to Causeway Bay, Nigel briefed Angela on the case. When he got to the part about the disappearing maids, Angela asked, "The Tommy-boys and Girly-girls?"

"Yes, the lesbian couples. You know." Nigel said.

"Oh... OK."

Ian parked on Lee Garden Road in a loading zone next to the Hysan Place Mall. The three detectives pushed through the crush of early Causeway Bay Sunday shoppers, traversed the Hennessy Road pedestrian bridge, and arrived at a gray tiled, twenty-story commercial building so narrow that there was no more than one small tenant per floor. The building entry was framed with advertisements for upper floor restaurants and hair salons. The Indonesian Legal Aid Foundation was on the fifth floor. The detectives brushed shoulders to fit into the undersized elevator.

On the fifth level they found themselves in an unadorned corridor, white walls and gray linoleum floor, a glass door in front of them marked 'Indonesian Legal Aid Foundation'. The office conveyed frugality, a scuffed blue linoleum floor and Ikea furniture. Tika came out of a conference room to greet them, followed by a woman carrying a notebook.

"Welcome," Tika said. "This is my assistant, Linda."

"Nice to meet you, Linda," Ian said smiling at Tika's assistant. "This is Inspector Nigel Ho and Officer Angela Cheung. Officer Cheung will be translating for us."

"Please, follow me," Tika said. "The group is in our conference room. I will introduce you first, and we can then do the interviews individually in an adjacent office." Ian, following behind Tika, who was in a charcoal skirt and white blouse, thought, *Still looks smokin' hot.* And then, *Keep it professional, Ian.*

Tika introduced the officers to the twelve women seated around the room. They were colorfully dressed and coiffed in street punk style, a gathering of tropical birds. Ian saw the hostility in their eyes, felt their distrust of authority. *This will be a difficult group to connect with.*

As Tika spoke to the women in Indonesian, Angela translated for Ian and Nigel, "She told them that you are concerned about the missing girls and are here to help them, and that you, Ian, are the brother of her personal friend, so they should trust you. She said that they should give you honest information, and that this is the only way to find out what happened to their friends."

"OK, let's start," Tika said in English. They walked into the adjacent office and Tika sat the three officers at a desk, Nigel at one end with tape recorder and pen, Ian in the middle, Angela on the other end. She then returned with Ruby, the woman whom Ian had met at Sedap Gurih.

"I thought that we would start with Ruby," Tika said as she and Ruby lowered themselves into chairs facing the officers.

Ian smiled at Ruby, her chopped hair had grown back a bit since the last time they had met. "Nice to see you again, Ruby. Could you please start by explaining why you ran out of the restaurant suddenly in our last meeting?" Ian asked. Angela translated.

Ruby fidgeted, and then looking at Angela, spoke softly in Indonesian.

Angela said in English, "A Southeast Asian man who had entered Sedap Gurih while she was talking with you she had seen before. He had given a flyer to her and her missing friend at Surabaya. The flyer was advertising for part time work. The next Sunday her friend went to apply for the job. Ruby never saw her again."

"Does she still have the flyer?"

"No."

"It's not still in her friend's possessions?" Ian asked.

"Remember, Ian, these girls live with their employers. Ruby would have no access to her friend's possessions," Tika said.

"Who was her friend's employer? Maybe they still have her things," Ian asked.

Ruby answered, "Don't know. Only knows that she took care of some Granny in Sha Tin." Angela translated.

Tika said, "The girl's employment agency would know who the employer was, however." In Indonesian she asked, "Ruby, do you know who the agent was?"

Ruby shrugged and shook her head 'no', sticking out her lower lip.

"Ruby, do you have any photographs of your missing friend?" Ian asked.

Ruby smiled and pulled out an IPhone. *How come everyone in Hong Kong, from taxi drivers to maids, can afford IPhones?* Ian wondered. After tapping in her password, Ruby scrolled through some photos, and then showed the screen to Ian. The photo showed Ruby with her arm around a giggling girl just a bit taller than her. They were standing in front of the Christmas display in the center atrium court at the IFC Mall.

"Here is my e-mail address. Please e-mail me the photo," Nigel said in Cantonese, passing a card to Ruby.

They thanked Ruby, and Tika brought in the next girl, Irene.

It was the same story, Irene confirming that the flyer was an advertisement to teach Indonesian to Chinese businessmen. After Irene's friend had called the number on the flyer, she had told Irene that the job interview was in Sham Shui Po.

Ian and Nigel looked at each other. "Shami Town!" Nigel exclaimed. He and Ian were frequently called to Sham Shui Po, a densely populated, working class monument to urban decay. 'Shami Town' had more than its share of domestic squabbles that ended in mortality. Last month Ian and Nigel had been called to a case where a wife had stabbed her husband to death as he slept, and then continued to stab him over a hundred times. "Please continue," Ian said.

"She went to the interview and never came back." Irene said.

It took two hours to question all the Indonesian women, with no additional information forthcoming. After the last one, Tika pulled Ian aside. "Can I speak with you privately? Let's use another room."

Ian followed Tika to another small office. They entered and she closed the door. As Tika leaned close, Ian felt his heart pumping at the intimacy.

"Have you spoken with Sarah lately?" Tika asked.

"No."

"She is really worried about George. She hasn't heard from him. He was supposed to have been home a few days ago."

"Oh, he's probably fine." Ian said.

"Maybe, but I suggest that you give her a call." Tika touched Ian's hand. "She feels that he's in some danger. Women have a sixth sense about things like that you know."

"Do they? Do you have a sixth sense too?"

"Most definitely," Tika said smiling.

*****

In the car heading back to headquarters Ian said to Officer Cheung, "Angela, thank you very much for translating today."

"May I put a thought in your heads?" Angela asked from the back seat.

"Sure."

"Please excuse me if I am being too forward, but if you planted an undercover operative where these girls hang out perhaps you could nab one of these guys passing out flyers."

"And you are suggesting that you go undercover for us?" Ian smiled as he turned to look at Angela in the back seat.

"I am suggesting more than that actually. I am suggesting that you transfer me to your department. My career goal is to be in Criminal Investigations." Angela shrugged. "Anyway, I think that in this case I could be good at undercover. Put me in a baseball cap and baggy jeans, and I could pass."

"A viable suggestion, Officer Cheung, we'll consider it. Let you know after we discuss it at tomorrow morning's strategy meeting," Ian said as he pulled the car into the headquarters parking garage.

The three split up, and Angela walked to the Metro to return to her apartment in Fotan. '*A Viable suggestion, Officer Cheung,*' Angela mimicked. *Those two are a bit stiff, but I could work with them,* she thought, hanging onto the strap in the rocking train car.

Arriving in Fotan, Angela walked to her gray concrete apartment building, hiked up the uneven steps to her fifth floor flat, and unlocked the metal door. She walked directly to the couch, kicking off her shoes, stripping off her policewoman's uniform, her brassiere, and her no-nonsense panties. Naked, she walked back to the narrow entry hall of the apartment and opened the closet door. A full length mirror hung on the back of the door. The opposite wall held another full length mirror, so that looking at the closet door mirror Angela could see the full nakedness of her back reflected behind her.

Starting at her buttocks was a tattoo of the East Kowloon ghetto that she had grown up in. Rising above the buildings of the slum was a giant bird, an Indonesian Garuda, wings spread across her shoulder blades, the Garuda's fierce head just below the base of her neck. Angela rotated her shoulder blades and the Garuda appeared to fly, to rise above the dangerous tenements and the poverty of her youth. With eyes half closed Angela watched the Garuda fly for thirty minutes.

*

Chapter 17

The intense Burmese sunlight radiating through the front picture window of the Jade City Hotel lobby illuminated sparkling dust motes and overwhelmed the hotel's modest air conditioning system, which bravely but ineffectively fought its daily feud with the sun. Aung and Tun Tun were sitting on the couch when George and Tan exited the stairwell. Aung greeted them, "Good morning, George, Tan. Sleep well?"

"Thanks for last night. It was really fun," Tan said to Tun Tun in Cantonese.

In Cantonese, Aung said, "I bet Tun Tun took you to see a Lethwei match. He used to be a champion when he was younger."

"A lot younger," Tun Tun added.

"Aung, you speak Cantonese also?" Tan said.

"Just a little," Aung said.

The four men left the hotel and climbed into the mud splattered Toyota parked in front. Tun Tun drove.

"Where's the rest of the Design Committee?" George asked.

"They meet us later. First show you mines and project site." Aung said.

The car bumped its way through the streets of Hpakant on an unpaved lane that paralleled the riverfront. They followed the winding, slow-moving river until Tun Tun turned the truck up a steep grade into the hills that bordered the town. He parked on a flat area below a small hillock.

The four exited the car and, following Aung and Tun Tun, George and Tan scampered up a loose gravel slope to the top of the hill. Below them was a pit so big that George believed the whole town of Gilroy, California, could fit in it.

The pit was conical, bigger at the top than at the bottom. Like ants in an inverted ant hill swarms of men labored below in the coffee-colored mud. Men trudged up the hill bent under the weight of straw baskets filled with rocks, while another line of men side-stepped down the hill with empty baskets. Men with pick axes at the bottom of the pit, brown-skinned men the color of the soil they labored in, beat the earth mercilessly, exposing boulders the size of grapefruits. At the top of the pit hundreds of boy soldiers hefting machine guns watched.

"Holy cow!" Tan exclaimed.

Aung explained, "Men bring up rocks. Other men test rocks, maybe have jade inside." Aung pointed to an operation set up adjacent to the pit. "Those men experts. They wet down stone, look for color. They tap with hammer. Rocks with jade go to storeroom. No jade in rock, we dump over there." Aung pointed to a vast rubble pit.

George looked at Tan, who was still standing with a gaping mouth looking at the scene below. "Tan, this is fantastic!"

"Fantastic? George, I feel mentally scarred. This is a glimpse of a purgatory that I could not have imagined. You know that most of those miners are HIV-infected heroin slaves, who will die very soon and very horribly, right?"

"Oh, right, but did you see that rubble pit, Tan, the rejected boulders? That's our building material. No stucco boxes. We use free native rock. Yes, one meter thick rock walls. Amazing insulation properties, keeps the units cool. A new vision, Tan! Forget *'Comfort in the Jungle'*, now it's *'Sustainability in the Jungle'*. We'll put a field of solar panels behind the hotel. These guys are going to love it!"

Tan stared at George and then back down to the sweaty, brown men crawling up and down the pit. Aung said, "Now we visit building site."

They scrambled down the hill and piled back into the Toyota. The truck's shock absorbers bounced in protest as they descended the steep road to the river. About fifteen minutes later the road ended at a gently sloping area of jungle about ten acres in size. Tun Tun turned off the truck and they got out.

"Road come from town to here," Aung said, pointing to the dirt road and Hpakant in the distance. "We put guardhouse here," indicating the spot where they were standing. "We build wall around hotel. No one gets in or out without our check."

"OK, high security," George said, standing in a pose with his hands on his hips, the international architect masterfully observing his site.

George and Tan spent an hour walking around the project site. Tan had a copy of the topography map which they frequently consulted as they walked the site. George made notes on the map. The jungle prevented access to some parts, but they were able to get a good feel for how the hotel might be positioned.

When they were done Aung said, "You go back room now and get good ideas. Then tonight we have dinner with Design Committee. Pick you up 6:30."

Back in the Toyota and heading to the Jade City Hotel, Aung turned in his seat and handed George a receipt for a wire transfer. "My associates transferred retainer fee through Bank of China Yangon to you HSBC account in Hong Kong."

"Oh, thank you, Aung. Really appreciate it," George said, relieved.

*****

At Jade City George and Tan set themselves up in the dining room of the hotel, ordering dishes of chicken rice and a couple of sodas. When the meal was complete and the plates cleared Tan laid the topography map over the table. George pulled out a roll of tracing paper and some felt- tipped markers and, placing it over the topography map, started sketching; big, bold boxes for the hotel blocks, red arrows for the guest circulation, blue arrows for service trucks. Behind the hotel he drew a field of squares and labeled it 'solar panels'. George also drew a thick black line indicating a wall around the perimeter of the site and a gatehouse at the access from the road, labeling it 'security wall'.

Tan moved to another vacant table and started drawing a detailed section and a one- point perspective of a typical room. His drawing illustrated thick exterior walls built of the rock that they had seen in the rubble pile with earth between, thicker at the base than at the top. Tan then drew a sun in the upper corner of the sheet. A thick red arrow traveled from the sun penetrating about halfway through the wall, reversed direction and went back out, which would illustrate the insulating properties of the thick walls.

Tan also drew a large 'K' in the other corner of the sheet with a thin blue arrow pointing to the rock material of the walls, 'K' for 'kyat', showing that the material was not only free, but would save them money on energy costs.

It took two hours until George and Tan, looking over the sketches, were satisfied that they had good props for the points that they were going to make in their presentation to the Design Committee. George looked at his watch. "It's 4:30, Tan, we have about two hours before we get picked up. I want to walk around the town. Want to join me? I'll put the drawings up in my room first."

"Sure."

*****

George and Tan stood on the narrow street in front of the Jade City Hotel not certain in which direction the main part of town was. "Was it this way, or was it that way?" George said, squinting up and down the narrow street.

""Hey, Brad Pitt, you look like you need a tour guide," a voice came from behind them.

"Brad Pitt?" George asked, turning around.

"I only know two American names, and you are the wrong color to be Barack Obama." The voice came from a diminutive boy about fifteen years old wearing shorts and a filthy T-shirt. He was leaning on a pair of crutches, his right leg amputated below the knee.

"You speak English?" George asked incredulously. "Where in the world did you learn?"

"Self-study, books on English. Also, my Dad was Thai, so I lived a few years in Bangkok, watched English TV stations. Even went to school for a while."

"We would love a tour guide. We've only got two hours. Can you show us around Hpakant?"

"That will be one U.S. dollar."

"Agreed," George said. "I am George and this is Tan. What's your name?"

"Tiger. This way, Gentlemen." Tiger, gave them a quick smile, and started off down the street at a fast pace despite his handicap. George and Tan followed on either side.

"If you don't mind my asking," Tan said, "how did you lose your leg?"

"I did not lose it. I know exactly where it is. It was blown into tiny pieces when I stepped on a land mine three years ago," Tiger said.

"Sorry about that."

"No, it's a good thing. It kept me out of the army, and also out of the mines. It launched my career as a tour guide," Tiger said.

As they turned into a broader street Tiger asked, "What are you guys interested in? Drugs, jade, women?"

"Actually, we are both architects. Could you show us any traditional Burmese architecture? Any temples?" George said.

"Hah!" Tiger laughed. "That's in Yangon, not in Hpakant. Only two kinds of temples in Hpakant, those to jade and those to drugs."

Tiger pointed to either side of the street they were on, the buildings looking like a hastily put together stage set for a Western movie. "See the signs for fancy watches and expensive booze? That is for the newly wealthy, those people who are winners in the jade game. They worship here."

They turned into another dusty street. In the middle of the street a long line of lean-to's had been built out of scrap wood and tin. "Heroin shooting galleries, for those that are the losers in the jade game. These are their temples."

At the end of the street they reached the Uyu River, and walked along the bank. "Does your Dad still live in Thailand, Tiger?" Tan asked.

"After Thailand we had settled in Myanmar close to the Chinese border, but then in 2012 my Mom and Dad were killed in the fighting between the KIA and the Burmese Army. What do they call it in the American press… 'collateral damage'? I was eleven."

Oh, wow, sorry to hear that," Tan said. "What did you do then?"

"What any eleven year old orphan would do in that situation. I came to Hpakant to earn some money in the mines. I was too angry at both militaries to want to join either side. Anyway, when I was twelve it was my karma to step on a land mine." Then, with a smile, Tiger added, "As you know, I then became the best, and actually the only, tour guide in Hpakant."

"Amazing story, Tiger!" George said. "Great attitude. I am sure that it would have been really easy for you to end up in one of those shooting galleries that we just passed."

"Can I be honest with you guys?" Tiger asked.

"Sure."

"You two are the biggest pussies that I have ever seen in Hpakant."

George and Tan laughed. "From what I have seen, I believe that you are right, Tiger," Tan said.

"You gentlemen are in need of some protection. I have something that will help, and I strongly suggest that you buy it." Tiger pulled from under his shirt a knife about twelve inches long in a leather sheath. "Only two U.S. dollars."

"You are quite a salesman, Tiger. OK, consider it sold." George took the knife and thrust it in his belt under his shirt.

"Hey, Tiger, I have a technical question," Tan said. "Internet access is blocked here and our telephones do not work in Myanmar with our Hong Kong Sim cards. Is there a place where we can buy a local Sim card to put into our phones?"

"That would have been difficult even in Yangon. No such place in Hpakant."

"So we are off the grid, cannot communicate with the rest of the world?" Tan asked, surprised at the panic this concept caused in him.

"Welcome to the jungle, Gentlemen."

They turned up a few winding streets and were suddenly back in front of the Jade City Hotel again. "Thank you very much, Tiger. It was a great tour," George said. "I don't have U.S. dollars, but I can give you twenty four Hong Kong dollars, which is the equivalent of three U.S., or I can give you kyats."

"I'll take the kyats." Tiger shoved the money into his shorts, turned, and waved good-bye over his shoulder as he disappeared down the road.

Back in the hotel lobby George looked at his watch. "Perfect, almost 6:30. I'll just go upstairs and get the drawings, Tan. See you back down here in ten minutes."

When he got to his room George picked up the roll of drawings that he and Tan had drawn, and as he was about to leave the room he remembered the knife that Tiger had sold him. He pulled it out of his belt and unsheathed it. The handle was wood, the blade sharp and tapered. *I'll never get this through airport security unless I check a bag,* George thought. He sheathed the knife and threw it in his suitcase next to Ruud's Samsung."

Tun Tun arrived in the lobby of Jade City punctually at 6:30. He said in Cantonese to Tan, "We will walk to a restaurant, meet everyone there."

Tun Tun led George and Tan through streets of block buildings and wooden shacks until they reached, by Hpakant standards, a fairly broad boulevard lined with leafy trees and colorful restaurants, all with outdoor dining areas. Threadbare men sat on plastic stools, eating, drinking, and smoking.

Tun Tun led the way through the outdoor area of one of the restaurants, weaving his way through the closely spaced tables into the crowded, spacious hall of the interior. Inside the restaurant ancient electric fans ringing the perimeter did their best to circulate the steamy, smoky air. Groups of diners reached happily into bowls of pungent dishes with spoons, chopsticks, and fingers, a forest of beer bottles on each table. The din of their animated conversations was deafening.

Tun Tun said some words to a waiter, and they were led to a private room in the back of the restaurant. Inside the other members of the Design Committee were already seated around a dining table covered in a stained tablecloth. George laid the topographic map down on the tabletop and then carefully placed the sketched site plan on top. "Aung, would it be better if I do the presentation in English and you translate, or would it be better for Tan to do the presentation in Cantonese and Tun Tun translate?"

"We all have a basic understanding of Cantonese."

"OK, then, I will do it," Tan said. He launched into an explanation in Cantonese of how the hotel could be designed as a series of stepped boxes cut into the gently sloping topography, saving money on excavation and fitting into the site naturally, rooms orientated around open courtyards. He then addressed concepts of site access, guest circulation, parking, and servicing. As he made each point he paused and let Tun Tun translate into Burmese before continuing with the next point.

Finally, Tan described using the discarded stone from the rubble piles as a free building material, as well as ideas about sustainability, saving money both in construction and property management, and the proposed security wall, using their sketches as props to illustrate his points.

When he was done, there was an energized conversation in Burmese among the Design Committee members. They then went silent, and with smiles on their faces, they suddenly all applauded. George and Tan beamed at the acceptance. George turned to Tan and said, "Yes! They liked it!"

"Good job," Aung said, shaking each architect's hand. "Now we eat." Soon bowls of steamed rice, spicy soup, plates of curried fish, boiled vegetables, fritters, and noodles started to arrive, as well as bottles of beer. The Design Committee chain-smoked throughout the meal and at the end, when the serious drinking started, Tun Tun pulled out some Cuban cigars and passed them out to all in the room.

At midnight the meal ended. Aung said to George and Tan, "Tun Tun will take you back to hotel. We will pick you up at 9:00am tomorrow, drive to airport in Myitkyina. I will fly back to Hong Kong with you."

"Great. What about the Design Committee?"

"They stay Myanmar, but I go back Hong Kong report to Zaw Than. Anyway, Design Committee will drive airport with us. Road from Hpakant to Myitkyina safer with big group."

"Sounds good," George said, glowing both from the successful presentation and numerous beers.

George, Tan, and Tun Tun walked through the darkened streets back to the hotel. As they approached Jade City a short figure on crutches stepped out of an alley. Tiger came up to Tun Tun and whispered something to him in Burmese, then disappeared back into the shadows.

"Hey, Tun Tun, you know Tiger also? He gave us a tour of Hpakant earlier. What did he say?" Tan asked in Cantonese.

Tun Tun was visibly upset. "Tiger is one of our lookouts. He said Burmese Army undercover agents are here looking for you two.

What the hell did you guys do?" Tan translated for George. Tun Tun already was on his mobile phone, speaking quickly in Burmese. Within minutes one the Toyotas pulled up. Tun Tun said, "Get in."

George and Tan got in the back. Aung was in the front seat. He turned around as the car drove away from the Jade City. "Burmese Army undercover agents waiting for you in hotel lobby. Why?"

"Don't know," George said.

"Wait, remember in Myitkyina, George?" Tan said. "That Dutch guy, Ruud. He said that there were two Burmese undercover guys watching us in the bar."

"Ruud! You know Ruud?" Aung exclaimed.

"We met him in a bar in Myitkyina. Do you know him too?" Tan said.

"Ruud is very bad man! Both KIA and Myanmar Army hate him. You have dealings with Ruud?"

"Oh, oh…" George said. Tan and Aung turned their attention towards George. "I forgot to tell you, Tan, I had a visit last night from Tony, Ruud's friend. He gave me a mobile phone to bring to Hong Kong to give to Ruud."

"What? George, that is stupid!" Tan blurted.

"Tony is mining engineer, Hong Kong guy, Ruud's partner. He give you telephone to smuggle out? Sim Card in telephone probably has information Ruud can sell to highest bidder. Don't know, but something bad for sure," Aung said.

"Sorry, I guess I was pretty naïve," George said.

"OK, new plan needed," Aung said, hitting numbers in his mobile phone and giving orders in Burmese. They drove around the block to the rear of the Jade City Hotel. Aung said, "You go up back stairs to your rooms and get suitcases. Then come down same way. We take you another hotel for tonight."

"Then tomorrow we leave at the same time for Myitkyina Airport?" George asked.

"No, KIA controls Hpakant, pretty safe here. Burmese Army controls airport in Myitkyina though. For sure they have back up waiting to arrest you at airport if undercover agents not find you."

"So where will we go?" Tan asked.

"We pick you up at 6:00 in morning. We smuggle you over China border, just like jade."

"I appreciate the concern, Aung," George said, "but that sounds like it will take some time. We really need to get back to Hong Kong. Maybe we should take our chances at the Myitkyina airport."

"Twenty years," Aung replied.

"Twenty years?" George asked.

"That is sentence for smuggling state secrets. Burmese catch you, you spend twenty years in Burmese prison. I suspect, though, you not survive more than few months," Aung said.

"We will take the route through China, Aung. Thank you very much," Tan said. Then, turning towards George he said, "George, you are determined to ruin my life, right?"

*****

As the pink tinged dawn appeared above the Hpakant hills George and Tan left the no-star hotel where they had spent the rest of the night and climbed into the back of the Toyota. The other Toyota contained the Design Committee, heavily armed and faces drawn with tension. George fingered the handle of the knife that Tiger had sold him under his shirt. He had tucked it into his belt before he left the room that morning.

The vehicles rolled away from the curb, and Aung turned to address the architects in the back. "We go northeast for China border. Burmese Army thinking we go southeast towards Myitkyina."

"So we will fool them," George said.

"Maybe," Aung replied.

The narrow dirt road they were on was potted and rough, and the Toyota bounced around as they made their way towards the border, Tan holding on to his stomach. They were two hours outside of Hpakant, on a straight stretch of road when the driver, looking in his rear view mirror, started cursing vehemently in Burmese. Looking behind them they could see that six Burmese Army vehicles had pulled out of the bush after they had passed and were now following them, two abreast.

On the road in front of them six more vehicles now pulled out of an opening in the jungle and stopped. They were blocked from the rear and the front. As their driver hit the brakes, Aung turned to George and Tan sitting wide eyed in the back and said, "This very bad!"

*

Chapter 18

As soon as the Toyotas came to a halt, Aung and the Design Committee flew out of the cars with drawn weapons. Half of them pointed their guns towards the cars approaching from the rear, the other half pointing their weapons towards the cars blocking their passage in front. Tan and George stayed seated in the back of the car. Tan felt the red dirt road, the green walls of the jungle, the humidity, all closing in on him, constricting him like the coils of a giant Burmese python that was crushing the breath out of him.

An obese man in a Burmese Army General's uniform exited one of the vehicles blocking the road in front. He ambled towards them with the gait of a pregnant woman, his stomach cantilevered over his belt buckle, his shirt strained at the buttons. His slick, black hair was combed tight over his square head. He smiled as he walked towards them, but it was not a smile of friendship.

A few steps behind the General two soldiers dragged a man whose hands were bound, dried blood under his nose and purple bruises on his cheekbones, his feet dragging in the dirt. When the General stopped in front of the Toyota the soldiers let their prisoner sink to the ground.

"Oh my god, that's Tony!" George exclaimed. He and Tan watched as Aung and two of his men walked up to the General and the bound man. An outwardly hostile discussion ensued, both men's hands resting on their holstered revolvers. After some animated finger pointing Aung gave an order to one of his men. The soldier ran to the back of the Toyota and removed George and Tan's suitcases. He returned to the group of men and ripped open the architects' bags in front of the fat Burmese General, dumping the contents on the road.

There, on top of the pile of George's rumpled clothes, sat the Samsung mobile phone that Tony had given him. Aung picked the phone up and handed it to the General, who opened the back of the telephone and removed the Sim card. He snapped it in half and then ground it into the dirt under his boot. He then tossed the phone into the jungle. Smiling, he raised his pistol and shot Aung between the eyes.

"Holy shit! They just shot Aung!" Tan screamed.

"Oh my God!"

As Aung dropped, both sides started shooting. The Burmese General, in as much of a crouch as his rotund belly would allow, retreated to his car behind the line of soldiers firing at the Kachins. One of his men hefted a grenade launcher to his shoulder and pointed it at the Toyota in which George and Tan were sitting.

"Out!" George screamed. He grabbed Tan's arm and dived out of the car, dragging the frozen-in-fear Tan with him. They scurried away from the car on hands and knees. A whoosh, a blaze of smoke, and the Toyota exploded into flying metal and broken glass.

Tony, abandoned by his captors, hands still tied behind him, ran to George, dodging the bullets whizzing around them. "Untie me, untie me!"

George grabbed Tiger's knife from his waistband and cut the ropes binding Tony's hands. Tony grabbed George's shoulder and over the sound of gunshots yelled in his ear, "Follow me!" He ran in a crouch for the jungle. George and Tan scooted behind him, bullets pinging the earth at their feet.

They crashed frantically into the dappled green light of the jungle, the razor blade edges of palm leaves cutting their arms, vines grabbing their bodies as if to hold them. They bulled their way through the vegetation. The three men ran for thirty minutes before stopping at a shallow stream slicing through a ravine. Panting hard, bent over, hands on his side, eyes wide, leg muscles burning, Tan said, "I can't run any further. Will they follow us?"

"Probably, once they get tired of shooting each other," Tony said. "Cross the stream, I know how we can throw them off the track."

"How?" George asked. Tony did not reply. He crossed the narrow stream and walked the ten feet across the earthen stream bank on the other side without entering the jungle. He beckoned George and Tan to follow.

"George, give me your knife," Tony said when the other two were standing next to him. With knife in hand he cut a large fern, returned to the stream bank, and walking backwards used the fern as a broom to erase their footsteps from the brown dirt.

When he got back to George and Tan he said, "Now very gently we will pass through the underbrush, as if we are on a Hong Kong rooftop doing Tai Chi. Slowly. Do not disturb a leaf, do not harm a twig, you are dancing with the jungle. They will see our footprints and smashed vegetation on the side of the river bank, but nothing on this side. They will think that we went upstream, walking in the water to not leave footprints."

"Cool, just like in a movie!" George exclaimed.

"A very bad movie." Tan said.

"I am no ordinary mining engineer, my friends. You boys are lucky to be with me," Tony said, entering the jungle, Tai Chi'ing his way through the thick vegetation. "Follow me."

"Lucky? If it wasn't for whatever illegal scheme that you were doing with that mobile phone, we would be happily on the airplane back home right now!" Tan said as he mimicked Tony's careful movements.

Ignoring the comment, Tony said, "Far enough, we can walk regularly now." He used George's knife, which he had not returned, to cut their way through the jungle vines as they returned to a quicker pace. "They will never know that we crossed the stream and entered the jungle."

"Do you even know what direction we are going in?" Tan asked.

Tony whirled on him. "I know exactly what direction we are going in, my friend, and I know exactly where we are going too."

"Don't call me 'my friend'. Where are we going?" Tan said.

"North, to the Chinese border. We'll make a small detour to get supplies from Dragon Ong. We'll then cross into Yunnan, depending on how it goes with Dragon." Tony turned back to hacking the trail through the underbrush, picking up the pace.

"Detour? Yunnan? Dragon Ong? What the hell are you talking about? You are mad!" Tan said following close behind.

Tony stopped again and spun to face Tan. "Mad? OK, smart guy, can you survive in this jungle? What are you going to do for water?" He then took the knife and cut off the top of a plant with a cup-shaped bulb. He turned the bulb upside down and a small amount of liquid poured to the ground. "See this? These cups are full of rain water. All around us, little cups of water. Did you know that? Would a mad man know that?" Tony turned and continued hacking a trail through the jungle.

By late afternoon the three men, their shirts drenched through with sweat, found a small clearing in the jungle. Tony said, "We'll camp here for the night. You two are architects, right? Build us a shelter. Use the knife." Tony handed the blade, handle first, to George. "I will find us some food." Tony disappeared into the jungle.

"A shelter?" George said. "Reminds me of a school assignment."

"A school assignment that your life depends on. You find branches, and I'll cut vines to lash them together." Tan said.

"How about that bamboo?" George said, pointing to a grove. "I'll cut the sections of bamboo that we will need with the knife, and you collect vines. If you need to cut the vines, use a sharp rock. Once you have the vines, take two or three strands and braid them together." The two architects set to their task. Soon there was a pile of six foot long Bamboo sections and braided vine ropes.

"OK," George said, handing Tan the knife. "Now while I lash the bamboo sections together with our vine ropes, you cut palm fronds." By the time Tan had gathered a pile of palm fronds, George had lashed together a bamboo frame. He then fashioned a ridge pole and two upright supports, their ends buried a foot into the ground. George leaned the frame against the ridge pole structure at an angle and lashed them together. The skeleton of the lean-to was finished. They then lashed row after row of palm fronds to the frame.

When they were done, George exclaimed, "Wish I had a camera. We could submit it for the cover of *Architectural Record*."

"Where did you learn how to build a lean-to?" Tan asked, amazed at the watertight structure that they had built out of nothing but jungle materials.

"Gilroy Boy Scouts."

Tony reappeared from the jungle carrying a brightly colored bird by the feet. Blood dripped from its head. "I nailed it with a rock." Tony looked at the lean-to bamboo shelter that Tan and George had built. "Not bad!"

"Gather some dry wood, and I will clean the bird. Knife?" Tony said, hand extended.

"Did you happen to notice that we are in a tropical rain forest? Where do you expect us to find dry wood?' Tan said.

"Yes, I did happen to notice, Dickhead. Did you happen to notice that native people build fires all the time? Use your eyes, look for wood protected by higher vegetation." Tony spat as he set to pulling the feathers.

When Tan and George returned with relatively dry sticks, Tony carved a point on the end of a short stick, and then hollowed out an indentation in a fallen log. With some small kindling to feed it, Tony put the end of the stick in the indentation and quickly rolled the stick between his hands until the friction caused smoke to rise from the log. It took thirty minutes, but finally they had fire.

As they sat around the fire eating the bird and swatting at the swarms of mosquitoes buzzing around their heads, Tan said to Tony, "You owe us some explanations, Tony. For starters, what was on that Sim Card?"

"I don't owe you squat, Dickhead."

George said, "Tan is right, Tony. We are in this situation because Ruud asked me to bring him his forgotten telephone. Obviously, I was played for a fool. I can live with that. However, we would appreciate knowing why we are now sitting in the middle of the Burmese jungle eating this flying rat and being injected with malaria by thousands of mosquitoes instead of safely sitting in a business class seat watching a movie."

"OK," Tony said, "Since you asked nicely."

"Thank you."

"Large sections of Myanmar's forests are being sold to the Chinese for logging by the Generals who run this place. Myanmar is being raped. The earth is torn up for the jade, the forests denuded for the trees," Tony said, munching on a leg from the jungle bird.

"So, what, you and Ruud are environmentalists?" Tan asked.

"No, we are businessmen. That fat General at the shootout, U Minh, was selling concessions on his own and not including the other generals in the take. The Sim Card had photos that I took of the licenses he sold. If the other generals found out, he would be dead within a day. If a Chinese businessman had that information, he would own U Minh, be able to get the most favorable concessions. We were going to auction off the Sim Card to Chinese bidders. Whoever got it would be king of the jungle."

"Why didn't you just bring it out yourself? Why get us involved?" George asked.

"Ruud and I are rather well known here. Both the Burmese Army and the KIA hate us. It's not so easy for us to travel around. You two, however, were golden, guests of the KIA."

"The Burmese hate you as well as the Kachins?"

"There was a disagreement a while back over some missing drugs. A Burmese heroin dealer, a sadistic nut who thinks he is a witch, accused Ruud of stealing it. Had his hand cut off, thought that would scare people more than just killing him. The dealer actually wears the mummified hand around his neck on a chain."

"Yah, bizarre!" George said.

"That is nothing." Tony said. "He's a cannibal too."

"A cannibal?"

"Yeah, the psycho dealer who cut Ruud's hand off feels that he gains power from eating human flesh. Ruud is lucky that he didn't eat him," Tony said. "Anyway, let's get some sleep. Tomorrow you will meet Dragon Ong. You'll need to be alert for that."

"Dragon Ong? Who is Dragon Ong?" Tan asked.

"You'll see."

Chapter 19

Tan was in the rear focusing on the uneven trail ahead of him, George and Tony walking in front. Since leaving their makeshift camp three hours before Tan and George had been following Tony through muggy, steamy jungle, the trail ascending steep hills and then dropping to streambeds patrolled by gangs of swarming mosquitoes. Tan was sure that Tony had no idea where they were going.

Suddenly Tan felt a presence walking behind him. He spun quickly, and screamed. Two Southeast Asian men were standing behind him. The men glared at Tan. George and Tony had also stopped when they heard Tan's scream. The two Southeast Asian men raised their rifles. Tony, with quick strides, walked back to the men and glared at them over their guns. In Cantonese he said, "We have business with Ong. Take us to him."

Also in Cantonese, one of the men said, "Your friend screams like a little girl." Then, without another word, the two put down their guns and proceeded down the trail in the direction that Tony had been leading them. Tony, George, and Tan fell in behind them. *So Tony knew where he was going after all,* Tan thought.

Within thirty minutes they arrived at a camp of thatched huts in an expansive river valley. As the jungle opened up, the sun scorching the earth mercilessly without the canopy of vegetation, they descended the trail to the village. The familiar chirping, screeching sounds of the insects and birds disappeared, replaced by unexpected sounds of electric guitar riffs and pounding bass tones of rock and roll.

The village was a scene from purgatory. Speakers positioned in the trees blasted the music, and groups of sweaty men staggered about the camp, doing drugs and drinking whiskey. All had guns and machetes. Skinny child soldiers strolled amongst the older men carrying rifles that they could barely heft.

Yea though I walk through the valley of the shadow of death, I will fear no evil, Tan repeated in his mind. Then, *Bullshit, I am fearing this evil big-time!*

They walked down a dirt path between the thatched huts, the men leering at them, pointing, laughing, shouting at them. One boy soldier pointed his weapon at them and then fell to the ground doubled over in laughter. The men appeared to George to be from all over Southeast Asia: Chinese, Thai, Filipino, and Burmese. Over the speakers Jimmy Hendrix sang 'All Along the Watchtower'. Tan and George walked as close to the two guides leading them as they could. *There must be some way out'ta here, said the joker to the thief.*

They arrived at a large weed and dirt circular clearing, in the center of which a huge man sat in a Thai rosewood chair carved with elephants and lotus flowers. As they entered the plaza their two guides disappeared and, led by Tony, the three walked towards the seated man. The man rose as they approached. George and Tan starred in amazement.

Dragon Ong was tall and wide. Samoan-big. He was wearing a red tank top shirt that said 'Lakers', black military boots, and a purple woman's summer skirt. From his ears dangled numerous gold hoop earrings. Between his thumb and forefinger he held a joint.

Tony stood directly in front of the colorful mountain of a man, inches from him. Dragon took a long pull on his reefer and handed it to Tony, who did likewise. Holding the smoke in their lungs they stared into each eyes intensely. They held it in. Finally after about one minute Dragon exhaled, coughing, and then Tony let his breath slowly out. "Still have better lungs than me, Tony!" Dragon exclaimed. The two men embraced, laughing.

"More chairs, more weed, whiskey!" Dragon yelled.

All were soon seated in a circle on intricately carved chairs, with a matching rosewood table set up in the center of the circle. On it was placed a bottle of Murray McDavid single malt scotch whiskey and a black lacquered Chinese box filled with joints. The bottle was passed from man to man, each man swigging from it, and four joints were lit and passed around.

"I never smoked marijuana before," Tan whispered in Tony's ear.

Tony whispered back, "Smoke or be smoked, Dickhead. Would be a major insult if you did not accept Dragon's hospitality."

Tony took a long pull on his joint, exhaled, took a drink of the whiskey, and as he passed the bottle to Tan, said, "Dragon, we are in need of some small assistance in getting our unworthy asses across the border. We are Hong Kong bound, and have zero money and no passports."

"Not a problem. The usual arrangement? I have a load ready to go."

"Fantastic, Dragon, I knew that you could help us," Tony said.

Dragon yelled in Burmese and one of his soldiers instantly appeared with a Polaroid camera. "Sit up straight," Tony said to Tan and George. "Passport photos."

After the photos were taken Dragon said, "By the way, how is Ruud, Tony? On the last load he shorted me."

"He shorted you? I am sure that it was accidental. Ruud has trouble with mathematics sometimes."

Dragon laughed. "Trouble with mathematics...that's funny! Anyway, tomorrow we talk business. Tonight is Carnivale!"

"Carnivale? You mean like in Brazil?" George asked.

"Yes! Carnivale exactly like in Brazil! Better even!" Dragon exclaimed.

George took another pull on his joint, looked at it and realized he was stoned out of his mind, and said, "This is some powerful shit."

"Yes it is," Dragon said. "By the way, our rude friend Tony did not formally introduce us. I am the one and only Dragon Ong. You are...?"

"George stood up and extended his hand towards Dragon, "I am George Washington Smith, and this gentleman is Tan Lam."

Dragon raised his huge frame out of the chair, but instead of taking George's hand he enveloped him in a bear hug. "Welcome, George Washington Smith and Tan Lam." He then pulled the very-stoned-for-the-first-time-in-his-life Tan out of his seat and gave him a hug also. "You gentlemen make yourselves at home. I need to make sure that all is prepared for tonight. When the sun goes down, the samba comes to town!" Dragon Ong left, leaving the three men still seated in a circle.

"I really like him!" George said.

"I do not know what is going on? Can someone explain to me what is going on?" Tan asked.

"What do you want to know, Dickhead?" Tony said, taking a swig from the whiskey bottle.

"Brazilian Carnivale in the Burmese jungle?" Tan asked.

"Dragon saw a video of the Carnivale in Rio de Janeiro once and got hooked. He had some local girls learn to samba, got them some costumes, got the music. The rest is just drugs and whiskey. He does it whenever he gets the urge. It's a party and a half. You guys will have fun."

"Why does Dragon speak such good English?" Tan continued with the questioning.

"He is Hong Kong Chinese, just like you, Dickhead."

"Why does he wear a dress?" Tan asked.

"Who knows? Dragon's got some weird parasite in his brain from eating bush meat. The parasite is crawling around his skull, turning his brain into Swiss cheese."

"That is so strange!" George explained. "Tony, if you do not mind, I have a question too."

"Shoot."

"Dragon said '*the usual arrangement*', that he has '*a load ready to go*.' What's that mean?"

"Dragon is a drug smuggler, we are his mules." Tony said.

"No way!" Tan blurted.

"Well, Dickhead, if you have a better idea as to how to get us across the border into Yunnan with no money, no passports, and no visas, please let us know." Tony paused, took a hit on his joint, exhaled. "No? OK. We are drug mules then."

Chapter 20

Carnivale started at sundown. The rock music came to an abrupt halt and the voice of Dragon Ong boomed over the loudspeakers, first in Cantonese, then in Burmese, and then in English, "Ladies and Gentlemen, this is your King of the Carnivale! Let the funky Samba begin!" The speakers in the trees began their mantra, the pulsating rhythms of drums and trumpets discharging at eardrum-annihilating volume.

From behind one of the huts a line of Burmese women paraded into the clearing gyrating to the music. They were wearing sequined bikinis and massive headdresses. Leading the procession, strutting with a graceful rhythm that belied his large size, was Dragon Ong. He was wearing a white sequined evening gown with long purple, yellow, and red tail feathers.

Barbecues had been set up along one side of the plaza as well as tables with whiskey, beer, and boxes of joints. Tan, who had not had a good meal since they left Hpakant, had positioned himself adjacent to one of the barbecues. Large fire pits had been ignited around the perimeter of the plaza casting a golden glow over the festivities. Tan counted over one hundred men cheering on the samba dancers, staggering and stoned, every so often one of them shooting his gun into the air.

After consuming a few skewers of barbecued meat, with a bottle of beer in one hand and a joint in the other, Tan circulated among the revelers. The world was spinning. He saw a blurry image of George dancing through the crowd, hooting and cheering. He noted Ong, tail feathers swaying with the beat as he danced with three women, naked except for their colorful feather headdresses. Enveloped in a fog of marijuana and alcohol, Tan felt his field of vision slowly narrowing until, like someone flicking a light switch, everything went black.

*****

Tan woke up slowly, the morning sun stinging his eyes and mosquitoes humming about his head. He was lying on a grassy patch in the middle of the plaza surrounded by empty beer and whiskey bottles. Ants crawled over him but he was too hung over to even swat them away. He gingerly stood up, and then bent over and puked.

George and Tony appeared. "I recommend a dip in the river," George said. "It will make you feel like a new man."

Two hours later, Tan's head still pounding and his stomach jumpy, he joined George and Tony in front of Dragon's hut. The circle of chairs had been set up again, but this time no drugs or booze. Dragon handed three passports to the men. "Gentlemen, you are now Frenchmen."

Tan held his new passport in his hands and thought, *French?*. He looked at the Bordeaux-red cover, the coat of arms embossed in gold, the words 'Republique Francaise'. He opened it and saw his picture looking back at him, the name Leon Guesde under the photo.

"I don't know about you guys, but I don't speak French," Tan said.

"No matter," Dragon answered. "Neither do the border guards. Just speak some gibberish that sounds like French if someone talks to you."

Three daypacks were brought: a blue one, a black one, and a gray one. "Legitimate travelers have 'stuff'. We have put some shorts and T-shirts in the packs. You may not want to actually wear them. I cannot vouch for their hygiene," Dragon said. "Now, if you three Frenchmen will remove your shirts."

They complied. Two of Ong's soldiers duct taped brown-colored bricks wrapped in plastic to each man's torso. "I have seen this on *Locked Up Abroad*. They always get caught! George, we cannot go through with this!" Tan exclaimed.

"I am not George, I am Jules Duclerc, international drug smuggler," George said in a really bad French accent. "Don't worry, Tan. You do this all the time, right, Tony?"

"Yes, it is very safe," Tony said. "Do not worry."

"Hearing you guys say 'don't worry' makes me worry twice as much," Tan whined.

When the men had their shirts back on, Ong gave Tony four more bricks. "Here are your visas, two for the guards on the Burmese side and two for the guards on the Chinese side." Dragon gave all three a bear hug, and they started out on the trail across the river valley towards the jungle and the border crossing with China, the packages taped to their sides uncomfortable in the humidity.

By three in the afternoon they started to see signs of civilization and by four o'clock they had reached the border crossing that spanned the Shweli River. On the Burmese side was the town of Mu Se, on the Chinese side was Ruili. They approached the guard post. After so much time in the jungle, the three-story concrete structure seemed like an edifice of urbanity.

"Let me do the talking. I know how to handle this," Tony said. "Give me you passports." He walked up to the six guards manning the post, engaged them in conversation in Cantonese, and handed them the passports and two of the bricks. They walked into the guard shack. Tony turned to Tan and George, winked, and signaled them to follow.

The three men were told to sit on filthy plastic chairs as the guards took the bricks and the passports into a back room. A noisy electric fan blew on them from a corner. Twenty minutes later two unsmiling Burmese guards came out and said in Mandarin, "Come with us."

George and Tan could sense by Tony's expression that this was not what he was expecting. They followed the guards into the room. On a table were the two brick 'visas', the packages opened. Sitting at the table was a young Burmese officer with his laptop, their three bogus French passports laid open next to it.

From another room a tall Burmese Captain entered. He said in Mandarin, "Do you three foreign dogs speak Mandarin?"

It took a short moment for them to remember that they were across the border from Mandarin speaking Yunnan. "Uh, yes, we do... or at least I do. Tan?" Tony said.

"Yes, I do too." Tan said, nodding.

"Good. Now can you explain to me why those two packages on that table contain dirt, and why you are carrying the passports of three Frenchmen who are wanted by the Burmese police for arranging fake Chinese brides for Burmese men?"

"Dirt! No way!" Tony went up to the table and inspected the

open package. "We have been double-crossed by Dragon Ong!" he howled, "Probably as payback because Ruud shorted him on the last shipment! Damn him!"

Tan thought he was going to puke again. "So, we are not in trouble, right?" Tan said to the Captain in Mandarin. "No harm done. No law against smuggling dirt. We will just go back into Myanmar and come back again another time."

The Captain smiled. "*Au contraire*, my three fake Frenchmen. True, no law against smuggling dirt, but trying to bribe border guards who are now pissed off because you tried to bribe them with dirt is quite serious. Also, I happen to know that the three Frenchmen whom you are claiming to be met their demise in the jungle at the hands of the Burmese that they ripped off. So you are using forged documents, also a serious offence."

"What is being said?" George asked, not understanding the Mandarin.

Tan turned to George and said, "Basically, George, we are fucked."

The Captain said, "We will arrange transportation to Bamaw prison momentarily, where you will be tried for your crimes, and then rot." In Burmese he gave orders to the guards. Tan, George, and Tony were escorted to a vinyl-floored, chalky-white room. There was one window with no glass, only metal bars. They heard the door lock click as they were left alone in the room.

Tan exclaimed, "This is not happening to me! No way! At our trial we can make the case that we were duped into this whole thing, tricked by Dragon Ong. It should be easy to prove that we are not those Frenchmen, that we only had dirt instead of dope."

"I am afraid that you do not understand the Burmese justice system," Tony said. "At the prison we will be put into a court room with other accused unfortunates. The judge will only be read a list of all our crimes at once, and then he will make one sentence for everyone. There is no discussion of individual cases, just a reading of the list of the alleged crimes of everyone in the room."

"We are going to be dropped into Hell, and there is nothing we can do about it!" Tan howled.

Tony looked out through the rusted window bars. Outside a line of traffic was stopped at the border crossing, mostly three wheeled motorcycles and small trucks stacked high with boxes of goods. A slat-backed truck carrying a load of pigs belched smoke from its exhaust as it idled in line. As Tony watched, a young boy walked by their window. Tony called to him in Mandarin, "Hey, friend! See these three new daypacks?" Tony held his pack up through the bars. "These will sell fast in Ruili, probably get 50 yuan a piece for them."

The boy looked up at the daypack. "What do you want me to do for them?"

"We are bored in here. See that load of pigs? It would be very entertaining if you snuck over and opened the gate of the truck," Tony said. "Do that and I'll drop the daypacks on the ground."

After a moment's reflection on the prospective reward versus the chance of getting caught, the boy, running in a crouch, was quick to the back of the truck, opening the slatted gate. The suddenly-freed, squealing porkers exploded from the truck, running in all directions. The driver, bellowing in Burmese, was instantly out of the truck, chasing the escaped beasts.

Other drivers also jumped out of their vehicles and joined the attempt to capture the escaped swine. They formed a circle to surround the desperate pigs as they darted erratically, squealing shrilly, ears straight up. People dove at the animals, rolling on the ground in missed attempts to grab the escapees, laughing and hooting at this sudden game breaking the monotony of the border crossing. Soon the border guards joined the fray also. People, pigs, and guards ran amok.

"This is our chance!" Tony said. He threw his shoulder into the door, the lock busting through the wooden jamb. The three men bolted out of the building, running as fast as they could toward the Shweli River.

As the pigs continued to evade the clumsy horde of would-be captors, the Captain watched the frenzied attempt at a roundup from the window of his office, shaking his head. *Time to put an end to this chaos*, he thought. He pulled out his revolver and calmly extending his hand out of his open window started shooting pigs. Everyone froze, stunned. The guards, the joyous laughter of the pig-catching game over, followed their Captain's example, emptying their clips until all the pigs lay still. "Problem solved," the Captain said, turning from the window and sitting back down at his desk.

Tan, Tony, and George let the current of the Shweli River carry them south, away from the border crossing. After about a mile Tony made his way toward the bank on the Chinese side, grabbing into the thick brush bordering the river and pulling himself onto the bank. The other two followed and all three rolled up onto solid land, crawling into the concealing jungle foliage. Tony rolled on his back and laughed, "Welcome to Yunnan Province, China, Gentlemen." He pulled up his shirt, "Remember to take off your packages of wet dirt!"

Chapter 21

Dita re-read the flyer, '*Teach Indonesian to Chinese businessmen.*' She tapped the number from the flyer into her Samsung. A man answered in Cantonese and gave her an address in Sham Shui Po. He said, "It's a butcher shop. It is where we have the classes. The owner of the butcher shop sponsors the program."

"You pay how much?" Dita asked.

"200 Hong Kong per hour."

"Wow! What time?"

"Be here at 2:00pm."

"OK." Dita said, hanging up and then dialing her friend, Abigail, who was sitting on the edge of the fountain in Victoria Park, enjoying the Sunday morning sun. "Hey, Abigail, I see you later tonight, O.K., cannot meet during day today, busy."

"Busy? With what, got another girlfriend?"

"No. Only you. I am going Sham Shui Po to teach Indonesian."

"That is weak lie. You have another girl friend."

"No. No lie! I see you tonight, at Surabaya. OK?"

"Sure, if you lucky!" Abigail hung up.

At 2:00pm sharp Dita walked up a narrow alley off of Li Kung Lane in Sham Shui Po to a squat industrial building streaked brown with rain water from overflowing gutters, the faded sign above the door reading 'He Hing Butcher'. She rang the buzzer on the wall next to the metal industrial door. It was opened by the same Southeast Asian man who had handed her the flyer at the Surabaya Club. "Please, come in," flashing a tobacco-stained grin.

Whether triggered by instinct, the smell of the slaughterhouse, or by the man's tone, some inner sense told Dita to turn and run. *Danger, do not enter!* Dita ignored the voice and stepped over the raised threshold into a concrete-floored lobby. The man said, "Follow me." He led her down a corridor lined with refrigerator doors to a small room with one plastic chair under a bare electric bulb. A second man was in the room.

"Sit," the man said.

Dita said, "One chair? What is this? Where do the students sit?" Her senses screamed at her, *Dita, run now! This is wrong!*

The second man, who was behind her, slapped a scopolamine-soaked rag over her mouth and nose. She could not move. The man lowered her into the chair. A blurry image of another man, bare-chested, dressed in a cloth skirt and a red headdress, entered her field of vision. *What is happening? I am drugged. Oh my God!*

They are leading me. Floating. I am naked. How did I get naked? Is that an altar? The man with the headdress is calling out in a foreign language. Who is he talking to?

The Witch finished his prayer to Nat and bowed. He then spun, removed a knife from the sheath tucked into his cloth skirt, and slit Dita's throat.

Chapter 22

Angela, dressed in black capris and a purple sweatshirt, sat alone in a far corner of the bar at The Surabaya Club facing the Sunday night crowd. When she got the approval to go undercover there was no question in her mind, she was going Tommy-boy rather than Girly-girl. She sipped on a Coke.

A dark-skinned girl in a white blouse sat down on the empty stool next to her. She looked at Angela and flashed a shy smile. Angela looked at her but did not return the smile. The girl said in Indonesian, "I have not seen you here before. I am Winnie."

Angela replied, "I don't party much, Winnie."

The girl looked away. Angela thought, *OK, need to play the undercover role.* "Hey. Winnie." The girl looked back at her. "I am Adi. Can I buy you a drink?"

A big smile from Winnie. "Sure, Adi, a margarita, please."

The margarita came and the girls tapped glasses. Winnie put her hand on Angela's thigh. "Where are you from, Adi?"

Angela stiffened at the other girl's touch, but then consciously forced her muscles to relax. "Jakarta. And you?"

"I am from Malang."

Angela's eyes had never stopped scanning the crowded bar, and she suddenly spotted a man with a cloth bag over his shoulder. "Winnie, come with me," Angela said, taking the girl's hand. "Let's dance."

Continuing to track the man with the bag, Angela took Winnie to the center of the dance floor. Winnie put her mouth up to Angela's ear and said, "Adi, I like your forcefulness."

Angela danced them towards the man with bag who was now talking to a couple standing in a far corner of the room. Angela saw him reach into the bag and hand a flyer to the women.

When they were next to the man Angela stopped dancing and said to the man in Cantonese, "Hey, what do you have there? Are you selling something?" She had to yell to be heard over the pounding thump of the music.

The man handed her a flyer. "A chance to earn some extra money."

Angela folded the flyer and put in her pocket without looking at it. "Thanks."

Angela turned to Winnie and said, "I am going to the bathroom." She left her standing on the dance floor. In the relative quiet of the ladies room Angela called Ian for backup.

Back in the club Angela did a turn around the edge of the dance floor with Winnie until she spotted the man again. She came up behind him and, drawing her revolver from the holster under her sweatshirt, put the barrel of the gun in the man's back. With her left hand she showed him her police badge. "We are going outside. Walk!"

The man complied. Angela walked close behind him, gun pressed in his back, as they descended the stairs to the street. When they passed the bouncers Angela hugged him close so the bouncers would not see her gun. Out the door and away from the pressing crowd to wait for the backup, Angela heard a voice call behind her, "Adi, Adi, wait!" It was Winnie. "Do you want my phone number? Are you on *Facebook*?"

The Burmese man took advantage of the distraction. He spun, leading with his elbow, catching Angela on the jaw line. As she collapsed to one knee on the sidewalk the man bolted, disappearing instantly in the crowded street. Angela's heart sank and she holstered her gun. She stood up just as the backup arrived, too late.

I am the Garuda, Angela said to herself, *I will catch him.* Instead of diving into the slow-moving crowd of Wanchai partygoers on the sidewalk she ran into the car lanes on Fenwick Street and, dodging taxis and minivans, got to the corner of Fenwick and Lockhart before the suspect. She spotted him in front of Mes Amis, the cloth bag still slung over his shoulder.

Angela cut back onto the sidewalk and dove, a bird of prey swooping down on a rabbit, tackling the man at his ankles. As the man hit the sidewalk two policemen from the backup who had followed her up Fenwick in the police cruiser were also on top of the suspect. In seconds he was handcuffed and whisked away into the police car. The crowd, who had parted for the scuffle and had stared in mild curiosity, closed ranks and continued their merry promenade.

*****

Sunday morning and the Ibuprofen were doing nothing to ease the pain in Angela's jaw. She sat at the conference room table at headquarters and studied the flyer with Nigel and Ian. "Great bust last night, Angela," Ian said. "Welcome to CID."

Another officer opened the door and said, "Hey, Ian, your desk phone is ringing."

"Thanks, Sammy." Ian walked to his cubicle and picked up the receiver, "Inspector Ian Hamilton."

The voice on the other end of the line said, "Oh, good, I was worried that I would not be able to get you on a busy Monday morning. This is Nakaji Sein, from the Burmese Embassy."

"Political Counselor Sein, what can I do for you?"

"Please call me Nakaji. I made some inquiries in the community, and found out that the dead man whom you are investigating did indeed work for Zaw Than, as you suspected."

"Really? Are you sure?"

"Completely. Zaw Than is very well know to all in our community," Nakaji said.

"Great information. Thank you," Ian said.

"Sure, but…that is not the real reason I called you, Detective. I have heard through my network that you arrested another Burmese citizen in connection with the case last night in Wanchai."

"How would that information get out so fast?"

"Hong Kong is a small city, Detective. Perhaps someone at the scene…"

"OK, well, it's true, last night we arrested a Burmese man whom we believe is another accomplice," Ian said.

"Before you question him I will need to confer with the man. It is international law, and I must insist that we follow formal protocol. Since the victim was Burmese I need to report to my superiors in Myanmar," Nakaji said.

"Yes, but…"

"I know what you are going to say, Ian. May I call you Ian? You were thinking, 'If this were Myanmar, international protocol would not be followed.' You are probably correct. However we are in Hong Kong, and I must insist. I can be at your police station in thirty minutes. Surely thirty more minutes will not impede justice too much, and I will get into serious trouble with my superiors if I do not follow procedure."

Ian hesitated as he contemplated this new annoyance. "OK, Nakaji. See you in thirty minutes." He put down the receiver.

Angela and Nigel were discussing interview strategy when Ian returned to the conference room. "We were waiting for you before we started the interrogation."

"Guys, sorry, but that was the Myanmar Political Counselor on the phone. We need to wait until he confers with the suspect before we question him. We have no choice. He'll be here in thirty minutes."

"Aiyaah! What an inconvenience," Angela said.

"However, I did get some interesting news," Ian said. "Zaw Than *is* involved in the case. The dead Kachin was in his employ. Meanwhile, we have the telephone number that was on the flyers. While we are waiting for Mr. Sein, Angela, let's give it try and see what we get."

Angela put the desk phone on speaker, and dialed the number.

The Burmese man in the *He Hing Butcher Shop*, about to enter one of the walk-in refrigerators, pulled the ringing mobile from his pocket and looked at it. His companion also stared at it. "We are good for this month," he said.

"Right," the other man said. "Let's finish packing and get to the camp." They ignored the ring.

The men put the butchered ribcages in a plastic lined vinyl bag packed with ice. No one on the Metro from Sham Shui Po to Central, nor on the ferry from Central to Mui Wo, suspected the gruesome contents of the red, white, and blue checkered vinyl bag carried by the two men.

*****

Political Counselor Sein arrived at the police station wearing a blue blazer and khaki pants. "Thank you for accommodating my request, Ian," he said as he shook hands with the three officers. "May I see the suspect now?"

Ian led him to a windowless interrogation room. Inside, the handcuffed Burmese suspect sat motionless, blankly staring at the white walls as if he could see through them, as if he could gaze all the way back to Myanmar and his Kachin village. "This will not take long," Nakaji said, and he entered the room, closing the door behind him.

Ten minutes later Nakaji emerged. "Thank you, officers. I can report to my superiors now that the suspect has been treated fairly and well by the Hong Kong police. He would give me no details of his crimes, but he did confirm to me that he is in the employ of Zaw Than, and that the dead Kachin was a colleague of his."

"No problem, Nakaji. Please let us know if you receive any more information." Ian turned to Nigel and Angela, "Let's proceed." The three, along with a Burmese translator, entered the interrogation room.

The suspect stared at them as they walked in. Ian began the questioning, but the suspect said nothing. The suspect said nothing for the entire interrogation.

*****

The two men carrying the checked vinyl bags arrived at the Mui Wo camp before The Witch. On the side of the clearing a shallow pit had been dug in which they made a small pyramid of charcoal. When the coals were glowing they spread them flat using a long-handled spatula and covered them with a metal grill. They placed the ribs, which they had rubbed with Char Siu BBQ sauce, on the oiled grill. The ribs would slow cook all day, the men adding more coals as needed and occasionally turning the ribs as they brushed them with additional sauce.

The Witch arrived at dusk. He went into his hut and emerged dressed in his headdress, the mummified hand hanging from a chain around his neck. A fire had been built in the center of the clearing. The Witch approached the flames, the orange glow reflecting off his skin, the sky indigo behind him. He raised his hands and face to the sky.

"Hear me, Nat! Another feast in your honor! Thank you for the protection which you have bestowed on me." The Witch threw a handful of reptile parts on the flames. The two men watched in awe. "I feel my enemies gathering about me. They think that we will run like the deer from the tiger. They will soon learn that I *am* the tiger, not the deer!"

The Witch sat down in a folding, aluminum frame beach chair that had been set by the fire. "Let the feast begin!" The men ran to the grill. Placing the cooked ribs in a metal pan, and, with paper plates and bottles of beer, they served The Witch his feast.

Chapter 23

It's going to be another drencher, Ian thought as he looked out the window from his cubicle at Police Headquarters, malefic gray clouds hanging low over the city. He dialed his sister. "Hey, Sarah."

"Oh, Ian, I am so worried about George. I haven't heard a thing. He was supposed to be back by now."

"He's probably fine. I think that where they were going has no internet service. Mobile phones probably don't even work. He's just off the grid, unreachable." Ian said.

"I know, Ian, but he should be back. I tried to check at his office and got nowhere. They must know what's happening. Maybe they'll be more cooperative with you. Can you call them?"

"No problem. I'll check on it." Ian said. "However, I would like you to do something for me also, Little Sister."

"Oh, yeah? What?"

"I can't really ask Tika out while the case that I am working on with her is active. However, if you went out with her for a drink, and I happened to be there too, well… that would be cool."

"Ah ha, you are interested in her!" Sarah exclaimed.

"Well, yeah, sort of."

"Ha! I'll do it. Thursday night OK?"

"Yeah. How about Red Bar at IFC?"

"Cool. I'll confirm once I talk to Tika. And Ian, thanks for checking on George for me."

Ian hung up and dialed the number of Robison Whitehorse and Grant. "Good morning, RWG, how may I direct your call?" a young woman's voice said in a British accent.

"Hi, my name is Ian Hamilton. I am a friend of one of your employees, George Washington Smith. We had expected him to be back from his trip to Myanmar by now, but it appears that he isn't. Is there someone that I can talk to about George?"

"Just a moment, please, I'll connect you."

A few rings, and a man's voice with an American accent came on, "Jerry Niles, may I help you."

Ian repeated his query. Jerry said, "We are aware that George is late coming back. Actually, another one of our architects, Tan Lam, is on the trip too. His parents called me six times yesterday, if you can believe that. As I told them, George and Tan are in the back country with no internet service, rough roads, and old cars. Could be anything, no telling what came up. They are probably just delayed. I am sure that everything is OK."

"Jerry, please excuse my directness, but that's a pretty fucking cavalier attitude. You do not have a clue as to whether George and Tan are OK. What is your company doing to find out?"

"Doing...aahh?"

"Nothing. Great. I suggest that you think of something, Jerry. When you do get some news, please call me, *Inspector* Ian Hamilton, Hong Kong Police Department." Ian gave him his number and clicked off.

Ian dialed Sarah's number. "Hi, Sarah. Just spoke with George's company and they are doing what they can to find out where George is. I have a better source, though. George's Burmese client, and yours', Zaw Than, just become a suspect in the missing Indonesian maids case. I will be bringing him in for questioning. I will also question him about what happened to George in Myanmar."

"Thanks, Ian. Oh, by the way, we are on with Tika for Thursday. Red Bar 8:00pm."

Ian dialed Nigel's extension on his desk phone. "Bring in Zaw Than. Do we have a good address for him?"

"Yes, I've got it. He lives on the Peak in one of those new yellow apartments that are supposed to look like bamboo reeds swaying in the breeze. His monthly rent is more than I earn in five years."

"Take Angela, bring him in."

"Sure. Angela was pretty upset about that interview yesterday with the Burmese guy. Hopefully she has chilled out by now," Nigel said.

"Yeah, I spoke with her afterwards, but have another talk with her in the car. If a suspect refuses to talk with us, losing our temper and cursing him is not helpful. She is Asian, she should understand about losing face."

*****

As the police cruiser navigated the curves of Stubbs Road up to the Peak Angela was still angry, "In Myanmar he would have not just talked for the police, he would have begged them to take his information. Jail for him in Hong Kong is like a vacation."

"Certainly you are not suggesting that we torture our suspects, Angela."

Angela glared at him and said nothing.

The cruiser pulled up to the entry of the stone, steel, and glass towers, the building appearing to twist as it rose from the steep hillside. Showing their badges to the sleepy-eyed, uniformed doorman, they were told to wait while he buzzed Zaw Than's apartment.

"No answer. That's strange. He just had another visitor about thirty minutes ago. I did not see him leave," the doorman remarked with a shrug, almost as if he was talking to himself. His eyes then glazed back over to their somnambulant state, back to daydreams of another career, another place.

"We'll go up and look around then." Nigel answered.

"I am sorry. I think that it would be best if you come back another time. Maybe you could make an appointment."

"No, screw that!" Angela exploded in Cantonese street slang, inches from the doorman's face. "We do not care what you think! We go up now, dog-fart!"

"OK,OK, relax. I was just suggesting…," the doorman said backing away from Angela, his eyes wide. He escorted them to the cherry wood interior of the private penthouse elevator to Zaw Than's apartment. They ascended to the top floor. The elevator doors opened, and they stepped into three thousand square feet of marble floors, designer furniture, and the most spectacular views in Hong Kong.

Laying on his back in the middle of the spacious living room, blood from a wound in his temple staining a white Berber carpet red, was Zaw Than, a revolver in one hand and a note clutched in the other.

Chapter 24

Tan, George, and Tony sat on granite boulders around a smoky fire. They had hiked east all day traversing the rugged hills and valleys of Yunnan, ascending from tropical lowlands and muddy streams to alpine forests. On the ground in front of them Tony had placed a pile of plants with large green leaves. "These are edible. Enjoy."

"Are you sure?" Tan asked, watching a small red bug crawl across one of the leaves.

"Sure I am sure," Tony said.

"Now that we are in China, how are we going to get to Hong Kong?" George said. "How far is it, Tony?"

"Far. We are in southwest China and we have to get to the southeast. We are within a day's walk of the city of Baoshan, which has an airport. They have one flight a day to Kunming. From Kunming we could catch a flight to Hong Kong." Tony said.

"I like the sound of those words, '*Catch a flight to Hong Kong*'," Tan said.

"We have to solve the issue of no money and no passports, however," George said.

"I have a plan for that." Tony said. "I have a contact in Baoshan. The drug route from Myanmar to Hong Kong is through Baoshan. They can hook us up."

George said, "No offense, Tony, but I have a bad feeling about you *'having a contact who can hook us up.'* You are comfortable with being a criminal. We, on the other hand, are not. All we need when we get to Baoshan is contact with the American Embassy."

"Whatever. Let's eat the plants and get some sleep," Tony said with a shrug.

*****

In the morning George could barely move, he felt like an old man. Sleeping on the ground was a challenge that he was not used to. He stretched his limbs gingerly as he stood up. Tony was already up and had re-started the fire. George looked at Tony and screamed.

"Oh my God! What happened to you?" Tony's swollen face seemed to be twice its normal size. It was bright red, and covered with white blisters.

"What?" Tony put his hand up to his face. "Aiyahhh!" Then looking at George, "You too! You look like a monster!"

The commotion woke Tan, who sat up, saw George and Tony, and then putting his hand to his own face, wailed, "What happened to us?"

George, now sitting on one of the boulders by the fire, said, "Tony, last night you said those plants were safe to eat."

"Well, I thought they were! Lots of plants look alike, you know," Tony said defensively.

Tan paced the campsite. "I hate you, Tony! Being around you is one disaster after another!"

"I am sure that our disfiguration is only temporary. Don't worry," Tony said.

"Don't worry? We do not even look human! No money, no identification, no food, wanted by the Burmese police, illegally in China, and now we look like monsters!" Tan howled as he strode around the campsite.

"Calm down, Tan. Getting agitated doesn't help anything," George said. "Let's continue to hike east and pray that our faces get back to normal soon."

The terrain became more mountainous and steep as they hiked. They skirted deep gorges, inching their way on narrow trails, muddy rivers snaking far below them. By the time that they reached the outskirts of Baoshan their facial swelling had subsided and the white blisters had disappeared. They merely looked they had very bad sunburns.

The first indication of civilization that they encountered was a sign for a tourist attraction. It was a brown sign with gold letters at the side of their trail. Tan translated for George, 'Site of Ancient Humanity Ruins, Reclining Buddha Temple'.

"Been there before," Tony said. "There is a paved road from the temple into the City of Baoshan. It is clear sailing from here, Gentlemen!"

They soon came to walled temple grounds with a stone gate and a multi-tiered terracotta tiled roof above it. Two stone lions sat on either side of stairs leading up to massive yellow-painted wooden doors in the gate. The doors were in the open position and Tan, Tony and George walked into the entry alcove.

At the side of the alcove a ticket booth had been built into the historic structure, a tiny wooden room with a thick sheet glass separating the ticket vendor from the visitors. Behind the counter a girl barely out of her teens was reading a novel. She looked surprised to see the three travelers.

In Mandarin Tony said, "Hello, we have a bit of trouble. Is there a telephone here that we can use here?"

The girl said, "Tickets are one hundred yuan each."

"No, we do not want to see the Reclining Buddha. We are in trouble and need to call someone," Tony said.

"Only sell tickets."

Tan pushed in front of Tony, pressing his angry, crimson face to the window of the ticket booth. "He asked if there is there a telephone that we can use? Did you not hear him say that we have an emergency? There *must* be a telephone, you dim-witted bitch!" Tan yelled in Mandarin.

"No. No telephone."

"Is there a manager or someone in charge that we can see then?" Tan asked through clenched teeth.

"No. Only me here."

"But what if there was a problem, like a fire or something? Wouldn't you have to call someone?" Tan said.

"Manager gets mad if I call. He has another job. He told me never call."

Tan switched to a friendlier tone, "Can't we use your personal mobile telephone then? This really is an emergency."

"No. You two talk funny."

"What do you mean that we talk funny? We are Cantonese."

"You are *mafan*, trouble."

"So shall we just go back into the forest and die of hunger and thirst then?" Tan asked, sarcasm creeping into his voice despite his efforts to control his temper.

"You have a *lao wai* with you."

"So what?"

"So you are *mafan*." The girl said, and she pulled down the metal shutter which closed off her ticket window, like a turtle pulling its head into its shell.

"Aahh!" Tan screamed, slapping the glass ticket window. "Can you believe that stupid farm girl!" Turning around he noticed that Tony had disappeared. He said to George. "Where's Tony?" George shrugged.

Tony appeared suddenly on the path coming from the cave which held the Reclining Buddha. "Sorry, guys, just wanted to get a peek at the reclining Buddha, back to my roots and all. Let's head out. Quickly now."

George shrugged again. They headed down the paved road which descended to the town of Baoshan. After another hour the urban sprawl of the city appeared on the horizon, a jumble of white, boxy buildings topped by a cloud of brown industrial haze.

"Civilization at last!" George exclaimed. "We can find a police station and get hooked up with our embassies."

"Do you realize how impractical that plan is?" Tony said.

"Why? Why would that be impractical?" Tan asked.

"First, the nearest embassies are in Chengdu. How would you get there? Do you think that the police will lend you money for food or transportation? They will lock you up first for being in the country without passports or visas. That is their job. They would then take their sweet time about notifying your embassies. You will then be at the mercy of some Chengdu bureaucrat getting your documentation filed and proving your identities. You would be stuck in Yunnan Prison for a long time."

"And your plan, Tony?" George asked.

"I buy a cheap phone and a Sim Card and then contact Ruud. He would get us out of China and into Hong Kong within a few days. You can then deal with the bureaucratic issues from home in Hong Kong, simply a matter of replacing stolen passports."

"How would you buy a phone and Sim Card? We do not even have one yuan," Tan asked.

"Yes we do. Remember when I went into the cave of the Reclining Buddha? I actually had a religious experience. I was going to tell you guys about it but I thought you would think me crazy. The Buddha spoke to me."

"He spoke to you?" George asked.

"Yes, as clearly as you are speaking to me now. He asked me to take the money in the donation box that people leave for the incense sticks. He said that we needed it more than him. That is a very Buddha-like thing to say, right? So, it had to be him."

"What? You stole the donation money from the temple! Not only are you bringing bad karma on your head, you idiot, but now we can't go to the police! They will be looking for us once that uncooperative ticket-taker reports us!" George exclaimed.

"Tony, I hate you!" Tan said.

"Well, I suggest that you consider my plan then, but you guys can do what you want."

In the first telephone store that they encountered as they entered the city Tony negotiated for a Nokia telephone and a Sim Card. The salesperson, a young man in his twenties wearing a crumpled white shirt and a thin blue tie, was sleeping hunched over on the glass countertop with his head on folded arms when they entered the store. He resumed his position as soon as they left.

Next door to the telephone store was a restaurant. Tony said, "We have enough money left over from our telephone purchase to feast, Gentlemen, at least in Baoshan."

As Tan ordered dishes of steamed chicken, noodles, mushrooms, broccoli, and cured ham, Tony called Ruud. They could only hear Tony's side of the conversation, a very brief synopsis of their adventures and where they were now. Tony then listened to the voice on the other end, and said, "That is absolutely fantastic, Ruud! See you tomorrow morning."

"Our luck has changed, Guys. Ruud is in the area, and will pick us up tomorrow morning," Tony said to Tan and George. "Here." He laid the Nokia on the table. "Anyone you guys want to call?"

Tan pounced on the phone and, after punching in the numbers, was soon talking to his parents, babbling in Cantonese, crying. Feeling awkward at the emotional display, George engaged Tony, "So how is Ruud going to get us to Hong Kong?"

"He didn't say, open telephone line, have to be careful. What he did say is that he was on his way to Hong Kong anyway, and so the route is already secured. We will meet him in front of the Black Dragon Teahouse tomorrow at 8:00am. It is only a few streets from here."

Tan had finished his call and handed the telephone to George, who walked outside for privacy. He tapped in Sarah's number. When the voice at the other end answered, George said, "Hey, Babe."

"George! Oh my god! Are you OK? Where are you?"

George relayed the whole story in detail. When he was done Sarah said, "What an adventure! You still need to get out of China. Is there anything that I can do?"

"If you could let Robison Whitehorse Grant know what's going on with Tan and me, that would be great. Mention to them that they should also contact our client, Zaw Than, and let him know about his people being killed by the Burmese Army."

"Oh, George, Zaw Than committed suicide the other day. It was headline news."

"You're kidding!"

"No. Ian is investigating it."

"Crazy stuff. Well, see you in a few days, Babe. Love you."

George went back into the restaurant where Tan and Tony were enthusiastically shoving chopstick-loads of Yunnan cuisine into their mouths. When the food was gone the three sat sipping tea. "I know of a cheap, zero star hotel around the corner from here where we can stay tonight. It will seem like luxury after sleeping on the ground." Tony said.

*****

In the morning haze they stood in front of the two-story, timber, three hundred year old Black Dragon Teahouse. It had been built on a raised stone platform, the massive wooden beams joined by doweling, the ends of the tiled, gabled roof sweeping upwards. The two architects, Tan and George, were delighted by the detailing of the old building, Tony was indifferent.

Their architectural admiration was interrupted when a giant tour bus turned slowly onto the narrow street, the smell of exhaust polluting the morning air. The sides of the bus were colorfully painted in yellows, blues, and greens, with large graphics of rainbows, mountains and lakes. In multi-colored Chinese characters and English letters were the words 'Cross Border Tours'.

The bus stopped in front of the teahouse and the door sprung open with a 'whoosh' of air from the pneumatic actuator. George expected a herd of tourists to stream out, cameras clicking. However, nothing happened, just the silent blackness of an empty doorway. Suddenly Ruud's giant frame appeared in the doorway. "Welcome aboard, my friends!"

"Ruud!" Tony exclaimed, and the three stepped up into the air-conditioned interior. Fifteen Burmese men at the back of the bus starred at them as they boarded. George and Tan took seats near the front of the bus next to Ruud.

"Ruud, what is with all the Burmese in the back of the bus? They do not look like tourists," George commented, turning to look at the sullen men behind him.

Ruud laughed. "They are far from the tourists. They are ex-KIA, and now they are in my army."

"Why do you need an army?" Tan asked.

"Because we are going to war, Gentlemen!" Ruud beamed at Tan. "We are going to war!"

Chapter 25

Ian, Tika, and Sarah sipped margaritas on the outdoor patio of The Red Bar admiring the view of Kowloon across Victoria Harbor. The typical Red Bar after-work crowd of young, urban professionals seated at the tables around them chatted and imbibed, beautiful people enjoying an evening full of promise.

"The prime suspect in the case, Zaw Than, is dead, a suicide. Do the police consider the case closed then, Ian?" Tika asked.

"Not at all," Ian answered. "We do not know yet if and how Zaw Than was connected to the missing Indonesian girls. He was only a suspect. And we are not sure that it was really a suicide."

"And your other suspect, that Burmese man that you just arrested in Wanchai, the newspapers said was just killed in Stanley Prison?" Sarah asked.

"Yes, stabbed by another inmate."

"But you have no other suspects, right?" Tika said. She raised her glass and said, "Let's drink to the right monsters being dead." They tapped glasses and drank. Ian refilled the glasses from the pitcher of margaritas on the table.

"Do you have any idea why Zaw Than would kill himself, Ian? He didn't seem like the suicidal type," Sarah asked.

"Drugs and jade, a lot of dirty money? Who knows what was on his conscience. Anyway, we have talked enough about depressing police business. Let's party, girls!" Ian drained his glass.

At midnight they found themselves at Dusk Till Dawn listening to a Filipino band and doing shots of tequila. They danced. Sarah went home. Ian and Tika danced some more. Ian pressed his body against Tika's. He could feel her body responding, pushing back against his. He smelled her hair and felt intoxicated. She lightly kissed his neck as they danced.

*****

Ian arrived at the office late, 10:00 am, short of sleep. He went straight for the coffee machine. "Rough night?" he heard behind him. He turned slowly, his foggy brain registered Nigel standing behind him.

"Yeah," Ian answered. "Anything new? Any leads on Zaw Than's mysterious visitor, the one that arrived just before he supposedly killed himself?"

"No. The video surveillance camera in the lobby of Zaw Than's apartment wasn't working. You don't believe that Zaw Than really committed suicide, right?"

"No, I don't. Zaw Than was a ruthless drug lord and illegal jade dealer. One of the requirements for the job is a lack of conscience. Those types usually do not commit suicide. Give me about thirty minutes for this coffee to kick in and let's meet in the conference room to review the evidence. Have Angela join us."

Half an hour later Angela and Nigel, seated at the conference table, watched Ian as he paced the room, his energy returned. He looked at the floor as he spoke, coffee cup in his right hand, his left behind his back, as if ruminating to himself. "I know that it would be easy to say that Zaw Than was a suicide. The killer is dead, his men killed as well, and the case is closed. We move on, *Mission accomplished.*" Ian looked up from the floor, stopped pacing, and turned to his team, pointing his coffee cup at them, "Do you believe it?" Ian did not wait for an answer. "No pissin' way! Not for a second! More credible is that Zaw Than was murdered by some knobhead that thinks we will accept the easy win and go home. The abductor of Indonesian maids is still out there!"

"Agree." Nigel said. Angela shook her head 'yes'.

"The note that Zaw Than had in his hand when you two found him read in Burmese '*My enemies are closing in on me.*' Drug dealers always have enemies closing in on them. No reason to kill yourself." Ian continued to pace. "What do we know about the gun that was in his hand?"

"It was a 9mm Browning HP, standard issue for the Burmese military." Angela said. "However, it is used by most militaries worldwide. No fingerprints on it other than the victim's. Could easily be a plant."

"Most importantly, we still have no idea what happened to the maids. They respond to a flyer which sends them to an address in Shami Town, and then they disappear, *poof*," Nigel said. "And the phone number on the flyer is a mobile number connected to a Sim card bought at a 7-11, untraceable."

Ian said, "Angela, this afternoon go to Sham Shui Po and snoop around. See if anyone has seen anything unusual. Shami Town might hold a key to solving our mystery, maybe we'll get lucky."

"Right," Angela said.

"Nigel, visit Cindy in the coroner's office. Try to find out if there is any evidence to prove that Zaw Than's death was not a suicide." Ian said.

Ian returned to his desk and went through the case files. It seemed like he was wrestling an opponent who anticipated his every move. He was losing the match and about to get pinned; *One, two, three, slam, career over!* At 5:00pm, frustrated with the lack of progress and groggy from a lack of sleep, Ian dragged himself out of his cubicle and headed home. When he opened the door to his apartment the smell of Indonesian cooking greeted his nostrils.

"I cooked." Tika said, standing in the middle of his living room wearing an apron. They embraced and kissed, and to Ian the world seemed right again.

*****

On the other side of Victoria Harbor in Kowloon Friday night was a slow night at Harry's Bar on Nathan Road. The Witch sipped his martini and watched the crowd.

Hidden CCTV cameras at the He Hing Butcher Shop had recorded Angela snooping about, trying the door, looking in the trash bin. He had recognized the female police officer. He had seen the determination in her face, and knew that it was time for him to push back.

Another sip of his martini. *I gave them an excuse to back off. Case solved, Zaw Than as the killer, and then his suicide. Plus I hired that*

*Triad prison gang to kill Zaw Than's supposed accomplice in jail,
everything wrapped up for them and delivered to their doorstep in
one nice, neat package.* Another sip. *However, they did not accept my
gift. Instead they insist on continuing to snoop around. Well, Nat, it
is time to show our fangs to these low level constables, time to show
them that if you provoke a cobra you will get bitten.* Another drink,
draining the glass and letting the olive at the bottom of the glass slide
into his mouth. *Kill the snoopy woman detective. That should send a
clear enough message.*

He scanned the crowd for the right accomplice, a tool that would
bring the policewoman into his reach. He needed an Indonesian-
speaking woman. His first attempt had been a fiasco. The Witch,
dressed in an *Ermenegildo Zegna* suit and *Ferragamo* tie, had spotted
a promising woman come in and sit down at the end of the bar. He had
walked over to her, sat down and smiled. As soon as he had engaged
her in conversation, however, he learned that she was a Filipina, not
an Indonesian. He awkwardly disengaged.

OK, another try. He spotted a dark-skinned Asian woman gyrate
her ample figure over to the bar. Her dress was a few sizes too small,
in an unflattering way. She took a cigarette out of her purse as she
lowered her posterior onto the stool. The Witch approached, lit her
cigarette, and asked her if she was Indonesian. She smiled and nodded
'yes'. The Witch estimated her age to be about forty, but hard to tell
in a dark bar and with layers of makeup.

"Can I buy you a drink?" he asked.

"Thank you," she said. "Tequila."

The Witch ordered her tequila and another martini for himself. He
leaned over and whispered in her ear, "I would like to hire you to
perform a service."

"You want *boom boom*?" The woman asked.

"No. No *boom boom*. I want you to make a telephone call in
Indonesian for me."

"A telephone call in Indonesian? That's all you want?" she said,
peering at him suspiciously. The Witch could not tell whether she was
drunk or just slow-witted. *Probably both, she's perfect.*

"You will use my telephone. This is exactly what I want you to say in Indonesian." The Witch handed her a piece of paper with the message written in English.

The woman squinted at the paper and then reached into her knock-off Jimmy Choo purse, pulling out a glasses case. Glasses on, she read the paper slowly, *"I have evidence on the disappearing maids, but I am afraid to speak with the men police. Can you meet me on the TST Promenade by the Hong Kong Art Museum, 8:00 pm tonight?"*

"That's right," The Witch said. She will ask you questions. Tell her you are too scared to speak on the telephone, and to come alone. The call will be on speaker mode. If she asks any other questions, you write her question on this paper in English and I will write the answer for you. You translate it." He then handed the woman five hundred Hong Kong dollars. "Easy money, right? When we are done I will give you another five hundred. What is your name?"

"Louisa," she said as she tucked the five hundred into her wallet. "OK."

The Witch put his telephone on speaker and handed it to her, along with the telephone number from Officer Angela Cheung's business card. Louisa tapped in the number.

When Angela answered, Louisa delivered the message in Indonesian. A brief exchange, and Angela asked, "Where are you calling from?"

The Witch wrote, *'I am in Wanchai, but too risky to meet here. Meet in TST.'*

"What's your name?"

"I am too scared to speak on the telephone," Louisa said in Indonesian.

Angela agreed to the meeting. Louisa ended the call and returned the telephone to the Witch. "Done. Now you want 'boom, boom'?"

"No. No 'boom boom'." The Witch smiled, returned his phone to his pocket, handed another five hundred Hong Kong to Louisa, gave her a kiss on her cheek, and walked out of Harry's Bar.

*

Chapter 26

"What do you mean, 'We are going to war'? I am going back to Hong Kong. I am not at war with anyone!" Tan said.

Ruud laughed as the tour bus sped out of Baoshan towards Kunming. "By 'we' I meant my Kachin friends in the back of the bus and I. But we may need your assistance at some point."

"Who are you at war with?" George asked.

"A witch. A very wicked witch," Ruud said.

"You are kidding, right? A wicked witch like in the 'Wizard of Oz'?" Tan replied. "Look, this was supposed to be just a business trip for us, a site visit and a design meeting. That's all! But, because we were stupid enough to recover your lost telephone which turned out to contain some ridiculous information about illegal logging, a shit load of bad things have happened to us."

"I am truly sorry about all the trouble," Ruud said.

"Sorry? You are sorry? You are out of your fucking mind, Ruud! Our clients were killed by the Burmese Army, we were forced to smuggle drugs for a lunatic who double-crossed us because you had ripped him off, we had to escape from Burmese border guards who were angry that the drugs that we were supposed to bribe them with turned out to be dirt, and we lost any chance of turning ourselves into the authorities in China because your deranged sidekick stole money from a temple. Now you tell us that you *may* need our assistance with your war with the Wicked Witch of the West? No way, Ruud! No fucking way!"

Ruud laughed again. "I can understand that you are frustrated. Did you notice, by the way, that my left hand is missing?"

"Of course we noticed." Tan said.

"The Witch cut it off. He wears it around his neck on a chain I hear. Do you think that we can just let him get away with that?"

"That has nothing to do with us. There is no 'we' involved with that," Tan protested.

Ruud acted like he did not hear. "That's right, Tan, he is going to pay. See that cooler in the back of the bus?"

George and Tan turned their heads, past the stern-faced Burmese men, and saw that there was a large white Styrofoam cooler at the rear of the bus.

"That cooler is full of hands," Ruud said.

"Hands?" George asked. Tan's face lost its color.

"Hands, yes, exactly. The Witch is quite the drug smuggler, a big operation. My friends in the back of the bus and I raided his compound in Myanmar and chopped the hands off all his people. A nice little gift for him, don't you think?"

"So you are going to deliver the hands to him?" Tan asked.

"That is only just for openers, of course." Ruud and Tony both were chuckling. Ruud pulled out a joint, took a long drag, and offered it to Tan.

"You are smoking dope in China? Are you crazy! Do you realize what would happen if we got stopped? They execute people for dope in China!" Tan said, refusing the joint. Ruud passed it to Tony.

Ruud guffawed as he blew smoke out of his mouth. "I don't think that a little Marijuana would be of much concern compared with the arsenal of guns and the cooler full of human hands that we have in the back of the bus." Tony laughed.

George said, "No offense, Ruud, but we would like to get off the bus please at the next big city. I am sure that Tan would agree."

"Totally agree. Prefer to take my chances with having no passport," Tan said.

"Suit yourselves, Gentlemen. Next big city is Kunming, we'll be there in a few hours," Ruud said.

As the colorful bus sped east, George and Tan dozed off, while Ruud and Tony continued to smoke weed. The ex-KIA soldiers-turned-mercenaries looked out the windows at the rolling, earth-tone colors of the passing Chinese landscape, umber hills interspersed with small duck and fish farms, houses made of plaster with traditional *Hakka*-style roofs. They were tourists on holiday.

Fifteen minutes outside of Kunming Ruud exclaimed, "I am

starving! This bus is stopping at Uncle Wang's, 'The Kunming Dumpling King'!"

"Uncle Wang, 'The Kunming Dumpling King'?" George asked, still half asleep.

The bus pulled up in front of a one story, red tiled building that looked like a Kentucky Fried Chicken franchise, only instead of 'The Colonel' the face of an elderly Chinese man smiled back from the pylon sign. Under the face the sign read *'Uncle Wang, The Kunming Dumpling King'* in both English and Chinese.

"Tony, go in and buy us about a thousand dumplings." Ruud said, thrusting a fistful of Chinese bills at Tony. "Buy all they've got! Oh, and some cokes too."

George said, "Hey, Ruud and Tony, this is a perfect spot for us to part ways."

"Oh. OK, sure," Ruud said. "Sorry you guys are going to miss the war."

"I have a super big favor to ask of you, however," George continued. "Can we have the mobile phone that Tony bought in Baoshan?"

"Sure," Tony said, handing the Nokia to George, "We got you involved in something that did not work out too well for you, it's the least we can do."

"Yeah, take some cash too." Ruud handed some one hundred RMB notes to George. "Get yourselves some dumplings."

Tony, George, and Tan walked through the aluminum-framed glass doors into the tiled entry of Uncle Wang's together, but as soon as they got in Tan and George hung back, detaching themselves from Tony. They sensed the craziness that was going to ensue.

At the counter the very stoned Tony placed his to-go order, "One thousand dumplings, please. Oh, and one hundred cokes." The teenage counter clerk thought that he was joking, but when he realized that Tony was serious they got into a heated negotiation. George thought that they might come to blows, especially when the clerk pointed his finger at Tony and derided his Hong Kong accent. Tony finally settled for thirty dumplings and seventeen cokes.

When Tony had left George and Tan placed their eat-in order of eight dumplings and two cokes with another clerk. George noted the layout of the restaurant, the red plastic laminate counter, the menu board, and said, "My God, this place is an exact replica of the KFC back in Gilroy!" He opened the Nokia and dialed Sarah.

"Hi, Babe, we need your help. Can you meet us in Kunming?"

"Of course!" Sarah said.

"Great. First go to both the U.S. and Hong Kong embassies and explain the situation. I am sure that we can get temporary passports fairly quickly, but find out how. Once you get here with cash and credit cards we can do whatever we need to."

"No problem."

"Also get whatever records you can from Robison Whitehorse and Grant on me. I am sure that they have my identity information as they sponsored me for my Hong Kong ID. They may have info on Tan too. I am going to hand the phone to Tan now so that he can give you his parent's contact information. From them you should get whatever identity information that they have for him, like a birth certificate, and bring all that stuff with you."

"I am on it, George."

"Love, you, Babe. Here's Tan."

As George handed the phone to Tan, he watched the tour bus pull out of the parking lot. He felt a sense of relief. *Those people were one disaster after another,* he thought.

On the bus, Ruud, with one of Uncle Wang's dumplings stuffed in his mouth, pulled out his IPhone and opened his e-mail. He typed in the address Nat01@biznetvigator.com. Extreme interrogation techniques were second nature to his ex-KIA mercenaries, and when they had raided the Witch's operation it was not very hard to learn the Witch's e-mail address. Ruud attached some pictures of the raid to the e-mail, including one of the cooler full of hands, lid open. He wrote, "Hey, friend! See you soon."

Chapter 27

By 8:00 pm, the Tsim Sha Tsui Promenade on the Kowloon waterfront was crowded with tourists. Across Victoria Harbor on the Hong Kong Island side the nightly laser light show was starting. Tourists were snapping photos as green laser lights, emanating from the tops of some of the most striking skyscrapers in the world, sliced the night sky. The tourists pushed and jostled up against the guardrail to get a good position. Classical music blared from speakers.

Angela stood on the Promenade in front of the Art Museum watching and waiting for her mysterious caller, feeling the adrenaline pulsing in her veins. She had instantly figured this meeting for a trap. When the call from Louisa on the Witch's phone had alerted Angela's suspicions she had sent a message to Nigel and Ian. Nigel had responded. Concealed in the crowd of tourists about ten feet away Nigel intently watched Angela.

Angela consciously relaxed her breathing and her muscles. She sensed it before she actually saw it; a man approaching with a camera and a hand-held flash gun. He thrust the flash in front of her face. A fraction of a second before he pulled the trigger to blind her she slipped the flash gun as a boxer would slip a punch. Then transferring all her weight from her right leg to her left, she twisted at the waist and snapped a powerful right hook to the Burmese man's jaw.

Behind her a second Burmese man moved in close, a rubber glove on his hand and clutching a rag soaked in anesthetic. Before the man could slap the rag over Angela's mouth, however, Nigel had slipped his left arm around the man's neck and pulled him backwards. Both men fell to the sidewalk. The Burmese man struggled in the choke hold trying to twist around to shove the drug-soaked rag in Nigel's face. Nigel wrapped his legs around the man's torso.

Angela meanwhile had the assailant with the flash gun handcuffed and lying face down on the ground. She pulled her revolver from the holster beneath her blouse, walked over to the intertwined pair wrestling on the ground, and slammed the butt of the gun into the temple of the second man. He went limp.

Nigel called for backup, and within minutes the two handcuffed men were being escorted to police cars. The crowd of tourists stared, the Victoria Harbor light show momentarily ignored. At the edge of the crowd the Witch watched as his men were captured.

How could this have gone so wrong? For the first time in his life he felt that Nat had deserted him. He felt a vibration in his pocket, and removed his Samsung, an e-mail from Dutchman@gmail.com. The Witch looked at the pictures of his operation under siege, his slaughtered workers, the cooler full of hands, and knew exactly who had sent the e-mail. He replaced the telephone in his pocket.

In a daze, The Witch turned and walked east to the Star Ferry. He had trouble breathing. He could only stare straight ahead as he rode the ferry across the Harbor to his serviced apartment at the top of the Four Seasons Hotel. *Nat, have you deserted me? Everything is going wrong!*

*****

The next morning Ian gathered his paperwork from his desk, picked up his coffee cup that read, 'Hong Kong Police – We Serve With Pride and Care', and said to Nigel and Angela, "Great work last night, both of you. Ready to interrogate our new friends?"

Nigel said, "Ian, this is Kyaw Thaw. He is from the Translation Services Division." From behind Nigel stepped a Southeast Asian man wearing a short sleeved white shirt and a blue tie. The man was so thin that Ian had not seen him standing behind his detective. *Has this guy ever eaten a carbohydrate in his life?* Ian wondered. Kyaw extended his bird-like hand towards Ian. "Kyaw is a contractor. His background has been thoroughly vetted and cleared by TSD. He is our Burmese translator," Nigel continued as Ian shook the man's hand.

"Nice to meet you, Kyaw," Ian said. "You are from Myanmar?"

"Yes. I have lived in Hong Kong for twelve years."

"Have you ever translated in an interrogation before?" Ian asked.

"Yes, sir, I have," Kyaw said.

"Key point, Kyaw; if I act angry, you act angry, if I act friendly, you act friendly. Try to translate my demeanor more than my words. Translate 'intent' rather than word-for- word. OK?"

"Yes, Sir."

Both of the Burmese men, handcuffed and dressed in orange jail jumpsuits, were sitting at a metal table in a windowless interrogation room. The light blue linoleum floor reflected the glare of the fluorescent ceiling lights above, the walls bright white. The side of one of the men's head was swollen with an angry purple bruise from Angela's gun butt. Ian had decided that he would interrogate the two together, feeling that if one started to cooperate, so would the other.

Ian, Nigel, and Kyaw seated themselves across from the suspects. Ian said, "Good morning, Gentlemen. Let's start by your giving us your names." Kyaw translated. The two men sat silent and stared back defiantly. Ian could see in their eyes just how hard these men were, how much deprivation they had been through in a life spent at civil war.

"OK, Gentlemen, I will tell you what, I'll start. Let's begin with the good news for you guys. In 1993 the death penalty was abolished in Hong Kong. With the evidence that we have on you two, you certainly would be executed if we had a death penalty. Instead, you will spend the rest of your lives in Stanley Prison." Ian waited while Kyaw translated, then continued.

"More good news, the Hong Prison system will seem like a five star hotel to you guys compared to a prison in Myanmar." Ian paused again.

The two men stared at Ian and said nothing.

"However, now the bad news." Ian opened his file and slapped a photo of their colleague who had been stabbed in prison on the table. Ian watched their eyes widen and looks of consternation replace their defiant stares. "Your boss had this done. He arranged for a Triad prison gang to silence your friend."

The two men stared at the photo and then at each other. Then Ian put another photo in front of them, a picture of their poisoned colleague lying on the floor of the Queen Victoria.

"Your boss seems to like killing his employees." Ian said. "He will of course have to silence you two as well, to protect himself."

The men continued to stare at the photos. Ian continued, "However, good news again, Gentlemen. The Hong Kong justice system likes to reward people who give us information that we need. What we desperately need is the name of your boss. I cannot say that you will go free, but your cooperation will definitely be taken into consideration when you are sentenced."

The two men listened to Kyaw's translation, looked up at Ian, and then at each other. Ian said, "I realize that there is probably some Kachin code of honor that you protect each other…"

One of the men said in Burmese to the other, "Let's cooperate. We are being sacrificed by the Witch."

The second man nodded in agreement.

Looking back at the police officers, the man said in broken English, "OK, we talk."

"Oh, you speak some English," Kyaw said.

"Our boss is Witch. He was Regional Commander Myanmar Army, not Kachin like us. He now do drug smuggling business, live Hong Kong."

"Why are KIA soldiers working in Hong Kong for a Burmese ex-commander? You are at civil war, no?" Nigel asked.

"We work Witch, good money, better life than Myanmar. Also nice not be at war for one time," The man answered.

"What are your names?" Ian asked.

"I Mya Myoe. My friend Than Hliang."

"So, Than and Mya, tell us about the flyers that you handed out to Indonesian women, and what happens to the women when they respond."

"Flyers bring women, sacrifice to Nat."

"Nat?" Ian asked. "Sacrifice?"

"The Witch gets power from Nat." Mya said. "Nat a spirit eats for human flesh. When Witch eats victims, Nat happy. In return Nat gives Witch protection and power."

"Your boss eats people!" Ian exclaimed." Why did he kill only the Indonesian maids?"

"No one cares about Indonesian funny girls. Many Causeway Bay. They no contact from family, employers not care, police not care, only friends is themselves. Easy victims."

"So when they called the number on the flyers, what happened?" Nigel asked.

"We tell them go butcher shop in Sham Shui Po. When they arrive, we put drug on face. Witch give them sacrifice to Nat."

"How would he sacrifice them to Nat?" Nigel asked.

"He has shrine butcher shop. He call to Nat to witness gift, and then cut they throats knife. We then cut and store ribs, throw of the other parts in the ocean. Once a month we bring ribs to camp Mui Wo for Witch eating Feast Day."

"You have a camp in Mui Wo?"

"Yes, we four lived in Mui Wo. Then we three. Then we two. Witch no lives there."

"What is The Witch's real name?"

Mya shrugged.

"Why would The Witch use Kachin soldiers to do his bidding instead of Burmese Army soldiers?" Ian asked.

"Same same Indonesian funny women, no one care about Kachin. Burmese Generals piss off if using Burmese soldiers for witchcraft. Burmese Generals supply Witch his drugs, so Witch uses Kachins, Burmese Generals no piss off."

"How do you get in touch with the Witch?"

"Mobile phone." Mya then recited the telephone number. Ian noticed that it was the same number from which Angela received the call asking her go to The Promenade.

"Than and Mya, it was the correct decision to cooperate. I am going to now put you together with some officers to whom you will describe the exact location of the butcher shop in Sham Shui Po and your camp in Mui Wo. Nigel and Angela, please come with me."

The two detectives followed Ian out of the interrogation room, down the corridor, and into another soundproof interrogation room. When they were in and the door closed Ian exclaimed, "As soon as Mya said that The Witch was not a Kachin, I knew the identity of The Witch!"

"Really? Who is he?" Nigel asked.

"I'll bet that he is Political Counselor Nakaji Sein from the Myanmar Embassy," Ian said.

"Yes! He spoke with our first suspect before we did, no doubt confirmed that he would keep his mouth shut. Also, he is the one that put the suspicion on Zaw Than, and then he must have killed him and disguised it as a suicide to make it seem that the case was solved!" Angela exclaimed.

"The guy ate the women! What a freak!" Ian said.

We need to get him off the streets." Nigel said. "One big problem though, wouldn't he have diplomatic immunity?"

"This case is too serious. I doubt that he will be able to escape prosecution," Ian said. "Step one, let's pick him up. Send a team to his office. Meanwhile you and I will try his apartment. The embassy will have an address for him. Angela. I want you to accompany the officers when they raid the Shami Town butcher shop and the Mui Wo camp."

*****

The Witch stood on his balcony at Four Seasons Place overlooking Victoria Harbor. He could see the Promenade on the other side of the harbor where the fiasco of the previous evening occurred. Around his neck he wore his mummified hand which had always brought him luck before. *Nat, tell me what to do. Are you abandoning me?*

Nat answered him clearly, '*I tire of your piddling sacrifices, one or two lambs a month. Am I not significant enough to justify a more worthwhile gesture?*'

The Witch answered, "Yes, Nat, I see my mistake now! Forgive me! I will give you worthy sacrifices beyond all expectations! You will be pleased!"

The Witch looked down from his balcony on Hong Kong below, seven million people squeezed into one of the most densely packed cities in the world. *Hong Kong is a stockade of lambs from which to choose an appropriate offering for Nat.*

The night sky was suddenly illuminated with a flash of lightening above the hills behind Kowloon. *Nat confirms. Meanwhile the police will have already interrogated my men, and probably already know my identity. I must hide quickly.*

He packed a suitcase with the essentials: checkbooks, credit cards, cash, passport, and an MP5 submachine gun. In his belt he tucked a Browning Hi-Power semi-automatic handgun.

Before The Witch left Four Seasons Place for the last time he e-mailed the man he answered to, the power who really ran the drug and jade trade between Myanmar and Hong Kong, the one who had the connections with the Myanmar Generals for drugs and the Kachin Generals for Jade.

'*Going into hiding, but still able to do business.*' The Witch typed in Burmese.

The answer came back immediately, '*You are becoming a liability. I also suspect that you were the one who killed Zaw Than. That is a big problem for me. No one to run jade business now.*'

The Witch replied, '*I will run the jade business. Zaw Than had become complacent, I will improve the trade. Can do both jade and drugs.*'

No answer. The Witch packed up the computer, grabbed his suitcase, and headed to Sham Shui Po.

Chapter 28

At the Myanmar embassy two uniformed officers collected evidence from Nakaji Sein's office as a distraught Consul General U Kham exclaimed to Angela, "Did you see what the Hong Kong papers are saying about us?" The headline of the 'Hong Kong Standard' on the Consul General's desk read *'Burmese Hungry for Hong Kong'*. "What an embarrassment to Myanmar! We were just developing Yangon as a tourist destination, and now the world will think that we are a country of cannibals!"

Angela shrugged, "Not my problem. Our big problem right now is finding Mr. Sein. We are afraid that if he makes it back to Myanmar we will never get our hands on him."

"He would never go back to Myanmar. He has made a fool of our country in the eyes of the world. Nakaji has many enemies in Myanmar, and his fate would not be pretty. No, he knows better than to return to Myanmar."

"Good news then. If he stays in Hong Kong we will catch him," Angela said.

When the two officers were done collecting evidence Angela sent them back to the station and then sent a meeting report to Ian and Nigel on her iPad, including the Consul General's remarks about the nature of Nakaji's welcome if he returned to Myanmar. She then headed for the MTR station.

It had been three months since Angela had visited her parents in East Kowloon. Sitting in the monotonous rocking of the subway car of the Kwun Tong Line, Angela dozed off. In her dream she was a young girl at the beach in Sai Kung with her parents on a family outing.

It was a brilliant day, blue sky and milky clouds. Her dad, Chinese, forty-five years old, a dragon head with the Hou Sai Lei Triad, sat on the sand and stared silently at the ocean. Her mom, Ira, twenty years old, Indonesian, beautiful, was standing next to her.

'Mom, what is that tall building?' Angela asked, pointing to a narrow wooden building on the edge of the sand.

'That is a barn, dear. See those big doors? They should never be opened.'

'Why not?'

'So that what is in the barn does not get out.' Her mother said.

The bright, sunny day suddenly morphed into night, a silver full moon in the pitch-dark sky. Angela was standing in front of the doors of the barn, which were open, casting long moonlight shadows on the sand. She was alone. It was cold.

She peered into barn. The sour smell of decay wafted out. The ceiling soared high above her. In the dim interior she could make out the forms of humanoid creatures hanging upside down from the rafters. They had human legs and were dressed in trousers and shoes. Instead of arms, however, they had long, leathery brown wings tucked around their bodies like bats. As she stared, one of the bat creatures raised his head and looked at her. It had the face of Nakaji Sein.

The creature screamed at her with mouth wide and full of needle-sharp teeth, a high pitched screech. Angela clasped her hands over her ears. The monstrosity then spread its mahogany-colored wings to their full six foot span, released its foothold on the rafter, and swooped down towards her. Angela cringed as it flew inches above her head and out of the barn. As it soared close to her she got a whiff of putrid decay. When it had passed Angela looked up and saw the beast's silhouette as it flew in front of the full moon.

Angela awoke, the terror of the dream fading. She looked around the subway car, happy to be returned the normalcy of the real world. *What a weird dream!* The illuminated sign above the train's door indicated with a blinking dot that the next stop was Lok Fu station, her stop. Angela chased the remaining grogginess from her brain and prepared to disembark.

The old neighborhood had barely changed. Some of the signs and shop fronts were different but many of the shopkeepers had known her all her life, nodding to her as she walked to her parent's apartment.

Sitting at the metal dining room table with a red plastic laminate top, the same one she had grown up with, her dad sipping tea, and Ira bringing out plates of Indonesian and Cantonese delicacies from the kitchen, it seemed to Angela that she had never left home. She inhaled the aroma of familiarity and felt safe and loved. They feasted on her mother's food and made small talk.

After they were done her Dad lit a cigarette, leaned back in his chair, and said, "So, Angela, everything good? The police OK?" Even though he was a leader of the Hou Sai Lei, Angela's dad had completely supported her decision to join the force. Too many of his friend's children who had followed in their fathers' criminal footsteps had ended up lying dead in the street.

"It's good, Dad. I would like to get your advice on something though."

Guanlong Cheung, Dragon Head of the Hou Sai Lei Triad, leaned forward in his chair, all business. "Sure."

"The police are looking for a very bad man, a Burmese man. He has disappeared in Hong Kong and I fear that the only way we would ever find this man is by pure luck or chance," Angela said.

"Ha, police could not find a dumpling in a bowl of *Hun Tun Mien*! I can find anyone in Hong Kong. This sounds personal, though, Angela."

"It is, Dad. He kills Indonesian women simply because they are defenseless. I want his head on a pole."

"OK, give me his description and a little time."

Angela got up and kissed her dad on the cheek, "Thanks, Dad."

*****

Ian, Tika, Sarah, and George were sitting in Cinta J's in Wanchai, a few blocks from the Queen Victoria, picking at a plate of *crispy pata*, fingers greasy from the Filipino delicacy.

"I'll bet that you are glad to be back in Hong Kong, George," Tika said.

"I most definitely am, and I am also eternally grateful to my girlfriend here for showing up in Kunming and saving my butt," George said, giving Sarah a kiss.

"Sarah said that you went right back to work, no time off?" Ian asked.

"It was better for me to dive back into work. Keeps my mind off the fact that because I was a nice guy and agreed to take some guy's 'lost' phone back to Hong Kong my clients got killed," George said.

"You shouldn't beat yourself up over it. It would be a better world if there were more trusting, nice guys out there," Tika said. "How's Tan doing?"

"Not too good. I heard that he won't get off his mother's couch. He just sits there watching TV and eating her Cantonese cooking," George answered.

"Yaah…that's bad. Hope he gets over it soon," Tika said.

"Forget that dreary stuff!" Ian said, raising his glass of Gray Goose. "Tonight we celebrate the return of George Washington Smith!" They all raised their glasses. "*Gambei* that shit!" They downed their drinks, and Ian ordered another round. An all-girl Filipino band started playing on a small stage set up at the back of the restaurant.

"Ian, what about The Witch? Think you'll catch him soon?" George asked.

"I hope so. Now, no more work talk! Got it?" Ian turned to the waitress, "Keep the Gray Goose's coming, Baby." At midnight they left Cinta J's and walked across the street to Spicy Fingers, where a diminutive Filipina woman with a powerful voice rocked the club. The four of them danced until the sun was peaking over the Hong Kong skyline.

*****

Hours before dawn at a private dock in Zhuhai near the Macao border crossing Ruud and Tony watched as the *Cross Border Tours* bus was driven onto a transport ferry. Loaded and underway on the open ocean heading towards Victoria Harbor, officially off Chinese soil, the transport blended in with the thousands of other vessels in one of the busiest shipping lanes in the world.

Their destination in Hong Kong was One Ear Chang's dock. Simon Chang, who was known as 'One Ear Chang' since losing his appendage in a gang fight when a teenager, was a Triad enforcer-turned-entrepreneur. Operating a dock on the backside of Lantau Island near Sunny Bay, One Ear charged a flat fee no matter what the shipment. Even though he always dressed in a filthy T-shirt and drove a rusted Toyota everyone knew that One Ear's had made Simon Chang a rich man, rich enough to send his daughter to Harvard and his son to Stanford.

On the forty-five minute boat ride from Zhuhai Ruud stood on the bow of the transport and admired the twinkling lights of Hong Kong's skyscrapers on the far shore. So many people, so many opportunities. Hong Kong was a dreamscape, and those living and working in those alluring towers lining the waterfront pursued the dream hard, like so many busy, little ants in an anthill. Ruud smiled and thought, *Here comes the anteater, my babies.*

Chapter 29

His mobile phone vibrated in his pocket. Ruud pulled it out and looked at the screen, an e-mail answer from The Witch. He had not expected a response to his '*See you soon*' e-mail.

The Witch's mail read, '*I understand that you are upset. However, if you can put that aside, I have a plan that would bring us both unimaginable wealth. Can we meet?*'

'*Where?*' Ruud tapped back into his telephone.

'*Statue Square 12:00 noon tomorrow,*' appeared on the Dutchman's screen.

'*Sure.*' Ruud tapped back.

Ruud left the bow of the transport and found Tony in the vessel's cabin. "We are going to meet The Witch tomorrow, just you and me. He wants to talk about a deal."

"A deal? I thought that we were at war?"

"Let's see what he has to say. We can kill him at any time," Ruud said.

*****

Statue Square at noon, an urban park close to the waterfront in Central, was crowded with tourists and office workers. Many were sitting on the tiled edge of Statue Square's shallow fountain eating their lunches. The park, bordered by the iconic HSBC Building on the south, The Prince's Building and Mandarin Hotel on the west, and the historic Legislative Council Building on the east, was safe, neutral ground for two old enemies to meet.

Ruud and Tony stood in front of the larger-than-life bronze statue of Sir Thomas Jackson, chief financier of Hong Kong's growth in the colonial era. As they peered up at the towering figure from behind them a voice suddenly said, "Very impressive, don't you think?"

They both spun. The Witch continued, "Although I never understood why anyone would aspire to have a bronze statue of themselves standing in some park after they are gone. I mean, they're still dead, right?"

"Nakaji!" Ruud spit out. "You have two minutes to catch my interest before I tear your head off."

Nakaji chuckled, "OK, then let me get to the point immediately. Jade. Got your attention?"

"Jade?"

"Yes, I have the Hong Kong side connected, and I have the Myanmar side connected. All I need is a partner to run the middle. I need someone to do the Myanmar pickup and transport without having most of the shipment disappear along the way. You know the route and have the experience, as well as the business smarts, to pull it off. You also know that if you rip me off again I will cut off your other hand."

Ruud's giant fist whistled out at Nakaji's head. The Witch, a former Lethwei practitioner, easily slipped under the blow, the calm smile still on his face. "Do you want revenge, or do you want to make more money than you'll know how to spend?"

"OK, keep talking," Ruud said.

Instead of discussing his jade business, however, The Witch's attention suddenly turned to the cooler sitting on the ground by Tony's feet. "Oh, Ruud, you have brought me a present!" Nakaji bent down, picked it up, and shook it as a child might shake a Christmas present to determine what was inside. "What could possibly be in here?"

Nakaji walked to the fountain, opened the cooler, and dumped the hands into the clear blue water. Office workers, screaming in horror, dropped their lunches and ran in all directions. A crowd began to gather, and two law enforcement officers patrolling the park walked towards the commotion. With a boyish grin Nakaji turned back to Ruud and Tony, "Think about it. Keep in touch." He dropped the empty cooler into the fountain and then disappeared into the scattering crowd and down the entrance to the subway like the white rabbit in 'Alice and Wonderland', leaving Ruud and Tony standing open-mouthed.

Ruud and Tony quickly slipped into the stunned crowd as the two officers approached, walking around the block before doubling back to the waterfront where they had parked the bus. "That didn't go well," Tony said.

"I don't know, he said he needs us to run his jade for him. Could be lucrative."

When they arrived back at the bus the Burmese mercenaries were standing outside on the sidewalk smoking. To the Burmese this trip so far had seemed like a holiday. They were not sure whom they were supposed to shoot, although they were pretty sure that eventually they would have to shoot someone. For now, however, they enjoyed the inactivity and riding on a comfortable, air conditioned tour bus in a foreign country.

Tony and Ruud got on the bus and closed the door and sat down alone, leaving the Kachins outside. Tony spoke first, "Ruud, so what do you think? An intro to the jade biz would be pretty amazing. I know that you're angry about your hand and all."

"I do not think that 'angry' adequately describes my feelings. And I *will* get revenge. However, I could put revenge off for a while until we made a few million in the jade trade. The question is, is he for real or are we being set up?"

"I think that he really needs us. He can't do everything himself, and we are about as experienced and qualified as it gets in moving contraband through Asia," Tony said.

Ruud thought for a few minutes and then whispered to Tony, "If we are not going to fight The Witch right now, we do not really need our Kachin friends who are standing outside of the bus then, do we?"

"Not really. Do you know how to get rid of them?" Tony whispered back.

"Yes, I think that I do."

The two exited the bus, and Ruud walked over to the relaxing men. In broken Burmese, he said, "Tony and I have another meeting, a very dangerous meeting, not far from here. We need to go alone. If we are not back in a few hours it means that we have probably been killed. OK?" The men waved and smiled.

Ruud and Tony walked off. "Can I buy you a drink in Lan Kwai Fong?" Ruud asked. "It's only a ten minute walk from here."

"We just leave them?" Tony asked.

"Nothing in that bus that we need. I have cash, credit, and ATM cards in my wallet, a Browning tucked under my shirt, and a bag of weed in my pocket. The bus is stolen anyway. In a few hours they will figure out that we are not coming back and will probably take the bus back home," Ruud said.

"I guess so, then. Lan Kwai Fong it is."

*****

Nat is again paving my way, I can feel him. He is happy with my promise, but I must deliver a worthy sacrifice soon, Nakaji thought. *'I know just who can help me do that.'*

The Witch exited the train in Admiralty. Reaching street level, he entered the first Pacific Coffee Shop that he found. Sitting at a low glass coffee table in an upholstered chair, a cappuccino in front of him, The Witch took out his phone and dialed Amir's number.

"Amir, Hi, how are you? This is Nakaji Sein. How long has it been, a few years, no?"

"Nakaji? You are kidding. I read about you in the newspapers. You were eating Indonesian women. Very cool! However, you are one wanted man. I want nothing to do with you." The telephone went dead as Amir hung up. Nakaji redialed.

"Amir, don't hang up, please. All those great ideas of yours about showing the establishment that they can't get away with the bullshit that they try to pull on society? This is the time to make our move, me and you. We can bring 'The Man' to his knees. That wasn't all just talk, was it?"

"Why now?" Amir asked.

"Because, as you mentioned, I am currently a fugitive, a wanted man, nothing left to lose. And, I happen to also currently have a fuck-load of cash."

A pause, and then Amir said, "Did you really kill and eat those women?"

"Just their ribs."

"Cool. Where shall we meet?"

Chapter 30

It took Amir thirty minutes to get to Pacific Coffee. Nakaji recognized him immediately. Amir was rodent-like. He entered the coffee shop in a hunched posture, nervously glancing left and right as he searched for Nakaji among the patrons of Pacific Coffee. A product of Pakistani and Indian parents, with a hooked, bulbous nose, a nest of gray-black greasy hair that he never combed and seldom washed, and a jumble of stained teeth in his mouth, he had an appearance that put most people off. However, he was a brilliant scientist, and that was what attracted Nakaji to him. That and the fact that Amir was a delusional, paranoid psychotic.

The two had first met three years ago introduced by a mutual acquaintance. Nakaji had needed a chemist to oversee the conversion of raw opium into bricks of morphine. Amir, who by day worked as a biotech researcher at Hong Kong Life Sciences, was keen to help, not so much for the money but as a way to help destabilize a society that he felt was corrupt. 'Poison the youth with drugs and no one will inherit the bastards' corrupt legacy,' Amir would rant.

"Amir, great to see you! Please sit. Would you like a coffee?" Nakaji said, standing as Amir shuffled over.

"No, no thanks," Amir said with a dismissive swoosh of his hand, continuing to sweep the shop with squinty glances as he lowered himself into a chair.

"How have you been?"

"How do you think I've been? The white bastards have strengthened their alliance with our yellow friends across the border to further exploit us of brown skin. Taxi's will not even stop for me now once they see the color of my skin."

"Amir, you're not that brown. I would say that you are more of a dark olive complexion."

"To the bastards that drive taxis I look brown."

"Wow, that's bad, Amir. And it is probably only going to get worse, right?" Nakaji knew how to goad Amir.

"Fuckin-A it's going to get worse! This year China will overtake the U.S. as the world's superpower. You know what the first thing they will do when that happens? They will throw us brown skins into their prison system so they can force us to slave in their manufacturing plants! I am sure that you know why they will do that."

"No. Why, Amir?"

"Because of white consumerism, of course! The over-consumption of useless shit by the white races fuels the economic growth of Asia. Plus, Chinese workers are demanding three times more money now than a decade ago."

"Really?"

"Fuckin- A really. So, the superpower motherfuckers will need free slave labor to offset the rising cost of the Chinese workers. Then they can continue to produce their cheap crap to sell to the white man!" Amir had raised the volume of his voice along with his adrenaline, and other patrons of the coffee shop had started to shoot glances at them.

"So, what if we, you and I, Amir, strike back? Take some of them down. That's what we've always talked about," Nakaji said.

"Yes, but something huge, big enough to get their attention!" Amir hissed.

"I completely agree, Amir. That is why I asked you here. Any ideas?" Nakaji asked.

"The plague." Amir said.

"The plague?"

"I have been thinking about this. The Black Death, the disease that wiped out one third of the population of Europe in 1348, was spread by the Oriental Rat Flea infected with the *Yersinia pestis* bacterium."

"I like it so far. So…how do we infest Hong Kong?"

"I can order the *Yersinia* microorganism from a company called Universal Culture Collections that supplies us with our bacteria cultures at work. For the fleas, Entomology Research Corporation, a U.S. company, can supply insects. It will be easy to infect the fleas with the bacteria."

"I see that you have already been planning this, Amir. That's great," Nakaji said. "Once the fleas are infected, what happens next?"

"There are many ways to deliver it," Amir continued, calm now. "Releasing a bag of infected fleas in the MTR, or on the Star Ferry, would be easy. How about in Hong Kong Stadium during the Hong Kong Sevens rugby match?"

"Amir, I knew that you would have the answers. I am so glad that we met. What is the timetable?"

"It will take about four weeks to order and get delivery. Meanwhile, I will need you to lease some industrial space where I can set up a laboratory. Once the fleas are infected we will need to move fast, fleas only have a lifespan of twenty-eight days," Amir said.

"Great, I already have industrial space that I use for warehousing drugs in Tai Po. We can set up there."

"This is going to cost, by the way."

"Money is not a problem, Amir. Just let me know what you need. I have accounts under fake names that are untraceable." Nakaji rose and shook hands with the scientist. "I will be in touch."

After Amir left, The Witch thought, *Things are shaping up nicely, Nat.*

Nat replied, '*Yes, very nicely indeed.*'

*

Chapter 31

Ruud and Tony were getting pleasantly buzzed on beer, sitting in The Whiskey Priest at a table facing the street watching the Lan Kwai Fong nightly procession of inebriated revelers file by. "So are we going to become jade moguls or not? You have to let The Witch know if we are 'in', right?" Tony asked.

"I like the thought of it, Tony. We could get very, very rich. I even like the sound of the word, 'Jaaade'. Jade is fucking awesome!" Ruud took out his mobile and sent a text to The Witch, '*OK, we are in. Next step?*'

In a few moments the reply came, '*Welcome! Will make arrangements and contact you in a few days.*'

Ruud turned to Tony and raised his glass, "We are now in the jade trade!" They tapped glasses and downed their beers. "We need to celebrate properly!" Ruud signaled to the waiter, "Six Jager shots, please."

*****

In Pacific Coffee, The Witch looked at Ruud's text message saying that he and Tony were 'in'. *Good. Now for a slightly more risky move. Give me guidance on this one, Nat.* Nakaji punched in some numbers and put the telephone to his ear.

A woman's voice answered. In Burmese, Nakaji said, "Mimi, how are you doing?"

Mimi Tun, Attaché to the Myanmar Embassy, was stunned. "Nakaji! What are you calling me for? I have nothing to say to you!"

"Mimi, please hear me out."

"You are a serial killer! Worse than a serial killer! Why should I listen to you?"

"Because I have a question for you, Mimi. How would you like to be one of the wealthiest and most powerful women in Hong Kong?" Nakaji said.

A long pause. "How?"

"I am setting up a jade trading business in the hole that was left open by Zaw Than's unfortunate demise. However, because of my recent notoriety in the newspapers, I need a representative. I cannot walk around publicly and do business. You would be perfect, Mimi, beautiful and ruthless, and Burmese. For all intents and purposes, everyone would think that you control the Burmese jade trade in Hong Kong."

Another pause as she thought it over. "Are you going to continue to kill Indonesian women?"

"No, no, Mimi, I swear, I am over that."

"OK. How soon?"

"I will arrange a meeting for you within the next few days with the CEO of Julies Auction House. He will be delighted to have someone replace Zaw Than as the face of the Myanmar jade trade. I will call you when it's arranged and I will rehearse with you what you should say and discuss our strategy. Mimi, you are going to be very rich."

*****

At the Whiskey Priest another round of six shot glasses of dark brown, 70-proof Jagermeister were placed before Ruud and Tony. Ruud said, "One, two, three…bang, bang, bang." He downed three shots in a row. Tony did the same. "Whooooooo!"

"Waiter, six more shots and two bottles of San Miguel."

As they sucked on the beers, Tony said, "Isn't that kind of expensive to just abandon the bus with the Burmese guys? I mean, how much did that bus cost? You could have sold it."

"I told you, the bus was stolen," Ruud answered. "OK, ready? One, two, three…bang, bang, bang!" They chased the three Jagermeister shots with the San Miguel's. "Waiter, six more, please, and two more San Miguel's."

"Oh yeah, you did say that it was stolen. Hey, Ruud, I need to talk serious with you," Tony said, slurring his words. "I am thinking that we have brought some bad karma down on our heads with that cooler full of hands. That was some crazy shit, even for us."

"You know, good point, Tony. Of course it was The Witch who disrespectfully dumped the hands in the fountain, but it is a true fact that we were complicit in their removal and transport." Ruud contemplated, and then exclaimed, "I have the solution! But first, one, two, three…bang, bang, bang!"

"Wha's the solution?" Tony asked. "Waiter, six more Jager's, please."

"The solution is, my drunken friend, that we go, right now, to Man Mo Temple, just around the corner, and ask forgiveness from the gods. They will be overwhelmed by our humbleness and sincerity, and bestow magnificent karma on our heads."

"What? That's crazy! Man Mo Temple is for students praying to get better grades on the examinations, not for people asking for forgiveness for chopping hands off! I know this stuff, I am from Hong Kong. Trust me."

"Tony, you can hook up with *any* god in any temple. I know this, trust *me*. First, one two, three…bang, bang, bang. Then we're off to get karma-tized."

Tony was staggering as they left the Whiskey Priest. The narrow, uneven sidewalks of Lan Kwai Fong had by now become packed with drunken partiers. As they walked by Bulldog's Bar Tony tripped over a piece of broken sidewalk and stumbled into two stunning Western girls dressed in tight, black dresses. "I am so sorry." Tony said.

"No problem." One of the girls said. "Hong Kong's streets are not exactly level."

"Are you tourists?" Tony asked.

"Yes, we are from Canada. I am Jennie and this is Anne."

"Well, I am Tony, from Hong Kong, and this giant man standing next to me is Ruud, from the Netherlands."

"Pleased to meet you, girls." Ruud smiled. "We were just on the way to the Man Mo Temple to get some good karma. Would you like to join us?" Ruud looked at the expression on their faces. "No, you're right. That is lame. Let us buy you a drink instead. Join us in Bulldogs."

Inside the bar the four found a corner and Ruud ordered beer and

Jager. They had to yell to be heard over the noise of the bar. "So what do you guys do?" Anne asked in Tony's ear.

"Global sourcing." Tony said.

Her lips brushing his ear again, "What is global sourcing?"

"We sell things to people who pay big money for them."

"What sorts of things?" Her cheek brushed against his, her hand on his waist. As Tony pressed his body into hers her hand went to the small of his back, where she felt the revolver in its holster under his shirt. "What's this?" She asked.

"A tool of the trade."

"Oh, you *are* a very bad man, aren't you?" She flipped up the lid of the holster and grasped the butt of the gun. Suddenly, a loud 'bang' as the Browning fired. Anne's eyes went wide, "Oh, my god! I am so sorry!"

"What happened? I've been shot! I've been shot!" Tony yelled as he looked back at the growing wet patch of blood staining the back of his jeans. "I've been shot in the ass!"

The two Canadian girls immediately disappeared, and no one in the crowded, loud bar seemed to notice that a gun had been discharged. "Ruud, I've been shot in the ass! I need to get to the hospital!"

"How did that happen? Where are the girls?"

"That bitch shot me! Get me to a hospital!"

At Queen Mary Hospital's emergency room, lying on his belly and with three stitches in his buttock, Tony said to Ruud, "How long are they going to keep me? I'm stitched up. We've been in this creepy place for hours. Get me my clothes and let's get out of here."

"No, this is great. Tony, don't you see? What a great place to hide out until The Witch contacts us, totally undercover. Act like you can't stand up when the doctor comes. Tell them that the room is spinning and that you have chills so they won't discharge you."

"This *is* kind of a safe place," Tony said.

*****

In Sham Shui Po, sitting on his bed in a ninth floor walk-up apartment in a moldy apartment building owned by the Liang Zai Triad, The Witch laid out his fake passports, ATM cards, and credit cards, all with his photo. The Liang Zai Triad had done business with The Witch for over three years, distributing heroin that he smuggled from Myanmar. The Triad, who owned about a quarter of the property in Sham Shui Po, had no trouble finding The Witch a safe haven to hide out in.

Nakaji put his ID's away, picked up his computer bag, and left the room. He hiked the nine levels down to the street. The stairwell smelled of mold, garbage, and burnt cooking. White, red, and blue tiles covered the too-small treads and too-high risers. The chalky white walls of the stairwell had large irregular, brown stains. There were no handrails. Bare electric wires hung like snakes from the ceiling. *This is not the Four Seasons,* The Witch thought.

Reaching ground level he walked east on Yu Chau Street past the roast ducks and sausages hanging in the window of the Happywood Restaurant. He turned the corner onto a narrow lane filled with street vendors selling umbrellas, electronic equipment, and DVD's, arriving at the Starbucks by the MTR station.

Nakaji got a coffee at the counter, sat down in one of the upholstered chairs, opened his computer, and connected to the free wifi. He sent three e-mails. The first, in Burmese, was to the man who supplied him the drugs and jade, the man that he answered to.

'Greetings. An update on our latest conversation; I now have a representative in place, Ms. Mimi Khaing, who can be the public face of our jade business. She is beautiful and clever, and I am sure that you will agree that she will be fantastic in the role.

I know that you were not delighted with my recent actions in regards to ZT, but we are both mature men who can supersede our minor differences. Let's look to the future and to expanding our business opportunities.

As to the other complications, I am secure and safe, and everything is in place to continue business as usual. I look forward to hearing from you soon. NS'

The second e-mail was in English.

'Ruud and Tony, everything is in place. Please go immediately to Yangon. Contact my associate Tin Shwe, T.Shwe@Hjadecorp.com, when you arrive. He will give you a package and twenty thousand U.S. dollars to bring to me in Hong Kong. NS'

Nakaji switched back to Burmese for the third e-mail.

'*Tin Shwe, soon you will be contacted in Yangon by a Dutchman and a Chinese man. Kill them. NS*'

Nakaji closed his computer with a smile and sipped his coffee. *Nat, the pieces are coming together, and I have not forgotten my promise to you to provide a worthy sacrifice. I have already put forces in motion. You will be very pleased.*

Chapter 32

By 9:00 am anyone walking on Gloucester Road felt like a dumpling in a dim sum steamer basket. Inside the air-conditioned comfort of police headquarters, Ian, Nigel, and Angela discussed the possible whereabouts of The Witch.

"Three possibilities," Ian said, standing in front of the white board. He wrote, '1. Flee to Myanmar. 2. Flee to another country. 3. Stay in HK.' He started to draw a cartoon of The Witch fleeing, but then glanced at Nigel and decided not to.

"The last known point that we can place him is at Four Seasons Place four days ago. He left with a suitcase and a laptop," Nigel said.

Ian mused, "We have officers watching the airport, the ports, and at the border crossings. Nothing so far. Of course, a drug smuggler will have ways to get out of Hong Kong, but our best chance of catching him is if he remains in Hong Kong."

A knock on the conference room door and two middle aged men in dark blue uniforms walked in. The three detectives in the room stood to attention. *Oh no, here comes the politics*, Ian thought. "Good morning, Commissioner Gu and Chief Inspector Chow."

"Good morning, Officers," Commissioner Gu said. "I will get right to the point. The public is panicked. A serial killer is on the loose. Indonesian groups and lesbian organizations are staging protests outside The Office of the Chief Executive. In the newspapers the word '*incompetent*' seems to be a common adjective in front of the words '*Hong Kong Police*'. We are in a bad light, and will continue to be until this sick bastard is caught."

"Request whatever resources you need, but catch this guy fast. Do we make ourselves clear?" Chief Inspector Chow said.

All three detectives said, 'Yes, Sir!"

"Come down to my office in thirty minutes, Ian. I want a synopsis of every detail of the case."

As the two senior officers left the room Ian realized that he had been holding his breath the whole time they were there. He exhaled. After the meeting, Ian sat alone in his cubicle, overwhelmed with the realization that this case could be excellent for his career or devastating for his career.

His desk phone rang. "Hey, Ian, this is Andy Lau down in Immigration. We've got fifteen Burmese illegal's down here that I believe are related to your serial killer case. They were picked up wandering around the Apple Store in the IFC Mall. One of them pulled a gun on a Mainlander when the guy cut in front of him in line. They were all armed to the teeth."

"Fifteen armed Burmese? What next? I'll be right down." As Ian headed out of cubicle and passed Nigel's station he called out, "Nigel, join me."

Kyaw Thaw, the Burmese translator, was already sitting with Andy at a large conference table in Immigration. Fifteen Burmese men with bemused expressions also were there, still acting like tourists on a holiday.

Andy said, "Thanks for coming, Ian. These guys claim that they were brought to Hong Kong by a one-handed Dutchman and a Chinese guy to be mercenaries in a war against some Burmese Witch."

"Ruud and Tony!" Nigel exclaimed.

"Good. I am glad that that makes sense to you." Andy replied.

"Kyaw, please ask them where the Dutchman and the Chinese guy are now." Ian said.

The Burmese men shrugged. One of them, a man with a jagged scar across his leathery face, spoke. Kyaw translated, "He said that they went to a meeting and never came back."

"Do they know where The Witch is?"

More shrugs.

"Andy, the Witch is Political Counselor Nakaji Sein, from the Myanmar Embassy. When you inform the Embassy about their wayward citizens here, be sensitive about that. Also, if you can avoid deporting them for a while, I would like Nigel to interview them one-by-one, see if he can fish out any leads to Ruud's, Tony's, or The Witch's whereabouts."

"Sure, Ian."

"Thanks, Andy." Ian looked at his watch. "Got a meeting with Commissioner Gu. Nigel, they are all yours."

*****

A few miles away in Pacific Place 3, Geoffrey Macmillan, CEO of Julie's Auction House Hong Kong, pushed the speaker function on his desk phone. When the tone sounded he jabbed in the four numbers of Sarah's extension. "Sarah, please come up to my office."

"Yes, Mr. Macmillan."

Sarah dashed from her cubicle, entered the elevator the executive floor, and opened the oversized mahogany doors of Geoffrey Macmillan's office. Notepad in hand she stood waiting for instructions, dwarfed by the two seven-foot tall ivory elephant tusks that stood on either side of Geoffrey's desk.

"Sarah, we have been contacted by our Myanmar trading partners. I am sure that you are aware of the unfortunate suicide of Zaw Than. His replacement is a Ms. Mimi Khaing."

"That is great news, Mr. Macmillan."

"Yes it is." Geoffrey pulled his calendar up on the computer screen. "I am free Wednesday afternoon next week. Please set up a meeting with Ms. Khaing. I will forward you her contact information."

"Yes, Mr. Macmillan." Sarah's high heels made no noise on the plush charcoal gray carpet as she left. Geoffrey walked to the floor-to-ceiling glass window of his office and looked down at Queensway Road far below. *The players are changing, but I hope that the game remains the same.*

*

Chapter 33

In his habitually hunched stance, standing behind a makeshift podium in the concrete industrial building that served as Nakaji Sein's drug warehouse, Amir addressed a group of twenty tattooed, pierced, and Mohawk-ed men and women standing before him. "Brothers and sisters of Apocalyption-X, our time has arrived! This is our 'Singularity', our 'Big Bang', the birth of our Universe! Look around you. This warehouse is now ours! We have always had the will, now we have the means. Welcome to the new home of Apocalyption-X!"

Murmurs of appreciation came from the audience. A thin man with flame tattoos on the side of his head asked, "Are we going to build bombs here?"

"Yes, Billy, but not the type of bombs that you are thinking of. Something much more elegant and newsworthy. We will build plague bombs," Amir said. "The headlines will read, *'Apocalyption-X unleashes Black Death on Hong Kong.'*"

Amir outlined his plan of infecting fleas with plague, and then releasing them on the public. "We will deliver our gift in zip-lock baggies on the MTR. When the train stops and the doors open, you will drop the open baggie full of our tiny friends on the floor. You then you step off the train, doors close. Simple."

A woman in the group said, "Hey, Amir, excuse my skeptical nature, but when you say that this lab space is 'ours', what exactly do you mean? Someone is funding this, right? What do they want? I would like to know who it is that thinks they are going to be controlling me."

Scattered murmurs of "Yeah" arose from the crowd.

"A good question, Carol," Amir said. "Our benefactor is currently a fugitive from the authorities. Because of the sensitive nature of his newly publicized infamy, I am reluctant to give you his name. I should also mention that, as of yet, he is unaware of Apocalyption-X. He thinks that it is just me carrying out this plan."

A muscular man with a silver ring through his left eyebrow said, "Screw him if he doesn't like it! We are driving the flea bomb bus! Apocalyption-X rules!"

"Apocalyption-X! Yeah!" Cheers and boot stomps from the group.

When the crowd calmed down Amir continued, "As the plague spreads through Hong Kong, there will be a run on antibiotics to control it, streptomycin specifically. I have already stockpiled a supply for our own use. As supplies of streptomycin run out there will be a vibrant trade in black market streptomycin. We will be at the forefront of the black market streptomycin trade. However, the pills that we sell as streptomycin will be filled with anthrax instead. The one-two punch; first the plague infested fleas and then the anthrax tainted medicine! We will bring the assholes to their knees!"

"Yeah, Apocalyption-X!" More cheering and boot stomping.

"Wake-up call, Hong Kong! You cannot exclude people of color, people without wealth, people who were not born into privilege, and not pay the price! The invoice has arrived, Hong Kong!" Amir slammed his hand down on the table. Then in a quiet voice, "Now, let's build us a lab."

The members of Apocalyption-X set to work with saws, drills, wood, steel, and gypsum board under Amir's direction. Amir scurried around the construction zone like a frantic rodent as they assembled, "Chemistry area will be here, biology there. This will be the wet zone. Culture storage is here. This will be the storeroom for the infected fleas. Work benches along this wall." Within a week they had built a laboratory that any scientist with a desire to annihilate a city's population could be proud of.

When the lab was complete Amir dialed The Witch's number. "Hey, Nakaji, I'd like you to come down and check out our lab. It's finished."

"Great. That was quick, Amir."

"Yeah...and this a little awkward, but I also want to introduce you to Apocalyption-X."

"Apoca-what?"

Amir explained. When he was finished there was a moment of silence from The Witch.

"And how many are there in your group?"

"Including me, twenty-eight."

Nakaji said, "You should have told me about your group sooner, Amir. However, I think it's wonderful that we have all these helpers. Tell you what, now that the lab is finished we should throw an appreciation party at the to keep everyone motivated and bonded. How about this Friday night at about 7:00pm? I will host a dinner at the new lab."

"Yeah, that would be super, Nakaji! I am glad that you're not angry. I'll tell them. See you Friday night."

Nakaji hung up. *Nat, you have once again shown me your path. Twenty-eight. Eight signifies prosperity. Twenty-eight, a two and an eight, two times prosperity. This is the sacrifice that you want, the twenty-eight members of Apocalyption-X!*

*****

The mood inside the new lab was festive. Outside it was a rainy Friday night. Every few minutes the sky strobe-flashed thin arms of crackling lightening as Nakaji drove up to his industrial building in a car that he had rented for the evening with one of his fake identities. He wore a long raincoat. The members of *Apocalyption-X* applauded as Nakaji stepped through the metal door into the lab. Amir walked him to the front of the group.

"Brothers and sisters, this is our benefactor!" Amir began. "Nakaji Sein, fugitive from the law, enemy of The Establishment, and the capital behind our operation. Nakaji, would you like to say a few words to your brothers and sisters?"

"Yes, I would Amir. Thank you." The group of would-be terrorists looked expectantly at the Burmese man standing before them. Nakaji stared back at them, and then slowly raised his face up to the ceiling, and loudly intoned in Burmese, "Nat, witness my gift to you. Thank you for all that you grant me. I am your servant, and this blood is yours!"

From beneath his raincoat The Witch withdrew his MP5

submachine gun and sprayed the audience, the report of the gun deafening, bullets that missed their mark ricocheting off the hard surfaces of the concrete room, smashing lab equipment and tearing up new cabinets. When it was over, Nakaji turned his gaze from the decimated bodies of Apocalyption-X, some still twitching, leaking blood onto the concrete floor of the new lab, to a stunned Amir. Nakaji said, "Did you really think that you could take the control of my project away from me? Amir, you are smart scientist but you have no common sense." Nakaji shot him in the head.

He returned to his rented car, opened the trunk, and took out an electric saw, a small barbecue grill, a jar of Char Siu sauce, and a bag of coals. He walked back into the building.

Chapter 34

"I found him," Angela heard her father's voice say over the telephone.

"Really? Great, Dad, where is he?"

"He is being protected by the Liang Zai. They have him in Sham Shui Po in an apartment on Yu Chau Street, next to Happywood Restaurant. He is in flat 9C."

"Wow, thanks, Dad! Love you."

*****

Two hours later Ian, Nigel, Angela, and twelve Special Duties Unit officers wearing Paraclete RMV body armor were standing in the SDU headquarters in Fanling being briefed by the Squad Leader. The men of the Special Duties Unit, the elite tactical strike force of the Hong Kong Police nicknamed The Flying Tigers, stood at attention as the plan was outlined.

"We will need to move fast. The Liang Zai will have lookouts posted so we will be spotted as soon as we enter Sham Shui Po. Therefore we will not have the advantage of surprise. They will have about five minutes to prepare for us before we hit them."

Angela observed with admiration the calm focus of the Flying Tigers. No fidgeting, each man standing coolly at attention.

The Squad Leader continued, "The buildings are too close for us to get our vehicles in behind, so when we pull up in front Squad A will go in the front door, Squads B and C will go up the fire stairs on either side. Move fast, move strong, but remember that the building will also be full of civilians. Any questions? No? Let's go."

The officers, along with Ian, Angela, and Nigel, jogged to the two Mercedez-Benz Unimog U5000 armored personnel carriers, hunched, muscular beasts crouched in the SDU vehicle lot. "Squad A in one vehicle and Squads B and C in the second vehicle!" The Squad Leader commanded.

Angela, Ian, and Nigel piled in with Squad A. Angela's adrenaline raced through her body as the powerful vehicles roared towards Sham Shui Po. She admired the firepower, SR-16 assault rifles and MP5 submachine guns and the serious men silently preparing themselves for battle.

As they sped through the narrow streets the sky became dark, thunder roared, and a deluge of rain started to fall. Lightening crackled repeatedly, exploding in the steel gray sky with flashes of blinding, bright white.

In Apartment 9C The Witch heard a knock on his apartment door and then it was flung open. A skinny red-pole enforcer barely out of his teens stood in the doorway. His head was shaved on the sides, the hair on the top of his head gelled to stand straight up. Nakaji thought he looked like a pineapple.

"You, come quickly now!" the red-pole demanded.

Nakaji grabbed his computer bag, suitcase, and guns and followed the youth, who led him to the fire stair. They sprinted up the stairs and exited through a graffiti-scrawled metal door onto the roof and out into the pounding rain. Water from the storm was already starting to pond on the old roof.

Lying near the parapet of the roof was a fifteen foot length of lashed-together bamboo poles. The boy lifted it and placed it from their building's parapet to the parapet of the adjacent building, creating a flimsy bridge over the ten-story drop to the alley below.

"Follow me, police are coming!" he yelled to be heard over the pounding rain. He then scampered, as agile as a monkey on a branch, across to the next building.

Nakaji looked down at the ground below and then at the slick bamboo poles spanning the two buildings. "You have got to be kidding!" he exclaimed, although the boy beckoning him to cross from the roof of the adjacent building had no chance of hearing him. As lightening flashed sporadically and thunder exploded in the distance, Nakaji thought, *Protect me, Nat!* Mentally preparing himself by imagining that he was walking on flat ground, he gingerly stepped up on to the wet bamboo bridge, sliding his feet one after the other until he was safely on the other side.

The boy then picked up the bamboo bridge, carried it to the other side of the roof, and laid it across to another building. They did this over and over again, the rain pounding them, Nakaji forcing himself to overcome his terror at every crossing, until they were six buildings away. The boy then led Nakaji to a square concrete structure that housed the exit stairs. Soaked through and still shaken from repeatedly traversing ten-story drops over wet, flimsy bamboo, Nakaji followed the skinny youth down open steel stairs to the fifth floor. Leaving wet footprints on the linoleum floor of a corridor that smelled of fish sauce and garlic they finally stopped in front of chipped wooden door. The soaked, dripping boy with the pineapple haircut handed Nakaji a key. "You live here." He then disappeared down the hall. Nakaji, shivering and drenched, let himself into the apartment.

SDU Squad Team A reached Apartment 9C first. They broke through the door, the jamb splintering as they hit the old door with a battering ram. Guns drawn and yelling 'Police!' the squad found an empty apartment.

"Damn!" Ian exclaimed. "Maybe they're hiding him on a lower floor. Angela, you check the lowest three levels, Nigel, you take levels four through six. I'll check the upper levels." Ian ran down the stairwell to level eight and exploded through the doorway into the hallway, gun drawn.

There was only one door on level eight that had not been boarded up with plywood. A hand written sign had been taped to the one usable door, black marker on red paper, reading '*King Kong School of Kung Fu*'. The door was unlocked, Ian entered.

The apartment had been gutted to form one large space, the floor covered with a blue vinyl mat. Along one wall was a wooden stand holding spears of various lengths, and next to them were kicking shields leaning against the wall. Three worn punching bags hung from brackets on the ceiling. In a corner was a wooden sparring dummy.

In the center of the blue mat stood the roundest man that Ian had ever seen, a bald beach ball of a man, mid-fifties, about as tall as Ian. *It looks like his butt starts at the back of his neck,* Ian thought. The man was wearing brown slacks and a cream and red, short-sleeved, checkered shirt. He was shoeless, brown socks on extra-wide feet. The man said in English, "Remove shoes."

Ian pulled out his badge and approached, "Police! We are looking for a suspect. I need to search your apartment."

Without understanding how he got there, Ian suddenly found himself lying on his back on the mat, looking at the ceiling. He jumped up and yelled, "What the hell are you doing, fatso? I said, 'Police'! That means I search your place, and you listen to what I ask and answer my questions!"

Ian came at the man, thinking that he would not be too rough on the fat man, just put a scare into him so that he got cooperation. Ian instantly found himself pressed against the wall. The fat man calmly pushed at a point just below Ian's collarbone with one finger. Ian found himself paralyzed, unable to move a muscle, no feeling in his body.

"I say 'remove shoes'. That means you remove shoes," The fat man said. He slowly released the pressure that he was applying with his finger, and Ian slowly regained the feeling in his body. "No matter, you already in."

"I am looking for...," Ian started.

"I know, I know. You looking for foreign man who stay upstairs, protected by Triad boys. Stupid boys, stink of weakness. They sell poison to our children."

"Yes. Do you know where that man is?"

"They take him away just before you get here. Up to roof. He not here anymore."

"I know that he's not here. Any idea where they took him, Mr. ....?"

"I King Kong. Many rat holes here, could be anywhere."

"So you heard them go to the roof?"

"Bridge to other buildings, no telling. Anyway, bad man have lady friend. You find lady friend, maybe it his weakness. "

"A lady friend?" Ian asked.

"Yes, two days back I eat lunch Happywood Restaurant. They at another table. He calls her 'Mimi'. She same country as him, she dress very fancy, smells like Western woman. They talk their country language, but tone sounds like they talk business, not boyfriend-girlfriend talk."

"Thank you, Mr. Kong. That could be helpful."

"You bring stupid boys to me, I make them tell where man is. They not afraid to go jail, they proud to go jail. They afraid of pain, though. They weak. Bring to me, I make them scream like little girls."

"I am afraid that that would violate police policy, Mr. Kong." Ian said as he left. "Thank you for the information."

He walked down the stairs to the street. King Kong's last words stuck in his mind, '*A woman named Mimi.*' Mimi Tun was the attaché that met with Ian at the Burmese Embassy. Not that Ian knew a lot of Burmese, probably 'Mimi' was a common name. *However, could it be the same 'Mimi'? Was she also involved in the drug trade with The Witch? They worked together at the embassy. Was she involved with the murders?*

*****

As soon as the red-pole had left him alone in the new flat, The Witch, shirt soaked from the run over the rooftops in the rain, exited the tenement building and flagged a taxi. *Someone in the Triad sold me out. Not going to stay in their flat and wait for another raid. Had enough of this ghetto life too,* he thought. "Driver, take me to the Ritz Carlton."

*

Chapter 35

Wednesday night was Ladies Night at Club Nova in Lan Kwai Fong. Sarah and Tika were drinking half-price house gin and tonics. George and Ian each had a bottle of San Miguel in front of them.

"Sarah, you look disturbed," George said. "Have a rough day?"

"Did you ever meet someone that you instantly didn't like but you could not put your finger on why? It's not because of the designer dress, the stiletto heels, or that she's more beautiful than you. You just don't like that person, plain and simple," Sarah said.

"Sure," George said. "That's your intuition telling you that you are in the presence of a predator. It's a hold-over trait from our Neanderthal days, a warning sign that the animal in front of you is dangerous."

"Did you have that experience today, Sarah?" Tika asked.

"Yes, I did. A woman came into Julie's named Mimi Khraing. She's with a Myanmar jade group and is taking over Zaw Than's position. I hated her instantly."

Ian reacted immediately, almost knocking over his beer bottle. "Mimi? Tell me about this, Sarah!"

"Mr. Macmillan and I met today with a woman named Mimi who is the new representative for the jade deals. What are you getting so excited about, Ian?"

"Tell me about Mimi," Ian said again.

"She's their new representative, high heels, gorgeous, obviously ruthless. I doubt that she will be able to fill Zaw Than's position though. You have to understand that Zaw Than created the market for raw jade in Hong Kong. Before that we auctioned only carved, finished jewelry and statues. Zaw Than was the one who had the idea that raw jade from Myanmar would be highly sought after. Mr. Macmillan took a chance on him, and it worked."

"Ian, you have a strange look on your face," Tika said.

"What if Mimi Kraing is really Mimi Tun from the Embassy? The Witch kills Zaw Than to make it look like the murderer is dead so that we stop the investigation. The Witch realizes after he kills him that there is a secondary benefit, an opening to get into the jade trade. He cannot just walk into Julie's, however, as everyone in Hong Kong has seen his picture in the newspaper. Therefore he contacts his friend at the Embassy, Mimi, to pose as his representative." Ian already had his Smartphone out. He found a photograph of Mimi Tun on the Myanmar Embassy's home page and showed it to Sarah. Sarah confirmed; Mimi Tun was Mimi Khraing.

Ian tapped in Nigel's number. "Nigel, pick up Mimi Tun, the Attaché from the Myanmar Embassy, and bring her to headquarters for questioning."

Nigel said, "Would like to, but something else just came up, Ian. We got a call from St. Mary's emergency room about a gunshot patient who sounds like Tony, accompanied by Ruud. The hospital always notifies us whenever a gunshot victim is admitted. These two sound like our boys; a Chinese guy shot in the ass brought in by a tall Dutchman with one hand. Angela and I are on way over there right now."

"That does sound like our boys. Good. I'll pick up Mimi myself. See you back at the station." Ian put away his phone and turned to Tika, gave her a kiss, and said, "Sorry, Babe, duty calls." It was a twenty minute walk from Lan Kwai Fong to Police Headquarters. At his computer, Ian found Mimi Tun's home address.

*****

"Well, Tony, time to go. We are off to Yangon. We just got an e-mail from Nakaji." Ruud said as he tucked his Smartphone back in his pocket.

Tony, lying spread-eagled on his stomach on the emergency room bed like a starfish on a rock, said, "Great, getting bored here."

A voice behind them said, "It will be a while before you go to Yangon. You gentlemen already have a date at Police Headquarters." Ruud spun. Nigel and Angela were standing next to a doctor a few paces away. They both flashed their police badges.

"No need to involve the police. Why would the police want to speak with us? My friend here is the victim of an accident. It is not police business." Ruud said.

"Him getting shot in the ass is the least of our concerns. Turn around," Nigel said, taking his handcuffs off of his belt.

"I think that you are going to find it difficult to put handcuffs on a one-handed man," Ruud said guffawing.

Nigel hesitated for a moment, and realized that Ruud was right. He clicked one end of the cuffs to Ruud's prosthesis. "OK, smart guy, how's this? Try to escape and I will shoot you."

"You too," Angela said, gesturing for Tony to stand up.

"I will need special transport," Tony said. "I cannot sit down."

"You are going to quickly learn to sit on one cheek, my friend," Angela said, roughly clicking the handcuffs into place.

In the interrogation room at Police Headquarters, Ruud sat and Tony stood. Tony paced as the pain killers wore off. When Angela and Nigel entered, Ruud said, "What are we here for, officers? We have done nothing wrong."

Nigel laughed. "How about being here in Hong Kong illegally to start?"

"Great, deport us then," Ruud said.

"And what about human trafficking? We take that very seriously."

"What human trafficking?"

"You brought fifteen Burmese citizens illegally into Hong Kong?" Nigel said.

"You caught those guys?"

"After you abandoned them they decided to go shopping for some Apple IPads. We picked them up at IFC Mall. By the way, where did you get that tour bus?" Nigel said.

Angela added, "And we would be remiss if we did not mention trafficking in human body parts. A cooler full of human hands, does that sound familiar? We have tape from CCTV cameras in Statue Square showing you with your gross little cooler. And dumping them in the fountain? That definitely violates about ten health and safety laws."

"We did not..," Ruud began.

"That's right," Angela said, clicking her fingers. "That wasn't you.

That was your friend, Nakaji Sein. Where is your friend, Nakaji, by the way?"

"Listen, I have no love for Nakaji," Ruud said. "I would be delighted to turn him in to you. However, I have no idea where he is, just his phone number."

"Are you saying that you will cooperate with us?" Nigel said.

"And if we do?" Tony asked.

"No promises, but the court would consider your cooperation."

"What would you like us to do?" Ruud said.

"Set up a meeting with The Witch."

*****

In Mimi Tun's tiny Shueng Wan bedroom her lover rolled off of her, exhausted. Mimi looked over at Consul General U Kham and wondered if he was going to have a heart attack. She was disgusted with herself. Twenty years older than her and fat as a village pig. *As soon as I get rich on jade, I think that I will have him killed,* she thought. Mimi smiled, being rich was going to be fun.

Ian's compact police cruiser fit nicely into a parking space two blocks from Mimi's apartment. He looked at his watch, 1:00am. When he reached her building he bounded up the two flights of stairs and knocked loudly with one hand while ringing the doorbell with another.

"What?" Who is that?" Kham shot out of the bed.

"I don't know." Mimi picked up a robe from the chair next to the bed, and walked to the door as she tied the belt. "Who's there?" She called out to the locked door.

"Police. Open the door!" Ian demanded.

"What do you want? Come back tomorrow, It's too late."

"Open the door now!"

Mimi turned the lock and opened the door a crack and looked out. Ian pushed his way in. "I need you to come down to the police station with me now, Ms. Tun, or should I say Ms. Khraing?"

Mimi turned white. How could she have been discovered? Did Nakaji double-cross her? "Can I come down in the morning? It's kind of late."

"Now." Ian walked behind her and put handcuffs on her.

"Is that necessary? I am afraid that I am going to have to invoke diplomatic immunity, Detective. As a member of the Embassy any cooperation that I would provide will be strictly voluntary, and I do not like the way that you are treating me. I am not going anywhere with you, take these handcuffs off of me right now."

"No diplomatic immunity in this case, Mimi. The crimes are far too major."

"Well, can I get dressed first?"

"Fair enough." Ian peaked into the guest bathroom off of the living room, and saw that there were no windows. "Let's get your clothes, and you can change in the bathroom."

Ian suddenly noticed a man's sport coat laying on a chair and loafers next to the door. "You know, I believe that you are not alone, Ms. Tun." Ian removed his revolver from his holster. "Let's find your friend together." Holding the handcuffs that bound Mimi's wrists in his left hand and his gun in his right, Ian walked her towards the bedroom.

Empty at first glance, Ian saw the rest of the man's wardrobe scattered about the room. Ian threw open the bedroom closet door. Fat belly overhanging his white boxer shorts, smelling like too much cologne, was Consul General U Kham. "Well, Consul General, what a surprise!" Ian said. "I was hoping for Nakaji Sein, though."

"This is not what it looks like, Detective," U Kham said.

"Yes it is. I am going to find out how you're mixed up in this. You are also going to the police station. Get dressed."

Driving to the police station in the back seat of the cruiser, Kham angrily berated Mimi in Burmese, "Are you involved with Nakaji Sein, you stupid bitch? This is going to cost me my career!" Ian did not know what the words meant, but he got the gist from the tone. He smiled to himself.

*

Chapter 36

By 8:00 am, the Witch had showered, ordered from room service, and was sitting at the desk in his room at the Ritz with his computer before him. As he sipped the last of his coffee he looked out of the floor-to-ceiling glass at Victoria Harbor below. He could barely make out in the hazy distance Lantau Island. He thought of his camp in the jungle behind Mui Wo.

Nakaji's computer emitted a beep tone alerting him that he had just received an e-mail. It was from Ruud. It read:

'Tony has been shot. Have back-up plan. Need to meet. 10:00am tomorrow at Statue Square?'

Strange news. Ruud is such a liability. Better to dispose of him now. He typed back, *'Let's make it at 11:00am. See you then.'* He picked up his mobile phone and tapped in the number of Spider Choi, the Dragon Head of the Liang Zai Triad. When Spider answered, Nakaji said, "We have a small problem. I need your help cleaning it up."

Nakaji turned his attention back to the window and the world outside his plush hotel room. He watched the boats far below in the Harbor leaving whitewater trails in their wakes. For the first time since he had been a young man, Nakaji contemplated the possibility that there was no Nat. It was just him, Nakaji Sein, alone. Things had been going wrong lately with too much regularity. *Maybe I am just misunderstanding Nat's direction. Or, maybe I have been deluding myself my whole life!*

*****

By 10:45am Ruud was sitting on the edge of the fountain wall in Statue Square enjoying the sun on his face, watching tourists, listening to birds chirping their mating calls. Around him eight heavily armed Special Unit Police waited undercover, disguised as business men, street vendors, and bums.

As he waited for the Witch to arrive Ruud thought how well things were turning out. He had come to Hong Kong to get his revenge, and now he would be instrumental in getting the Witch arrested. *Too bad that there is no Capital Punishment in Hong Kong. I should have brought him down in Mainland.*

While Ruud was enjoying the morning sun, accelerating toward Statue Square on a brilliant-red Kawasaki Ninja, its engine wailing at each gear shift, a Liang Zai red-pole steered recklessly through late-morning traffic. He wore a red helmet that matched his bike, the visor tinted dark gray.

When he reached Statue Square he jumped the powerful bike over the curb and, gunning the engine loudly, navigated the motorcycle through the tourists and office workers, screeching to a stop in front of Ruud sitting on the edge of the fountain. It happened so fast that Ruud's mind did not have time to process the fact that something unusual was happening.

Two shots, one in Ruud's forehead and the other in his heart. The big Dutchman fell backwards into the fountain, two expanding tornadoes of red swirling up from his wounds in the clear water, his eyes still open in shock.

The red-pole put the gun back in his belt, accelerated his bike into a wheelie, and sped off towards the street and escape. The undercover police drew their weapons and all fired at once. Most of the bullets found their mark and the gangster flew off the Kawasaki, dead before he hit the ground. The rider-less bike continued to careen forward, running into a woman from Iowa and knocking her flat before coming to rest on the pavement. A Japanese tourist who had been shot in the leg by a bullet that missed its mark lay on the plaza and screamed in pain, the statue of Sir Thomas Jackson looking down on him in bronze indifference.

*****

At police headquarters Ian asked the caller from SDU to repeat the information. "Ruud's dead? Shot by a Triad enforcer?" He looked up at Nigel and Angela, who were standing next to his desk and had overheard. Ian hung up the telephone.

"The Witch knew that it was a trap," Nigel said. "Damn, this guy is always a step ahead of us."

"We'll catch him," Ian said. "Nigel, have our Myanmar Embassy friends, Mimi and Kham, brought up from Holding. Put them in separate rooms. Angela, contact SDU and find out the details of Ruud's shooting."

Thirty minutes later Ian and Nigel entered Interrogation Room A. Mimi glared at the two detectives as they entered, her elegance and attitude had been dissipated by a night in a holding cell.

"You make bad choices, Ms. Tun. To get involved with Nakaji Sein was probably the worst choice you ever made," Ian said as he and Nigel seated themselves across the table.

"Nakaji is slime, agreed. However, I did not do anything against the law," Mimi said.

"Murder is most definitely against the law." Nigel said.

"I had nothing to do with Nakaji's disgusting indiscretions. I just posed as a jade dealer," Mimi said.

"The only way that we can verify that is to find the real killer. Where can we find Nakaji?" Ian asked.

"He is living in a tenement in Sham Shui Po, next to the Happywood Restaurant. I met him there once," Mimi said.

"He *was* there, but he has relocated. Where is he now?"

"Don't know."

"We will need more cooperation from you than that, Ms. Tun. Otherwise, you are our only suspect, and the public wants this case brought to a close. You also just admitted that you met with a known fugitive and failed to inform the police of his location. It would be a shame to spend the rest of your life in Lo Wu Prison," Ian said.

Mimi started to cry, "I was only getting involved in his jade deal, nothing else! I didn't even do anything. I just went to one meeting!"

"Did you know that Nakaji killed Zaw Than?" Ian asked.

"What? No, that was a suicide!" Mimi said.

Nigel took over in a gentler tone than Ian had been using. "Look, Mimi, chances are you were not involved in the killings. That's why we need you to be very truthful with us and tell us absolutely everything. If we find that you lied to us, or left something out, we will have to assume that you are very deep into this: the killings, the drug trade, the jade trade, everything gets put back on the table."

"I will tell you everything, I promise," Mimi blubbered. "I was not involved in any killing, I swear, or the drugs. U Kham, you talk to him about the drugs."

"The General Counsul was involved with Nakaji's drug business?" Ian asked.

"He took a cut. He was aware. Everyone in the Embassy was aware. But Kham could have made it difficult for Nakaji if he wanted to. So he took a fat payment every month to not notice."

"Do you have any evidence that he might have been aware that Nakaji was a serial killer?" Nigel asked.

"No, I don't think he was aware of that."

The two officers continued interrogating Mimi for another hour. They then moved to the adjacent interrogation room. Consul General Kham, hair disheveled and eyes bloodshot, was furious, a cornered animal showing his teeth. "How dare you treat a Consul General like a common criminal? Stop this game immediately or this is very quickly going to become an international incident!"

"Please accept our apologies for any inconvenience, Consul General, but we need to know exactly how involved you were with Nakaji Sein's criminal enterprise," Ian said.

"I was not involved at all! I also have diplomatic immunity. Now release me!" Kham demanded.

"Sorry, this case is just a bit too serious for you to play the immunity card, Consul General. We have evidence that you took payments from Nakaji to facilitate his drug trading. That is indeed involvement.

Kham slammed his hand on the tabletop. "I took payments from Nakaji to *not* get involved! Yes, I turned a blind eye. That is no big deal."

"You also were screwing his accomplice in the jade trade. Nakaji's jade venture is connected to the murder of Zaw Than," Ian said.

"I certainly knew nothing of Zaw Than's murder, the jade trade, or Mimi's involvement. I was simply screwing my Attaché. I had nothing to do with Nakaji Sein's indiscretions."

"Indiscretions?" Nigel said. "Serial murder is usually described in a little stronger terms than 'indiscretions'.

Ian said, "I will be frank with you, Consul General. Your diplomatic immunity can probably give you a free pass on a lot of this stuff. However, if you were involved with the murders of the Indonesian maids, you will be spending the rest of your life in a Hong Kong prison."

Kham softened his tone, running his hand through his uncombed hair. "Look, I am telling you the truth. My only crime was being in the wrong place at the wrong time. I find what Nakaji Sein did abhorrent."

"Our only interest is in finding Sein. Do you have *any* information on where he might be?"

"No. I swear, Detective. I would tell you in a second if I knew, believe me."

"I actually do believe you, Consul General. However, if you do get some information on Sein's whereabouts, please let us know." Ian turned to Nigel and said, "We do not have enough evidence to continue to hold the General Consul or his Attaché. Please release them."

Ian and Nigel left the interrogation room. As they walked back to their cubicles, Nigel said, "Are you sure about cutting them loose?"

"We would need solid evidence to hold them with their diplomatic status. Also, if either of them knew where The Witch was, they would have already given him up. Both have no love for The Witch."

"So…what do we do next?" Nigel asked.

"We need a lucky break, my friend, a very lucky break."

*

Chapter 37

Nakaji Sein peered intently at the map of the world displayed on his computer screen. My enemies are too close and I'm getting no direction from Nat. Maybe there is no Nat, only Nakaji! I am alone and I feel powerless. It is time to run! Where to run?

Nakaji moved his mouse in a tight circle over the globe on his screen, the white arrow on the screen rotating over Hong Kong. He then moved the arrow west until it hovered over North America. Shall I run to America? No, Americans are full of themselves, empowered. They make me feel even more powerless. I hate Americans. He moved the arrow north. Canada? No, less annoying than America, but almost as bad.

Nakaji moved the arrow back east, and stopped momentarily over Myanmar. No, too many enemies at the moment. The mouse continued its path, the white arrow drifting around Asia.

Suddenly, his hand stopped. Yes! Perfect! Japan! The Japanese are a race with an inferiority complex. Psychologically they are always expecting imminent doom. I feel more powerful just thinking about living there! And I also know how to gain an entry.

Nakaji picked up his telephone and tapped in the number of Spider Choi. In Cantonese he said, "Spider, I have a business idea."

"What business idea?"

"You now have some small business with Japan, right? I know how to make it big business," Nakaji said.

"O.K. Meet at Happywood tonight, 10:00 o'clock."

*****

At 10:00pm Happywood Restaurant was busy. A bowl of pork dumpling soup steaming in front of him, Nakaji sat at a round table opposite the Dragon Head of the Liang Zai Triad. Four of Spider's red-pole enforcers also were at the table, picking at plates of vinegary black mushrooms, shredded potatoes, and green beans while they glared at the other customers.

"Tell me about your business idea," Spider said.

"You told me once that you do methamphetamine trade with the Japanese, right? Small profit. Japan, however, is ripe for the heroin trade, Spider. Big profit," Nakaji said.

Spider said nothing, only stared expressionless. Nakaji did not know if his proposal was being well received or not. He stared back at the Triad boss and waited for a response.

"I hate the Japanese," Spider finally said.

"Everyone hates the Japanese, Spider. That's OK, this is business."

Spider said to the red-poles, "Get Matsumoto. Bring him here." Spider turned back to Nakaji, "Hong Kong getting too hot for you, Nakaji? You want to hide in Japan?"

"I thought that it would be a good idea."

"Mmm. You ever been to Japan before, Nakaji?"

"No."

Spider smiled and said, "You are a funny man. Let me tell you some things." He put a pork dumpling in his mouth. "I will connect you with the Chikuzen-Kai Yakuza. One of the smaller families, but their main business is drug dealing. Most other Yakuza gangs avoid drugs. Matsumoto is my Chikuzen-Kai contact in Hong Kong. He speaks Cantonese."

"Is Matsumoto high enough to deal with us?" Nakaji asked.

Spider laughed. "No, he is a flea in the organization. He will need to connect you to his Oyabun, the boss."

"And how hard will it be to develop our trade in heroin?"

"Very hard. You should understand that the Yakuza are tolerated by the Japanese government. They even have offices with their signs on the front. When it comes to drugs, however, Yakuza have made a deal with the government; government doesn't bother them with 'soft' drugs like methamphetamines, and they do not deal in 'hard' drugs like heroin or cocaine."

"Oh."

Spider laughed again. "Not all bad news though, Nakaji. First, Japan is an untapped market for heroin. We will have no competition.

Second, the Chikuzen-Kai is the most radical of the Yakuza families. They just might go for it. Their Oyabun is particularly crazy."

Thirty minutes later Fumio Matsumoto was sitting with them at the table. Fumio, dressed in gray slacks, white shirt, and gray sports coat looked like any Japanese businessman, except that he was missing the last joint of the pinky and ring fingers on his left hand.

After an explanation of their business proposition by Nakaji in Cantonese Fumio sat back and pondered. He had screwed up twice before and had had to send the tips of his fingers in a jar to the Oyabun to make amends. However, this was just the kind of lunatic idea the Oyabun liked. It might get him back in good standing. Fumio stood up, bowed, and said, "It will be my honor to arrange a meeting for you in Japan, Nakaji-san."

Nakaji stood up and also bowed, "Thank you, Matsumoto-san." He handed Fumio a business card, "This is my contact information. Please disregard the name on the card, Aung Tat is an alias. I leave for Japan tomorrow."

*

Chapter 38

Friday morning, and Ian was talking to his coffee cup, "Come on, wake me up, do your magic." His desk phone rang. An operator said, "There is a Winnie Li on the line. She says that she has information on your serial killer case."

"Please put her through," Ian said. *I could use a break. Let this be good!* "Hello, Ms. Li, this is Detective Ian Hamilton. You have information on our case?"

Ian finished the call and exploded out of his cubicle. "Come on!" he yelled to Nigel and Angela as he passed their desks. "I'll explain in the car." The two detectives gave each other a glance and then raced after him.

As the police cruiser sped toward the Kowloon tunnel, Angela in the back and Nigel in the passenger seat, Ian said, "I just received a call from a Winnie Li. She is a housekeeper at The Ritz. She recognized Nakaji from his picture in the newspaper, and he's registered at the hotel under the name 'Aung Tat'. This could be our lucky break!"

Ian pulled up fast under the *porte cochere* of the Ritz Carlton, almost sideswiping a Rolls Royce, coming to an abrupt stop in front of the hotel's entry. The three officers bolted for the elevator, leaving the police cruiser blocking the drive. At the ninth floor lobby they hurried across the hushed, carpeted elegance to the front desk. Ian flashed his badge in the desk clerk's face. "We need someone to let us into one of your guest's rooms immediately!"

The clerk calmly said, "Yes, Sir, guest's name?"

"Aung Tat."

The clerk's fingers tapped at his keyboard. "I am sorry, Sir. Mr. Tat checked out early this morning."

"Damn it!" Ian slapped his hand down hard on the imported Italian marble of the countertop. "Has his room been cleaned yet?"

More tapping on the keyboard, "No, Sir."

"Room number?"

"1087, Sir, on the one hundred and eighth floor."

"That room is now off-limits to your staff," Ian said. "Angela, you take the room. Call headquarters for a forensic team to assist you. Nigel, find the doorman who was on duty. Find out if Nakaji took a taxi after he checked out? Usually the doorman asks you where you are going and they then tell the driver, especially for a foreigner." Ian turned to the desk clerk. "What time did he check out?"

The clerk looked back at his screen. "6:43am, Sir."

"Please call the manager." Ian said.

"No need to call. I am the manager," a voice smoothly intoned. A Western man dressed in black suit with slicked back blond hair had walked up behind Ian. "I am Vitaly. May I help you?" He said, extending his hand.

"Vitaly, I am Detective Ian Hamilton. Is there somewhere that we can talk?"

"Please follow me." Vitaly led Ian behind the front counter to a small office. "Can I get you some coffee or water, Detective Hamilton?"

"No, thanks, Vitaly…you are Russian?"

"Yes."

"I have to inform you that a fugitive has been staying in room 1087. He checked in under the name Aung Tat. His real name is Nakaji Sein."

"Nakaji Sein…Oh, that is the name of that serial killer, isn't it? I read about him in the newspapers."

"Yes. We will take possession of the room until our forensic work is done. Meanwhile, any information that you or your staff could provide would be helpful: where he ate, any visitors, anything. One of my officers is trying to find the doorman who was on duty this morning to question him."

Vitaly scooted his chair to a desk with a computer. After some tapping on the keyboard he said. "It looks like your friend was a creature of habit. Every morning room service brought him scrambled eggs, bacon, and coffee. Every lunch they brought him a hamburger and French fries with a coke. Ah, dinner varied, sometimes a steak, sometimes spaghetti Bolognese. He was definitely a fan of room service. I suppose if you are a fugitive, though, you would want to stay in as much as possible."

"We will need copies of his all credit card receipts. I am assuming that he paid his hotel bill with a card?"

Vitaly peered at the screen. "Yes, a Visa card registered to Aung Tat. That should be fun for you to trace."

"Could you please print the receipts out?"

"Sure," Vitaly said, pushing the 'print' button on his computer.

There was a knock on the office door, and Nigel entered. "I found the doorman who was on duty. He remembers getting a taxi for a Southeast Asian man at about 6:45am. He said that he was going to the airport."

"Leaving the Ritz at about 6:45am, his flight had to be around 9:30am. The ticket was probably under the name 'Aung Tat' but check all Burmese sounding names if you don't get a hit on that." Ian handed Nigel the printout of Nakaji's credit card receipts. "Check this Visa card under the name 'Aung Tat'. If we are lucky he would have paid for his airline ticket with that card." Ian threw Nigel the car keys. "Take the car back to the station. I'll stay here and help Angela process the room."

After Nigel left Vitaly said, "I hope that we can keep this quiet, Detective. You know, out of the newspapers."

"'This'?"

"Yes, 'this', the 'Cannibal of Hong Kong' staying at the Ritz Carlton 'this'."

"We are not in control of the newspapers, but I can assure you that the Hong Kong police will be as discreet as possible."

"Thank you. You will of course have the hotel's full cooperation in your investigation."

Ian took the elevator up to the one hundred and eighth floor. *How tall are they going to keep building these buildings? This is freaky! How would you get down if there was a fire?* Angela was carefully stepping around the room following first responder procedures until the forensic team arrived. "Anything interesting?" Ian asked.

She shook her head 'no'. Ian walked into the room's bathroom. A pile of used towels lay on the floor, the shower stall still wet from

Nakaji's last shower. *Tons of DNA and fingerprints, but we already know who we are looking for,* Ian thought.

As Ian exited the bathroom he saw a thin, middle-aged Chinese woman in a housekeeper's uniform standing at the doorway staring into the room. Ian instantly knew who she was. "Are you Winnie?"

"Yes, I am."

"Winnie, I am Detective Ian Hamilton. We spoke on the telephone earlier. Thank you so much for your assistance. Citizens like you make a difference."

"You catch him?" Winnie asked.

"No, he checked out early this morning. But we are on his trail."

Winnie sneered, her mouth showing that she had only half her teeth. "Stupid *gwai lo* policeman, always too late," she said in Cantonese.

"Auntie Li?" Angela asked in Cantonese.

"Angela? You are with the police?"

Ian turned to Angela, then back to Winnie. "You two know each other?"

"From the old neighborhood," Angela said in English, and then switched to Cantonese. "Auntie Li, no one knows my dad is Triad. Need to keep it quiet. OK?"

"OK. Great to see you, Angela. I expected you to be dead by now, tough girl like you. So many of the young ones dead now."

Angela switched back to English, "Auntie Li used to have a vegetable store in the neighborhood where I grew up."

"Great, Angela. Please focus back on the case. We need to find out where Nakaji went." Ian said.

"He went to someplace colder than here." Winnie said in English.

"What?" Ian asked.

In Cantonese, Winnie said, "This one is really slow-witted. He is your boss?" Then in English, "The man that you are looking for, he went to someplace colder than Hong Kong."

"How do you know?"

"Yesterday in his closet he had a new winter coat."

"Winnie, you are quite the detective!" Ian said.

Winnie smiled her gap-toothed grin, and in Cantonese, "Working with this guy must be very amusing for you, Angela."

Ian's telephone rang. On the other end, Nigel said, "Got it. Aung Tat was on ANA flight NH912, left Hong Kong at 9:40am, lands in Narita at 3:00pm Tokyo time."

Ian quickly looked at his watch. "It's 11:00am here, so it is noon in Japan. We still have time!"

"I have initiated contact with Tokyo police using one of our Japanese translators to intercept him when he lands." Nigel said.

"Fantastic! We've got him, Nigel!"

"Well, maybe not." Nigel said. "Our Japanese translator said that the way that the police representative from Japan said 'yes' was more of a 'no'. He said that it could go either way."

"What? Why wouldn't they cooperate?"

"I don't know."

"I'll be back at headquarters in twenty minutes. Have the translator there. We'll call and check on the progress."

As Ian rushed out of the hotel room he brushed past Winnie Li. She smiled her snaggly-toothed grin and said to Ian, "Let the Japanese keep him, a gift from Hong Kong."

*****

As Ian lowered himself into his seat back at the police station he looked at his watch, *11:30am. We have two and a half hours before he lands.* Ian nodded at Nigel and the Japanese translator, Sammy Liu. He pushed the 'speaker' button, and then tapped in the international number of the Tokyo Police Liaison Unit.

Five rings and then, *"Hai, mushi mushi."*

Ian said, "Do you speak English?"

"Gomen nasai……."

Sammy said in Japanese, "That is OK, Sir. We speak Japanese. We are checking on the status of the request that we made an hour ago for you to intercept a fugitive for us on ANA flight 912."

"Ahh, yes, very difficult," came over the line. Sammy translated.

"What do you mean 'very difficult'? What does that mean?" Ian exclaimed.

"Current politics is not auspicious. The LDP requires any Chinese request to be approved by them before any action is taken. Have to submit the forms, and then they will take it into consideration." Sammy translated.

"Chinese? We are from Hong Kong, not China! I don't get this! Do you realize that there is a serial killer on board an airplane that will land in Tokyo two and a half hours from now, and if you do not apprehend him he will no doubt start killing your own citizens?"

"Yes, very bad. That is why I submitted the forms immediately after your last call," the voice said on the other end of the line.

"Forms won't do it, you moron! What is going on there?"

"Ahh… the Senkaku Islands dispute, very bad. Any action with China must be approved first by LDP."

"The dispute is with China, not Hong Kong! We are the *Hong Kong* police! It is a different country!" Ian yelled, now on his feet.

"It is *'One Country, Two Systems'.*" the Japanese officer said calmly.

"Let me speak with your supervisor!" Ian yelled.

"Yes." The Japanese officer said, and then hung up.

The three Hong Kong officers looked at each other stunned. "I need to go to the Police Commissioner," Ian said, and ran from the room.

By the time that the proper calls to higher-ups in Japanese politics were made and the proper people of influence filtered the proper directions down the hierarchal chain, Nakaji Sein was on the bus from Narita Airport into downtown Tokyo.

Ian sat at his desk dejected. *I lost him twice today. What more could go wrong?*

Ian's mobile phone rang. He looked at the screen. It was from George. "Hey, George." Ian said.

"She's gone, Ian! She's been taken!"

"What? Who's gone?"

"Sarah! She's been kidnapped by The Witch!"

Chapter 39

Ian raced the police cruiser towards Sarah's Soho apartment, calling forensics on the way and weaving around cars as the police siren screamed its warning. Double parking the car on Staunton Street, he took the elevator to the eighth floor of Sarah's building. *Why? Why Sarah? Did The Witch take her to get at me?*

George, frantic, was standing in the middle of Sarah's two-bedroom apartment. There had obviously been a struggle. A chair lay broken on its side and a coffee table had been upended. "Ian! Finally you are here! Who would want to harm Sarah?"

"I don't know, George. The forensic team is on the way. Do not touch anything. When did you get here?" Ian asked.

"At about 4:30. We were going to catch some of the happy hours on Elgin Street, work our way down to Lan Kwai Fong. When I got here the door was open, and the place looked like there had been a wrestling match. I called you immediately."

"This is a police investigation, George, but I can tell you that I am going to find whoever did this and am personally going to tear their head off!"

"Do you think that it could be related to your investigation of that serial killer? Sarah was involved in the Burmese jade deals with her company. Someone she had met with was a suspect in the murder case, right?"

"We cannot jump to conclusions, George, nor can we rule anything out. Forensics will be here in a few minutes. Let's see what they can tell us." Ian took out his telephone. "I'll call Tika, let her know."

"Dammit, Ian, The Witch has her, doesn't he? He's going to eat her!"

"Calm down, George. We can't jump to conclusions."

"Screw being calm, The Witch is going to eat Sarah!"

*****

Nakaji had put on his new coat. November in Tokyo was colder than what he was used to. He got off the airport bus at Shinjuku and made his way through the chaos of Shinjuku Station, through the crowds in the underground arcade of the busiest transport hub in the world, to the Keio Plaza Hotel. In the over-lit lobby Nakaji handed his passport to the desk clerk, who said in English, "Aung-san, welcome to Keio Plaza."

He was shown to his clean, no-frills room which had a spectacular view of the lights of Nishi Shinjuku's skyscrapers twinkling outside the window. After storing his luggage Nakaji sat at his desk and thought, *New city, new adventure.* He e-mailed Cho Suzumura.

Nakaji had first met Cho in a tiny ramen restaurant that he frequented on Tang Lung Street in Hong Kong. They had instantly become friends, recognizing in each other a disdain for what society would call 'normal behavior'. Cho Suzumura, a Tokyo native, was a sometimes bouncer, sometimes bartender, sometimes waiter. He was fluent in English from four years spent in Los Angeles trying to open a gym on Melrose. When the gym failed and he found himself serving ramen in a restaurant on Olympic Boulevard, Cho left L.A. to try his luck in Hong Kong. Eventually he had returned to Tokyo, where he now worked as a sometimes bouncer, sometimes bartender, sometimes waiter.

'Cho, I am moving to Japan for a business venture. Need a translator and bodyguard. Interested? NS.'

Cho had instantly e-mailed back, *'Sure!'*

Nakaji answered, *'Keio Plaza, Shinjuku. Meet in lobby at 8.'*

Cho looked out of place amid the businessmen and the families of tourists, his muscular and tattooed frame spread out on a couch in the lobby of the Keio Plaza. He had taken off his Indiana Jones style leather jacket and a sleeveless workout shirt exposed his gym-toned biceps. In torn jeans and with a knit cap on his head, he exclaimed "Hey, Nakaji, long time, man!" as he spotted Nakaji walking towards him.

"Yeah, long time, Cho. Let's grab a drink someplace where we can talk," Nakaji said.

"Sure. Follow me, great *yakitori* place around the corner."

With sticks of grilled chicken and bottles of Kirin Beer in front of them Nakaji explained his plan. "So, Cho, as soon as we get a call from Fumio Matsumoto we head to Fukuoka to meet with the Chikuzen-kai."

Cho said, "You realize of course that the Chikuzen-Kai is the most vicious of all the Yakuza families."

"So I have heard," Nakaji said. "Can you handle it?"

Cho pointed to the tattoo of a demon *Hannya* mask on his forearm. The face of the demon was deep red, her wispy black hair blowing in the wind. Two gold-colored horns protruded from her forehead. She had golden eyes with jet black pupils, her brow furrowed in anger, and her mouth, in an open grimace, was filled with canine-like gold teeth. "This is how a jealous woman is portrayed in Japanese Noh Theater, very dangerous. Believe me, I have had my share of jealous women. The Yakuza will be easy," Cho said.

"Good. Can you get us some guns?"

"No, Japan is the land of gun control," Cho replied. "Even Yakuza have difficulty getting guns. More chance that we will get chopped up by swords than shot."

Nakaji's phone vibrated. He looked at the text, and then said to Cho, "It's from Fumio. Tomorrow we go to Fukuoka. Better get us some swords then."

*****

The next morning Nakaji felt like he was starting to get used to the sting of the wintry air. He and Cho stood on Platform Fourteen in Tokyo Train Station waiting for the bullet train to Fukuoka. The long, aerodynamic nose of the white train slid up to the platform noiselessly, exactly on schedule. Nakaji blew out his breath and watched it condense into a cloud. *I am a smoke-breathing dragon.*

The landscape merged from urban to rural as the *Shinkansen* express train left Tokyo behind and smoothly accelerated to two hundred and seventy kilometers per hour. He turned to Cho, "How long until we get to Fukuoka?"

"Five hours."

"Cho, I read about a race of 'untouchables' in Japan. Tell me about them."

"'Untouchables'? Oh yeah, the *Burakumin*. Goes way back to the feudal era. People who had unclean jobs, like leather tanners and undertakers for example, were considered impure. They had to live in their own ghettos. Still today they're discriminated against. Every time someone applies for a job, the company will investigate to see if they are *Burakumin*. Can't get a good job. Marriage too. They can only marry their own kind."

"'The *Burakumin*. I like the sound of the word. Do they still live in ghettos?" Nakaji asked.

"Yeah, in fact one of the biggest Burakumin ghettos is in Fukuoka, where we are going," Cho said.

"This is sounding better all the time. So, if there was a crime committed in the *Burakumin* community the police would not be that motivated to investigate, right?"

"Probably not." Cho said. "Know who they got to clean up the Fukushima nuclear plant disaster? The *Burakumin*. They are considered a disposable people."

"I think that I am really going to like Fukuoka." Nakaji said smiling, turning his attention back to the green hills and small farms whizzing by outside the train window.

*****

The Nishitetsu Inn, three stars, catering primarily to businessmen, was directly across the street from the Hakata Train Station in Fukuoka. Cho checked them in. Nakaji asked, "We are supposed to meet Fumio at 5:00 at the Jotenji Temple. Is it far from here?"

Cho asked the desk clerk. "No, not far. A five minute walk."

At 5:00pm Jotenji Temple was deserted, and the fading sun combined with a chilling wind made Nakaji shudder. Fumio was on time. "Ah, great, you have a translator with you," he said to Nakaji in Cantonese, bowing to Cho. "Now I switch to Japanese. Much easier. Please walk with me."

As they strolled through the temple grounds, Fumio said. "We will meet Kodaira-san, my Oyabun, at our headquarters in an hour. I must warn you, he is a little unusual, not a typical Japanese."

"I have heard of him," Cho said. "His nickname is 'Choku', right?" Cho explained to Nakaji in English, "Many Japanese words to describe modern things mimic the English words. For example, the English word 'computer' is '*computa*' in Japanese. '*Choku*' means 'choke'."

"Right," Fumio continued. "Kodaira-san has one of his lieutenants choke him, almost to the point of suffocation, when he wants to get a good idea. He believes that getting choked makes him think clearer. Because of his choke-play his nickname is '*Choku*'. In one incident he went too far, cut off too much blood to his eyes or something, and one of his eyeballs has gotten bigger than the other. Looks very strange."

"Sounds like an interesting guy, this Choku-san," Nakaji said.

"Better not to call him 'Choku-san'. 'Kodaira-san' or 'Oyabun' is better," Fumio said. "What I want to talk you about, though, is the best way for you to discuss the heroin deal with him."

"Good. I appreciate the advice," Nakaji said.

"Wanting you to be successful with Kodaira-san is actually selfish on my part, Nakaji-san. Japan is a very small market for the methamphetamine business, so your Triad friends squeeze us. Price goes up, makes me look bad. If I look too bad I may have to send another finger, or worse."

"Understand, Fumio," Nakaji said. "This is a chance for you to raise your image."

"Exactly. Kodaira-san gets bored very easily. Your proposal therefore must be quick, get to the point immediately. Most important part will be his questions. Answer honestly. He is also a genius. He will already know the answer. If he is interested he will ask you about the financial details."

"If he is not interested?"

"He will kill you."

They chatted as they walked through the temple cemetery, square gray tombstones packed tight together, only enough room needed to entomb an urn of ashes. They strolled through an ornate gate, past some small Shinto shrines alongside a Zen sand garden, and suddenly arrived at the point where they had originally entered the temple grounds. In front of the temple a stretched, black limousine with two rock-solid Japanese men dressed in suits standing alongside it was waiting for them.

"Please get in," Fumio said, indicating the open rear door of the car. The three climbed into the spacious leather and wood-trimmed interior. They rode in silence, and within forty minutes reached the Fukuoka Tower Building in Momochi Seaside Park, soaring seven hundred feet above Hakata Bay.

As they stood in the lobby of the modern tower waiting for the elevator Nakaji read the directory and exclaimed, "This is amazing! In Hong Kong the Triads hide. Here, the Yakuza have offices in modern office buildings with their name on the building directory!"

When they exited the elevator into an oyster-colored lobby, two uniformed receptionists who looked like twins stood up from behind a cherry wood counter up and bowed. Above them on the wall were the words "Chikuzen-kai" in stainless steel letters. It looked like any legitimate office.

Fumio led the way past the receptionist twins through a pair of cherry wood doors. The resemblance to a standard office immediately disappeared. There were almost no walls or partitions in the space, just a vast expanse of open area with floor-to-ceiling glass windows and a magnificent 360 degree view of Fukuoka. The floors were *tatami* mats. Fumio indicated that they should remove their shoes before entering.

Scattered throughout the huge room were low, maroon lacquer tables and brown cushions on the floor. In the center of the room at a grouping of the low tables a gathering of men sat on the cushions playing *oicho-kabu,* a card game popular with the Yakuza. The men were all bare to the waist, exposing their multicolored, full-body tattoos.

As Nakaji and Cho shuffled shoeless following Fumio across the *tatami* mats they were given a hard glare by the Yakuza. Seeing that they were with Fumio the men went back to their game, growling and snapping retorts at each other like irritated junkyard dogs, slamming cards and yen on the *tatami* mat.

Fumio led Nakaji and Cho past the gamblers. They exited the large space through an ornate sliding shoji screen door, stepping into an enclosed room. As they entered their eyes had to adjust. The windows in the room that they just entered were covered with heavy purple curtains and the lighting was muted. The floor was carpeted in a black plush Berber with a pattern of small, gold squares. Along the rear wall of the room was a purple suede couch on which sat Choku Kodaira, dressed in Swarovski crystal-studded loafers, no socks, blue jeans, and a leopard-patterned jacket. He had a skull earring and dark sunglasses. Standing next to him in a semi-circle were his six 'Big Brothers', *Kyodai*, all dressed in black suits and ties.

Fumio bowed deeply. "Oyabun, may I present Mr. Nakaji Sein."

"Sein-san, it is a pleasure to meet you," Kodaira said, standing up and giving a short bow.

Nakaji bowed back. "Thank you for making time to meet with me, Kodaira-san." Cho translated.

"Please, sit down." Kodaira pointed to two upholstered chairs opposite the couch. He clapped his hands, and from a dark recess of the room a woman in a yellow kimono appeared with a tray of tea.

"I have brought you a small present, Kodaira-san," Nakaji said, taking a gift-wrapped box from his coat pocket. One of the *Kyodai* took it from him and handed it to the *Oyabun*.

"Thank you very much," Kodaira said, as he unwrapped the gift. When he saw what was inside he howled like a wolf. "I am going to like you very much, Sein-san!"

Kodaira removed Ruud's mummified hand on a chain from the box and put the necklace around his neck. He clapped his hands, took off his sunglasses, and shouted, "Bring me a mirror!" As Kodaira admired himself wearing the mummified hand in the handheld mirror Nakaji tried to not stare at the Oyabun's left eye. The eyeball was extended out of the socket, bloodshot, and almost twice as big as the right one.

Kodaira finally put down the mirror and said, "How much 'snow' can you deliver, how much will it cost, and when can you deliver, Nakaji-san?"

They discussed terms for fifteen minutes. "Good, deliver in ten days to Fumio in Hong Kong. He will handle the details to get the delivery to Japan." Kodaira stood up, replaced his sunglasses, and gave a short bow. He then said to Fumio, "Take them to Club Taru."

"*Hai, Oyabun!*"

As they descended in the elevator Fumio exclaimed, "That gift was genius, Nakaji-san!"

"Thank you. What is 'Club Taru'?"

"It is a bondage club that Kodaira owns. '*Taru*' means 'barrel' in Japanese. The club is designed to look like the inside of a barrel."

"A bondage club? I have never heard of such a thing. What goes on?"

"You can tie up the waitresses, or have them tie you up. You can lightly choke them if you want to. Sorry, he would know if we did not go and it would seem rude. Just a few hours, have some drinks."

"No, it sounds interesting. I am looking forward to it," Nakaji said.

*****

Club Taru had no sign over the door and no windows. There was just a heavy wooden door in a blank wall, in front of which stood a man in a black suit. He was weight-lifter large. When he saw Fumio he bowed deeply and held the door open, looking like his enlarged biceps would rip out of the tight suit if he flexed.

The walls and ceiling of the bar, paneled in wood siding, formed a curved cylinder so the effect was that you were within a giant oak barrel lying on its side. As soon as they walked into the bar the three were greeted by a woman wearing a business suit, her face powdered shocking white, her lipstick vivid, glistening red.

"Ah, Fumio-san. We were expecting you and your guests." She bowed and walked them to a semi-private booth, plush low sofas arranged around a low glass table. On the table was a bottle of Johnnie Walker, cans of tea, and a pitcher full of ice. The woman kneeled and poured the pitcher half full of whiskey and half full of tea.

In English, Nakaji said to Cho, "They are ruining good whiskey."

"Got to flow with the culture, Man," Cho said, smiling.

As they sat down three young women, also dressed in business attire, arrived and sat down with them. In Japanese, Cho said, "Do any of you beautiful ladies speak English?"

"I do," one said in English. A rearrangement of seats took place, so the English speaker was next to Nakaji.

Fumio raised his glass and stood up. In Cantonese he said, "Nakaji, I cannot tell you how much I appreciate this opportunity. Here is to a long and prosperous relationship! Konpai!"

Whiskey/tea after whiskey/tea was downed, until two and a half bottles of Johnnie Walker stood empty. In a fog, Nakaji looked at Fumio and Cho chatting up the girls. Fumio was chain smoking. The barrel shape of the room seemed to spin and Fumio and Cho drifted in and out of focus.

Nakaji whispered in Cho's ear, "Hey, Cho, didn't Fumio say that we could tie these girls up and then choke them?"

"I think so. Ask her. She speaks English," Cho said, pointing to the girl sitting next to Nakaji.

"Hey, uh... what did you say your name was?" Nakji said to the woman.

"Keiko."

"Keiko-san, I heard that this is a bondage bar," Nakaji said.

"Yes. We can tie each other up. Do you like that, Nakaji-san?"

"I have never done it. Do *you* like it?" Nakaji asked as he downed another glass of the whiskey/tea. Keiko refilled his glass.

"Yes, I like it, Nakaji-san."

"And I can choke you?"

"Yes."

"I would like do it, Keiko," Nakaji whispered in her ear. And then in Burmese he said, "You will be the first sacrifice to Nat in the new land."

Keiko looked at Nakaji, smiled, and then said, "Just a moment." She got up and spoke to one of the attendants. A wooden chair and a twenty foot length of hemp rope were brought. Keiko sat in the chair. When they noticed what was happening Fumio and Cho applauded, "Hey, Nakaji-san, you are getting into it. Great!" Fumio said.

The girl sitting next to Cho said something to Nakaji in Japanese. Cho translated, "She wants to know if you would like her to show you how to tie *Shibari* knots. They are elegant traditional Japanese knots."

Nakaji stood up, dizzy, steadying himself by grasping the back of the chair. Rope in hand, he said, "No! Nat does not care about elegant knots. He only cares about the blood!"

"Who is Nat? What blood?" Cho asked.

Nakaji looked up at the rounded ceiling of Club Taru and exclaimed loudly in Burmese, "Nat, I feel your spirit! You are back with me! In this new land I offer you this first sacrifice!"

Nakaji started at Keiko's right ankle, tying it to the chair leg with the braided hemp rope and cinching it tight. As he did so Keiko made little cat-like whining noises. More applause came from Cho, Fumio, and the two girls. He then wrapped the rope around her other ankle, and continued working his way up her body.

He got as far as just underneath her armpits, and then, with about six feet of rope left, Nakaji stepped behind the chair and looped the rope around Keiko's neck. Raising his face again to the ceiling, he yelled in Burmese, "Nat, I give you your sacrifice!" Nakaji pulled the rope tight with all his strength.

Keiko's little cat noises turned into a gargled scream. Her eyes went wide as she realized that this was no longer play-acting. Nakaji continued to yell in Burmese as he choked Keiko. Cho jumped up and grabbed Nakaji, trying to pry his hands off the rope. "Nakaji, stop, stop! It is only play choking!" The two other girls started screaming.

One of the screaming girls suddenly picked up a flower vase from the table and smashed it over Nakaji's head. Nakaji stopped his exhortations to Nat, his grasp on the rope went limp, and he fell to the floor. A crowd had gathered around the unconscious Keiko. She was untied and her limp body was carried away. Three angry looking bouncers came towards the group.

Cho dumped a pitcher of whiskey/tea on the prone Nakaji. "Get up, Nakaji! We've got to get out of here!" Cho and Fumio helped Nakaji to his feet and led him past the bouncers and out the door. Fumio hailed a taxi. He pushed Nakaji and Cho in, and said, "I'll take another taxi. I'm going in a different direction. Talk to you guys tomorrow."

Cho gave instructions to the driver, and as the car pulled away from the curb, he turned to Nakaji and said, "What the hell happened to you in there?"

Nakaji, his hair still dripping whiskey/tea, said, "Cho, this country was made for me. I am going to love it here!"

*

Chapter 40

Angela picked up a piece of golden Hainan Chicken with black chopsticks from a red plate as she listened to her father talk. Father and daughter were sitting in a narrow restaurant in Kowloon Tong, the laminate tabletop covered with specialty dishes of southern China.

"You were correct, Angela, Nakaji Sein did go to Japan. He is backed by the Liang Zai Triad's connections to start a heroin business with the Chikuzen-kai Yakuza."

"Great, Dad, that is really helpful. I won't ask you how you found out and how many Liang Zai red-poles suffered before they gave up that information. How to find Sein in Japan is the next question. We have finally obtained the cooperation of the Japanese police."

"The Liang Zai Triad connection with the Chikuzen-kai Yakuza is a Japanese man living in Hong Kong, Fumio Matsumoto. He got back to Hong Kong a few days ago. Shall I grab him for you?"

Angela laughed. "No, you have done enough already, Dad. We will pick him up. Do you have an address for him?"

The next morning at headquarters Angela and Nigel pulled rolling chairs into Ian's cubicle. Angela relayed the information that she had learned about Fumio Matsumoto and the Chikuzen-kai.

Ian said, "I have to ask you, Angela, what is your source? First you came up with The Witch's location in Sham Shui Po, and now you bring information that he is dealing heroin with the Yakuza, and even the name of the Yakuza's Hong Kong contact."

"Can't reveal my source." Angela said, jutting her chin towards Ian.

"OK, fair enough, for now. We need to catch this..he looked at his notes, Fumio Matsumoto, doing something dirty. Put a watch on him. He might sell out Nakaji to get out of a lengthy jail sentence if we can catch him with that heroin."

*****

The heroin shipment from Myanmar came into One Ear's in a tan Samsonite suitcase. It was picked up by a skinny Liang Zai red-pole on a Kawasaki Ninja 500. He strapped it securely to the back of his motorcycle, gunned the engine, and peeled off on the forty minute drive to Fumio's Dynasty Heights eighth floor apartment in Shek Kip Mei.

Angela and Nigel were staked out in an unmarked car in front of Fumio's apartment. "There it is!" Nigel said, as the boy parked his bike on the sidewalk and sauntered to the building lobby, rolling the suitcase behind him.

"Yep, that is a Triad walk, for sure," Angela said. "Walks like he owns the world."

When the red-pole strutted out of the building lobby, minus the Samsonite, Angela was standing next to his motorcycle. As the gangster walked towards her she slowly raised her leg, placed her foot on the Kawasaki, and pushed it over.

"Hey! What are doing, you crazy bitch-woman!" The boy screamed, running at Angela. When he was almost upon her, she held out her badge in one hand and removed her revolver from her back holster with her other. Nigel came up behind the gangster and put handcuffs on him.

With the red-pole sitting in the back of their car, Nigel and Angela banged on Fumio's door. It was a while before they heard him shuffling toward the door. "Who?" The door was opened by a short man wearing only rumpled blue boxer shorts, stick-thin arms, a pot belly, and a full body suit of tattoos.

"Fumio Matsumoto?" Nigel asked, shoving his badge in Fumio's face.

"*Hai.*"

"Please get dressed. You are coming with us."

At the police station Fumio scowled at the two detectives from across the interrogation room table, arms folded. He refused to acknowledge that he spoke Cantonese so they called in police translator Sammy Liu. When the translator finally arrived Angela and Nigel returned to the interrogation room, and Angela said to Fumio in Cantonese, "You have wasted a lot of time. We know that you can speak Cantonese, but no matter, now the translator is here."

Fumio growled a phrase at her in Japanese. The translator said, "He told you to perform oral sex on him."

Angela smiled, still speaking Cantonese, "Here's the thing, Matsumoto, we have a suitcase full of high-grade Burmese heroin that we found in your apartment and we have the Triad punk that delivered it. Your life is over. Thirty years, maybe forty years, in Stanley Prison. I think you are the one who is going to be performing the oral sex."

Nigel said, "Also, I don't know if you are much a history buff, Mr. Matsumoto, but the Japanese were particularly nasty to the Chinese in World War Two. A Japanese prisoner on his own in Stanley Prison, I can't imagine what kind of hell your life will be like."

"What do you want?" Fumio said in Cantonese.

"Oh, now he speaks Cantonese, a quick learner!" Angela exclaimed. "We want Nakaji Sein. No promises, but hand him to us and the prosecutor will take your cooperation into consideration when sentencing. You might get out of jail before you need a wheelchair."

"No. The deal is, I tell you where to find him and I go free. No jail time."

Nigel laughed, "You are in no position to deal, Matsumoto. That won't fly."

"We are going to get Nakaji Sein, with you or without you," Angela said. "If you can make it easier for us, however, it would be in your interest. Think about that." Angela and Nigel got up, thanked the translator, and left the in interrogation room. "Take him to lock-up," she said to the guard.

The air conditioning system was losing the battle with the blazing Hong Kong afternoon sun, as Ian, sweating through his shirt, listened to Angela and Nigel relay the morning's events in the conference room. He stood up and closed the conference room door.

Ian's hands shook. "Look, Guys, I can't sleep, my stomach feels like I have just been sucker-punched. I am numb. I cannot focus on anything but my sister right now. I am afraid that The Witch has her. I cannot accept that he killed her before he went to Japan, but it is a possibility. Even if he hasn't, he may have his Triad friends ship her there."

"Yahh.. that would be bad if The Witch ate your sister," Angela said.

"Angela, statements like that are not helpful," Ian said.

"Sorry…"

"I want you two to go to Japan and track down this sick motherfucker. I need to stay here and search for Sarah in Hong Kong. I believe that she is still here."

"No problem," Nigel said.

"Since the Sein case is international, we will need to involve the Police Commission and arrange a contact with the Japanese police," Ian said. "This has to be a joint operation. I will arrange the meeting with the Commission and help you present a plan of action."

"I have an idea." Angela said. "We know that The Witch will be waiting for Matsumoto to contact him once the drugs are delivered in Japan. I suggest that we let the load of drugs go through. We have Matsumoto's phone. We can text The Witch into a trap after the Yakuza and The Witch get the drugs."

"Yes, let the drugs go through and follow their path to the Witch. However, if The Witch calls Matsumoto in response to the text, the plan would fail. Too many things could go wrong." Ian said. "To trap him in Japan with any chance of success, we will need to take Matsumoto to Japan. Will he cooperate over there?"

"I think that Matsumoto will cooperate if we can offer him jail time in Japan instead of Hong Kong," Nigel said.

"Good. Lean on him. Once he is in line, write up a proposal and review it with me. Then we can approach the Commission."

Chapter 41

Angela handed her work plan, which she had titled *Operation Japan,* to Ian. "Did Matsumoto agree to help us trap Sein?" Ian asked.

"Yes. He went for it." Angela said.

"*'It'* being what?"

"*'It'* is him doing his time in a Japanese prison instead of over here. Once he helps us connect with Nakaji Sein, we hand him over to the Japanese police."

"No, you will hand Matsumoto over to the Japanese police as soon as you get on Japanese soil. Your main role will be escorting Matsumoto to Japan and then escorting Sein back to Hong Kong. Nigel will go with you."

"I have never been to Japan before." Angela said.

"No worries, it's a very civilized place. The Japanese police will give you their cooperation..should be easy."

*****

The video conference was set for 2:00pm Hong Kong time, 3:00pm Japan time. In the executive conference room were Commissioner Gavin Gu, Chief Inspector Tommy Chow, Ian, Nigel, Angela, and a Japanese translator. Precisely on time, the blank video screen came to life showing four Japanese men, sitting stiffly as if posed in a vintage photograph. There were two older men in blue dress uniforms, and two younger ones wearing white shirts with open collars.

One of the younger men spoke first, in perfect English with very little accent, "Hello. I am Detective Shuji Nakagawa. This is Superintendent Kotaro Yamamoto, Chief Inspector Mizuho Kozuki, and Detective Ryosuke Inoguchi." Each man nodded his head as his name was mentioned. The younger men smiled, the older men frowned.

Commissioner Gu introduced everyone on the Hong Kong side. Then, "We appreciate your cooperation, Gentlemen. The Nakaji Sein case is our most visible case. I am sure that you understand the politics involved."

Detective Nakagawa said, "We understand. You will have our full cooperation. We will meet you at the airport, where we will take custody of the prisoner. I, along with Detective Inoguchi, will then lead the capture of your suspect, Nakaji Sein. Your team can accompany us, but they will be observers only. When the suspect is captured, we will turn him over to your team at Narita Airport for transport back to Hong Kong."

"Understand and agree, Detective Nakagawa," Ian said. "Detective Angela Cheung and Detective Nigel Ho are scheduled to leave here with the prisoner tomorrow morning. They will be on Japan Airlines Flight 736, arriving Tokyo, Narita, at 4:05pm."

"Detectives Cheung and Ho, do not disembark the airplane when you arrive at Narita," Nakagawa said. "We will come on the airplane to take custody of the prisoner."

"We will wait on the airplane," Nigel confirmed. Everyone on the Japanese side bowed, everyone on the Hong Kong side awkwardly followed suit, and the screen went blank.

*****

Angela had the window seat. Fumio sat next to her in the middle seat, handcuffed and manacled. Nigel had the aisle. The Japan Airlines jet roared out of Chek Lap Kok Airport, hitting turbulence, rocking and shaking as it ascended into the clouds. Angela turned white and gripped the armrest of the seat. She had never flown before.

Fumio, sensing her discomfit, looked at her and smiled, "Afraid to die?" he asked in Cantonese.

"Shut up," Angela growled, not releasing her death grip on the armrests.

The flight smoothed as the airplane hit cruising altitude and Angela relaxed. Fumio turned to Nigel, "What makes you think that I will uphold my end of the deal? Once I am in Japan, what if I don't call Nakaji-san?"

"Then you will be back on the airplane back to Hong Kong and Stanley Prison immediately, you moron," Nigel answered in Cantonese.

"Moron? No need to be unprofessional, Detective. I did not have much of a choice in my profession, you know. I am a *Burakumin*, untouchable. What should I have done, clean toilets for a profession?"

"I am not interested in what your career options were. It's only three more hours to Tokyo. Just sit there and shut up," Nigel said.

The other passengers stared at the man in handcuffs whenever they passed their aisle. A Japanese boy of about eight stopped for a minute until his mother came up and shooed him on. "I am popular," Fumio said to Angela. "They are looking at me like I am a caged tiger."

Angela sniffed, "A caged monkey is more like it."

The landing at Narita was bumpy. As they touched down and started to taxi to the gate, Nigel turned on his mobile telephone and dialed Detective Nakagawa, "We've landed."

"Great, just stay on the airplane. We will wait until all the passengers get off, then come on and take possession of the prisoner," Detective Nakagawa said.

When the airplane was empty ten uniformed officers in bullet proof vests trotted on, led by Detectives Nakagawa and Inoguchi, both dressed in open collar white shirts, gray slacks, and London Fog overcoats. Angela noted that both Japanese detectives were about thirty years old. Nigel slipped out of his seat and the uniformed officers pulled Fumio to his feet. They then tied a length of thick hemp rope around his waist and led him off the airplane.

"Rope? Isn't that a little old fashioned? He's manacled," Angela said to Nigel in Cantonese.

Nigel shrugged and said, "I read that the Japanese culture embraces both the modern and the old ways."

As the uniformed officers led Matsumoto away, both detectives bowed deeply to Angela and Nigel. "I am Detective Shuji Nakagawa and this is Detective Ryosuki Inoguchi. Inoguchi-san speaks English also. Let's collect your suitcases and we will take you to Headquarters."

"Oh, shit!" Angela said, looking at the detectives' London Fogs. "I forgot that it would be cold here. I didn't bring a jacket."

Shuji smiled. "Don't worry. We will stop at Takashimaya on the way to Headquarters. You can buy a coat there."

Angela said. "But I heard that everything in Japan is unbelievably expensive."

Shuji laughed. "That is the old Japan. Economy is now so bad that prices probably are cheaper than Hong Kong."

The black and white Mitsubishi Diamante police cruiser negotiated downtown Tokyo traffic, Angela and Nigel in the back seat. Evening was descending on the city and the lights of Tokyo were starting to come on in the gray, shoe-box skyscrapers outside the car's window as they inched through traffic.

Shuji turned to the Hong Kong detectives, "When we get to Headquarters we will have to ask you to surrender your weapons. You will then meet Chief Inspector Kozuki. Meanwhile, our team will be processing Matsumoto-san into our system."

"First time you come Tokyo?" Ryosuke asked.

"Yes, Inosuke-san."

"Please, call me Ryo. My English poor. Shuji-san go University Michigan, his English perfect. I only learn university Japan."

"No problem understanding you, Ryo," Nigel said.

"It take time process Matsumoto-san into system. You two like try real Japanese *ramen* on way?" Ryo asked.

"That would be fantastic!" Angela said.

After stopping first at Takashimaya Department Store where Angela bought a down parka, the two Hong Kong detectives found themselves sitting on stools at a wooden bar in a restaurant so narrow that Nigel felt that he could stretch his arms out and touch both walls.

Ryo philosophized about ramen."So many ramen shops Tokyo, but every one different. Each makes noodles and soup, but each also make art. Broth always special chef's recipe. Noodles hand-pulled, hand-cut, cooked perfect, not one second too early, not one second too late. Pork, bamboo shoots, soft boiled eggs, seaweed, completely fresh. You get bowl of hard work and love. *Wakarimashitaka?*"

Shuji laughed and added, "It is actually a survival instinct from samurai days. If a samurai did not like your ramen, or whatever product that you produced or service that you performed, he could cut your head off. As a result, merchants in Japan became very detailed oriented."

Angela took a taste and exclaimed, "This is the best ramen I have ever had!"

*****

When they arrived at the eighteen story, gray-stone Metropolitan Police Headquarters building in Kasumigaseki, Ryo dropped them off at the entry. Angela and Nigel followed Shuji through the security checkpoint, up an elevator, and past cubicles full of assiduous officers. Nigel commented, "All police stations look alike."

Chief Inspector Mizuho Kozuki's office had no pretentions and no personal touches. Mizuho stood up and stiffly bowed as Nigel and Angela, accompanied by Shuji, entered his office. In Japanese, he said, "Welcome to Japan. Please have a seat." Shuji translated.

"Thank you for your cooperation, Chief Inspector," Nigel said.

"You two are observers only while in Japan. Understand?" Mizuho said.

Before Nigel or Angela could answer, a young officer rushed into the office, bowed deeply, apologized profusely, and then, walking over to Mizuho, whispered something in his ear. The Chief Inspector's expression went from gruff to I-have-just-been-dropped down-an-elevator-shaft.

Mizuho quickly jumped up and as he ran out of his office with the young officer, yelled at Shuji, "Come with me! Tell the foreigners to wait here!"

Angela and Nigel looked at each. "I wonder what that's all about?" Angela said. Nigel shrugged.

Ten minutes later Shuji came back into the office, head bowed, shoulders slumped. "Something wrong, Nakagawa-san?' Nigel asked.

"I regret to inform you that Matsumoto-san is dead."

*

Chapter 42

"How can he be dead? He was in police custody!" Angela exclaimed.

"Yes. We are so sorry." Shuji bowed almost to his waist level.

"'Sorry' doesn't explain it! What the hell happened?" Nigel said.

"Suicide. He was in his cell, he swallowed wet toilet paper until he suffocated."

"Take us to him," Angela said.

"No, I cannot. This is a Japanese investigation. You should not involve yourself."

Angela jumped to her feet and screamed, "Take us to him! Now!"

Shuji was shocked by the outburst, but still objected. "I will get into trouble."

"Not as much trouble as you will get in if we make this an international incident. This is a high profile case. There will be a lot of anti-Japanese backlash in Hong Kong if the *Standard's* headline reads '*Japanese police interfere with capture of serial killer*'," Nigel said.

"So no matter what I do I will get in trouble. OK, please follow me," Shuji said. The two Hong Kong detectives followed Shuji down white-washed corridors and gray metal stairs until they got to a level of small cells.

"This is our Isolation holding area," Shuji said. They walked down a corridor that smelled of sweat and fear, pitted concrete floors and rows of five foot by ten foot cells, white bars with chipped paint. The walls of the cells were painted sea foam green at the bottom, creamy white above. On one side of each cell was a narrow bed, in the opposite corner a stainless steel toilet and sink. A steel shelf next to the toilet held a roll of toilet paper.

Fumio's cell was crowded with guards wearing plastic gloves, his body spread-eagled on the floor. As Angela and Nigel tried to enter the cell their way was blocked by one of the guards. "Get out of my way," Angela said in English, her hands balled into fists.

"It's OK," Shuji said to the guard in Japanese, who moved aside.

Angela knelt next to the body. Fumio's open mouth was stuffed with wet toilet paper, the empty cardboard roll lying next to him on the floor. Angela pried opened his shut eyes, and then she put her face inches from Fumio's neck as she carefully studied his skin.

Angela stood up and announced, "This was no suicide. Our prisoner was murdered. Come on, Nigel." Angela marched out of the cell.

"Wait! Where are you going? Why do you say he was murdered?" Shuji sputtered as he trotted closely behind Angela.

Angela was silent, marching back to Mizuho's office. The Inspector was seated at his desk reading a document. He looked up in shock at the sudden intrusion.

Angela turned to Shuji, who, red-faced, had just caught up. "Translate!" She ordered, and then turned back to Mizuho. "Our prisoner was murdered while in your custody. It was not a suicide, and you tried to cover it up. Are you going to give us an explanation?"

"Women should not be so forceful," Mizuho said. Shuji translated.

"You have a problem with women? Then tell my partner your answer instead of me if it makes your tiny penis feel even smaller to explain yourself to a woman," Angela said.

"I will not translate that," Shuji said in English. "Can you please give us the reason, Angela-san, why you are saying that Matsumoto-san was murdered?"

"Matsumoto's neck had petechial hemorrhaging. Those are tiny purple spots on the skin caused by bleeding from manual compression. In other words, he was choked to death."

Shuji translated. Mizuho said nothing.

Angela continued, "Also, the tube from the empty toilet paper roll was laying on the floor on Matsumoto's right side. Matsumoto was right handed, and so would have therefore held the roll in his left hand while he tried to force the paper down his throat with his right. The tube should have been lying on his left side."

"Oh," Shuji said.

"And one more thing, De-tec-tives," Angela said. "The bed was made, the covers still tight. No one had sat on it after it was last made. Matsumoto would have sat on the bed, probably even lay down on it, at least until the guards had left and he was mentally prepared to commit suicide. He was killed somewhere else and brought to that cell."

Mizuho sat without saying anything for so long that Angela wondered if Shuji had translated correctly. Finally he said, "Please have them wait somewhere else so that we can discuss this privately, Nakagawa-san."

Shuji brought Angela and Nigel to an adjacent conference room. "Please wait here and let me find out what is going on. I am very sorry."

Back with the Chief Inspector, Mizuho said, "This rude *gaijin* hag is going to be trouble." Your job was to control them."

"*Hai*, Mizuho-san, but that is difficult when I am kept in the dark. Can you tell me what really happened? I think that only the truth will save our face at this point."

"He was put into the General Population instead of Isolation. I don't know why. That was obviously a mistake. Another inmate killed him."

"So it was murder."

"*Gaijins* think that Japanese commit suicide all the time, so we assumed that they would accept that explanation. Less of an embarrassment for our department…"

"Of course they would find out something like that! Did you really think that we could hide it?"

"That directive did not come from me, it came from higher up. Your failure to control these *gaijins*, however, has exposed us to this loss of face. This is your fault!" Mizuho said.

Ignoring the accusation, Shuji said, "Sir, let's keep in mind that their goal is to catch their serial killer and bring him back to Hong Kong. I would suggest that we help them to find him and they might forget about Matsumoto-san, whom they really had no interest in."

Mizuho considered Shuji's statement, his face a frowning mask. "Good, we will divert their attention away from Matsumoto's death and back to the real reason that they came here. You and Inoguchi-san take them to Fukuoka, out of Tokyo and out of my jurisdiction. I will contact Onuma-san in Fukuoka, let him know that you are coming and brief him on the sensitivities of the case. I am leaving this in your hands, Nakagawa-san. Do not screw it up!"

"*Hai*!" Shuji bowed deeply.

Angela and Nigel looked expectantly at Shuji as he returned and seated himself across the conference table from them. He looked down at his hands for a while, and then said. "Matsumoto-san was obviously handled incorrectly by us, and we are very sorry about that. He was killed by another prisoner in General Population."

"You were right, Angela!" Nigel exclaimed.

"However, please remember that Matsumoto-san was not the goal. He was just a tool. Capturing the serial killer and returning him to Hong Kong was always the main objective. Ryo and I will accompany you to Fukuoka tomorrow and with the help of the Fukuoka police we will capture your killer."

"Why go to..where did you say?.... Fukuoka?" Nigel said.

"Matsumoto-san was Chikuzen-Kai. They are based in Fukuoka. If Sein-san is doing business with the Chikuzen-kai, he would need to be in Fukuoka."

"May we see the tape?" Angela said.

"What tape?"

"Matsumoto was killed in General Population. It would have been recorded on your CCTV security cameras. We would like to see the tape."

Shuji hesitated, this would only get him further in trouble with Mizuho. However, Angela was right, whoever killed Matsumoto may be connected to finding Sein. "Well, I am already in trouble. OK, please follow me."

They took the elevator to the basement, Shuji leading them to a dark room lit by an array of video screens. Five officers were sitting in comfortable rolling chairs watching the screens. When Shuji entered they all jumped to their feet and bowed.

Shuji returned the bow and then requested the General Population room video be played back for them at the time of Fumio's murder. More chairs were rolled over and the three detectives were seated in front of one of the monitors.

The black and white image came to life. "There," Shuji said, pointing to a man standing by himself. "There is Matsumoto-san." They watched as Fumio shuffled around the room, not making eye contact with the other inmates.

"He looks nervous. I think he knows that something is going to happen, that his being placed in General Population was no accident," Angela said.

"No accident?" Shuji said. "Are you suggesting that the police were complicit in his murder?"

"Just saying…" Angela said, staring hard at the screen.

"Look, he's being approached! Three guys with full body tattoos," Nigel exclaimed.

"Yakuza!" Shuji exclaimed.

They watched as two of the men engaged Fumio in conversation while the third circled around behind him. Fumio was obviously agitated, shaking his head 'no', hands up in front of his body defensively. He backed up into the third Yakuza behind him who wrapped his arm around Fumio's neck in a triangle choke hold, applying pressure to the carotid artery.

Within a minute Fumio's body went limp and the man released his grip. The three Yakuza walked away and were quickly absorbed into the rest of the population, Fumio's lifeless body lay on the bare concrete floor, ignored by the other prisoners as if it was not there.

Angela timed it, five full minutes before the guards appeared on the tape and, without a word, lifted Fumio's body and carried him off.

"The Yakuza knew that Matsumoto was here to cooperate with us. They shut him up," Nigel said.

"If the Yakuza knew, Sein also knows. We have lost our advantage of surprise," Angela said.

"Today has been a setback, I know, but tomorrow we go to Fukuoka and follow new leads. When we get there we will have the cooperation of the Fukuoka Division. Ryo will take you to your hotel now and you can rest up for tomorrow," Shuji said.

"OK. Thanks for your help, Shuji. We realize that you didn't orchestrate this," Nigel said.

Ryo was waiting outside the Headquarters building for them in the black and white Mitsubishi police cruiser. "I taking you Tokyo Prince Hotel, three stars, close to Tokyo Tower."

"Thanks, Ryo. You heard about Matsumoto?" Nigel asked.

"Of course, very sorry. Anyway, tomorrow we go Fukuoka. I pick you up your hotel at 8:00am."

Nigel said to Angela, "When we get to the hotel we can make a call to Ian and update him. I am sure that he will want us to stay here and continue to pursue The Witch."

*****

Standing naked in front of the full-length mirror in the Tokyo Prince, her back towards the mirror, her head turned looking at her reflection, Angela rotated her shoulder blades. The Garuda flapped its wings. *I am the Garuda. The prey will not escape. I will not leave Japan until my talons are planted firmly in his flesh.*

Chapter 43

Nakaji stared at his computer screen. The e-mail was from Spider Choi. 'Our Japanese friend went to the hospital. He decided to cooperate with the doctors. They accompanied him to Japan for an operation. Don't worry. I have informed his Japanese relatives.'

The Witch read it a few times to be sure that he understood Spider's meaning. Fumio decided to cooperate with the police? What happened to gangster machismo? And the Hong Kong police have followed me to Japan?

Nakaji's telephone rang. It was Cho. "A car is coming to pick us up in thirty minutes."

"To take us where?"

"I don't know. You may not have noticed, Nakaji, but Japanese gangsters are not real talkative. Just, 'We will pick you up at your hotel in thirty minutes…click'."

"OK. See you in the lobby in thirty minutes."

It was easy to spot the Yakuza as soon as he walked in the lobby of the Nishitetsu Inn: the sneer, the aggressive stare, and the I-own-this-place walk. Seeing Cho and Nakaji, the man in the black suit motioned for them to follow him. Leading them to a black Toyota Avalon, he opened the rear door for them and then slid in next to the driver. Without a word from the two goons in the front seat the vehicle accelerated into Fukuoka traffic.

The driver soon directed the vehicle off the main streets into lanes so narrow that the Avalon's mirrors barely missed scraping the buildings. The car stopped in front of an industrial building. There was no sign, only a green metal door in a tan plaster wall. The man in the black suit turned to Cho and growled, "Get out and knock on the door."

Cho, Nakaji behind him, timidly knocked on the door. They heard dead bolts thrown open on the other side and the door slowly creaked ajar. They were not expecting what they saw on the inside.

A long-legged woman in a mini-skirt and high heels held the door open. "Welcome," she said, bowing deeply. "Please enter."

Behind her was a high-ceilinged industrial space converted into what looked like a clubhouse. Green, red, and blue disco lights flashed throughout the large room. An array of tables and a fully stocked bar were along the side wall. Michael Jackson's Thriller was playing loudly in the background. Cho and Nakaji stumbled in, disoriented. The door was shut and bolted behind them.

The woman bowed again and led them to a table. "Please, sit down. Would you like a drink?" Cho counted five other mini-skirted women sitting at the bar, smoking and staring at them.

"No, no thank you," Cho said. With no idea what they were getting into, the last thing that Cho wanted was for their senses to be dulled by alcohol.

A metal door at the rear of the room was flung open and six men strutted in. Nakaji recognized the one in the lead as one of Choku Kodaira's lieutenants from their first meeting. The man, who was wearing a French beret, seated himself opposite Nakaji at the table. He removed his beret, clipped the end off a long Cuban cigar, and as he lit it with a lighter that looked like a miniature blowtorch, said in Japanese, "I am Jiro."

Nakaji starred open-mouthed at the top of Jiro's bald head. It was tattooed with a Kappa, a mythical beast with the body of a turtle and the beak of a bird, a mischievous creature who lives in mountain streams. Its favorite meal is human children. The Kappa tattoo, in vivid greens, yellows and blues, appeared to be reclining on top of Jiro's head as if sunning itself on a rock, its clawed, webbed hands folded under its chin, a malicious grin across its frog-like face.

"Matsumoto-san became a traitor. We took care of him. I am now your contact for the drug deals," Jiro said.

Cho translated, adding, "I think that is what he said."

"You think?" Nakaji asked Cho, "Aren't you both speaking Japanese?"

"He is speaking Yakuza Japanese," Cho said. "Notice the way that he trills his 'r's'? He is also leaving out consonants, changing sentence structure, using strange Yakuza words, and every other word is a curse word. That's how Yakuza speak. Add on top of that the Fukuoka dialect, and I am getting about seventy percent of what he says."

"Great..Tell him that I had heard about Matsumoto from the Triad. It was surprising, but I'm glad that he took care of it."

Jiro nodded as Cho translated. He then said, "We heard that the first shipment went through and is on its way, but what about the next shipment?"

Nakaji said, "Matsumoto was taking delivery in Hong Kong. Do you want me now to deliver directly to you in Fukuoka?"

"Yes. Can you?" Jiro asked.

"No problem. What is the safest port of entry?"

"We own the southern portion of Fukuoka Port. Next shipment in one week?" Jiro asked.

"Done."

Changing the subject, Jiro's serious countenance turning into a roguish smile, "Do you like this place? Pretty cool, huh?" Jiro swept his arm in a circle. As he did so his suit jacket fell open, and Nakaji noticed a foot long knife in a wooden sheath tucked into Jiro's waistband.

"Yes, very nice, Jiro-san." Nakaji felt awkward making small talk with the gangster. He also found the Kappa distracting.

"I run the largest ward in Fukuoka for Kodaira-san, so I have lots of soldiers. I keep them happy and loyal by providing this great headquarters. Cool lights, music system, full bar, women. There is even a full kitchen with a chef back there." Jiro pointed in the direction of the bar. Nakaji smiled, wanting to leave, sensing an ominous energy brewing.

"Good. Then if business talk is done, I have a gift for you." Jiro said.

"A gift for me?" Nakaji said. All his senses were on high alert. He saw that Cho had also tensed with Jiro's announcement, wondering what sort of a gift such a man would provide.

"I heard that you crossed some boundaries at the Taru Bar the other night." He noticed Nakaji's discomfort, enjoyed it. Laughing, "Don't worry. Gaijins can get away with a lot in Japan. A line that is very clear to a Japanese can be invisible to a foreigner. Actually, I think that your actions were very cool. To seriously choke that bitch must have surprised the hell out of her!"

"I did get carried away. Sorry," Nakaji said.

"No, no need for 'sorry'. I have brought her here for you to finish what you started." Jiro clapped his hands.

From the back of the darkened room two gangsters led a bound and gagged Keiko to the table. Her eyes were wide in terror. She was still dressed in a smart businesswomen's suit. Her neck was bruised dark blue from her previous encounter with Nakaji.

Jiro pulled a six foot length of rope from his jacket pocket and held it out to Nakaji. "Would you to like to finish the job?"

Cho, under his breath, hissed to Nakaji, "This is a test!"

Nakaji smiled and stood, walking up to Keiko. He stared into her eyes. He then calmly turned to the seated Jiro and slowly pulled open Jiro's suit jacket. With his right hand Nakaji grasped the handle of Jiro's knife and pulled it out of its sheath. "The rope is actually not my style."

He raised the knife to the ceiling and screamed in Burmese, "Nat, the sacrifice has returned! This is the blood you want! First sacrifice in the new country!" The gangsters watched, captivated, the Burmese incantations of The Witch electrifying. Suddenly The Witch spun and with one quick slice blood spewed in a geyser from Keiko's neck. The Witch raised his head to the ceiling and screamed in Burmese, "For you, Nat!"

As Keiko started to slide to the floor, Nakaji caught her. He raised her expiring body above his head. A waterfall of red from her sliced neck showered him, splashing the astonished gangsters. He then slammed her body down on the table face-up. Jiro jumped to his feet, his Kappa tattoo dotted with blood.

With Jiro's knife still in his grasp, Nakaji cut away Keiko's business suit, exposing her midsection. "For Nat!" He drove the knife into her, and expertly, deftly, cut out a section of her ribs.

He handed the rib section, dripping blood, to the astonished Jiro, who put out his hand and accepted it with a bow, his face pale, his body shaking. Nakaji said, "Tell your chef to grill this up for me."

"What? Grill it up?....Hai." Jiro said, another bow, and he

obediently turned towards the kitchen, walking slowly and carefully, the ribs held out before him as if he were carrying a bomb about to explode.

"Oh, and Jiro, one more thing." Nakaji said. Jiro stopped and turned back towards The Witch. "Have him put some teriyaki sauce on it for me." Cho translated.

Another bow, and the white-faced Jiro returned on his path to the kitchen, holding the rib section before him in his outstretched hand, leaving a trail of blood on the floor, his clubhouse sound system playing J-Pop in the background.

Nakaji smiled at the astonished Cho, "Did I pass the test?"

"With flying colors!"

Chapter 44

Ian stared out the window at the haze hanging over Hong Kong from his cubicle in police headquarters. The ring of his desk phone snapped him out of his daze. "Ian, this is Officer Sam Wong over at Stanley Prison. One of our inmates has requested to see you."

"Why?"

"He says that he knows who kidnapped your sister."

"What? I'll be right there!"

Ian knew that he was acting irresponsibly as he drove the police cruiser much too fast on the blind corners of the two-lane, undulating road between Central and Stanley. He put on the siren. *I should have asked Officer Wong which prisoner. Why would a prisoner in Stanley know who nabbed Sarah? Was it not The Witch? An accomplice of The Witch? Almost there!* With brakes screeching Ian pulled up in front the eighteen foot high walls of the maximum security facility and sprinted for the entry. He signed in and asked for Officer Wong.

A middle-aged officer with a relaxed demeanor arrived in minutes, affably shaking Ian's hand. "Detective Hamilton, I am Sam Wong. Do you know one of our newer guests named Tony Fan? He came in here with a gunshot wound to the ass."

"Tony Fan? Ruud's partner Tony? *He* is the guy who knows who kidnapped Sarah?"

"So he says. Follow me. I have set him up for you in an interview room," Sam said.

Stanley Prison was opened in 1937, and new layers of paint could not mask the years of pain and cruelty that had transpired there. 'Black Christmas', 1941, the Japanese had taken over Stanley, and prisoners were starved, tortured, and executed. Ian always felt uncomfortable walking the prison corridors, felt like he had stepped into a scene from a vintage horror movie, the ghosts of the unfortunates floating around him.

Tony, manacled and in a prison jumpsuit, was sitting in one of the interrogation rooms. An electric fan ineffectively swept the room, producing more noise than breeze. Ian sat down opposite him, "You have some information for me, Tony?"

"I do, but you know how this give and take works. Can you get me out of here?"

"I can't. However, if your information is helpful, I can bring your cooperation to the attention of the prosecutor, maybe get you transferred to Pik Uk Prison. Pik Uk is five-star compared to Stanley. That is all I can promise."

"Not much of a promise."

Ian exploded across the table and grabbed the front of Tony's jumpsuit. "Another way of looking at it, Tony-boy, is that if you withhold information from me and Sarah gets hurt because of it, you will be an accessory, and I will make sure that you never, ever get out of here!"

"Relax, Detective, I'm cooperating. I would just like to get some benefit for me out of it."

Ian released his grip, and Tony smoothed out his crumpled jail-wear.

"Give it up!" Ian demanded.

"OK, your sister is George Smith's girlfriend, right? George wouldn't shut up about her the whole time that we were hacking through the jungles in Myanmar. All that flamer spoke about was his girlfriend Sarah and her brother, Ian, his good friend, the police detective."

"Yes, Sarah is George's girlfriend. So?"

"A few days ago I had a visitor. I did not know who he was at first because he was wrapped up in a blanket. When he started talking, however, I recognized him. He was Tan, that wimpy-assed architect who was with George and me in Myanmar."

"Tan Lam?"

"Yeah, him. I said, 'Where did you get the blanket?' and he looked at me really crazy, like everyone wears a blanket, and said, 'It's from my mother's couch'. Then he said to me, 'Who's the dickhead now, Dickhead? You're in jail, where you belong.' He then went into a long rant about how George and I destroyed his life. He said that I got what I deserved, and that he was going to make sure that George also paid, that George would find out what it was like to lose what you love. He said that he was going to take George's girlfriend."

"Take her, what does that mean? Take her where?"

"He didn't say. That was the end of the conversation. I don't think that he even knew I was there anymore, just muttering to himself and drifting off towards the door still wrapped in that ridiculous blanket."

"So Tan took Sarah. Tony, thank you." Ian said. "If this information helps us locate Sarah I will talk to the prosecutor about your cooperation. Call me if you think of anything else."

Ian drove slower on the trip back to Central. He called George as he navigated the narrow bends of the road. No answer. He let it ring until the message recording came on, *'This is George Washington Smith, international architect saving the world from bad design. Please leave a message.'*

"George, Sarah was taken by your colleague, Tan Lam. Meet me at police headquarters as soon as you can so we can brainstorm where Tan might have taken her."

As Ian drove, he thought, *Nigel had spoken to the Lam's when Tan was lost in Myanmar. He said that they were decent people. Maybe they can give me a clue as to where Tan might be now.*

Ian parked the cruiser in front of the Lam's apartment in an old part of Kennedy Town, walked past the sleeping guard to the tiny elevator, and ascended to the fifth floor. A woman in her fifties answered the door, the weighty smell of Cantonese cooking wafting out behind her. "Mrs. Lam, I am Detective Ian Hamilton with the Hong Kong Police. You spoke with my colleague, Nigel Ho, about a month ago. I would like to ask you some questions about your son, Tan."

Without saying anything the woman gestured for Ian to come in. She led him to a couch, pointed for him to sit down, and then inexplicably walked out of the apartment, leaving Ian sitting by himself. Ian looked around the room. Shelves of books and mementoes lined the walls as well as numerous family photos of a happy Tan, he and his family posed in various vacation places around the world: the Eiffel Tower, the Sydney Opera House, Fisherman's Wharf, Waikiki Beach. Same pose in each photo. On the wall were a number of amateurish oil paintings of flowers and fruit. The furniture was vintage 1960.

Mrs. Lam returned with a thin Chinese girl of about twelve in a white school uniform. The girl sat next to Ian on the couch and Mrs. Lam sat in a chair facing them. "Mrs. Lam doesn't speak English. I live next door." The girl said to Ian.

"I appreciate your translating then. I am Ian, what is your name?"

"Susie Chiu."

"Susie, could you please ask Mrs. Lam when the last time that she saw her son, Tan, was."

Mrs. Lam started sobbing and replied in Cantonese. Susie translated, "She hasn't seen Tan in over a week. She says his spirit has been stolen."

"His spirit stolen?"

"That is gibberish of course. He has PTSD." Susie said.

"PTSD?" Ian asked.

"Post Traumatic Stress Disorder, just like what soldiers get when returning from war. We learned about it in school."

"Does she have any idea where Tan is now?" Ian asked.

"No. Tan grew up in Hong Kong. He knows every inch. He could be anywhere." Mrs. Lam said, dabbing her eyes with a balled-up tissue.

Ian's telephone vibrated in his pocket, a text message from Nigel, 'Call me. Urgent.'

"Excuse me a moment," Ian said to Mrs. Lam and Susie. He tapped in Nigel's number.

As soon as it rang, Nigel picked up. "We received a call from Robison Whitehorse and Grant, your friend George's architectural office. He was just taken at gunpoint from the office by Tan Lam, wearing a blanket. They left in a gray VW Jetta. We've sent a team over there."

Chapter 45

Ian hung up, stunned. "Mrs. Lam, could I please see Tan's room?"

Tan's room was small, even by Hong Kong standards. The bed was neatly made, architecture books lined up on the shelves. By the window was a small desk. On it was a framed photograph of a smiling, skinny teenage Tan. Surrounded by wild underbrush, the young Tan was standing in front of two concrete tunnels, dark openings about three feet wide by six feet tall which disappeared into a hill. Street names were embossed into the concrete above the openings to the tunnels in large letters. One said *Shaftesbury Avenue* and the other said *Oxford Street*. Next to the tunnel entries was a sign in English and Chinese reading '*Danger. Desolate Trench. Do Not Enter.*'

"Where was this photograph taken?" Ian asked.

"Oh, that is at the Gin Drinker's Line. It was Tan's favorite place to play when he was a kid. He took me there once," Susie said.

"The Gin Drinker's Line?"

"Part of Hong Kong's history, we learned about it in school." Susie lectured, "Completed in 1938, a defensive line of trenches, tunnels, and pill boxes were built by the British from Gin Drinkers Bay to Port Shelter stretching across Kowloon to hold the Japanese advance on Hong Kong. They gave the various tunnels names of London streets so that the British soldiers wouldn't get lost in the tunnels. The whole thing was worthless, of course, and was easily overrun. The Japanese breached it in less than three hours in 1941, actually the same day that they bombed Pearl Harbor."

"Tan took you there?"

"Yes. He loved it. I hated it. It is full of nasty Rhesus monkeys."

"If I showed you a map, Susie, could you show me the exact point where this photo was taken?"

Susie reached into the pocket of her white dress and pulled out her

Samsung. A few taps and she held up an enlarged map. "It is here, right by the Shing Mun Reservoir. Give me your number, I'll forward this to you."

"Thank you, Susie. You are an impressive young lady. If you would like a career in law enforcement when you grow up, give me a call."

"I am going to be a veterinarian." Susie stated.

Mrs. Lam, still patting her eyes, spoke to Ian in Cantonese. Susie said, "She wants you to understand that Tan is a good boy. His spirit has been stolen, that's all. Please do not hurt him."

Ian looked at Mrs. Lam and said, "I understand, Mrs. Lam."

Back in the cruiser and heading to Shing Mun, Ian called Nigel. "It's just a hunch, but I think Tan is holding Sarah and George in the tunnels of the Gin Drinkers Line. Do you know it? I am heading there now, and I need backup."

"Yes, but the Gin Drinkers Line is over ten miles of tunnels. Where on the Gin Drinkers Line?" Nigel asked.

"Next to the Shing Mun Reservoir there is a trail which leads to two tunnel entries. *Oxford Street* and *Shaftesbury Avenue* are the names of the tunnels." Ian said.

"OK, got it. That part of the Gin Drinker's line is called the Shing Mun Redoubt."

"Nigel, bring some fire power with you. I don't know how crazy Tan really is."

"You will need fire power for more than Tan. That area is home to thousands of seriously vicious monkeys." Nigel said.

Despite Susie's map Ian got lost, so he and Nigel, in a van with six other officers, arrived at the Shing Mun Reservoir parking lot at the same time. They found the trailhead and began the hike to the redoubt. Nigel said, "Look", pointing at tire tracks in the mud of the narrow trail. "They took the car up the trail."

"They didn't get far." Ian said. Ahead of them blocking the trail the Volkswagen was wedged between two trees, its sides crumpled. The officers inspected the vehicle and then walked around it, continuing up the path towards the tunnels.

"Here, this is the spot in the photo that was on Tan's desk!" Ian exclaimed. They had arrived at a clearing in the overgrown vegetation. A metal sign bolted to a wooden post read, '*Danger. Desolate Trench. Do Not Enter.*' In front of the sign were two tunnel entrances at ninety degrees to each other; *Shaftesbury Avenue* and *Oxford Street*.

"This one," Nigel said, pointing to fresh footprints in the mud at the entrance to Oxford Street. The officers took out their flashlights and, with Ian in the lead, entered the narrow concrete passageway.

The dark tunnel angled first left and then right and then back again, Ian's flashlight beam bouncing off walls green with mold. Every so often the tunnel would open up to a trench from which the British had planned to fire at the Japanese invaders. In places the tunnel roof had collapsed and daylight streamed in, giving relief from the disorientation and claustrophobia that all were feeling.

Ian suddenly stopped and held up his hand. In a whisper he said, "Voices!" The sound was coming from a side tunnel which branched off to their right. Ian hurried down it, the other officers following. They passed a sign on the tunnel wall which read '*Pillbox 402*'. The tunnel opened up to a twenty foot by twenty foot room. The roof of the pillbox had collapsed years ago, and vegetation had started to grow within the open-air room.

"Ah, the Officers of the Law have arrived." In the center of the room stood Tan Lam, wrapped in the blanket from his mother's couch, a Smith and Wesson .38 in his hand. "Welcome, Gentlemen. I was just explaining how the world works to my guests." He pointed to the side of the pillbox where George and Sarah sat amid the overgrown weeds, their hands and feet bound with vinyl, blue-and-white-striped laundry line.

Ian started to rush towards Sarah but Tan raised his gun, "No, no.... not one more step, Detective or I'll shoot her." Ian stopped in his tracks. "As I was saying, I was just explaining to our very pompous and self-absorbed friend, George Washington Smith, how the world works," Tan continued, pointing the gun at George. "How is this for *Shock and Awe*, George? Do you not feel safe? I never feel safe, George, not since you brought me on our little Burmese adventure."

"Tan, you have had a traumatic experience. We can get you help. You can get over it," George said. "Put down the gun and untie us."

"Giving orders again, George?" Tan sneered. "By the way, do you like this place? It was my favorite place to hang out when I was a kid. I would play that I was defending Hong Kong from invaders, sitting in my pillbox with my machine gun, shooting monsters attacking the city. I would imagine that I was a hero."

"George is right, we can get you help." Ian said.

"You shut up too, Detective Hamilton!" Tan commanded. "Now, how the world works... I am not a hero in real life. I know my limitations. There are people in the world, however, that *think* they are heroes. However, they are not heroes either. They just screw up other people's lives and then when things go wrong they say, '*Oh, sorry, my mistake. Get over it.*' These people are assholes. George here is one of those assholes."

"Tan, I told you, I am sorry for what happened." George said.

"'*Sorry*' is not helpful, George! I want to hear you say, 'Tan, I am an asshole.'"

"Tan, there is no question, I can be an asshole."

"Not '*can be*', George!" Tan yelled. " '*Am*'! I, George Washington Smith, *am* an asshole!"

"OK. I am an asshole!" George squawked.

"Like you mean it!"

"I am an asshole!" George screamed louder.

"Good." Tan threw his gun at Ian's feet. "There are no bullets in it."

The officers jumped on Tan and had him handcuffed in seconds. Ian ran to Sarah and untied her and then untied George. The three hugged as Tan was led out of the tunnel by the Hong Kong Police, his mother's blanket still draped around his shoulders.

By the time they got back to the police cars at the Shing Mun Reservoir the sun was setting behind the hills and the sky was darkening. Tan was placed in the back seat of one of the cruisers. Ian opened the door of the cruiser and said. "Tan, you scared the shit out of me by kidnapping my sister, and also distracted me from an important case. I know that you are mentally fucked up from your little ordeal in the jungle and everything, but Tan, *you* are the asshole." Ian slammed the car door hard and walked back to his own vehicle.

Chapter 46

It was 7:00 pm, and the restaurants in the Soho district of Hong Kong were starting to fill as the glowing lights of the city were coming to life like a million fireflies. There was a promise of wild times in the air. The smell of world-class cuisine from a myriad of international restaurants scented the air. Outside of a French bistro on Elgin Street throngs of people jostled by on the narrow sidewalk: wealthy entrepreneurs, mid-level managers, minimum wage cooks, maids, retailers, students, tattooed twenty-something's, couples on dates; all intent on securing their fair share of a Friday night's celebration.

Inside the French bistro the ambiance was calm, European, sensible. Walnut trim on the walls, a chalkboard menu hanging over the bar, lights on curlicue metal sconces, wooden ceiling fans lazily stirring the air above, and one could imagine that they were in the French countryside. Tika sipped a Beaujolais. Ian sat across from her drinking a martini.

"I can't believe how lucky that bastard is! Our main Japanese connection killed. It does seem like he has some spirit watching over him," Ian said, then looking down at his drink, "Wow, excellent martini!"

"Relax, Ian. At least the psycho is far away from Hong Kong," Tika said.

"It would be nice to catch him though," Ian said. A plate of escargot arrived smelling of olive oil and garlic.

"I agree. But in this life you sometimes have to settle for '*at least*'," Tika said as she tore off a piece of warm bread from a basket in the center of the table and dipped it into the oil surrounding the snails. "At least he's not killing Hong Kong's Indonesian helpers anymore."

"He's probably killing someone somewhere, though," Ian said. He picked up one the escargot with a pair of tongs and, using a tiny fork, dug the morsel out of the shell and popped it in his mouth.

"Angela and Nigel are on his trail, no?" Tika asked, taking the tongs and choosing herself one of the escargot. She followed the delicacy with an oil-dipped piece of the bread and a sip of her wine.

'Yeah, but they are only observers in a foreign country. I am hoping that the Japanese police will follow through for them and capture the freak."

"Hey," Tika said changing the subject, "I got an e-mail from Sarah. She and George are having a great time in Bali. Sarah said that George has changed since their kidnapping experience."

"He changed?"

"Yeah, she said that he's not so self-absorbed. The whole incident has had a positive effect on him."

"George was self-absorbed?"

"You're kidding, right?"

*****

On the top floor of the four-story Fukuoka Police headquarters Angela, Nigel, Shuji, and Ryo sat across a conference table from Chief Superintendent Hirofumi Onuma and Captain Shigeru Makiyama. Onuma frowned as Shuji briefed them on the case.

Shuji concluded by saying, "We have therefore come to Fukuoka, Onuma-san, to find and capture the foreign serial killer, and we are asking for your assistance."

Onuma rubbed the back of his head and sucked air in through his teeth, "*So nan ka naa...* of course we will cooperate, but it will be difficult. The Chikuzen-kai is quite a strange group to deal with." Shuji understood Onuma's wording, an indirect way of saying, '*No, there is too much possibility for screwing up and getting a negative review*'.

"We are aware of that, Onuma-san, however this is an international investigation, and many eyes will be on our performance here," Shuji said. Onuma understood Shuji's wording, '*Any non-cooperation would be made public, which would also result in a negative review*'.

More head rubbing and air sucking. "Ahhh, yes, that is unfortunate.

But of course, we are honored to help." Onuma gave a slight bow, more of a head-bob.

"Good. Thank you, Onuma-san." Shuji said with a slight head-bob back.

Makiyama, who had been sitting straight-backed and expressionless, said, "As this is an international case, we could assign Officer Kotaro Yamamoto. Yamamoto-san trained with the Canadian police in our exchange program last year. If things go bad, it could be blamed on the exchange program."

"Yamamoto-san has very strange ideas, a very rash suggestion, Makiyama-san." Onuma said.

"Yes, Superintendent, please excuse my rashness." Makiyama gave a slight head-bob.

Nigel spoke up, "Wait, we have no idea what you are talking about. Could someone please translate?"

"So sorry, Nigel-san," Shuji said. "Captain Makiyama suggested that an Officer Yamamoto be assigned to assist us as he has had international experience."

"Great. Thanks." Nigel said.

Shuji said to Onuma, "They accept Officer Yamamoto."

"Ahh, there's nothing more for it then. It would look like we are indecisive if we did not assign him. *So nan ka naa*…. 'Unusual Yamamoto' it is then." Then, looking at Makiyama, Onuma said, "Now things have the potential to really get out of control. Better start researching the exchange program, Makiyama-san. We will need to divert blame quickly when things go bad."

"*Hai*, Superintendent," Makiyama said, bowing deeply this time. Then to the group, "Please follow me, I will bring you to Yamamoto-san." They were led to a conference room on the second floor, and Makiyama left to summon Yamamoto. Five minutes later, he returned and introduced Officer Kotaro Yamamoto.

Yamamoto looked young to Angela, certainly no more than twenty-five. *Handsome for a Japanese, though. And he projects strength,* she thought.

"Yamamoto-san is fluent in English. He spent a year with the Canadian police," Makiyama said.

"So then, we can speak English with you?" Shuji asked in English.

"Please do. I do not get very many chances to practice my English." Kotaro said with a bow. Makiyama bowed and left as the conversation switched to English.

Shuji explained the case to Yamamoto, with Angela and Nigel filling in some of the Hong Kong details. When Shuji had finished, Kotaro sat back in his chair and nodded, "Very interesting. We usually do not get such interesting cases in Fukuoka."

"So, what do you suggest as a first course of action to capture The Witch, Yamamoto-san?" Nigel asked.

Kotaro smiled and said, "I believe that Superintendent Onuma probably told you that I am not typical Japanese, that I do not follow typical police procedures. Makiyama-san even warned me not to screw up the investigation with my unusual foreign methods as he walked me up here. However, my superiors sometimes misinterpret my behavior and label it 'non-Japanese' because I act like a samurai, not like a feudal merchant afraid to make a move that will upset someone with superior rank. I suggest, therefore, that we go after your suspect like we are samurais."

"How would a samurai proceed then?" Nigel said.

Kotaro continued, "Nigel-san, do you know about the sport of *kendo*?"

"A couple of guys in protective clothing whacking each other with bamboo swords?" Nigel asked.

Kotaro laughed. "It is very much more than that, more than just sword fighting. It would be a long explanation, so let's just say that my methods of investigation are based on what I learn practicing kendo. Take the initiative with a strong and fast attack, show our spirit and strength, move forward; one step – one blow."

"I like the sound of that." Angela said. "But how do we do actually do it?"

"You had said that your killer is using the alias *'Tat Aung'*. I can have our hotel database checked for anyone under that name, or for any Burmese that checked in recently. We not only raid the hotel, but with the same slice of our sword we strike the offices of the Chikuzen-kai as well. A strong, unexpected assault will expose their weaknesses, maybe create an opening. If we do not get your suspect in our first raid we will at least have unbalanced our enemy. An enemy off balance is easy to defeat."

I can see what Onuma-san was afraid of, he sounds unstable. Very untypical to raid a Yakuza office without over-whelming evidence of a crime, Shuji thought.

"If you want to put it into Western terms, Detectives, we are going to kick some Yakuza ass; one step- one blow." Kotaro said.

"I like this guy." Angela said to Nigel in Cantonese.

Chapter 47

Nakaji sat alone in his room in the Nishitetsu Inn staring at his computer screen as he transferred money from his Hong Kong bank account to his new Japanese account, all under a fictitious identity. His mobile vibrated. It was from Cho.

"Nakaji-san, we need to get out of the hotel immediately! I just got a call from Jiro. The police have found our location and are on the way!" Cho blurted as soon as The Witch answered.

"Where shall we go?"

"Jiro is sending a car. We will meet him at the rear of the hotel in five minutes. Grab your stuff and let's get out of here!"

The black Toyota sped through downtown Fukuoka, Nakaji and Cho sitting in the back seat, Jiro, beret on his head, was in the front. He turned and said, "We have an informant. The fucking police are going to storm the Nishitetsu Inn and then, unbelievably, are going to raid our offices in Momochi Seaside Park. Very aggressive behavior for the police! We were surprised. We are ready for them though."

"So where are you taking us?" Nakaji asked.

"An apartment that we own. Very safe. It is in the *Burakumin* neighborhood. The police will not even go into the community," Jiro said. "Do you know about the *Burakumin,* Nakaji-san?"

"Yes, I do. I am very interested in *Burakumin*. This will give me a chance to find out more about them." Nakaji said.

"Nothing very interesting. Most of our gang are *Burakumin*."

*****

The police descended on the hotel hard. Kotaro wanted to make an impression. No nicely asking for the key to the room. Frightened hotel staff and guests scattered as Kotaro and his platoon of thirty *kidotai* special riot police, with Angela, Nigel, Shuji, and Ryo following, raced through the lobby and up the stairs. With a battering ram they smashed down the door to Nakaji's room.

"Empty! No suitcase, no personal effects. He was warned! Damn it!" Kotaro exclaimed.

The strike force turned and sprinted back to their vehicles. Sirens *whooped* as they raced towards Momochi Seaside Park for their next strike. "This means that the Yakuza know we are coming. We are going to meet an opponent whose sword is already drawn," Kotaro said, clenching and unclenching his hands.

As they exited the vehicles in front of the Chikuzen-kai headquarters Angela noted that Kotaro took a *katana*, a short sword, from the car and strapped it in a sheath to his back. The *kidotai* charged into the building lobby like a herd of bulls, the glass in the entry doors shattering, the granite floors scuffed black by their boots. A new problem, "The elevators are turned off!" someone yelled. "The Chikuzen-kai own the building!"

"The only route up is the stairs, eighty floors. A trap!" Kotaro said. "It is like the one, narrow path into Himeji Castle, where attackers were defenseless as the castle archers rained arrows down on them. We cannot take the one opening that they are offering us. It would be suicide."

Shuji, spotting a metal service door, disappeared into the service corridor. He returned quickly and announced in a hissing whisper, "The service elevator is still working!"

To the Captain of the riot platoon, Kotaro said, "Take the group up the stairs. Rest every ten floors. I will take the service elevator with the Tokyo guys and the foreigners. We will surprise them while they focus on your team climbing the stairwell!"

The riot police went through the double doors of the stairwell and began their ascent. The Yakuza had cut the electricity to the stairwell, leaving the tower completely dark. They police filed up in the blackness like children entering a haunted house, no longer a herd of enraged bulls, hugging the walls, feeling their way. The Yakuza waited for them at the top, calling down obscenities which echoed off the concrete walls through the floors of darkness. "Hey, come up and meet my blade you fucking cops."

The five officers in the metal-sided service elevator did not talk, preparing themselves mentally for whatever confrontation was coming. Angela noticed Kotaro's slow, deep breathing, his intentional calmness. When the elevator doors slid open they stepped into a bare corridor, a fluorescent tube hanging from the ceiling, a line of trashcans along the wall. On the far side of the corridor were a pair of doors. They walked as silently as they could through the doors and found themselves in a large, empty *tatami*-floored room. The adjacent office was also dark and empty. They followed the cries of the Yakuza's vulgar calls. Led by Kotaro, they entered the reception area and came up behind ten Yakuzas yelling down into the stairwell.

"What have we here? Scrawny, tattooed roosters crowing in the barnyard?" Kotaro said loudly as he grabbed the first one, left hand on the man's collar and right hand his belt. Kotaro dragged the man backwards, and then lifted the Yakuza by his belt and dumped him unceremoniously on his butt. The man howled in surprise. The rest of his gang turned.

"What the hell are you doing, you snooping-dog Cop?" Growled one of the Yakuza, as he drew a twelve inch blade from his belt and approached Kotaro. The man lunged, knife first.

Kotaro stepped to the side and, his movements a blur, pulled the *katana* from the sheath on his back. One smooth movement, a blur of silver in the air, and the man's hand was cleanly sliced off. It lay on the gray granite tile floor of the office lobby, still clutching the knife. The Yakuza sunk to his knees, his stump spouting blood, a look of surprise on his face. The others stood frozen, soundless.

"Where is your *Oyabun*?" Kotaro demanded.

"He is not here. Are you blind, or just stupid?" One of the gangsters snapped.

Kataro's sword flashed again, coming to a sudden stop at the gangster's eyelash. "Blind? You are lucky I am not."

"Go to hell, Cop."

"Where are you hiding the fugitive? Where is the Burmese man?" Kotaro demanded.

"He's up my ass. Want to search for him, Cop?" another one of the gangsters sneered.

Kotaro's kick snapped powerfully into the man's ribs, propelling him backwards into the wall. Shuji and Ryo's guns were drawn, keeping the remainder of the Yakuza at bay.

The police platoon finally arrived at the top of the stairwell, visibly winded from their long climb to the eightieth floor. "Take these scum into custody." Kotaro said to the commander. "The elevator machine room should be one floor up on the roof, so you can turn it back on and won't have to walk down."

Before any of the police could respond, however, one of the Yakuza, shirtless, his body covered with tattoos of flowers, fish, and devils, yelled "Bastard Cops!" He pulled a knife from his waist band and drove the blade to the hilt into Nigel's side.

Nigel collapsed backwards, his hand clasped to his wound, blood running between his fingers, his eyes wide with shock. While two policemen bludgeoned the Yakuza who had stabbed Nigel unconscious, another officer radioed for medical help. Nigel was instantly surrounded by a team of men trying to staunch his bleeding as he was lowered gently to the floor. One of the officers sprinted for the elevator room.

Within fifteen minutes the ambulance staff had arrived. They strapped the wounded Hong Kong detective to a gurney. Angela held Nigel's hand as they wheeled him off. Trotting alongside the gurney, Kotaro on the other side, she said, "Don't leave me in Japan alone, Nigel! I am not going to back to Hong Kong without you, you hear me?"

Chapter 48

Shuji and Ryo returned to headquarters with the platoon while Kotaro and Angela accompanied Nigel to the hospital. The flashing blue roof light of the ambulance parted the Fukuoka evening traffic.

Japan or Hong Kong, hospital waiting rooms all look the same, Angela thought as she and Kotaro were ushered into the hospital's waiting area. Nigel had been wheeled away to Intensive Care, a sextet of white-uniformed nurses surrounding his gurney.

Angela dialed Ian's number. Kotaro sat next to her on a worn blue couch. *How many anxious relatives have sat on this couch, waiting for news?* When she heard Ian's voice on the other end, she said, "Nigel was stabbed."

A pause, then, "How bad?"

"The doctors say that he will live, but it is a pretty deep wound. He's in ICU." Angela filled him in on the raid.

"Damn. And The Witch is still at large?"

"Yeah."

"I am flying out there tomorrow."

"You don't have to."

"Yes, I do." Ian hung up.

Angela put away her phone and asked Kotaro, "Any update?"

"No, he is stabilized and sleeping. I do not think that there is much more going to happen tonight." He looked at his watch. "Can I take you to dinner?"

A short taxi ride away, Angela found herself in a tiny tempura restaurant sitting at a wooden bar, she and Kotaro eating deep fried shrimps, vegetables, and drinking chilled sake. The tempura chef, wearing a blue cotton coat with black trim and a blue bandana on his head, deep fried the delicacies in front of them as they watched. Angela inhaled the aroma of the delicately frying food and the earthy fragrance of the sake.

"I thought sake was supposed to be served warm." Angela said, as she sipped from her cup.

"In the old days, yes, but that was when all sake was brewed in wooden barrels. The sake took on the strong flavor of the wood, and warming enhanced the flavor. Today, however, sake is brewed in steel containers. The best sakes have very complex flavors, not just the flavor of the wooden casks. Warming them would mask the delicate flavors."

"Tastes great, I love it." Angela said as she sipped the chilled brew. They finished the small bottle, and Kotaro ordered another.

"Back to business; we have a big problem, Angela." Kotaro said. "An informant must have tipped off the Yakuza. We cannot gain the advantage until we find this informant."

"He's in your department, you think?"

"Could be." Kotaro said, pouring more sake into his and Angela's cups.

"Oh, by the way, my boss, Detective Ian Hamilton, is coming to Japan, probably will be on a flight tomorrow."

"I will call Shuji and let him know. He can coordinate meeting Ian-san and escorting him to Fukuoka."

"I'll go with them." Angela said.

As Kotaro chatted with Shuji on the telephone, updating him on Nigel's condition and asking him to make arrangements to meet Ian at the airport, Angela continued to sip the sake from her small, porcelain cup. Soon drained, Kotaro ordered another bottle, as well as some *edamame* and dried squid. Angela said, "Hey, Kotaro-san, your face has turned bright red. Are you a light-weight drinker?"

"All Asians get red-faced when they drink." Kotaro said with a grin.

"No they don't. *You* get red-faced. I am also Asian, in case you hadn't noticed, and I am fine." Angela said.

"Hah!"

"Hey, cutting off that guy's hand today, you don't get in trouble for that here? In Hong Kong you would have had some explaining to do."

"Here, I am a 'corner desk man', not worth reprimanding."

"What the hell does that mean?"

Kotaro laughed. "In Japan when an employee falls out of favor he is dispatched to a corner desk by the window. His career is over. No one pays him any attention. Because they think that I have learned crazy ideas from working in Canada they consider me 'un-Japanese', and I have been so dispatched. I am not worth the trouble."

"You learned crazy ideas working in Canada?"

"Not at all. I have always been this way, I am very traditional Japanese." Kotaro drained his cup and poured another. "Angela, do you ever feel like you are possessed by a spirit, by a powerful force from outside yourself?"

"I do, Kotaro-san! You do also?"

"I am possessed by the spirit of Miyamoto Mushashi! Do you know who he is?" Kotaro was beginning to slightly slur his words.

"No."

"He was the most famous Japanese swordsman! He was never defeated. He also was a painter and a writer. Besides 'The Book of Five Rings', the definitive book on sword strategy, he wrote 'The Way of Walking Alone'. When I read those books I feel like I wrote them myself."

Angela, also feeling flush from the alcohol, decided to open up to Kotaro. "Kotaro, I feel possessed by a spirit too. I am host to the spirit of the Garuda."

"The Garuda spirit?"

"It's a mythical Indonesian bird. They are guardians and protectors. The Garuda has brought me out of a life of poverty and hopelessness. When its spirit enters me I am more than I am when alone. The Garuda gives me power."

"Yes! Mushashi's spirit gives me power too!"

Kotaro started to order another sake, but Angela put her hand on his arm. "I have had enough, Kotaro-san. Can you take me to my hotel?"

As he ordered the bill, Angela whispered in his ear, "Or you can take me to your place."

*****

Kotaro traced his index finger over the lines of the Garuda on Angela's back as she slept, and wondered if he should get a tattoo of Miyamoto Mushashi on his.

Chapter 49

By 9:00 am everyone at the Fukuoka Police Station knew that Officer Kotaro Yamamoto had exceeded his usual misadventures. Not only had the suspect escaped capture, one of the foreign detectives had gotten stabbed. It was a loss of face for the whole department.

Kotaro stood, head bowed, in Chief Superintendent Onuma's office. Onuma and Captain Makiyama glared at him. After five minutes of silence, Onuma exclaimed while scratching the back of his head, "Sssss…..again, Yamamoto-san! When are you going to stop embarrassing us?"

"I am sorry for my incompetence, Chief Superintendent."

"What did I do to deserve the likes of you on my force? Why did I think that assigning you to the foreigners was a good idea?"

"I am sorry, Onuma-san."

"You are a fool! *Bakayaro*! What shall we do, Makiyama-san?"

Makiyama said, "Detective Hamilton from Hong Kong is arriving in Tokyo today. Nakagawa-san and Inoguchi-san will take the woman detective to meet him at Narita Airport and escort him back here. When they get to Fukuoka, Yamamoto-san should present to the foreign detective a detailed report in English on the status of the investigation and apologize for the stabbing of his colleague. It will be better to look like organized bunglers rather than just common bunglers. Or Yamamoto-san can commit *seppuku*. That would be appropriate in this situation."

"No need for Yamamoto-san to commit suicide, the Western detective would not understand the gesture." Onuma said. "The report should be sufficient."

"*Hai*, Makiyama-san!" Kotaro said, bowing deeply from the waist.

"Please try and not embarrass us anymore between now and then!"

"*Hai!*" Kotaro said, bowing again as he backed out of Onuma's office.

*****

Angela marveled at the beauty of Japan as forested rural hills and ancient plaster and wooden houses sped by her outside the window of the bullet train speeding towards Tokyo, Shuji and Ryo in the seats next to her. She was listening with only half her attention as Shuji explained the relationship between the Yakuza and the police. The other half of her mind was on the night before spent with Kotaro.

"It is very complicated, Angela-san," Shuji said. "The Yakuza are entwined with legal society, including financial companies and the stock market."

Ryo added, "There is also cooperation between police and Yakuza. We are not total enemy."

A vendor selling boxed lunches wheeled a stainless steel cart down the aisle. "Would you like a *bento*, Angela-san?" Ryo asked.

"Huh? Oh, no thanks." Angela's focus returned to the inside of the train car. "Could you please call the hospital and check on Nigel's condition?"

After a brief conversation on his phone, Ryo said. "He doing well. Can return Hong Kong about one week."

"Great. Let's focus on Nakaji Sein then. How are we going to find him?" Angela asked.

"Sein is a foreigner. Foreigners are easy to find in Japan. They are obvious. We will catch him very soon," Shuji said.

"Well he hasn't been obvious so far," Angela answered, and went back to starring out the window.

At Tokyo Station they transferred to the Narita Express for the airport. They arrived early so they took seats at Tully's Coffee.

"Do you think that your suspect will have trouble getting the heroin out of Hong Kong?" Shuji asked, sipping his coffee.

Angela answered, "No, it's easy enough for him to get the drugs into Hong Kong from Myanmar, it should be no trouble getting it out. His Triad partners will smooth the way for him. What about getting it into Japan on this end? Difficult?"

"The Chikuzen-kai controls the Fukuoka Port. It will be easy for them to get drugs in here also."

"So how do we mess them up?" Angela asked.

"Can you track the heroin in Hong Kong, follow it to Japan?" Shuji asked.

"A good suggestion, follow the heroin. The trick would be locating the shipment, but with some luck maybe a possibility." Angela made a mental note to see if her Dad could find out the details of the Liang Zai shipment to Japan. She looked at her watch. "Let's head to the gate. Ian's plane should be landing."

From two tables away a thin Japanese girl in a pink cotton dress watched them, sipping a cappuccino and pretending to read a paperback. Kiwi Watanabe looked like a typical teenager, although she was twenty-three years old. Always smaller than her classmates, at the age of nine her sister had nicknamed her 'Kiwi' after the fruit and it had stuck.

Kiwi had always felt awkward in the world. Even when in a group she felt alone. She considered herself ugly, with ears too big for her tiny body and a mouth full of uneven teeth. The large ears were the worst part, a stick of a girl with the ears of an African elephant.

She thought back to her high school years. "Can you hear me, Kiwi-san?" one of the 'popular girls' would taunt her, alluding to Kiwi's generously-proportioned ears protruding between the strands of her thin, stringy hair. "I don't think that you can hear me, Kiwi-san." The other 'beautiful girls' would then slice Kiwi to pieces with their laughter, sharp as any *katana*.

At the beginning of her senior year Kiwi had started plotting. She surprised herself at how quickly she had devised a plan. First she studied the habits of what she called *The Project*. She followed *The Project* wherever she went. Kiwi was delighted to learn that the skill of blending into the background unseen came easily to her. *I am a ninja!* She liked surveillance. To see without being seen thrilled her.

Every Tuesday night *The Project* would go to English Study Session, walking home alone when the class ended at 9:00pm and crossing the Shuto Expressway at the Wakami-cho overpass bridge at exactly 9:15pm. *That is where you will meet your demise. I am going to really do it, not just imagine doing it. Can you hear me now, Bitch?*

On a moonless Tuesday night Kiwi positioned herself against the guardrail at the center of the overpass bridge and covered her body with a blanket. *I look like a pile of rags on the ground.* The bridge at that hour, as always, was deserted, dark except for circles of illumination cast by the two light poles at the ends. Kiwi felt calm as she waited under her blanket. *The Project* was the interloper in this new 'Kiwi World'. *I am a dangerous ninja hidden from the world.*

Finally she heard the pad of sneakered feet on the pavement. She could picture the white, low-top sneakers and white leggings on *The Project's* perfect calves. As the footsteps passed she sprung from underneath the blanket.

Throwing the blanket over *The Project's* head, she spun the 'beautiful girl' in circles. Then, using the momentum of the surprised girl, flung her towards the rail of the bridge. *The Project* grabbed for the rail as she catapulted over, hanging for a few seconds by one hand before she dropped into the traffic of the busy Shuto Expressway twenty feet below. *I can hear you now, Popular Girl.*

Kiwi had giggled in delight all the way back home. She had found a purpose, a path in life. *I am an assassin,* she had said to herself, *and a damn good one at that.*

As Angela, Ryo, and Shuji stood up to walk to the gate, Kiwi said out-loud to herself, "They are going to the gate now to meet the Hong Kong detective. Kill them before they get to Fukuoka, Kiwi-san." A couple at an adjacent table turned to stare at the thin girl talking to herself. Kiwi could not stop herself from giggling, hand over her mouth to hide her uneven teeth, as she followed *The Projects* to the gate.

Chapter 50

Jiro had put Nakaji and Cho into a two-bedroom apartment in the *Barakumin* ghetto. The community was the antithesis of a Japanese neighborhood, missing the quintessential ordered neatness of typical Japan. Masonry walls were scrawled with graffiti and the streets were littered. Uncollected, stinking piles of garbage decorated every block. The averted glances and polite demeanor of traditional Japan were replaced with brazen looks of challenge and hostility.

As Nakaji and Cho sat in their new living room drinking Kirin Beers and watching baseball on an ancient TV, the Fukuoka Hawks playing the Hiroshima Carps, Cho's mobile vibrated. It was Jiro. Nakaji could hear the guttural tones of the gangster over the speaker. Cho hung up and said, "Good news. The shipment has arrived. Jiro-san says Choku wants to celebrate with us. They will pick us up in thirty minutes."

As Cho and Nakaji stood outside the apartment building waiting for the car, an old man on a red bicycle peddled up to them and stopped. Six small Japanese flags on wooden sticks flew from the handlebars of the man's dented bike. On the man's head was an upside-down spaghetti strainer to which he had sewn the ears of a teddy bear doll. The tattoos on his flabby arms protruding from his worn T-shirt attested to his Yakuza past.

"Good evening, foreign men. I am The *Tenuki*, the badger," the old man said.

"I am not a foreigner," Cho said.

"You are not from this neighborhood. In this neighborhood you are a foreigner," The *Tenuki* said.

"OK, point taken." Cho chuckled. Nakaji watched with curiosity, having no idea what was being said but noted the man's strangeness.

"Badgers have huge testicles," The *Tenuki* added.

"Good for you." Cho stared at the man, hoping that the car would come soon.

"I can offer you protection. This is a dangerous neighborhood. The police do not even dare to come in here."

"We do not need your protection," Cho answered.

"No, you do. Do you think that The *Tenuki* does not know that you are guests of the Chikuzen-kai? A badger is smart as well as fierce."

"So we do not need you," Cho said.

The Chikuzen-kai cannot protect you here. This neighborhood is *Barakumin*. No fear of the Yakuza, or of anyone. It will only cost you five hundred yen per week."

Cho laughed. "Sorry, Old Man. Take your huge testicles someplace else."

The car arrived and Nakaji and Cho climbed in. "What was that about?" Nakaji asked.

"That old man was trying to shake us down for protection money."

"Typical. Do you know where we are going?"

"Jiro said it was a club called *Okuri-inu*. The *Okuri-inu* is a mythical dog-spirit who follows travelers through the mountain woods and rips them apart if they stumble."

"Nice. Let's not stumble tonight."

The car navigated narrow lanes until it pulled into a circular drive, the sound of decomposed granite grinding beneath the wheels. They stopped in front of a large, European style, stone-faced building. The massive entry doors of the structure were flanked by two neon sculptures of slathering, wolf-like creatures with long, menacing claws and teeth.

Nakaji and Cho were greeted at the door by a woman in a yellow kimono embroidered with purple peonies and blue butterflies. Two muscular goons in black suits stood next to her.

"Welcome to *Okuri-inu*," the woman said with a deep bow. "Kodaira-san is expecting you. Please follow me." She turned and, with her stride restricted to tiny, shuffling steps by the tight kimono, appeared to float down a hallway of black marble floors and ochre-colored plaster walls.

The hallway ceiling was covered with wood lattice, lit from below by sconces on the walls. Every once in a while they would pass a *tokonoma*, a recess in the wall, which would contain either a flower arrangement or a hanging scroll. Nakaji and Cho obediently followed their seemingly weightless, ghost-like guide. She led them to a raised foyer of dark wood. The woman bowed and pointed to a wooden shoe rack along the wall.

"We need to remove our shoes." Cho said to Nakaji. They were given slippers and then were led down a winding corridor, their kimonoed guide stopping at a pair of sliding screen doors. The doors were painted with a flock of white and black cranes flying through white clouds on a gold background. The woman got on her knees, slid open the golden doors for them, and from her kneeling position bowed until her forehead touched the floor.

Nakaji and Cho entered an expansive room the size of a concert hall and gaped in amazement at the scene before them. In the center of the *tatami*-floored room was a circular, three foot high, red-earth sumo ring. A thick hemp rope circled the edge of the ring. Radiating outward from the raised circular sumo ring, brown pillows were strewn on the *tatami* floor. About fifty shirtless, tattooed Yakuza lounged on the pillows around the ring, drinking beer, smoking, placing bets, and yelling encouragement to the combatants in the ring.

The combatants, however, were not the massive mountains of men traditionally found in a sumo ring. They were dwarfs, females, wearing only a *mawashi*, a cotton loin cloth. In the center of the ring, between the two dwarfs, was a full size man, the referee, also wearing only a *mawashi*. He had a full tattoo body suit and was holding a wooden fan. The two women, glistening with sweat, glared at each other from either side of the ring.

At a call from the referee, the dwarf wrestlers strutted to the center of the ring, throwing salt in the traditional fashion, slapping their *mawashi*, and crouching down in the ready squat. As soon as their knuckles touched the earth, they launched themselves at each other. Their bodies accelerated powerfully, slamming together with a *thwack*, each locking a grip on the other's *mawashi* as they tried to push each other out of the ring. The audience's screams of delight and encouragement were deafening as the women strained in their efforts, each trying to unbalance the other. Bets were yelled from men waving notes of various denominations above their heads.

Cho spotted a man in a black suit walking towards them. The man bowed curtly and motioned for them to follow him. He walked them to a privately screened alcove where five gangsters sat around a glass coffee table. In the middle of the group, ensconced on a purple couch, wearing a pirate's patch over his bad eye, sat Choku Kodaira. Dressed in yellow slacks and a green sports jacket, with no shirt underneath, he wore Ruud's mummified hand on a chain around his neck.

When he saw Nakaji and Cho, Kodaira stood up, and, as his jacket fell open, flowing tattoos of mythical creatures, ghosts, and demons came to life on his bare chest. Sitting on the table in front of him were the ten bricks of Burmese heroin that Nakaji had sent from Hong Kong. Jiro, the kappa tattoo contentedly smiling from atop his bald head, stood behind Kodaira. "The snow has arrived. Your people delivered, as promised, Nakaji-san. Thank you." Cho translated.

Nakaji said, "No problem, Kodaira-san. Would you like the next shipment in one week or two weeks?"

"Jiro will work out the details with you. Meanwhile, please sit down and enjoy the evening." He indicated with a sweep of his hand that Nakaji and Cho sit next to him on the couch. Jiro clapped his hands and the heroin bricks were whisked away.

Four kimono-clad women then brought small plates, chopsticks, and shallow bowls containing soy sauce and bright green *wasabi*. A large dish of artfully arranged sashimi was placed in the middle of the table, slices of tuna, yellowtail, and sea bass. Also, two bottles of Gray Goose vodka and glasses appeared.

"Ah, my favorite vodka. It is French," Kodaira said, as the woman poured four glasses. "To a long and successful relationship! Kompai!" Kodaira held his glass up and then drained it. Nakaji, Cho, and Jiro followed.

"How are your accommodations?" Kodaira asked Nakaji.

"Very nice. Thank you for your hospitality, Kodaira-san."

"Very nice?" Kodaira laughed. "Good! However, I know what you are planning. Forget about it."

"What? What I am planning?" Nakaji asked as Cho translated.

Kodaira drained another glass of the Gray Goose. "I know all about your tastes, Nakaji-san. Actually, I think it is pretty cool. You are planning on harvesting the *Burakumin* women in your new neighborhood."

Nakaji was caught by surprise. "No, I, uh…."

'I would be if I were you. Anyway, forget about it." Kodaira said. "The Yakuza are mostly *Burakumin*. They are our people, under our protection, off limits to you."

"I assure you that I will not….." Nakaji stammered.

"However, not to worry, Nakaji-san. There is other game to be had," Kodaira said.

"Other game?"

"Koreans. Nobody cares about Koreans in Japan." Kodaira clapped his hands. A chubby Korean girl, pudgy fingers and double chin, in a short, white dress, high heels, and a tight blouse, was led in and directed to the couch. "This is a Korean girl. She thinks that she is supposed to have sex with you. No one will miss her. When you leave tonight, take her to Jiro's place. You can use his kitchen." Kodaira whispered to Cho, "I thought that he would like a girl with some meat on her bones."

Chapter 51

The seats on the express bullet train returning to Fukuoka from Tokyo rotated, so Angela and Ian could sit facing Ryo and Shuji. Once the speeding *Shinkansen* left the lights of urban Tokyo and reached full speed, the only illumination outside the windows were the pinpoints of stars in the darkness. Ryo and Shuji stood up and excused themselves to go to the smoking car.

Three seats back, head down and pretending to read a novel, Kiwi said to herself, *Ah, the two Japanese detectives went for a smoke; a good chance.* She stood up and moved towards *The Projects*, putting on a pair of plastic gloves and taking her gun, a SIG Sauer Mosquito with silencer attached, out of her Hello Kitty handbag.

She planned to slip unnoticed into the empty row behind *The Projects* and silently pump a bullet into the foreign man's obscenely giant body through the seat. Then the Asian woman would be next. She would leave the pistol in the pouch at the back of the seat, the weapon untraceable to her, and then slip away unnoticed back to her seat, an innocent young woman on her way to a Fukuoka holiday.

As she stood up she noticed a salary man in a wrinkled white shirt reading a comic book in the next row of seats. He had taken off his shoes. Kiwi froze. *How crude of him! Does he think that everyone wants to smell his feet?* She imagined the smell of man's feet, imagined a pervasive stench fouling the air of the train car. The thought of the odor overwhelmed her. It was consuming her, polluting her. She started gagging. Kiwi had always been like that, one irritant would so take over her mind that she could think of nothing else. *Focus, focus! Forget about that rude person! There is a* Project *to kill.* Her left hand rubbed her temple trying to erase the distraction.

Her concentration overwhelmed by the salary man's rudeness, she forgot to conceal the gun that she was clutching in her right hand. A young woman in a blue uniform with a white apron pushing a *bento* cart entered the train car from the other end. She saw the gun in Kiwi's hand and screamed, a sharp, metallic '*eeee*'.

Already agitated by the salary man and his lack of consideration for her olfactory senses, the scream of the *bento* girl triggered an immediate reaction from Kiwi. "Shut up, Bitch! Popular Girl!" she yelled, and fired a bullet into the girl's forehead. The 'phhtt' of the silenced shot, and the salesgirl's scream stopped abruptly. A red dot, like a Hindu's *bindi*, appeared as if by magic above her eyes. She fell backwards.

The horrified passengers then watched as Kiwi shouted, "And you put your shoes back on, you rude man!" Kiwi put a bullet into the head of the salary man, who had looked up in confusion from his comic book at the commotion. "Rude, horrible man!" Kiwi yelled again, pumping more bullets into him until her clip was empty.

Ian jumped to his feet as soon as the red circle appeared between the *bento* girl's eyes. He saw the thin girl with the gun take aim at the man in the row behind him, the man go limp as life vanished from his body. Ian dove, and in seconds Kiwi was on the floor and disarmed. Shuji and Ryo, returning from their smoke break, came running. Kiwi, spitting invectives, was handcuffed to a seat.

The train police also arrived, but, used to nothing more serious than the occasional pickpocket, deferred to Shuji and Ryo in regards to the prisoner, busying themselves with moving the passengers to another car and radioing the conductor to stop at the next station. Ryo called ahead to the Shin-Iwakuni station, notifying the local police to meet them with a coroner.

Ian rotated the seat in front of the handcuffed Kiwi to face her and sat down. Shuji sat next to him to translate, Ryo stood next to them. As they sat down, Kiwi, like a captured feral cat, snarled, hissed, and spat on the officers.

"Are you OK? I hope that I did not hurt you when I tackled you. Would you like a bottle of water?" Ian said as he wiped the spittle from his face. Shuji translated.

Kiwi responded to Ian's tone, her glare relaxing, eyes half-closing, "That would be nice, thank you." Kiwi said. Ryo ran for a water bottle.

"Why did you kill those two people?" Ian asked.

"I did not intend to, you were whom I was intending to kill, and I would have too if those rude insects hadn't distracted me." Kiwi eyes flashed back to anger.

"You wanted to kill me?" Ian continued. "That's OK. I do not take it personally that you were going to kill me. It's only business, right?"

"Yes, of course it is just business. People are cockroaches. It is of no matter to eliminate them. You are just another cockroach." Kiwi said.

"True, I understand your point. But you were hired by one of those cockroaches, right? Well, I want to eliminate that cockroach. Can you give me his name?"

"That would be unprofessional of me."

"What is your name?" Ian asked, changing the subject.

"Kiwi, like the fruit."

"Kiwi, I am Ian."

"I know who you are, stupid. I was hired to kill you, remember?"

"Kiwi-san, acting professional doesn't matter anymore. Your business is over. The truth is, you will no doubt be executed, or at the very least, spend the rest of your life in prison or a mental institution. Give up the cockroach that hired you. Let me rid the world of one more insect," Ian said.

"You are just talking nice to me because I have information that you want. However, I know what you are thinking. What you are really thinking is, *'Her ears are much too big for her head'*, aren't you?" Kiwi responded.

"I didn't notice your ears, Kiwi. Whatever I think doesn't matter. This is your last chance to add one more cockroach to your list before you go to jail."

" *'Big ears'*, I am sure that is what you are thinking!" Her lips curled back in a snarl, revealing her mouth of uneven teeth. She spat on Ian again.

After wiping off the new spit, remaining calm, Ian asked. "Who hired you, Kiwi, the Yakuza?"

"The Yakuza? No, they do their own killing in Japan. Why would they hire Kiwi?"

Angela had walked up, and, standing next to Ian, said, "That is a beautiful jade pendent you are wearing around your neck, Kiwi. Did a Chinese client give you that?"

"Yes." Kiwi said beaming. "It *is* beautiful! Triad from Hong Kong gave it to me as a deposit."

"A Triad hired you to kill us? Which Triad?" Angela asked.

Kiwi shrugged. "No idea. Chinese guys. Spoke really bad Japanese, but I could understand mostly. Two hundred thousand yen for each of you. Four hundred thousand yen for the Burmese guy. They were unfamiliar with Japan, so they hired a Japanese professional," Kiwi said with pride.

"They wanted you to kill Nakaji Sein also? How did they contact you?" Ian asked.

"Through my website. You should visit, *kiwikills4u.com*. You can 'like' me on my Facebook page too. I send links to all international criminal organizations: mafia, Triads, Columbian drug smugglers, Russian extortionists. They have web pages too."

"They have websites?" Ian asked incredulously.

"Yes. Twitter too." Kiwi said. "You are pretty stupid."

The four detectives left Kiwi handcuffed to the seat and went to a bank of seats at the back of the train car.

"What a nut case!" Angela said.

"Yes." Ian said. "Shuji and Ryo, please take her back to Tokyo. See if you can find out which Triad hired her."

The train slowed down, pulling into Shin-Iwakuni Station. As soon as the doors opened a team of twenty police entered the car. The train became a crime scene. Everyone was evacuated except those passengers unfortunate to have been in the car when Kiwi started shooting. Their statements were taken for hours. The local coroner took possession of the bodies. It was 11:00pm by the time Angela and Ian were able to catch a local train to Hiroshima and then transfer to the 11:25pm *Shinkansen* express to Fukuoka.

As the bullet train sped at 200 kilometers per hour towards their destination, Angela said to Ian, "There is one guy in the Fukuoka police department that we can trust."

"Oh, yeah?"

"His name is Kotaro Yamamoto."

Ian thought, *That is a strange thing for Angela to say. She is usually skeptical of everybody.* "OK." he said.

"I wonder if there is wifi on this train." Angela said, looking at her phone. "I am going to pull up Kiwi's webpage. I cannot believe that assassins have web pages."

She tapped in '*www.kiwikills4u.com*'. The English on Kiwi's webpage was bad, and would have been comical unless you realized that she was offering to murder people. At the top of the page was a red banner band with yellow stars. Under the banner the heading read, '*Celebrity of Killer in Japan. Very True Professional*'.

Underneath the heading were four 'selfies' of Kiwi, different backgrounds but all in the same pose, holding her gun next to her head pointed straight up and smiling demurely: Kiwi in a garden, in a hotel room, in a bathroom, and in front of Tokyo Tower. Under the photos the tag line read, '*Kiwi on Assignment*'.

Angela clicked the 'About' button in the banner. Two more 'selfies' came up; same gun, same school girl smile, different outfits. The text below the photos read, '*I am Kiwi, very professional killer in Japan. I am best choice if you need relationship dead*'.

Angela clicked the 'About Me' button. *About me, I am not beautiful. My ears very big and my breasts very small. I wish I was born opposite, small ears and big breasts. However, victims expect killer to be handsome man, not girl with big ears and small breasts. So I good at discreet.*'

Angela clicked the 'Contact' tab, and Kiwi's full name and telephone number came up, as well as a link to her Facebook page. Under 'Rates' were a few more 'selfies', and '*20,000 yen for easy job. Give quote for more challenge assignment*.'

"Is no one checking this stuff?" Angela asked. "How can killers advertise like this?"

Ian shrugged.

They arrived in Fukuoka at 1:00am. Kotaro met them at the Fukuoka train station and brought them to their hotel. The tall, box-like skyscrapers and streetscapes of neon that they passed were, to Ian's exhausted eyes, a psychedelic blur outside the fogged windows of the car.

"The first thing that I want to do in the morning is visit Nigel in the hospital," Ian said.

"No problem. I will take you," Kotaro answered.

*****

Nigel was in good spirits when they walked into his room at the hospital, sitting up in the hospital bed sipping juice from a plastic cup. "Hey, great to see you guys! The doctors said that I will be able to go home in two days."

"That's good news. Angela will make the arrangements. Take off as much time as you need to when you get back," Ian said.

"I can work a desk when I get back, no problem. Rather not lay around my apartment thinking about how much fun you guys are having chasing the bad guys," Nigel said. "I feel like an idiot for getting stabbed. I was just standing there watching the action like it was a TV show. I should have been on guard, more alert."

"Do not blame yourself. You only had the authority to be an observer. I, however, was responsible for your safety. I am the one that should be blamed," Kotaro said, bowing.

"Hey, no blame for anyone. It's a dangerous profession. It happens," Ian said.

"Yeah, no one's blaming you, Kotaro. Have you guys made any progress tracking down our Burmese serial killer?" Nigel asked.

"Nothing new," Angela said." But we are not leaving Japan until we have that psycho in custody."

Ian put his hand on Nigel's shoulder and said, "Hang in there, Buddy. We'll be cruising down Gloucester Road together again in a few weeks."

The morning air was crisp as Ian, Angela, and Kotaro exited the hospital. Ian inhaled deeply, "Hospitals stink. I need a coffee."

"There's a Starbucks just down the street. We can walk," Kotaro said.

As they walked to the coffee shop, Ian hugged himself against the piercing cold. He watched the steam of his own breath and was reminded of England, the only other time in his life he had spent in a cold climate where winter was actually cold. Jet lagged and in a new environment, the coffee shop seemed a lot further to Ian than 'just down the street'. Finally, ensconced amid the familiar branding of Starbucks, the ochre's and brown's of the coffee house walls, sitting on yellow and purple upholstered chairs, Ian felt his body start to defrost and relax.

Sipping a cappuccino, Kotaro began by saying, "Yesterday a body was found floating in the Mikasa River, a woman whose throat had been cut and whose ribs had been sliced out."

"Missing her ribs? It sounds like our serial killer has started to practice his hobby here," Ian said.

"She was identified as Keiko Hashimoto, a worker in one of the Yakuza's clubs. The Medical Examiner said she had been killed about two days ago," Kotaro said.

"Why would the Yakuza be OK with that?" Angela asked.

Kotaro shrugged, "I guess employees are not that difficult to find here."

"More puzzling is why the Triad hired Kiwi to kill both us *and* Sein," Ian said. "'Us' I understand, but who wants Nakaji Sein dead and why?"

Kotaro's telephone suddenly vibrated. He looked at the screen and then put it to his ear. "*Hai, Mushi Mushi!*"

Kotaro's expression turned serious, and then ashen, as he ended the call. "That was one of my colleagues. A flower vase with a black orchid in it was on my desk this morning."

"What does that mean?" Angela asked.

"It means that I have been marked for death by the Black Dragon Society," Kotaro answered.

Chapter 52

"What is the Black Dragon Society?" Ian asked.

"The Black Dragons are a secret organization of police who do illegal things, like making extra income helping the Yakuza, beating suspects to get confessions, extorting shopkeepers. A flower vase with a black orchard on my desk means that they have marked me as a potential threat to their activities and will try to kill me.

"Oh, that sounds bad, Kotaro-san," Angela said.

"Nothing to worry about," Kotaro shrugged.

Kotaro's phone vibrated again. His eyes went wide as he listened to the caller on the other end. When the conversation ended, he replaced his telephone in its pouch and said, "Chief Superintendent Onuma went crazy this morning. He is killing people. We need to get back to Headquarters."

"He is killing people?" Angela asked as they hurried from the Starbucks.

"Worse than that," Kotaro said. "He has hostages, and he is asking for me."

*****

When they reached Police Headquarters hundreds of evacuated administrators and officers were standing in the parking lot looking befuddled, the routine of their day disturbed. Riot police barricaded the front doors. Kotaro identified himself and they were quickly escorted to a command center which had been set up in Superintendent Atsumu Watanabe's office. Watanabe, a portly man with wispy hair combed over a bald spot, was sitting at his desk, a computer and a video conference screen in front of him.

On the video screen the face of Onuma peered into the room. His eyes were red rimmed. Behind Onuma on the floor three secretaries could be seen cowering, their whimpering cries audible in Watanabe's office.

When Kotaro walked into the office, Watanabe turned off the screen and put the voice function on mute, "Chief Superintendent Onuma is locked in his office. He has killed five officers so far, is holding three people hostage, and he is calling for you. What do you know about this mess, Kotaro-san? Why is he asking for you?"

"I do not know. I suspect that it is because he doesn't like me."

Watanabe slammed his hand on the desk. "Because he doesn't like you? That is a ridiculous answer! Tell me the truth, Kotaro-san!" Watanabe demanded.

Ian interrupted, "Kotaro, could you please translate for me?"

"Who the fuck is this foreign devil? Oh, yeah, we have foreign detectives here because one of their criminals fled to our country, right? These are them?" Watanabe asked.

"Sorry, Watanabe-san, yes, he is Detective Ian Hamilton from the Hong Kong Police Force, here pursuing an international suspect. The Chief Superintendent's breakdown may be related to his case. He has asked me to translate for him."

"OK, so translate for him!" Watanabe exclaimed.

Kotaro gave a nod to Ian, "Go ahead."

"Superintendent Watanabe, I feel that Onuma-san has information that may be useful in tracking down our suspect. Therefore, I ask that you make every effort to capture him alive." Kotaro translated.

"Take him alive? Doesn't this foreign idiot know that the only decent way out of this situation is for Onuma to kill himself? Anyway, tell him, 'Of course we would like to take him alive'," Watanabe said.

After Kotaro translated, Watanabe, thrusting a finger at the video conference screen, said, "Well, Yamamoto-san, what are you waiting for? He has been asking for you! Go sit down and talk to him!"

Kotaro sat down in front of Watanabe's computer and switched the mute off and the screen on. "Hello, Chief Superintendent Onuma."

"Ah, you have finally arrived," Onuma's distraught image once again projected on the screen as it flickered back to life. Onuma scratched the back of his head, still weeping,. "Saa... Yamamoto-san, you have caused me much trouble. Your foreign ways have been a nuisance. Now they will be the end of me. I wanted you to know before I moved on. I want you to see the end. You will feel guilty for the rest of your miserable, foolish life." Onuma brought his gun up to his temple.

"Wait! Onuma-san, what are you talking about?" Kotaro said.

"*Bakayaro!* What am I talking about? I am under Yakuza control. I am an informant. Because of your embarrassing raid on the Yakuza headquarters the other day they will kill me. Their enforcers are just waiting to get me alone and then I am done for. I would rather kill myself."

"How did you get yourself in trouble with the Yakuza in the first place?" Kotaro asked, realizing that when their conversation ended, Onuma would shoot himself and their video screen would show Onuma's head exploding like a dropped watermelon.

"I am Black Dragon. I first got involved protecting their gambling dens. Then started gambling myself. Gambling debts mounted up," Onuma lamented. "They gave me credit, a little at first, and then a lot. Soon I owed them so much that I could never hope to repay it."

"And you demanded to see me just so that I could watch you kill yourself?" Kotaro asked.

"Of course. I hope that it becomes carved into your foreigner-corrupted mind for the rest of your pathetic life, you crazy bastard! I hate you! May you go to hell, and still remember this moment while you burn!" Onuma raised the gun to his temple again.

"Wait, Onuma-san! Do you know where the international suspect is being hidden?" Kotaro asked.

"With the *Barakumin*." That was Onuma's last statement, he pulled the trigger. The video screen showed his demise in gory detail. Like back-up singers in a rock band, the three hostages screamed in the background.

Watanabe yelled orders into a walkie-talkie, sending a platoon of riot police racing to Onuma's office. "Over," he said. A curt bow to Ian, and Watanabe left the room.

"What did Onuma say?" Ian asked.

Kotaro shrugged. "He said that your suspect is being held in the *Barakumin* neighborhood. That was all."

"OK, where is this Bara..whatever neighborhood?" Ian asked.

"I will take you there tomorrow. It is a likely place for the Chikuzen-kai to hide your suspect. However, the police are not respected there, we may have difficulties."

*****

Back at the hotel Angela dropped into her bed and instantly fell into a deep sleep.

She was a young girl on Poi O Beach. No mother or father in sight, she was all alone. She walked up to a barn-like building on the edge of the sand. The door to the barn opened, and Onuma walked out, pistol in hand. He pointed the gun to his head, and his eyes caught Angela's. He smiled, lowered the gun, and then pointed the gun at her. She could not move or scream.

Angela awoke groggily to a thumping sound. Slowly she realized that someone was knocking on her door. She stumbled to it, and asked, "Who is it?"

A voice from the other side said, "It is me, Miyamoto Mushashi."

Chapter 53

A rented blue Nissan pulled slowly into a gravely parking lot at the rear of a three story apartment complex in the *Barakumin* ghetto of Fukuoka. Three Chinese gangsters got out of the car. A hatchet-faced boy of seventeen with a Mohawk and a lanky hoodlum in his late twenties smoking a cigarette emerged from the front seats, and from the back a Triad red pole dressed in expensive jeans and a multi-colored sports jacket with the sleeves rolled up to his elbows got out. They looked around the parking lot and up at the building like predators sniffing the air for prey.

The one with the Mohawk said in guttural Cantonese, "Hey, Lee, how come you know where that Witch guy is hanging out?"

"Some old man with a spaghetti strainer on his head told me. The information cost me five hundred yen. We go up the back stairs, Apartment 3C."

When they had ascended to 3C Lee lowered his center of gravity as if facing an opponent on the streets of Wanchai and with flat bottom of his foot kicked the door in. Nakaji and Cho were sitting on the couch watching baseball. As the lock burst through the wooden jamb with a splintering crash they looked up in shock. Cho, wearing a cut-off denim jacket, launched his tattooed, muscular body at the intruders.

Mohawk-hairstyle removed a pair of nun chucks from his belt and cracked Cho across the skull as the second man hacked a slice into Cho's side with a meat cleaver. Cho slumped to the floor clutching his side.

Nakaji, still sitting on the couch as, said, "Who are you and what do you want?"

"What the fuck you think we want? We want you to die! There's a contract out on you, Dog Fart, you and those Hong Kong detectives who are trying to catch you." Lee said.

"That's ridiculous. Look, the Yakuza will pay more than whoever put the contract out on me. How much do you want?" Nakaji said as he got up from the couch.

Lee threw a spinning hook kick that landed square on Nakaji's jaw. "Doesn't work that way, Witch." Nakaji rolled with the blow, avoiding falling to the floor, but wondering if his jaw was broken.

The hood with the meat cleaver approached Nakaji. He drew his arm back to deliver a vicious slice, but Nakaji was quicker, launching himself at the man, driving a knee into the enforcer's midsection and then following with a slashing elbow to the cheekbone, sending the man to the carpet.

The young punk with the Mohawk came up behind Nakaji as the first hood went down, slamming the back of Nakaji's head with the nun chucks. Nakaji crumpled to his knees. Howling with rage, the man that Nakaji had elbowed rose from the floor and, twirling his arm in a figure eight, cut Nakaji repeatedly across the face with his cleaver. Mohawk also pulled a meat cleaver from his belt and added a few whacks.

The two triad enforcers then turned their attention to the wounded Cho, rolling him onto his back, outstretched his arms, and with railroad spikes and hammers nailed Cho to the apartment floor. They gagged him with a towel to silence his screams. They then did the same with the wide-eyed Nakaji Sein.

To his two enforcers, standing above the men crucified to the floor, meat cleavers hanging limply in their hands, Lee said in Cantonese, "You guys know what to do. Green Box Boy style, right? Finish them with the cleavers and then photograph the hell out of it. We'll send the pictures to our client to prove we delivered, and then also hit the social media to boost our reputation. Meanwhile, I am going downstairs to keep a lookout. Join me when you're done."

*****

At 9:00am most of the shops in the *Burakumin* neighborhood were still shuttered. Ian, Angela, and Kotaro walked down the narrow streets. They felt the hostile stares, smelled the piled up garbage. "This doesn't seem like Japan," Angela commented.

Kotaro asked people they passed on the street if anyone had seen a Southeast Asian man in the neighborhood. No answers, people just turned their backs on them.

As they rounded one corner in front of a ramen shop, an old man on a bicycle wearing a spaghetti strainer on his head pedaled up to them. "I am the *Tenuki*," the old man announced. "My testicles are huge."

"Good for you," Kotaro said.

"I know who you are looking for," the old man said. "An Asian foreigner and a Japanese punk."

Kotaro exclaimed, "Yes!" Can you tell us where to find them?" Then in English to the detectives, "This guy knows where Nakaji Sein is!"

The old man said, "Of course I can tell you where to find them. After all, I am the *Tenuki*, guardian of the neighborhood. However it will cost you five hundred yen."

Kotaro pulled out his wallet and withdrew five hundred yen. The old man snatched it and said, "Follow me!" He peddled away, the Japanese flags on his handlebars snapping in the wind.

"Let's go!" Kotaro said to Angela and Ian as he started to trot after the *Tenuki*.

The *Tenuki* stopped his bicycle by a nondescript apartment building, in front of which was a six foot high concrete block wall with an open gate. "Third floor, apartment C." The *Tenuki* quickly sped off, peddling furiously, disappearing around the corner.

Ian started for the gate but Kotaro grabbed his arm, putting a finger to his mouth. He then pointed to the ground beyond the gate. The shadow of a man standing behind the wall could be seen on the concrete path that led through the opening.

From under his coat Kotaro silently drew his short sword and walked on his toes to the gate. Quick as a snake strike, he reached around the wall and grabbed the man's lapel, jerking him out from behind the wall. With his other hand Kotaro smashed the hilt of his sword into the man's head. The surprised man fell to his knees, and as he did so Kotaro snapped a pair of handcuffs on him.

"Who are you? Identify yourself!" Kotaro demanded in Japanese.

"Kotaro-san, you are wasting your breath. He doesn't understand you," Angela said.

"What?"

"He is Chinese, not Japanese. I know this slime bag," Angela said.

Kotaro stood the man up. "You know him? Who is he?"

"He is 'Cat Boy' Lee, a red pole enforcer with the Green Box Boys Triad," Angela said. She ripped open the man's shirt. On his chest was a large tattoo, a yellow triangle with a green box inside. In Cantonese Angela said, "What are the Green Box Boys doing in Japan?"

Cat Boy sneered at her, "What is the daughter of the Dragon Head of Hou Sai Lei doing in Japan?"

Angela cupped her hands behind Cat Boy's head and forcefully pulled his head down waist high as she drove her knee up into his face. Blood erupted from Lee's nose and upper lip. "I do not expect a question back when I ask a question. Understand? Now, let's try again. What are you doing in Japan?"

"You broke my nose, you violent bitch!" Cat Boy exclaimed, spitting blood.

From the rear of the apartment came the sound of a car's ignition turning over and tires squealing as a vehicle quickly raced away. Ian raced to the back of the apartment just in time to see a sky-blue Nissan Sentra disappear down the street.

Ian returned and said, "Are those your friends in the Nissan? Where are they going? Do they have Nakaji Sein with them?"

'Cat Boy' smiled. He said in Cantonese to Angela, "Your *Gweilo* friend sure has a lot of questions."

"And you had better start answering those questions, Cat-Shit Boy, or I am going to do some more face rearranging," Angela snarled. "First question; what are the Green Box Boys doing in Japan?"

'Cat Boy' shrugged. "OK. A hit was issued to kill the three Hong Kong detectives and the Burmese drug dealer."

"By whom?" Angela asked.

"He is some guy super-connected in Hong Kong and Myanmar. Don't know his name."

"Why kill both us *and* Sein?"

"You were getting too close to capturing Sein, and Sein could identify the guy who put the hit on him. Easiest just to kill all of you."

"Were you the guys who hired that Japanese woman to kill us?" Ian asked after Angela translated.

"Yeah, what an incompetent bitch she turned out to be!" 'Cat Boy' said, switching from Cantonese to English. "We found her on some website. Thought we could save some travel time, have her take the risks, and still get paid. Bad idea. When she failed we decided to do the killing ourselves, which we should have done to begin with."

"So I am assuming that those were your friends who just sped off with Nakaji in that Nissan." Ian said.

"Those were my friends, *Gweilo*, but Mr. Nakaji Sein is no doubt dead and gone, lying in a pool of his own blood upstairs." He then added, "Green Box Boy style, *Gweilo*."

Kotaro called for back-up and, dragging the handcuffed 'Cat Boy' along with them, they entered the apartment building and swiftly ascended the stairs to the third floor. Kotaro had sheathed his sword, and now held his revolver in his hand.

The door to 3C was ajar. Kotaro slowly pushed it fully open with his foot and, revolver first, entered the room. Crucified to the floor with railroad spikes were the bloody bodies of Nakaji and Cho. A meat cleaver protruded from each of their chests.

"Damn, we do good work!" Cat Boy exclaimed.

"Shut up, Asshole." Ian said.

Kotaro kneeled next to the two bodies and checked for any signs of life. "These guys are gone." He said. "It was not a quick death, they suffered."

Ian said to 'Cat Boy', "Where would your friends go? To the airport and back to Hong Kong?"

"I wouldn't if I were them," Cat Boy answered. "There were four contracts; three detectives and the Burmese. Why go back home with only one-fourth of the money? I would stay and go for the full payday."

"Unfortunately I agree with you," Ian said. "We are still in danger. Angela, call Nigel and fill him in. Make sure that he gets on a plane back to Hong Kong immediately, I am sure that he can travel by now. We cannot protect him in Japan."

"Right." Angela then turned to 'Cat Boy' and said in Cantonese, "We need the identity of the guy who put the contract on us. You must have some idea who he is, Cat Feces. If you cooperate with us I will do everything in my power to ensure that you are deported back to Hong Kong. If you do not cooperate, I promise you that you will never leave this stinking island alive. This is very personal for me. You know who I am, so you know that these are not empty words."

Before 'Cat Boy' could answer, eight Japanese policemen stepped into the apartment, crowding into the small living room. They were all wearing black motorcycle helmets, with the tinted visors down.

"Oh, the back-up that you called for has arrived, Kotaro-san," Angela said.

"Not exactly," Kotaro answered. "These guys are not back-up. They are from The Black Dragon Society."

Chapter 54

The Black Dragons fanned out in a semi-circle around the small room and drew revolvers. Kotaro pulled from his jacket pocket two smoke grenades. "Dive for the floor!" Kotaro yelled in English.

He pulled the pins and tossed the grenades, smoothly sliding his sword from the sheath on his back. *I am Miyamoto Mushashi!* The room was instantly filled with smoke so thick it was like a living creature swirling within the room, visibility reduced to inches. The Black Dragons fired their weapons blindly into the enveloping fog. Ian and Angela lay flat on the floor, their faces buried in the cheap shag carpet.

For years Kotaro had practiced kendo blindfolded, a training practice used by his hero, Miyamoto Mushashi. He would block and counter as his opponent struck, 'sensing' the blow before it arrived rather than relying on sight, 'feeling' the location of his training partner.

He spun into the smoke, became part of the smoke. He moved around the room silently, sensing his enemies, everywhere and nowhere, slicing and stabbing as the blind Black Dragons fired haphazardly in panic. The sound of their gunfire was interspersed with the screams of their comrades as Kotaro's lethal blade cut them down one by one.

Finally there was silence. Angela crawled to a window and opened it, the smoke slowly dissipating. Eight slashed bodies, helmets still on, lay about the room. On the couch 'Cat Boy' Lee also was dead, a crimson, circular bullet wound staining the yellow and green tattoo on his chest.

The three detectives surveyed the carnage. Kotaro slowly lowered his blade. He grinned, "The 'Mainichi Shimbun' headline will no doubt read, *'Ten valiant police officers were killed today in a shootout with a Chinese Triad gang'*.

Ian, also smiling, said, "Better than it reading, '*Two Hong Kong detectives and a Japanese officer killed by Chinese Triads.*'!"

*****

The blue Nissan Sentra idled on a side street. The Mohawk-ed, younger of the two Green Box Boys said in Cantonese, "Shall we go back to Hong Kong now? We got the Burmese guy."

The older one at the wheel of the car sneered, "You are truly as stupid as you are ugly. How do you think that we would be greeted when we got back? *'Oh, you guys got one of the four targets. Great work!'* No, we get them all. Then we go back to Hong Kong."

"How will we get them then?" Mohawk haircut asked.

"We will smash into them with our car. If that doesn't kill them we will then finish them off with cleavers," the older gangster said.

"But if we smash our car into theirs won't we also be injured or killed?"

"There is your ignorance showing up again, like a stupid puppy dog. You have to understand physics. I understand physics. I know exactly at what angle to smash their car with ours so that we are undamaged."

"Wow," the younger one said, visibly impressed.

*****

In the Japanese police car on the way back to the police station Ian said, "Well, our work in Japan is done. Is Nigel on his way back to Hong Kong, Angela?"

"Yes, he will be on a plane this evening. He is pretty much healed."

"Great, we'll leave too as soon as we can get a flight back."

Kotaro said, "I would say that this ending is not bad. A killer has been put out of circulation, even though it was not as you expected with a trial and a sentence. The Triad did your work for you."

"Yeah, justice has been served, for sure," Ian said.

"The Wicked Witch is dead!" Angela exclaimed. "Not a bad ending at all."

Kotaro said, "Please excuse me, this is a very un-Japanese thing to do, but when good things happen I like to sing it to the world...".

Kotaro slipped a CD into the console above the radio and turned the knob to full volume. Willie Nelson singing 'Blue Skies' blasted out of the speakers. Kotaro sang along at the top of his lungs.

'Blue skies smilin' at me.
Nothin' but blue skies do I see.
Blue birds singin' a song.
Nothin' but blue skies from now on.'

Angela and Ian joined in.

'Blue skies smilin' at me.
Nothin' but blue skies do I see.
Blue birds singin' a song.
Nothin' but blue skies from now on.'

They never saw the sky-blue Nissan Sentra speeding toward them.

The world went black for a period of time. It may have been a second, or it may have been a few minutes. Kotaro was unsure, but at least he knew that he was alive. He was unable to move however. The steering wheel was pushing into his chest, pinning him to the seat. A sharp pain emanated from his left leg. *Probably broken,* he thought. Through the shattered windshield of the police car he could see the Nissan smashed on the side of the roadway. It had rolled after it had struck the police car, and now sat broken and smoking.

The younger of the Green Box Boys, sitting dazed in the front passenger seat of the *Sentra*, yelled. "Physics, my ass, you stupid dog fart! You don't know shit about physics!"

He was wasting his breath, however. The older boy, who had not fastened his seat belt, was hanging partially out of the smashed front windshield, his skull crushed. The younger one, with only an open gash on his forehead, unfastened his seat belt, pried open the crumpled passenger door, and, tears in his eyes and heart pumping in terror, limped off into the Japanese countryside as fast as he could.

"Angela, Kotaro, you guys alright?" Ian asked from the back seat of the police cruiser.

"I'm pinned, and I think that my leg is broken, but OK." Kotaro said.

"I'm OK." Angela said. "I think......"

In the distance they could hear the *'Whoop, whoop'* of an approaching ambulance.

Chapter 55

Monday morning was a radiant December day in Hong Kong, Christmas vacation looming around the corner. Nigel had taken the first week back in Hong Kong off. When he did come back to the office he was still moving stiffly, but Angela felt that it was just a sympathy play. The Hong Kong headlines had screamed '*Hong Serial Killer Murdered By Triad in Japan*' for a few days, but by now it was old news.

The three detectives sat at the conference table by their cubicles. "I take it personally." Ian said, pausing and looking at his detectives, none of them impressed with the perfect weather outside. "When someone puts a contract out on me, I take it very personally. The son-of-a-bitch who put the contract on us is still out there, free to continue with his illegal businesses. We need to find him. We will find him. This case is not over."

"Do you have a plan? We don't have a thread to follow." Nigel asked.

"Not true. Our thread is the Myanmar Embassy. Everything that has happened in the case is connected to Myanmar, and those guys in the embassy are somehow involved up to their eyeballs. Nigel, call the Embassy and tell them we are on the way over."

*****

Nigel was reminded of their first visit to the Embassy as they walked past the gold-colored plaque that read in black letters, '*The Embassy of the Republic of the Union of Myanmar*', and were paraded into the same burgundy-carpeted conference room. They were kept waiting exactly the same fifteen minutes.

However, all similarities stopped as a different man, with a different assistant, entered the room. The new ambassador, no more than five feet tall and thin, was wearing an expensive, oyster-gray suit. He looked to be in his fifties. The woman was large, especially for a Burmese, towering over her boss, with copious makeup and gravity-defying fake breasts. Her outfit was professional, but just barely, revealing acres of cleavage, broad shoulders, and powerful legs. The three detectives stared speechless at the unusual duo.

Extending a business card, the man said, "I am Ambassador Extraordinary and Plenipotentiary Khin Khin Myint. This is my assistant Lilly."

Ian looked at the card. It really did say *'Ambassador Extraordinary and Plenipotentiary'*. The large woman also extended a card to Ian, and Ian gave her one of his cards. Her card only said *'Lilly';* no last name, no title.

"Nice to meet you, Ambassador Myint and Lilly. We were expecting Consul General Kham and Attaché Mimi Tun." Ian said.

The Ambassador laughed. "Please call me Khin Khin, Detective. Consul General Kham and Attaché Tun were disposed of."

"Disposed of? You mean 'let go'?" Ian asked.

"No, I mean 'disposed of'. They were an embarrassment to us: having an affair, arrested by your department, involved in illegal drugs and jade trading. Not the kind of image that we want to project."

"Oh." Ian said. "Well, in that case I will ask you the same questions that I was going to ask them."

"Ask away, Detective."

"We are looking for a Burmese man in Hong Kong who is involved with the killing of your former Political Counselor, Nakaji Sein, in Japan. We are asking your help in finding this man. Does your embassy have knowledge of whom this person might be?"

Khin Khin laughed, as Lilly glared stone-faced at the detectives. "I like your directness, Detective. Westerners are so much more direct than Asians. I think that I can help you. I believe that you must mean 'The Bilu'. The Bilu is the man that you are searching for." he said.

"'The Bilu'?" Ian asked.

Khin Khin said, "Yes. A Bilu is an ogre in Burmese mythology. What a creative nickname, don't you think? I wish that I had thought of it! I would add it to my name card. I would imagine, however, that you would want to give 'The Bilu' a medal instead of trying to track him down. After all, he killed your serial murderer, right? Nakaji Sein is a man that we hope everyone forgets very quickly. Do you know how badly he affected our tourism industry? The Bilu is a hero."

"Sorry about your tourism industry, Ambassador, but as well as killing Sein, The Bilu tried to have us killed. I am going to find him." Ian said.

"I am sure that you will, Detective. You seem to be a very determined and competent person."

"Do you know the Bilu's real name, or where we might find him?" Ian asked.

"I am afraid that I do not. However, if I hear anything of this Bilu character I will be sure to let you know." The Ambassador stood up and shook hands with the three detectives.

*****

As the police cruiser slowly crept through late morning traffic back to the station, Nigel said, "'Disposed of'...that means they killed them, right?"

"That is the way I took it," Ian said. "What a creepy pair! They seem like people that you find in a circus rather than in an embassy, a man the size of a Chihuahua, and a Great Dane of a woman."

"The assistant, Lilly, never said a word, just gave us that nasty stare," Nigel said.

"I have never seen such a large Southeast Asian woman! Maybe she's not pure Burmese," Ian speculated.

From the back seat Angela said, "You two are so stupid."

"What?" Nigel asked, turning his head around to look at Angela.

"That was not a woman, de-tec-tives. That was a ladyboy."

"Holy cow, you are right, Angela!" Ian exclaimed.

"I've got more news for you; she's not Burmese, she's Thai," Angela said.

*****

As soon as the three detectives left the Myanmar Embassy, Khin Khin said to Lilly, "Close the conference room door and get 'The Bilu' on the phone."

Lilly slid the telephone in front of Khin Khin, tapping in the numbers and pushing the 'speaker' function. She then sat down next to Khin Khin.

When The Bilu answered, Khin Khin said in Burmese, "They're not giving up. They are continuing to pursue you."

"How did they find out about me?" the voice asked.

"Don't know."

The answer came back, "Kill them then."

Lilly hung up and said to Khin Khin, "Why you tell detectives about Bilu? That make trouble, no?"

"Oh, but isn't it more fun that way, Lilly?" Khin Khin laughed.

Chapter 56

The license plate on the front of the gleaming, ebony Rolls Royce Phantom read 'JADE'. The twenty-foot long behemoth doubled-parked in front of the Myanmar Embassy. A figure clad in a blue blazer and khaki pants emerged from the rear seat and dashed into the Embassy building. The car eased back into traffic.

Across the street in an unmarked car parked illegally in front of Pacific Coffee, Nigel watched. *Ah, what have we here?* Ian had assigned him to stakeout the Embassy, his intuition telling him that here was some connection between the strange new ambassador and 'The Bilu'.

Thirty minutes later the Rolls returned and the blazer-clad figure exited the Embassy. The man jumped into the back seat and the car pulled into traffic like a whale merging into a school of smaller fish. Nigel started the engine and pulled his undercover car into the flow, following closely.

Dialing Ian's number on his mobile as he drove, Nigel said, "I am following an interesting visitor to the Myanmar Embassy, a Rolls with the license plate 'JADE'.

Ian said, "Just a sec." He pulled up the Hong Kong Transport Department database and tapped in the license. "Whoa, that car is registered to Geoffrey MacMillan! He is CEO of Julie's Auction House in Hong Kong. He is Sarah's boss!"

Ian hung up. *So there is a connection between Julie's and the Myanmar Embassy. Very interesting.*

While Nigel continued to follow the Rolls through stop-and-go traffic, at Headquarters Ian called Angela into a small conference room. "Angela, since you have been working with us you have consistently come up with solid information on the Triads, like knowing who that Green Box Boy was in Japan, and putting us on to the Liang Zai when The Witch was hiding in 'Shami Town'. I am not going to ask you where this knowledge comes from, for now that's your business. I do want to use your connections to our advantage, though."

"OK…" Angela said.

"The way I see it, The Witch was tight with the Liang Zai, and when he fell out of favor with The Bilu, The Bilu went to The Green Box Boys to eliminate him. He could not have very well gone to The Liang Zai as they were The Witch's people," Ian said. "Agree so far?"

"Sure."

"All that Myanmar drug business, therefore, that the Liang Zai was doing with The Witch ended with the death of The Witch. That business therefore will now go to their competitor, The Green Box Boys. The Liang Zai knows a lot more about this than we do. After all, it was their business. They may even know who 'The Bilu' is. That is what we need to find out, Angela. Can you arrange a meeting for us with the Liang Zai?"

"Yes, I can, but, no offense, I think that the information would be more forthcoming if the meeting was just with me," Angela said.

"I don't like sending you in alone. What if you brought Nigel?"

"Best if just me."

"OK, Angela. I am going to trust your instincts on this. Set it up."

*****

The meeting was set up in The Happywood Restaurant in Sham Shui Po. Angela's father had arranged it. Spider Choi looked at Angela over a bowl of shrimp won ton noodle soup. "Why in the world would I help the police?" Spider asked.

"Because you know that if we take The Bilu out of action another scumbag will replace him, and that new scumbag will be your opportunity to get the business back." Angela picked up a square of fried tofu, dipped it in spicy sauce, and popped it into her mouth.

"If I wanted to take out The Bilu I could do it myself. Don't need you police dimwits to do it for me." Spider slurped up a mouthful of noodles from his soup.

"Maybe, or maybe that would start a war with the Green Box Boys that you would rather not have. A war would be bad for business."

Spider shrugged. "All you want me to do is tag his ass, and you and your uniformed monkey's will do what.....arrest him? He will have a team of trickster lawyers at your throats in minutes."

"Look, Spider, I'm not asking you for any long term commitment here. All I'm asking is for you to tell me who the fuck he is. No one will know you are the one who told me, and if, *just if,* we are lucky, we will take him out of action, high priced lawyers or no." Angela plucked a sliver of Hainan Chicken from one of the plates and put it in her mouth. "Either you help us or just cut the bullshit and enjoy your damn shrimp won tons."

Spider laughed. "You are your father's daughter, for sure." He inserted a piece of roast duck in his mouth. "I don't know the identity of The Bilu, Angela, but I do know how he operated. Nakaji used to talk about him. The Bilu has two businesses; one is drugs and the other is illegal jade. He used some guy named Zaw Than to operate the jade trade. Nakaji Sein ran the drugs for The Bilu. Nakaji, being greedy, wanted to run both businesses, jade and drugs, so he killed Zaw. He gambled that The Bilu would be so desperate with Zaw gone that he would automatically give the jade part of the business to Nakaji also."

"Following you so far. We suspected that Nakaji killed Zaw Than." Angela said.

"Nakaji gambled wrong, though. His sensational public exposure as a killer and cannibal, and the fact that he knew the identity of The Bilu, made him a huge liability. Logical that The Bilu would want to kill him."

"So, Spider, we knew all that. Tell me something that we didn't know."

"The Bilu is a white guy. I'll bet that you didn't know that."

"A *Gweilo*? Are you serious?"

"White as a water deer's ass."

*

Chapter 57

The Rolls Royce Phantom smoothly navigated the precipitous curves of the road up to The Peak after it left the Myanmar Embassy. Geoffrey thought about his meeting with Khin Khin. He and Khin Khin had grown in different directions over the years. Geoffrey's business acumen had expanded, and along with it an obsessive desire for discretion to protect himself and his businesses. Khin Khin, however, had become more outlandish in his behavior. There was nothing discreet about him. Even the title that he had put on his name card, 'Ambassador Extraordinary and Plenipotentiary', was outrageous. Geoffrey wondered about the wisdom of his decision to bring Khin Khin to Hong Kong and set him up as the Ambassador to Myanmar.

When Nakaji had introduced Mimi Tun into his jade business, Geoffrey had found it a threat, especially when she and Ambassador Kham had gotten arrested. They were suddenly in the spotlight, and he worried that the attention from the police and the press could illuminate Mimi's and Kham's connection to Nakaji, and ultimately to him. He therefore came upon the idea to make his old friend, Khin Khin, the Ambassador. A perfect match. Who in the world could he trust more?

When Geoffrey had suggested the ambassador change to the Burmese Generals, his relationship with the Generals was so strong and his businesses such a major contributor to their bank accounts, that they had readily agrees to replace Ambassador Kham with Geoffrey's man to protect their business interests.

Contacting Khin Khin was easy. Over the years Geoffrey had kept erratic contact with him. Khin Khin still lived in Pattaya, and when Geoffrey had proposed the idea to Shrunken Boy, Geoffrey was surprised at how quickly his friend agreed to move to Hong Kong. He then remembered how Khin Khin had always been quick to agree to any new adventure, any new challenge.

He had not, however, expected Khin Khin to show up with a ladyboy friend, and a crate containing a twenty foot Burmese python. The snake was the largest python that Geoffrey had ever seen, its girth like a tree trunk and a head the size of a suitcase. It weighed almost two hundred pounds.

Lilly was also strange to Geoffrey, so surly, very different than the vivacious ladyboy friends that he remembered Khin Khin attracted to before. Lilly was more weightlifter than runway model. "She is a first rate assassin, Bilu," Khin Khin had said. Geoffrey could easily picture her as 'a first rate assassin'.

Khin Khin and Lilly had fed Mimi and Ambassador Kham to the snake.

*****

The Globe, one of the more popular beer bars in Soho, serving a large selection of exotic micro brews, was packed by 7:00pm. At one of the wooden tables Sarah, Tika, George, and Ian were each on their second mug.

"Before we get too far along with the brews, Sarah, I have some work-related questions that I would like to ask you." Ian said.

"Oh, you want to interview Sarah like she is a suspect?" Tika asked with a giggle. "This should be fun."

"Not a suspect, and this is serious." Ian said. "Sarah, I need information on your boss, Geoffrey MacMillan. How connected is he to Myanmar?"

"Very connected." Sarah answered, a moustache of beer foam on her upper lip. "Myanmar jade is our chief commodity. There are always muckiddy-muck Burmese Generals parading through our office like fat peacocks to meet with Mr. MacMillan. They used to come in with Zaw Than in the old days, but now that Zaw is gone they come in alone."

"Like fat peacocks?" Tika asked.

"For sure. They wear those crazy green uniforms with braided gold decorations, covered with colorful medals, high peaked hats, strutting through our office like they own it." Sarah took another sip of the amber beer.

"Have you been in the meetings with the Generals?" Ian asked.

"No, and even if I was, I would be clueless. They speak in Burmese. Mr. MacMillan is fluent."

"Your boss is fluent in Burmese?" Ian asked.

"Yeah, he grew up there."

"MacMillan grew up in Burma? Very interesting!" Ian exclaimed. "Have you ever heard him called the name 'Bilu'?"

"Sure. I think that is Mr. Macmillan's Burmese name. Whenever the Generals come in they greet him, *'Hey, Bilu!'*

Ian sat back in his seat stunned. *We have found The Bilu! And he's a Hong Kong socialite!*

Ian pulled out his telephone and started to send an e-mail to Angela and Nigel, but then reconsidered. *No, we need to proceed strategically on this one. We are going to need indisputable evidence before we make a move on Geoffrey MacMillan, CEO of Julie's Hong Kong. Sarah saying that she had heard him called 'Bilu' will not be enough to arrest him. But, we now know who he is!*

"Waiter!" Ian called. "A round of tequila shots, please! *Herradura!*"

*****

Angela sat starring at her computer screen wearing only her bra and panties. Even though her Fotan apartment sweltered like a sauna in the Hong Kong humidity, she preferred to be frugal and sweat rather than switch on the air conditioning unit. On the screen was the latest e-mail from Kotaro.

'Garuda-san, how are you? My leg is healing. The cast will come off in one week. I am looking forward to returning to kendo training. When can you visit Japan again? Miyamoto Mushashi.'

Angela smiled. She pictured the Japanese detective writing her the e-mail, remembered the first night that they had spent together in Tokyo, eating yakitori and drinking sake. She replied to the e-mail.

'Mushashi-san, good to hear that your leg is healing. Why don't

you visit Hong Kong instead of my going to Japan? There are plenty of restaurants with great yakitori and sake here. The Garuda.'

Angela stood up, stripped off her bra and panties, and went to her mirrors. She watched the Garuda fly, but this time his voyage was different. It was not the usual angry Garuda taking flight, rising up fiercely from the Kowloon ghetto. On this flight the Garuda swooped and soared happily over the rooftops of Hong Kong, joy in its heart.

Chapter 58

In the morning Angela and Ian arrived at the office at the same time. Both were energized, wide-eyed, and could not wait to share what they had learned with the team.

"Ian, I've got information on The Bilu!" Angela exclaimed.

"Me too, but you go first, Angela," Ian said with his boyish grin.

Nigel arrived. He could feel the excitement in the room. "What, did you two drink too much espresso? What's going on?"

"Angela has some information on The Bilu. Go ahead, Angela."

"The Bilu is a Caucasian!" She exploded. "I met with The Liang Zai Triad, Nakaji Sein's old partners. Spider Choi said that Nakaji used to talk about The Bilu, and that he was a white guy."

"That is true, Angela. In fact, I happen to know who The Bilu is." Ian said, again flashing his smile.

"You know who The Bilu is? Well, who is he?" Angela asked.

Nigel interjected, "Man, you guys have all this great information and I have nothing. All I did was follow a rich guy in a Rolls Royce."

"Actually, Nigel, you were following The Bilu," Ian said.

"I was?"

"Yep. The Bilu is Geoffrey MacMillan, CEO of Julie's, proud owner of a black Rolls Royce Phantom, license plate 'JADE'."

"Let's pick him up!" Angela said as she moved towards the exit.

"Angela, no, we need to get our case together first, solid. Otherwise it will be like trying to bring down a rhino with a sling shot. Geoffrey MacMillan is a powerful adversary. I will talk to the Commissioner this morning. Meanwhile you two try to find out all you can on MacMillan's history, build a case with substantial evidence. Focus on finding a link with The Bilu and that new ambassador in the embassy. My intuition tells me that he is Geoffrey's man, and dirty."

*****

Angela and Nigel dove enthusiastically into the research. "Hey, Nigel, check this out." Angela sat at her computer in her cubicle starring at her screen. Nigel rolled his chair over next to hers. "Based on the Ambassador Extraordinaire's assistant being Thai, which is unusual for someone working in the Burmese Embassy, I did a database search for Khin Khin Myint / Thailand. It turns out that Mr. Myint owns a string of ladyboy bars in Pattaya."

"From bar owner to ambassador? That is quite a career leap," Nigel said.

Angela squinted at the screen, "It looks like he went into partnership on the bars with someone named Eggplant Payakaroon in the early eighties, but inherited the whole operation when Eggplant went to prison in 1992 for property fraud."

Ian had walked up behind Nigel and Angela. "Interesting, but we need a connection to MacMillan. Can you place MacMillan in Thailand in the eighties with Khin Khin?" Ian said.

"Not yet, Ian. However, when I searched Macmillan/Burma I got lots of info on Geoffrey's father, Arthur MacMillan. He was the Burmese Minister of Tourism, the only Westerner at the time living in the country during the '60's and early '70's. Geoffrey's mother disappeared when Geoffrey was five. Arthur was arrested in Burma in 1973 and died in prison. No information about what happened to his son."

"Geoffrey and Khin Khin Myint are about the same age. What if they were friends and left Burma together when Geoffrey's father was arrested?" Nigel asked.

"And went over the border to Thailand. That makes sense," Ian said.

"So shall we pay another visit to the Ambassador?" Angela asked.

"No. Assuming he and Geoffrey are connected, a visit to Ambassador Myint will alert MacMillan to the fact that we are on to him. I do not want to do that until we have a stronger case," Ian said.

*****

Bilu and Shrunken Boy had taken the ferry from Central to

Discovery Bay and were sitting at Hemingway's outdoor patio watching the last vestiges of the sunset, a dramatic show of dark purple clouds outlined in pink, the silhouette of Dragon Head in the distance. On the calm bay in front of Hemingway's patio a fisherman in a wooden rowboat pulled in his net full of tiny, silver fish. The two old friends were slipping pleasantly into inebriation as they ordered their third martini.

"You ever think that you might give it all up one day and return to Burma?" Khin Khin asked.

"Only as a last alternative, Shrunken Boy. If it was go to jail or go to Burma, I would choose Burma," Geoffrey answered. "What about you?"

"I dream about returning to Burma. Not Yangon, but out in the countryside. I would like to return there someday," Khin Khin said, savoring the peacefulness of the evening. "That's why I suggested we have drinks here in Discovery Bay instead of the commotion of Central. I relish calmness at this point in my life." He downed his martini and ordered another. "A life of leisure living in a thatch hut in the Burmese countryside sounds perfect."

"I think that I am more of a City Boy," Geoffrey said. "Hey, Shrunken Boy, I don't know about you, but I am snockered on these martinis. Don't have the stamina anymore that I did back in the old days when we did 'The Crawl'. I am going to call it a night."

A waiter brought Khin Khin's martini. "Please bring us the bill," Khin Khin said to him. He raised the glass by its delicate stem and then downed it like it was a shot. "The next ferry to Central is in fifteen minutes, Bilu. We shall be on it,"

Geoffrey's driver met them when they exited the ferry terminal at Pier Three in Central after the twenty-five minute boat ride. As they drove up to the peak, The Phantom's custom audio system playing the Beatles' 'White Album' from 1968, Khin Khin and Geoffrey sang along vociferously.

Blackbird singing in the dead of night
Take these broken wings and learn to fly

All your life
You were only waiting for this moment to arise.
  Blackbird singing in the dead of night
Take these sunken eyes and learn to see
All your life
You were only waiting for this moment to be free.

At the Residence of The Ambassador of the Union of Myanmar, a white, rambling mansion built in 1877 with spectacular views of the city lights, Khin Khin staggered out of the Rolls towards his front door. "Bye, Bilu, great night." *I can't believe how wasted I am after only four martinis. Not like the old days.*

Getting the key in the lock was a challenge but Khin Khin finally was able to let himself in. He wandered through the marbled entry hall and formal front living areas of the mansion to the rear of the house, towards the kitchen. He followed the sounds, '*thwack, thwack, thwack, thwack*', echoing through the residence. Four solid 'thwacks' and a pause, and then it repeated.

In a space next to the kitchen he and Lilly had hung a punching bag. Lilly, glistening with sweat and wearing a sports top and shorts, with six ounce gloves on her hands, was working out on the bag. Left round kick, right cross, left hook, right cross. Crisp explosive shots; '*thwack, thwack, thwack, thwack*'. Bob and slide, move in again, she worked the combination over and over.

She paused when she saw Khin Khin. "You drunk," she said, and turned back to the bag.

"Yes, madam, I am afraid that I am." Khin Khin weaved as he stood. "I am going to go downstairs and feed Big Boy."

"That stupid idea. You drunk."

"No, it's a fine idea. He loves me." Khin Khin walked with unsteady steps to the stairway leading to the basement.

Lilly heard him fumble with the lights, stumble at the bottom of the stairs, and call out, "Big Boy....I'm here to feed you, Baby." She turned back to the punching bag and started a new combination; slip right, right hook to the ribs, right hook to the head, left knee, right elbow.

The giant python stirred. It was hungry, its tongue flicked out, tasted the air. It smelled a warm blooded animal in its space. In a room next to the cage was a cooler containing chicken parts which they fed to the giant constrictor with a pair of long tongs. This time, however, Khin Khin passed the tongs and reached in with his hands. He turned drunkenly toward the cage. "Here, Big Boy...Shrunken Boy has some nice chicken for you." The snake aggressively moved toward him as he opened the cage door, its tongue flicking the air. The reptile could not distinguish between keeper and prey, they both smelled the same.

The snake raised itself up until it was eye to eye with Khin Khin and then came in fast. Two hundred pounds of muscle slammed him to the floor like a professional linebacker running into a girl scout. Rows of blade-sharp teeth clamped onto Khin Khin's shoulder as the snake coiled its massive girth around his body. Whenever Khin Khin exhaled the snake squeezed tighter. Unable to take a breath, his arms pinned to his sides, Khin Khin was helpless. The only visible parts of Khin Khin were his feet protruding from the coils on one end and his head on the other. As Khin Khin's life started to ebb the snake released its powerful grip on his shoulder and moved its mouth to his head. It began to swallow him.

"*Thwack, thwack, thwack.*'....Lilly paused as she heard the screams from the basement. She looked for a moment at the dark opening to the basement stairwell and then turned back to the bag and finished her set. Taking off her gloves, she walked upstairs to the bedroom, took a shower, dressed, and packed a suitcase. She then called a taxi.

On the way to the airport Lilly rummaged in her purse until she found Ian's business card. It was after-hours so she left a message on Ian's voice mail, "You come Myanmar Ambassador residence. Look basement. You find accident."

*

Chapter 59

The Hong Kong Standard's headlines broadcast 'Myanmar Ambassador Eaten By Pet Snake'. The article went on to read, 'The new Myanmar Ambassador to Hong Kong, Khin Khin Myint, after a night out with a friend came home to feed his pet snake, a twenty foot long Burmese python. The snake mistook him for its dinner. His assistant called police, but by the time police arrived, the Ambassador was just a lump in the python's body.' The article continued about the dangers of keeping large snakes, and admonitions about never feeding a snake over eight feet long by hand, or by yourself, or while smelling like a chicken, or while drunk.

Geoffrey tossed the newspaper on the coffee table. If I had not brought Khin Khin to Hong Kong this never would have happened to him. Am I responsible? No, Khin Khin brought this on himself. He brought the snake to Hong Kong. It was his decision to feed it by hand when he was drunk. Geoffrey remembered their last night together. Funny how Khin Khin talked about returning to Myanmar and settling in the countryside just before he died. Was that a message to me from the Universe? Is that what I am supposed to do now?

*****

Angela and Nigel's computers both beeped at the same time, indicating an IM from Ian. It said, 'Come to the conference room.' They both rose from their seats and gave each other a quizzical look over their cubicle walls.

When they walked into the conference room a woman Angela and Nigel had not seen before was seated at the table with Ian. The woman, looking to be in her fifties, had a broad faced, no make-up, and short hair. She rose and gave each of the detectives a firm handshake. "I am Linda Yu, Superintendent of Financial Investigation, Narcotics Bureau."

"One more bad guy down, although I would not wish the death that Ambassador Myint suffered on anyone," Ian said when everyone was seated. "I am not, however, going to rest until the last player in this drama falls too, the bastard who tried to have us killed, Geoffrey MacMillan."

"Yes!" Angela exclaimed.

"The best chance of us catching Mr. MacMillan with his jade-encrusted underpants down will be to gather information on his dirty money. That is why I have invited Superintendent Yu to this meeting to educate us on exactly how to do that."

Linda said, "Thanks, Ian. You are correct. Drug dealers earn gigantic amounts of cash, and cash is very unwieldy. How do you transfer it when it is illegal? Exchange it? Deposit it? You can't very well deposit a million dollars cash into HSBC without bringing attention to yourself. Even transporting it and storing it is a problem. One million dollars worth of heroin weighs forty four pounds. One million dollars in cash weighs two hundred and fifty six pounds."

Ian picked up the discussion, "So therefore a drug dealer's biggest problem is getting his tons of money into the banking system. To do this he must launder it. The money laundering business is rampant in Hong Kong. If we can track down where and how The Bilu launders his dirty money, we can connect him to his crimes and make an arrest. Linda and her team are experts at this."

"Knowing the top end, who the ultimate beneficiary is of the laundering, makes it easier. We now have to track down the bottom end and connect the dots. My staff is already tracing accounts and shell companies that can be associated with Geoffrey MacMillan, both in Hong Kong and off-shore." Linda said. "What we need from you detectives is information on who his money launderer might be."

*****

Angela and Nigel returned to their cubicles, but as soon as Angela saw an opportunity to leave the building unnoticed, she slipped out. She walked to the corner of the police campus along Gloucester Road. Standing under a large recruitment poster reading 'Join The Police – Reach Full Potential', both in English and Chinese, Angela dialed her dad's number. "Hey Dad, do you know anything about money laundering?"

"Yeah, sure."

"Who is the biggest and best? Who would the biggest drug dealer in Hong Kong use?"

"The best is under the Canal Street fly-over at Lockhart Road. You know the 'Villain Hitters'?"

"You're kidding! Those crazy old ladies that superstitious people go to so they can cast curses on their enemies? The Da Siu Yan?"

"Yeah, Da Siu Yan. The leader of the gang is Number 37. For sure she is the biggest and best money launderer in Hong Kong. The rumor is that she used to be a vice president at HSBC."

*

Chapter 60

"What?" Ian asked. Angela and Nigel were standing next to his desk in his cubicle. "The 'Villain Hitters'?"

"Yeah. I am sure that you have seen them, the old ladies under the Canal Road fly-over between Wanchai and Causeway Bay? People go to them to put curses on their enemies. The 'Villain Hitter' writes the victim's name and birth date on a piece of paper, and then hits the paper, usually with an old shoe, sometimes even burns it. A lot of Chinese people believe in that black magic stuff," Angela said.

"And they are also money launderers?" Ian asked.

"The best in Hong Kong. If I was MacMillan, with the amounts of cash that he generated, I would use the best that I could."

"And the leader of this gang of money launders is someone named Number 37? You expect me to believe that under a gloomy, filthy, smelly concrete fly-over is the headquarters of the most sophisticated money laundering operation in Hong Kong? Run by old ladies in pajamas?" Ian asked.

"It's actually brilliant, if it's true," Nigel said.

"OK, well…. pick up Ms. 37. I will ask Superintendent Yu to join the interrogation when you guys get back with our Villain Hitter."

*****

In the police car on the way to Lockhart Road and the Canal River fly-over, Nigel suddenly turned to Angela and said, "I know who you are."

"What do you mean by that? Of course you know who I am," Angela retorted.

"I mean that I know who your dad is."

"Oh."

"Don't worry, I won't tell anyone. Just wanted to let you know that I know," Nigel said.

"OK. Please keep it quiet."

Finding Number 37 was easy. Each Villain Hitter had a small stand placed around the massive gray-tiled columns supporting the flyover. Each stand had three or four child-sized, plastic stools in front of it for customers to sit on. An upside down cardboard box, draped in red paper, served as a table.

On the tables were small pyramids of oranges and sticks of burning incense. Alters made of red-papered cardboard boxes surrounded the 'Villain Hitter's' stands, and within each alter porcelain figurines of Chinese deities stared celestially out at the customers. On the ground next to each stand was a metal can used for burning the slips of paper on which the name of the victim and birth date had been written. There was also on each table a wooden block, and next to the block was an object such as an old shoe with which the Villain Hitter could strike the paper before burning.

Number 37 had the prime spot next to the first column. There were no other Villain Hitters around her. A large '37' was drawn on a cardboard sign next to her stand. Angela and Nigel sat down on her tiny, blue plastic stools.

"You want a curse put on your enemies?" The woman asked in Cantonese. She looked to be about sixty years old. Her head was shaved bald, and she was wearing black pajamas. A necklace with a large jade pendant hung from her neck. She clutched an old high heel shoe.

"Yes, we do," Nigel said. "A very bad man."

Angela held her police badge in front of the woman's face. "He launderers his dirty money through you."

The old woman erupted from her seat with a scream, a Fury from the darkness of Hades. Angela flashed on her daydream of a bat-like creature swooping out of a darkened building as she stood helpless on the beach. Number 37's shoe made a whistling noise as she swung it heel first at Nigel's head. Angela moved fast, wrestling her to the ground before the shoe connected with the stunned and immobile Nigel's cranium. Angela was surprised at the strength of the old woman. She handcuffed the Villain Hitter and led her to the police car.

At the police station Villain Hitter 37 was processed. Her handcuffs were removed so that she could be fingerprinted. Then, still in her black pajamas, she was locked into a windowless interrogation room. Thirty minutes later she was joined by Nigel, Angela, Ian and Superintendent Yu. They sat down around the room's one table. The old woman's eyes, sunken, hostile and dark-rimmed, followed from one to another, a trapped, skeletal creature in silk pajamas.

Linda placed a thick file folder on the table and said pleasantly. "Hello, Ms...... Let's see, what shall we call you? Villain Hitter 37? Or shall we call you Winnie Lo?"

The woman's expression remained blank. She starred at Linda as if she were watching a bad movie.

"Your fingerprints, Ms. Lo, they prove that you are the famous, or I should say infamous, and missing, Winnie Lo. Everyone was wondering where you had gotten off to, Winnie." The woman fidgeted, but said nothing. "Ian, have you heard of Ms. Lo?"

"No, I have not. Who is she?" Ian asked.

Linda opened the file and read, "Winnie Lo; graduated with honors from Hong Kong University, went on to earn a master's degree in finance from Stanford. She then had a short, illustrious career with Goldman Sachs, and finally landed a position as a vice president with HSBC." Linda looked up from the file, "But then there was that issue of.. what did the papers call it, Winnie? Embezzlement? A harsh word, but you could understand why everyone would be upset. Millions disappeared. And '*poof*', Winnie disappeared too."

"And here she is now, living monastically as Villain Hitter 37. An amazing story." Ian said.

"Well, not so monastically." Linda pulled from her file an issue of Hong Kong Socialite Magazine. "Here's a photo of Winnie, wearing a wig, standing in front of her Ferrari. By the way, Winnie, you look much better with hair. The shaved head thing is not a good look for you."

Ian glanced at the photo, and then jabbed his finger at a picture of Winnie in a sparkling sequined blue evening gown standing next to a man in a tuxedo with his arm around her. "That's Geoffrey

MacMillan!" The caption under the photo read, '*At the* Evening of Jade *annual ball.*

Linda closed the magazine and returned it to her file. "Detective Hamilton's enthusiasm is understandable, Winnie. You see, he has been trying to get evidence on Mr. MacMillan for some time, and now he has it." Winnie glared at the Superintendent. Linda continued, smiling, "Oh, no, don't worry, Winnie. We won't need your cooperation to get Detective Hamilton his evidence. I mean, you wouldn't give it to us anyway, as you know that you will be spending the rest of your life in prison whether you cooperate or not. No, we have your phone records, and that is the trail that will lead us directly to Mr. Geoffrey MacMillan." Linda removed a sheaf of papers from her file. "Calls every ten minutes to the same number from your telephone. By the way, Winnie, congratulations, you are no doubt the only Villain Hitter with the very latest Samsung smart phone, not a fake either."

Winnie raised her right hand and gave Superintendent Yu the finger.

Linda ignored it and continued, "Anyway, we traced the number to an industrial building in Kwun Tong. An army of police officers are speeding there now where I am sure that they will find an office full of your loyal employees, transferring dirty money from bank to bank until it smells fresh and clean. Within all those records Detective Hamilton will, no doubt, find more evidence on Mr. MacMillan than he ever dreamed possible."

Linda stood up, closed her file, and said, "Have a nice life in jail, Winnie."

As Linda stood up to walk out of the interrogation room, Winnie screamed, "Die, Bitch!"

Linda Yu turned back towards Winnie, smiled, and raised her right fist, her middle finger pointing towards the ceiling.

Chapter 61

The story of the Myanmar Ambassador to Hong Kong being eaten by his pet Burmese python was such a sensational tale that it even made it to the English language newspaper 'Pattaya Today'. Khin Khin was well known and well liked in Pattaya, and the community was shocked. His three bars, Ice Cream I, II, and III, were overwhelmingly popular.

When Khin Khin had accepted the Ambassador position in Hong Kong, he had left the running of the Ice Cream empire to his partner, Marc Bouchet, a Frenchman who had been living in Thailand for twenty years. Marc was devastated by the news of Khin Khin's death. Khin Khin had been his mentor, the impetus that had steered him from a life as an alcoholic drifter to a life with purpose. When he read the news Marc felt he was once again balancing on the edge of the alcoholic crevasse that Khin Khin had pulled him out of.

His melancholy was lessened when, a few days after learning of Khin Khin's demise, he was contacted by Geoffrey MacMillan's lawyer. "Mr. Bouchet? This is Harvey Albright of Albright and Taylor. We represent the interests of Mr. Geoffrey MacMillan who was a very close friend of your ex-partner, Mr. Khin Khin Myint," the voice over the line had said.

"Yes, yes, Geoffrey MacMillan! Khin Khin spoke often of him." Marc had said with his heavy French accent.

"Mr. MacMillan plans on shipping Mr. Myint's body back to Thailand. He believes that Pattaya will be the most comfortable final resting place for him. He feels that Khin Khin has many friends there who would like to attend his funeral."

"Absolument! Fantastique! I will make all the arrangements. We will do a Buddhist ceremony. Will Mr. MacMillan be attending?"

"Yes, Monsieur Bouchet. Mr. MacMillan will attend," Harvey said.

*****

Geoffrey had decided to fly into Bangkok and then hire a car for the two hour drive to Pattaya. As the hired Mercedes smoothly purred south down Highway 3 Geoffrey thought back thirty years, to the time when he and Khin Khin had run from Bangkok to Pattaya with the Thai police searching for the two young foreign *yaa baa* dealers. They had felt immortal in those days.

The car pulled up in front of the largest bar on Diamond Street. An outdoor patio ran the entire length of the pub. Across the face of the building above the patio a neon sign read *'Ice Cream I'*, each letter as big as a man and each a different color. Geoffrey exited the car, removed his suitcase from the trunk, and walked into the dim interior. Alannah Myles singing *Black Velvet* was playing on the sound system.

A foreigner walked out from behind the bar and said, "Geoffrey?" He then hugged him and kissed both of Geoffrey's cheeks.

"Nice to meet you, Marc."

"I have heard so much from Khin Khin about you over the years I feel like you are an old friend. You must be tired after your journey. Please sit. A beer?" Marc said.

Without waiting for an answer Marc went back behind the bar and returned with two bottles of Chang Beer. Geoffrey, holding the frosty bottle, traced his finger over the familiar green and gold label with the two white elephants, remembering his life in Bangkok so long ago. It had been thirty years since he had drunk a Chang.

"Everything is arranged: the monks, the guests. It starts tomorrow morning. It will take place here in the bar." Marc said.

Buddhist funeral rites in Thailand are usually a multi-day affair. Khin Khin's funeral started with the Bathing Rites, his body covered with a cloth. Scented water was poured over his hand. He was then placed in a coffin surrounded by wreaths of flowers, incense, and candles. Monks in apricot-yellow robes chanted from the *Abhidharma*.

For two days guests came in and out, visiting, feasting, playing dominoes, the monks chanting and praying. On the evening of the third day it was time for the cremation. Banana leaves were placed on the ground from the doorway of the bar, through the outdoor patio, and out into the street. Marc, carrying a white banner on a long bamboo pole, with Geoffrey by his side, led the procession.

Behind the two foreign men walked ten monks. They carried a broad yellow ribbon that was attached to the coffin. The coffin itself, carried in an elaborately decorated cart pulled by an ox, was followed by two rows of ladyboys dressed in black and carrying silver bowls of flowers. Next came a small flatbed truck in the back of which a band had set up. Not a traditional funeral band, these were the rock musicians who were regulars at the Ice Cream bars. They had a small generator and amp in the truck with them and they played gospel, rock, and pop as the procession wound its way through the streets of Pattaya. In the rear of the procession walked friends of Khim Khim, numbering in the hundreds. As they passed bystanders *waied* in respect, their palms pressed together.

The funeral parade ended at Pattaya Beach. A funeral pyre had been built out of bricks on the sand halfway to the water. Geoffrey wondered about the legality of burning a body on a public beach, but as no one else seemed concerned, and as there were numerous policemen in uniform in the procession, he figured that it must be OK in Pattaya.

The guests were handed small 'flowers' made of wood. Each guest walked up to the coffin, which was now resting on top of the brick pyre, and placed the wooden flower in a tray beneath the coffin. They would then knock a few times on the coffin, *wai,* and say a short prayer. When all had done this the monks put lit torches beneath the coffin. It was evening, and the band played *Swing Low Sweet Chariot* as the flames illuminated the purple sky with an orange glow, sparks dancing like fireflies.

After it was over and the fire had reduced to embers, Marc and Geoffrey wandered over to Ice Cream II on the Walking Street. They sat at the bar drinking martinis.

"Will you return to Hong Kong, Geoffrey? You are always welcome here you know. The bar business is good."

"I know, Marc, thanks. The night he died Khin Khin was talking to me about returning to Myanmar. I feel that it was a message, like sometimes when you have a dream and it seems important, not just another dream, like you should pay attention to it."

"Return to Myanmar? That sounds like a strange choice to me," Marc said. He then called to the bartender, "Keep these martinis coming, Ruby."

With two fresh martinis in front of them, Geoffrey said, "Khin Khin's death really had an effect on my thinking. It is like the fire that has driven me all my life has been put out. My anger is gone. Anger has always been a close friend of mine."

"Isn't your anger being gone a good thing?" Marc asked.

"Maybe." After a hesitation, Geoffrey said, "No, not 'maybe'. It *is* a good thing. I just feel lost without it, I guess."

"You have lost two friends; Khin Khin and your anger. You need some time to recover, Geoffrey."

"You know, you are absolutely right, Marc, and where better to do that than in some small village in the countryside of Myanmar. I am going to follow the trail that Khin Khin showed me." Geoffrey raised his martini and he and Marc tapped glasses.

"Ruby! Keep those martinis coming!" Marc yelled to the bartender.

*****

Geoffrey spent two weeks in Pattaya. After the first week he made a telephone call to Albright and Taylor to instruct them as to how to liquidate his Hong Kong assets and to transfer the funds to his Yangon account. Harvey Albright started his end of the call by saying, "Mr. MacMillan, I have to tell you, Winnie Lo has been arrested and all of her records seized."

A long pause. "Khin Khin was a prophet, Harvey," Geoffrey said. "If I was in Hong Kong I would be in jail right now. He has sent me here, and then to Myanmar, where I will be untouchable by Hong Kong authorities. This is the first spiritual experience of my life. It is profound."

"Well, I do not know about Khin Khin being a prophet or the spiritual part, but it is a very good thing that you are not here. I suggest that you get yourself to Myanmar as soon as possible, Mr. MacMillan."

Chapter 62

Sitting in her Fotan apartment, Angela read the e-mail twice. 'Garuda-san, my life has changed. I have taken a sabbatical from the police department. I will be in Hong Kong tomorrow, ANA flight 769, arrives 5:00pm. Will explain when I see you. Mushashi.'

'OK, I will meet you at the airport. Your life has changed?! Can't wait to hear. Garuda.' Angela tapped back.

******

Terminal Two at Chek Lap Kok Airport was crowded at 5:00pm. An international cross-section of ethnicities navigated the modern terminal trying, sometimes unsuccessfully, to not collide with each other as they pulled rolling bags or pushed metal trolley carts. Fatigued businessmen with 'another day -another city' expressions dragged wheeled, black bags, rushing to find a taxi stand to take them to one more four-star hotel. Vacationing families with energized children riding on top of suitcases stacked on the trolleys, wide-eyed at new adventure, hair wild from a long flight, gazed around the modern terminal at the colorful circus of milling people. Every age and every hue, human beings shot out of the gate in every direction like particle beams in a science experiment. Returning Hong Kong residents relieved to be home joined the milieu exiting the gate, while lovers and spouses leaned on the guardrail and waited, glowing in anticipation of reunion. Angela was one of these.

They hugged when Kotaro, wheeling a black suitcase behind him, arrived. He was wearing a maroon sweatshirt that read 'Fukuoka Sanix Bombs Rugby'."You look good, Angela-san," Kotaro said. They held hands as they boarded the Airport Express train which would whisk them from Chek Lap Kok into Central. The high-speed train smoothly and powerfully accelerated them towards the city center. Angela said, "So tell me, Kotaro, what are you doing in Hong Kong and why did you take a sabbatical from the police department?"

Kotaro put a finger over his lips. "I will tell you over dinner, Garuda-san. You are going to get me some authentic Cantonese food, right?"

When they disembarked in Central Angela took Kotaro to a local restaurant close to the Airport Express station. After she had ordered in Cantonese, Angela said, "OK, so what's up? You took a sabbatical? Your life has changed? Give it up, Kotaro-san."

"A very long story. It started when I got my tattoo."

"Your tattoo? You got a tattoo?" Angela exclaimed.

"Yes, just like you, Garuda-san. The image of Miyamoto Mushashi is now on my back. Very beautiful, you will see tonight. Anyway, the tattoo artist that I chose is very skilled. He has a samurai spirit. His name is Kokai Nakagawa. Very famous guy, maybe you've heard of him? No?"

"No."

Kotaro leaned forward, "Angela, while I was getting my tattoo I learned that Kokai knows the location of the lost 'Hongjo Masamune'!"

"That is supposed to mean something to me? Hongho Masa…whatever?" Angela asked.

Kotaro sat back and smiled, "Ah, you don't know. Of course not. I will explain, Angela. The samurai sword embodies the soul of Japan, and the 'Hongjo Masamune' is considered to be the finest sword ever made. Its maker, Goro Masamune, is venerated as one of Japan's best sword-smiths ever."

"So you are talking about a sword?"

"Yes, a famous missing sword. The 'Hongjo Masamune', used by General Shigenaga Hongjo in the battle of Kawana Kajima in 1561, disappeared after World War II when the Americans insisted that the Japanese relinquish all weapons, including family swords. The 'Hongjo Masamune' was turned over to an American soldier and was never seen again. The blade is a Japanese National Treasure. To someone with Budo spirit, finding the missing sword would be the greatest achievement possible in this lifetime."

"So you took a sabbatical from a paying job to find this sword on the basis of some tattoo artist's wild story? You are kidding. Whom did he say has the sword?"

"That's the amazing part, Angela, and why I know the story is true! Geoffrey MacMillan! The lost 'Masamune' is in the private collection of your suspect, Geoffrey MacMillan! In your e-mail you said that the Hong Kong police had frozen his assets. Your police therefore must have the sword!"

"Kotaro, if your tattoo artist knew who had the lost sword why didn't he just go after it himself?" Angela asked.

"He has no legs."

"No legs?"

"Yes, makes it difficult. He needs a partner. That's me."

"How did he learn that MacMillan had the 'Hongjo-Masawhatever' sword to begin with?"

"Eight years ago Kokai-san was in Hong Kong to tattoo some client. In those days he had legs. He attended a Julie's auction while he was in Hong Kong: old Japanese artifacts, porcelains, netsuke, kimonos, and swords. He had spent his life following the way of the samurai. His knowledge of famous swords is vast. In the Julie's preview the day before the auction he spotted the 'Hongjo Masamune'. He recognized it immediately."

"So he bid on it?"

"No, Kokai-san didn't have that kind of money, and he could have lost it to another bidder. He naively thought that Julie's would do the right thing once they realized that the sword was a Japanese National Treasure. Kokai-san therefore immediately contacted the CEO of Julie's and told him the provenance of the sword, and that the sword must be returned to Japan. He was thanked for his information and told that the sword would be pulled from the auction and turned in to the proper authorities. The next day it had been removed from the auction."

"And the CEO was MacMillan and Kokai believed him, right?" Angela asked.

"Of course. An honorable man expects honorable action from others. However, on returning to Japan Kokai-san discovered that no Japanese authorities had been contacted. MacMillan-san had bought it privately from the owner and he had added it to his own private collection. He is a dishonorable man."

"Yes, he is."

"When Kokai-san found out he returned to Hong Kong and angrily confronted MacMillan-san at his office. The CEO denied ever having met Kokai-san or having any knowledge of the sword. He had Kokai-san physically ejected from his office. The next day a bomb exploded in Kokai-san's rented car. He lost both legs."

"And you left your job and took up this quest to find a lost sword based on this crazy story? Kotaro, you are chi sin, nuts! It is like looking for the lost Ark! You have no proof of any of this!" Angela exclaimed.

"No, Angela, the spirit of Mushashi has guided us all along. That is the proof! Our meeting, the inspiration to get a tattoo, Kokai-san having been maimed by your suspect, the lost Masamune, it is all connected! Can you not feel the divine guidance? And now your police department has MacMillan's assets."

Angela shrugged. "I hate to tell you this, Kotaro, but before we closed the loop on MacMillan his crooked attorneys shipped quite a few crates to Yangon. We froze his bank accounts and fixed assets like his property and cars, but something like a sword probably got away."

Kotaro frowned. "I suspected that the road would not be so easy. Is there an inventory of what was seized?"

"Of course. We can check the inventory tomorrow. I'll arrange a meeting with Linda Yu," Angela said.

Kotaro smiled. "Thanks, Garuda-san. I appreciate it. For now, let's eat and then go to your apartment. I would like to show you my tattoo."

*****

Tika and Sarah were drinking Mojito's, George and Ian downing tequila shots. George had the waiter bring them each three shots at once, and they were lined up on the table. The Filipino band was excellent, with both a male and female lead singer. Dusk 'Til Dawn at 11:00pm was just starting to fill up with an alcohol-glazed crowd.

"So he just a sent an e-mail to the entire company?" Ian asked.

Sarah, sipping her drink, said, "Yes. It said, 'Effective immediately, I retire from my position as CEO at Julie's Auction House. It has been a wonderful experience working with all of you, and I wish all of you the best of luck. Sincerely, Geoffrey MacMillan.' No forwarding address or anything."

"That must have caused some shock waves. Has he been replaced yet?" George asked.

"Not yet. I am boss-less for the moment."

"I'll drink to that!" George said raising his shot glass.

"Poor little Ian, he finally had a case solidly documented against the bad guy and then no one to arrest." Tika said, rustling Ian's hair and giving him a kiss on the ear.

"You know, I'm actually OK with it all. The Witch is dead, and the Witch's boss has run away. I have saved Hong Kong again," Ian said, raising his shot before downing it. "And career-wise, I look golden."

"The Wicked Witch is dead!" George said as he slammed back another shot.

"How did your team take it? I mean about the bad guy getting away." George asked.

"Angela at first wanted me to send her to Myanmar, in her words, 'To track the bastard down and drag him out of the country'. She relaxed a bit when she learned that we could freeze most of his Hong Kong assets. Nigel took it in stride, nothing fazes him."

"I read in the papers that you guys also took down the law firm of Albright and Taylor. Is that right? That's quite an accomplishment. They were fairly prestigious, like David toppling Goliath." George said.

"They were complicit in MacMillan's drug dealings. It was really Linda Yu and her team who built the case against them and should get the credit. However, I will never forget the image of Angela slapping the cuffs on Harvey Albright. When he called her a 'meddlesome bitch' she was this close to slamming his fat ass down on a desk. I saw the anger flame up in her eyes. But then she controlled herself and calmly handcuffed him. I was proud of her."

"So it's over," Tika said. "I assume that you are on to new cases with new bad guys."

"There is no shortage of bad guys for me to save Hong Kong from." Ian said.

"Waiter!" George called. "Another shot for The Savior of Hong Kong, and a round for his entourage as well!"

*****

Angela and Kotaro spent the next day meeting with Linda Yu. They thoroughly went through the inventory of all of Geoffrey's frozen assets. No swords.

"You must be disappointed, Kotaro." Linda said. "I am sorry."

Kotaro smiled, "No, not a disappointment but a chance to polish my spirit. I knew this path would be a long one when I took it. Thank you for taking the time to review your inventory with me, Linda-san."

That evening, in Angela's apartment, Kotaro lay on his stomach as Angela traced her finger over the tattoo of Miyamoto Mushashi on his back. It was an intricate work of art. Miyamoto, in colorful, flowing kimono, his bushy brow furrowed in anger and with a sword in each hand, was depicted slashing at unseen opponents. The tattoo seemed to move, to have its own life. It had a power and energy that Angela had never seen before in a tattoo.

"Damn, your artist was good!"

"A master." Kotaro said.

"So what will you do now, Kotaro?" Angela asked.

"I will follow the road that Mushashi has set me on. I will go to Myanmar to find the lost 'Hongjo Masamune'. My destiny is to return the sword to the people of Japan."

"That will not be so easy, Kotaro. You can get to Yangon, but if MacMillan has gone to the countryside or to Kachin territory there is no way you can get to him. Myanmar is one of the most closed societies on earth. To even make an inquiry about someone under the protection of the Burmese generals could get you killed. Actually, your idea is crazy. How do you say 'crazy' in Japanese?"

" 'Kichigai'. Not as kichigai as you think, Garuda-san. My cousin works in Myanmar for the Japanese government. He is a Buddhist and is connected to a sect of underground monks that the Western media labeled 'The Saffron Revolution' when they protested the government's policies in 2007. He and his Buddhist friends will help me."

" 'The Saffron Revolution'? I read about that. The newspapers in 2007 said that most of those monks were killed or imprisoned."

"Do not believe everything that you read in the paper, Angela-san. For one thing, in Myanmar Buddhist monks' robes are maroon, not saffron. So the newspapers are not always accurate. Anyway, I am not going alone."

"Not alone? Who is going with you?"

Kotaro turned to look up at Angela, "Miyamoto Mushashi will be accompanying me, of course."